SIGGA *of* REYKJAVIK

SIGGA *of* REYKJAVIK

a novel by Solveig Eggerz

BACON PRESS BOOKS
WASHINGTON, DC

"The Midwife," excerpted from the book, won first prize for fiction in 2009 Golden NIB Contest, sponsored by the Virginia Writers Club.

"Saved," was published in *Delmarva Review,* Volume 9.

Originally titled, *Curve of the Earth,* the manuscript won recognition from William Faulkner—William Wisdom Creative Writing Competition

Published in Iceland as *Forargata, Reykjavik* by Tindur, 2018

Published in the United States by Bacon Press Books, Washington, DC
www.baconpressbooks.com

Cover Design: Alan Pranke
www.amp13.com

Editing: Lorraine Fico-White
magnificomanuscripts.com

Interior Design: Lorie DeWorken
mindthemargins.com

Author photo: Ann Cameron Siegal

ISBN: 978-0-9971489-8-5

Library of Congress Control Number: 2019932183

For Guðný

Table of Contents

SIGGA *of* REYKJAVIK

Chapter 1

I was in the shed shoveling cow dung. When I heard the new calf bawl for its mother, I entered its dark pen, placed my arms under its soft belly, buried my nose in its spicy smell, and raised it off the ground. When I set it down, it nuzzled me. I rubbed the strings of saliva into my sweater, so Mama wouldn't notice. She didn't like the lifting, didn't believe I needed to build my strength to defend against the men on the farm. I was ten years old, but one day I'd be Sigga the Strong and break somebody's jaw.

That evening, I sat on the edge of the bed I shared with Mama in the loft and pulled off my socks. Sleeping directly above the cow shed, we got the warmth of the animals from between the floorboards. Below, my calf bawled as if to say, "I want my mama." I ran to the end of the loft and told him, "Tomorrow I'll lift you higher."

"Come to bed," Mama said. I scurried back. She plucked a red calf hair from my shoulder.

I crept under the covers and nested in Mama's arms, her soft bosom against my shoulder blades. Across from us, in the beds that lined the wall, snored the male workers. Their mouths hung open, showing broken, yellow teeth. I smelled their dirty socks and oily hair. I hated them. "Let's leave," I whispered.

"Quiet, Sigga."

"I don't like living here."

"We must obey the old laws," she said.

I bit down on my pillow until I gagged. Borghildur, asleep in the bed next to ours, had told me I couldn't leave the farm until I got a job in town

1

or on the docks. But I'd heard her whisper, "Unless something unexpected happens." I prayed for something unexpected.

Borghildur was fifty years older than me, but we were still best friends. I admired her. She was brave. And . . . she taught me how to read. I sniffed out books and newspaper scraps in every corner of the farm. When the farmer and his wife were outside, I felt my way along the dark passage from the loft, past the kitchen and storage rooms, to the room at the front of the farm where they lived. I picked up old newspapers and hurried back to the loft to read. Under my pillow I had a clipping from 1918 with the headline, "Iceland Is a Free and Sovereign Nation." Free from Denmark. The word "independence" came up. I rolled it around in my mouth. Like a melting sugar cube, it filled my mouth with sweetness. I, too, *would* gain my independence.

The farmer sold things in the village and brought back newspapers. The farmwife wrapped her good dishes in them, stuffed newspaper wads into her church shoes, and tore strips for the outhouse. Like a mouse collecting scraps for her nest, I gathered up bits of newspaper and read them, especially the advertisements. In Reykjavik, women worked as maids, in tailor shops, and in fish plants. With the money they earned, they bought coats, eggbeaters, and sewing machines. I discovered pictures of the Danish king and queen wrapped around the farmwife's teapot. Their names were Kristjan X and his wife, Alexandrine. I learned about the ocean and how it connected us to the outside world. In the ocean there had been a war. Torpedoes sank our new trawlers. Fishermen died. And their children lost their father. I never had a father.

One dark evening, we bent over our work in the loft. The only sounds were the treadle of the spinning wheel, the click of knitting needles, the cursing of men fixing reins and bits, and the sputter of the oil lamp. On the bed across from me sat two women, dressed in black skirts, combing wool. Suddenly, Borghildur stood up and opened a book, the story of the people of Laxar Valley. I knew the story because Borghildur had read it to me. The husband of Breeches Auður divorced his wife for wearing men's pants. In the twelfth century they had laws about clothes. I rubbed my hands over the torn overalls Mama had begged from the farmwife. Her son, stupid Lárus, had outgrown them.

Borghildur turned to me. "Do you have something for us, Sigga?"

I blushed down to my shoulder blades. I always had something because I carried wadded-up newspaper articles in my pockets. I pulled out a report I'd found at the bottom of the bridle chest about the other king, Kristjan's father, King Frederick VIII, when he visited Iceland in 1907, a year before I was born.

I smoothed out the crinkled paper and read, "The king and his wife stepped off the ship onto a red carpet. It was raining, but pretty young girls in white dresses ran up and offered flowers to the king. All the residents of Reykjavik crowded close and clapped and cheered."

An old woman across from me dropped her sewing and placed her hand on her heart. "Ahhhh, the king."

Borghildur spat over her shoulder into a dark corner. "The king can go to the devil. We need our independence."

I clapped. The men made round eyes. I would become strong like Borghildur.

Chapter 2

It happened often but one memory stands out. I was eight years old.

"Get me some liver and blood sausages," the farmwife commanded. Of course, I obeyed. Swinging my dipping spoon, I crept down the dark passage and felt my way along the moist wall. I passed the shadowy place where the farmer kept broken-down saddles, ropes, boxes, blades for scythes, cracked leather reins, and driftwood scraps. I thought I was alone. But I wasn't. A man leaned against the wall. I recognized his bushy head. The farmwife's brother. In my nightmares he was the hairy man. I hurried past him and into the sour-smelling room lined with barrels of liver and blood sausages, sheeps' heads, feet, testicles, bladders, roe, sharks' flippers and gills. I pulled up a stool, stood on my toes, and peered into the dark liquid. My eyes watered from the pickling smell. A sausage floated by. I caught it with my dipping spoon, lifting it out of the barrel. An arm encircled me. The hairy man. He pinned me against his hot chest. I choked on the smell of his beard. Plop. The sausage dropped back into the brine. His arm flattened my lungs. I couldn't breathe. Hard as pliers, his hand moved under my chin. The other wandered between my legs. "Sweet little honey bunny. I'll find a sausage for you."

I screeched, kicking him backward hard as I could. But he held on. I sank my teeth into his hand. It tasted like blood and leather.

"Aaaaaaiiiiiii! You filthy little mink." He let go and ran down the passageway.

Later, in bed, I whispered, "The hairy man caught me. I bit him."

Mama's thin body trembled against my back. "No, Sigga—"

"He did bad things."

"Shhh. Nobody must hear you." In the next bed, Borghildur breathed like rattling stones. Mama stroked my hair, trying to calm me, but I threw off the blanket and padded to the tiny window at the end of the loft and stared out at the stars. Beyond them was Reykjavik where women earned money and went shopping. I would go there. I'd find Papa. He would take out his hunting knife and stab the hairy man until his blood gushed out. I padded back to bed, stepping carefully on the floorboards. I hated splinters.

Next morning while the workers pulled on their trousers, I sat on Borghildur's bed and watched her fasten her black skirt and wrap her crocheted wool shawl around her shoulders. "Yesterday I did a brave thing," I said.

"What's that, little Sigga?" she said, smiling at me the way Mama never did.

I put pride into my voice. "I bit the hairy man."

She dropped her comb. Holding me to her bosom, she talked into the top of my head. "My poor baby girl. Did he bleed?"

I nodded "yes" against her bosom, felt her flinch.

"You mustn't brag about it," she whispered.

She pushed me away but kept her hand on my shoulder. "I was here the day you were born. When your mother wouldn't tell your papa's name, somebody said to leave you behind the waterfall to die. But you had the prettiest little nose. I fought to keep you here."

After the bite, Mama sewed me a dolly from the farmer's old torn sock with black buttons for eyes. I kept Dolly tucked under my arm and whispered to her about bad men. A few days later, I stood at the creek bank, imagining how the water flowed toward Reykjavik. I didn't hear Dísa, the pig-nosed farmer's daughter, behind me. I turned too late. She gripped Dolly by the leg and threw her into the sky. Like a shot bird, Dolly fell with a splash into the water, floated for a few seconds, then sank. I couldn't swim, so I couldn't save her. I whirled around, swung my fist, and punched Dísa's nose so hard she slipped and fell on the muddy bank. I straddled her and ground her face into the mud until her ugly pig snout bled.

Footsteps on the soft ground. Fingers dug into my shoulder and pulled me to my feet. "Girl," Mama hissed into my face. "You think life's bad now. It can get worse." I swallowed snot and tears. Still I was glad I'd bashed the pig girl. And I'd learned something about my body. Anger made my arms and legs strong.

A few days later, I was helping Mama wash work clothes in the big tub in the shed. I picked up some pants stiff with dirt. In the dim light from the kerosene lamp, the pants looked like a runaway troll. I shook my arms and made it dance. "Look, Mama. He's running to Reykjavik."

"Drop those pants," she said.

I carried them to the tub.

But she took the pants from my hands and threw them aside. "No. You. Take off your clothes and get in."

I stood nailed to the floor. The only bath I knew was the icy cold creek.

"Fast. Right now."

I fumbled with the buttons on my tattered overalls, slipped off my undershirt, and stepped out of my bunched-up cotton underpants. Mama's lips formed a tight line. She kept looking around. Finally, I stood in front of her, naked and shivering.

"Quick," she said, and hoisted me over the edge of the tub. I slid under the water up to my nose. It held me in a warm hug as if it loved me. Mama rubbed some green soap onto a brush and scrubbed my neck, arms, bony chest, and up and down my ribs. "Give me your feet, girl," she said. In and out, between my toes, her fingers went. She brushed the soles of my feet, tickling me. Wiggling and laughing, I slid under the water and came up sputtering.

"Quiet. Get out," she said.

I stepped out of the tub and dripped on the floor. Mama wrapped me in a towel and rubbed life into every cell of my body. My blood rushed to the surface to meet my mother's fingers. When my skin was pinked-up and tingling, she held me against her apron for a tiny moment, then pushed me away. I grabbed her funny mood to ask the old question.

"Where is Papa?"

Her shoulders stiffened. Her hand rose. I swayed my back so she could not swat my bottom.

"Where is he?" I called.

"Get dressed."

"His letter," I whispered, pulling on my clothes.

"Tonight, when we're in bed."

In the evening, the loft trembled with sleep sounds when Mama crept out of our bed. I helped her lift the mattress. Under it, next to the long wooden box where she kept her knitting needles, was the letter from Papa. Holding the letter, she lowered the mattress. I climbed into bed. Leaning into the sliver of moonlight from the window, she read, "I wish I could be with both of you. Tell my little girl that her papa loves her. One day I'll come and see her."

The words wrapped themselves around my heart and warmed me.

I reached for the letter. "Let me see it."

But Mama swung her arm out of reach, folded the letter, and slid it under the mattress. Back in bed, I snuggled in her warmth. "Did he ever write another letter?" I asked.

No answer.

―――――――

By the time I was eleven, I was tall, with square shoulders and strong arms. I turned hay and baled it. I shoveled dung out of the shed until it formed a mountain at the edge of the farm. And I tended the angelica garden. But evenings in the loft, Mama made me knit and sew. I knitted a stack of woolen patches to lay inside sheepskin shoes or rubber shoes for the farm folk. I didn't mind Mama selling the leftover patches in the village, but I stomped my feet when she sold my angelica root. Those coins should have been mine.

Angelica cured constipation, cramps, wind, bronchitis, and coughing. I dug the bulb and its legs out of the ground with a root digger. I picked angelica leaves and collected the seeds. Sometimes the farmwife boiled parts of the plant and made sick workers drink it three times a day. When we had no fish or meat, she sliced it and fried it in butter. Maybe I'd become an angelica farmer. The plant could buy me my independence.

Anger lived inside me like a wild animal. Sure, Mama was a coward. But mostly I was angry at men. They brought it on themselves. They couldn't take off their own socks and shoes—or even their pants. Every woman in the loft was assigned a man. She knitted his socks, sweaters, and mittens, cleaned and fixed his overalls, sewed his fishskin, sheepskin, or calfskin shoes, and stitched oilskin suits for him when he went to sea in the winter months. Unfair.

Men did almost nothing, just little things like repairing rakes, bridles, and reins, and plaiting rope from horsehair. Some shrank woolen mittens and socks, immersing them in water, to make them last longer. In spring and summer, they cut grass with a scythe. And men *never* served women the way women served men.

One evening, I was combing wool while Mama twisted yarn onto a spindle.

"Did any of those men ever thank you?" I asked.

A tiny gleam crept into her eyes. "Back on the other farm, before you were born—yes. I knitted all his socks and mittens. But then I got sick. And *he* did the knitting. Can you imagine? *He* did the knitting."

I drew in my breath. "Who?"

"He had big hands. When he scrunched and crumpled the wet wool, it shrank quickly and became very tight and strong. My mittens and socks lasted longer than any others on the farm."

I heard the pride in her voice, saw how her thin cheeks glowed.

"And he made things from wood," she said. She went to our bed and pulled back the mattress and took out the long, wooden, knitting needle box. I'd often played with the box. "He carved this box for me," she said.

I set down my wool and ran my fingers over the letters spelling my mother's name: Hansína. I saved the big question for later.

Finally, when we were under the covers, I asked, "Mama?"

"What?"

"Mama. Was that man my father?"

"What man?"

"The one who shrank the socks and carved a box for your knitting needles."

The mattress jiggled. Irritation? Shyness? I couldn't tell.

"What was his name?" I asked.

"Guðmundur."

While she pretended to be asleep, I dropped the name into my tiny collection of information about Papa. I filled in the rest with my imagination. On bad days when I needed a protector, my lost father was a lion who would rip my enemies to shreds with his huge teeth. One of his big feet pressed the chest of the man who'd stroked my bottom. The man writhed on the ground begging for mercy. Roar! My father sank his teeth into the man's neck, bit his head off.

Mama also served strange men who arrived wet and dirty after hard riding. Drunk men. One day I'd destroy them. I'd use the farmwife's butcher knife to cut them at the collarbone. It would be easy. I knew how to split the cooked head of a sheep into two halves. Blood would spurt. Mama and I'd run away with the man in the moon.

One night, I had a book under my pillow. I'd borrowed it off the farmer's shelf. When the book's corner poked my chin, I woke up. The spot next to me was still warm, but Mama was missing. Voices came up from the dark passage below.

"Pull on me, woman," a man said.

I crept down the steps and hid in a dark corner and saw Mama pull on his boots so hard she staggered backward and fell against the wall.

The man snickered as Mama scrambled to her feet. She grabbed his other boot. "Har. Har. I'll give you something else to hold onto."

As Mama peeled off his wet socks, the beast took out a flask and tipped it up to drink. He rose to his feet and swayed. Mama rushed to his side and held his arm.

My fists tightened.

"Let me lean on you, woman," he said. Mama bowed under his bulk.

Something exploded inside me. I leaped out. "Don't go with him, Mama."

"Who's this goddamned little girl?" the man asked.

I rose up to my full height and swung my fist, catching him on the chin. He groaned, swayed, but surged up again. Snap went his teeth. Mama slid out from under his arm. He lost his balance and staggered toward the wall. I prepared to swing again.

"Sigga, stop," she said, throwing her arms around me and pinning my arms to my side. On his hands and knees now, the ugly critter felt his way along the wall until he came to the pile of rags where the dogs slept on cold nights. As he lay down, he groaned like a rusted machine.

I took Mama's hand. "You can't let them push you around like that," I said as we climbed the steps.

"Yes, I can," she said.

In bed, I chose my words carefully. "In Reykjavik, women work for pay. I read about it in the papers. They work in tailor shops. They clean houses. They clean fish. They get paid in money. We don't have to stay here."

"Stop it. Just stop talking."

Soon she was asleep, but my hot blood kept me awake. I must go to Reykjavik. I must find Papa. He loved me. His letter said so. An idea came to me. I had never read his letter myself. I jumped out of bed. The floor was cold under my feet. Carefully, I rolled back the mattress, shifting Mama's weight toward the wall, and thrust my fingers under the mattress until I touched paper. My letter.

I pulled the envelope toward me. My fingers trembled as I unfolded the page. A sliver of dawn peeked through the window, giving me just enough light to read Papa's words of love. I started at the top. My lips moved. "Two kilos potatoes, flour, chicken netting, lard, sugar." And the prices. At the top was the name of a store in the village. I sat on the floor, hugged my knees, and wept silently. I looked at my mother, her lips sweetly parted in sleep. Silently I called her names. *Lygari. Lygari.* Liar. Liar.

Chapter 3

For the next several years I sharpened all the skills that might help me escape and gain independence. I planted and harvested the best angelica garden in the county. Sewing made me crazy, but I volunteered to stitch work clothes and repair the farmer's shirts. I practiced my skills. I spent a lot of time around the animals, milking the cows, watching how they gave birth. I sheared the sheep and learned the habits of chickens.

Then Jónas arrived.

The hired hands were in the field turning hay. I was in the farmhouse brewing coffee for them. I glanced out the window and saw a man ambling up the road toward the home field. When he knocked, I ran to the door. I hardly ever saw strangers. This one had coal black eyes and bushy eyebrows, a face like the sharp side of a mountain.

His voice creaked. "I'm Jónas, the tutor. Is nobody home?"

I pointed to the line of people in the outer field. "I've got some lovely porridge from breakfast. Want some?"

He set down his bag and sank into the chair. While I stirred the pot, I studied the top of his head. I sensed he knew things I needed to know. "Why are you here?" I asked.

"I stay on farms. I can cut hay, feed animals. And I teach any young people who need teaching." I watched him gulp down the porridge. At last he looked up and wiped his mouth on his sleeve.

"I'm Sigga. I'm fifteen, never been to school. I need a teacher."

He got to his feet, stretched, and groaned. His eyes were on me, but they didn't gleam in the way of some men. I was glad.

"We start tomorrow evening. Be sure to come," he said and headed for the door.

I watched him cross the field to meet the farmwife. Funny-looking fellow, like birds that fly in from a distant place and only spend a season.

Next evening, after bringing the cows to pasture, I raced down the dark passage and entered the living room, hot and panting. Jónas and the farmer's son and daughter, the two dolts, Lárus and Dísa, sat around the table. Dísa fixed her swine eyes on me. I wished I wasn't wearing Lárus' old sweater. Mama had patched the elbows with leftover blue yarn.

A piece of paper and a pencil lay in front of me. I picked up the pencil and doodled.

"Sigga," Jónas said.

I dropped the pencil.

He walked around the table and stood behind me. "We're talking about the Age of Settlement and the first Alþing at Þingvellir. Lárus, can you repeat to Sigga what I just said?"

Lárus doubled over into a fake coughing fit. Dísa made yawning sounds. So Jónas repeated the whole lesson. I tried to memorize every word. Over the next few days, I learned the history of our country, starting with the settlement. The parts that stayed with me were the beheading of the Catholic bishop because of something called the Reformation and the volcano that erupted in 1783.

"So big," Jónas said, "it started the French Revolution."

It was a dark snowy day just before Christmas. Jónas showed us a newspaper clipping from December 1, 1918. I kept the same one under my pillow.

"What happened on that day?" he asked.

Dísa licked her lips. "The ships brought crates of apples and oranges for Christmas."

"Wrong," I said quickly.

Dísa slapped the back of my head. I whirled around. Before I could twist the girl's ears, Jónas swung his ruler. Rubbing my hands in pain, I shouted, "We became a sovereign nation in a personal union with the king of Denmark."

Jónas smiled. "Of course, we still have the Danish king, but one day—"

Lárus let out a cracking fart. Rap. The ruler landed on his head. Jónas ran his thumb and forefinger along the wood of his ruler. Checking for blood?

"You're giving me a headache," Lárus yelled and walked out of the room. Dísa followed.

Jónas watched them go, and his craggy features softened. He looked different from most people. He must've come from far away. "Are you from up north?" I asked.

"No. Reykjavik."

"Why did you come all the way out here?"

A sad look crossed his face. "I lost most of my family—my brother, my little sister, my parents—in the Spanish flu. Too many memories—I had to leave."

"I hardly know about the flu," I said.

He sat down and cracked his knuckles. "Half the town was sick in bed or in the grave. Boats froze to the pier. Polar bears crossed over from Greenland on icebergs."

Couldn't be. Into Reykjavik?

"If you walked along the shore, you heard seals coughing," he said. "Coughed until they died. Pneumonia. Coal ran out. People used peat or seaweed in their stoves. Children rocked on their beds to keep warm. Old people hid under the covers. But the flu found them."

Jónas folded his arms over his chest and stayed silent for a moment.

"I never even went to their funerals," he said sadly. "Doctors wouldn't let us. Police buried the dead. If you stood near the open grave, the fumes of the dead could make you sick, they said. Police came to your house, put the corpse into a van, delivered it to the morgue. But the morgue filled up. I heard that," he sighed, "my mother and father lay in the pile in the graveyard. Bodies had to take their turn getting buried."

I closed my eyes, tried to picture all those bodies.

In the loft, Mama trod the spinning wheel. Knitting needles clicked. A man carved spoons from wood. Boys braided horsehair into ropes. I fell asleep combing tangles out of wool, but I woke up to Borghildur's big voice.

"Melkorka was the daughter of an Irish king, but the Vikings brought her to Iceland as a slave. When Melkorka's son Olaf sailed for Ireland, his mother gave him a gold arm ring that her father, the Irish king, had given her when she cut her first tooth. When Olaf arrived in Ireland, he showed the king the arm ring his mother had given him."

I dropped my carding combs and leaned forward.

"When the king saw the ring, his face grew red."

"That's when the king knew Olaf was his grandson," I called out. I shivered. Papa was alive. I just knew it.

Borghildur chanted a gloomy verse. "*Yfir kaldan eyðissand, einn um nótt ég sveima.* Over cold northern desert, I wander alone at night." We all muttered the sad words of loss, singing in different voices and changing keys, coming down hard on, "*Nú er horfið Norðurland. Nú á ég hvergi heima.* The north country has disappeared. Now I have no home."

The wind whined at the window. Raindrops pelted the small windowpane. Would I dare flee the farm? It was the only home I knew.

Borghildur clapped her hands. "It's almost Christmas. Let's sing about Jesus."

"To hell with Christmas," a grumpy old fellow said.

My friend crossed to the men's side of the loft and thrust her face into his. "And to hell with you, old man." Turning to the rest of us, she said, "All together now, praise Jesus." She began deep and low. Mama took the high voice. The men rolled in behind Borghildur's singing and delivered the old psalm right up to Saint Peter's gates.

"*Jesú, mín morgunstjarna, með náð lýs þinni hjörð, þinn ljóma þiggjum gjarnan á þessa dimmu jörð fyrir þitt friðarorð.* Jesus, my morning star, through your grace illuminate your flock; gladly we receive your glow on this dark earth through your words of peace."

Borghildur sat down and picked up her crocheting.

"Sing all you want," the grump said. "We'll be stuck here knitting socks on Christmas, same's ever."

"No, we won't. We'll all go up the hill to church," Borghildur said. "All except you. You'll stay here and get smashed to bits by the night troll." She was on her feet again, singing into the grumbler's face. "'Show me your pretty hand, missy, missy. Show me your hand.' Haven't you heard the troll on the window Christmas Eve? He's trying to get you, old man. Look at the troll, you get turned to stone. Keep your back to him, say, 'My hand's never touched filth, you ugly troll.' He'll go away. And you'll live another day, scumbag."

The old man threw back his head and laughed so we could see all the spaces where his teeth had once been. "I'll wrestle with the troll," he said between snorts of laughter.

We all hammered the floor with our feet.

Borghildur pointed at me. "Sigga?"

My cheeks went hot. "What do you think of the new Icelandic flag?" I blurted out. "Do you like the blue?"

"We should never, ever have given up the old Danish flag," the old man said.

"Don't you believe in independence?" Everybody stared at me, so I made a speech. "We're Icelanders, not Danes. We have our own trawlers. We don't need the stupid king."

Mama sent me a killing look.

Jónas sat at the end of the loft, fiddling with some reins. He winked at me. Later, in bed, I asked Mama, "Whatever happened to that man?"

"What man?"

"The one who carved you a knitting needle box? Guðmundur?"

"Oh, him," she said. "He climbed some cliffs looking for angelica. Never came back." I felt the tension in her body, how she was trying to say those words as if she didn't care what had happened to him.

"When was that?"

"Before you were born."

I didn't believe her. Papa was alive, and I would find him.

"Mama—"

"I'm tired."

My fingers dug into her arm. "You are *not* tired. That story about Melkorka and the Irish king . . . When the king saw the arm ring, his face turned red. He knew it was from his daughter." I couldn't finish. I was Melkorka. I might have to cross the sea to Ireland to find Papa.

From under the covers came Mama's muffled song. "*Hættu að gráta, hringaná, heyrðu ræðu mína, ég skal gefa þér gull í tá.* Don't cry, my little girl. Hear my words. I'll drop gold in the toe of your sock."

I heard the youngest calf bawl for its mother in the shed below.

Next day I wore overalls that only reached to my shins. One of the straps was broken. My brown sweater had belonged to one of the men who died of exposure fetching sheep. They'd taken the sweater off him before they buried his body.

"How was Iceland affected by the war?" Jónas asked as I entered the room.

Silence but for Lárus' fingernails scratching his crotch.

"We had food shortages and started sailing to New York," I said, taking my seat.

Lárus gave me a look of hatred, then jumped to his feet, knocking his books and papers to the floor. He bent to hiss into my ear.

"Trashbag."

I smelled cardamom seed liquor, laced with fermented shark, on his breath. Every year, he dipped into his mother's holiday food. After he stormed out of the room, I saw him from the window, stomping the snow, kicking up flowerpot shards in the yard.

For the rest of the winter I avoided Jónas' lessons. I didn't want to be near Lárus. His anger made me edgy. I went back to teaching myself. I scrounged around for old newspapers and read what I could. Going through the farmwife's cupboard and unwrapping plates, I found an advertisement different from all the others.

Help Wanted at the Lingerie Shop, Hafnarstræti.
Five-week corset construction class. Contact Magdalena.

Next to the words was a drawing of a corset. Construction? What could that mean? I studied the drawing. I loved its complexity. The corset seemed to be pieced together from several panels. If I was going to be independent, I needed an education. I would take this class. I tore out the ad and put it in the pocket of my overalls.

At the evening reading, I patted my pocket. Corsets would set me free.

One of the men asked Borghildur to read *Egilssaga*, which featured lots of killings.

"No," Borghildur said. "We'll read about his grandson, Kjartan, and Guðrún, the woman he loved."

The women clapped.

"When Guðrún was an aged nun," Borghildur read, "her son asked her which man she had loved the most. She didn't answer but discussed the qualities of her four husbands. Her son repeated the question. 'Which man did you love the most?' Then the old woman answered, '*Þeim var ég verst er ég unni mest*. To him I was worst whom I loved the most.'"

Guðrún ran her own life. I admired her.

The next day, I grasped the long wooden handle, pushed the iron spike into the earth, and burrowed under the angelica root. Putting all my strength into it, I popped the bulb and legs out of the earth, spraying myself with soil. Once I had a pile of bulbs and legs, I washed them off, buried them in dirt, and covered the pile with turf. One day the farmwife would ask me to dig up some angelica from my special burial place. Because I was a good gardener, this year we had more angelica than we could use. I was furious when the farmer tied a bag of *my* angelica to his saddle. Mama mounted the horse next to him. They would sell *my* angelica in the village.

"Take me," I said and ran alongside his horse until the dust from the hooves made me sneeze. When they were gone, I found a scrap of paper and wrote the following to Magdalena, the owner of The Lingerie Shop in Reykjavík:

> I have no money for the corset construction
> lessons, but I can already sew. Every evening of
> my life I've been sewing here on the farm. Can
> we make an agreement? You teach me how to sew
> corsets, and I will clean the shop.

Not just corsets. I'd do nightgowns, underpants, brassieres, and garter belts, all the ladies' things I'd seen in newspaper advertisements. But Magdalena didn't answer my letter. I studied the drawing of the corset on the advertisement and imagined how the parts were measured and sewn together. I needed a real corset so I could see how it was assembled.

Meanwhile, my anger was killing me. Mama bowed to the farmwife and all the men on the farm.

"Yes, ma'am."

"No, sir."

"Of course."

"Right away."

Was everyone else worth more than she was?

One day I was in the tool shed when an old lecher came at me with his fly unbuttoned. "Touch it. Just once."

I waved my root digger at his crotch, tried to hook his dick with it. My shoulder hit a glass jar. Crash. Mama made me crazy, apologizing to the farmwife.

"Sigga's so clumsy. Sorry. We'll clean up the pieces."

For days after that, the lecher tried to trap me in the animal shed, where only the warm, breathing animals could see us.

It was summer, and I was raking hay. I kept my head turned southwest toward Reykjavik, saw myself constructing a corset inside a cozy tailor shop. One day during coffee break, Jónas caught me staring at the horizon. "What are you thinking about?"

"About those U-boats. You know. During the war," I said.

He poured himself some coffee from the workers' thermos. "Sigga, why did you stop the lessons? You were my star pupil."

Out of the corner of my eye I watched Lárus, hands in his pockets, slouch toward the farmhouse. His mother would feed him cake and encourage him to take a nap.

I took The Lingerie Shop advertisement from my pocket. "This is what I really want," I said.

Jónas' charcoal eyes rolled down my hips. "God almighty, you don't need a corset."

Blood flooded my face. "I don't want a corset. I want to *make* corsets."

"You're not beautiful, Sigga—" he said, his breath warm on my upper arm.

"You . . . you . . . resemble the side of a cliff."

"You didn't let me finish. You're not beautiful, but you look good. Men want to keep their eyes on you. It has to do with how you walk in a straightforward way with your shoulders back. I noticed it the first time you came to the lesson."

He bent his head over his coffee cup as if the sun and the moon lived there.

My cheeks were on fire.

"You're a smart girl, but you don't understand. Men want you. Not for love."

I ran my big toe between the tufts of grass.

"Sigga, be careful," he said.

"I am," I whispered.

I stood rooted to the spot. I became aware of myself in a new way. I'd never been sure of how I looked. I had no mirror. But now I sensed how my bones were stacked inside my body, how my muscles were attached, and how each organ was in its right place. Every part of me was strong and ready to move forward.

Suddenly Mama stood next to me. I saw the unease in her eyes. I took her arm. "Let's leave this farm," I said. "In Reykjavik, we can sew, clean fish, be maids—"

Backing away, she held up both hands.

My irritation bloomed into forbidden words. "Why did you lie to me about Papa?"

Like a pale moth, her hand fluttered to her chest. "Lie?"

"The letter. I found the letter. He didn't write it."

The color left her cheeks. Instantly I was sorry and placed my arms around her thin shoulders. Her small body heaved against my big guilty self.

"I did the best I could," she said.

"Why did you lie?"

She moved away from me and looked belligerent. "He disappeared, died at sea."

"You said he fell off a cliff."

Bewildered, she looked at her feet. She'd made up the love story between her and Guðmundur, the shrinker of mittens. But I wouldn't let her steal Papa out of my imagination. He would tear my enemies apart, starting with the hairy man.

Chapter 4

The following spring, Borghildur woke up one morning and decided not to get out of bed. After that, she barely ate and hardly talked. One afternoon, I was catching cobwebs in the loft. Nobody but Borghildur was there.

"Sigga, come here," she said.

I went to the edge of her bed.

"You're a pretty girl."

A shiver went up my spine as I recalled Jónas' words. I wanted to be strong and brassy, not pretty. Now an unfamiliar pleasure rippled through me. I stood up and ran my hands along my square hips.

"Be careful, little Sigga," she whispered.

With my temper?

"Promise me . . . promise me you won't kill anyone on this farm."

"I promise." But if the pig-nosed girl got in my way again, I'd drive a pitchfork through her heart.

"Check the foot of my bed—under the covers."

I tugged until the tightly tucked-in blanket came loose and Borghildur's pale blue feet twitched in the cool air. Her toenails were long and unclean. Under her feet lay a piece of pink and white clothing.

"Take it out," she said.

I shook it and hugged it to my chest. It was a sleeveless sundress with a design of floppy red flowers. It smelled old.

"I wore it when—"

"When what?"

She shook her head. "You take it, Sigga. It'll be beautiful on you, but beware. When you hear men panting, run to the nearest cave."

"You hid in a cave?"

Her voice grew stronger. "I never hid from anyone."

"But you—"

"Quick girl. Before I forget. Put your hand in the pocket."

In the shallow pocket of the dress, my fingers touched a short metal thing. I took it out.

"It's called lipstick," she said.

I'd seen drawings of big lips, advertisements for this thing.

"Take off the lid."

I pulled it off and peered into the little cylinder.

"Give it to me." With her thumb and forefinger, she pushed a small knob upward. A chunk of red grease appeared. She dabbed her lips with it, rubbed them together, handed it back to me. "Try it, girl."

It tasted of rancid fat. Still, as I sensed the scarlet color of my lips, my breasts tingled. I pouted. The whole world was waiting for my kiss.

Borghildur's gray hair radiated out from her head on the pillow. Her face was white and bloodless, but her red lips seemed to smile on a memory. Holding the dress on my lap, I sat down on the edge of her bed and waited for her to speak again. But breathing was all she did. And then she didn't do that either. I bent over her and touched my lipstick to her lipstick. We had shared so much in my lifetime. "*Bless, Borghildur mín.* Goodbye, my dear Borghildur."

Next day I washed the dress and hung it on the line to dry. At her funeral, we sang her favorite song about Jesus. "*Jesú bróðir besti, barna vinur mesti.* Jesus, best brother, greatest friend of children." After we buried her, I got her bed.

―――――――――

When I wore Borghildur's dress, all the parts of my body that had been hidden under my sweater and overalls came alive. The breeze blew right through the armholes from one side to the other, tickling my breasts. It played with the hem of my dress and made me aware of the length of my legs, from the toes all the way up to where they were attached to my hips.

It was a sunny day with no outlook for rain. Through the thin fabric of my dress, the sun warmed my skin. I practiced different ways of walking as I balanced my rake on the end of my finger. My feet toed the grass. I took short strides. I took long ones. I swung my hips and pleasure rippled through my body. The wind tossed my hair as I got in line to rake the hay.

Mama turned and frowned at me. "You need a sweater over that dress."

Ignoring her, I moved my rake across the hay and breathed in the smell of freshly cut grass. Lárus slipped into the space behind me. I heard his rake scratching the earth, his cursing when the rake lodged itself in a clump of earth. After we turned the row of hay over to dry, his overalls brushed my bare arm. My ear sensed his warm breath, and my nostrils twitched at the smell of coriander brandy.

"Pretty girl," he whispered, his eyes burning the backs of my legs.

I threw down my rake, whirled around, and punched his chest. He stumbled, landed on his back, and lay there giggling and staring up at the sky. I picked up my rake and hurried to catch up with the other workers. When I looked back, he was gone.

In the evening when it was time to load the hay onto the horses' backs, Lárus reappeared. I snorted when I saw the pillow creases on his cheek. He'd been napping like a baby. He took the reins of the lead horse and headed for the barn. My thoughts softened as I set aside hay scraps for the "hidden people," the invisible creatures who helped the farm prosper.

It was nearly midnight when I climbed the steps to the loft. I slipped out of my dress, hung it over the end of the bed, and slid into my cotton nightgown, stitched together from old flour bags. These days it reached to my knees. I stretched my long body—first my legs, then the arms—touching both ends of Borghildur's old bed. The loft window framed the bright sky of the summer night. I heard the tired workers breathing. I joined their rhythm and fell into a deep sleep. I didn't hear the footsteps on the stairs, but I shuddered awake when boots stomped the loft floor. I raised my head.

Lárus stood at the front of the loft, muttering to himself. He paced the loft, lurched against bed frames, cursed, picked himself up, and lumbered to the window at the opposite end of the loft. Bedclothes rustled. Those hired hands didn't fool me. They weren't sleeping. They were listening. When he neared my bed, he peered in and saw me. He sat down.

I pushed myself against the wall. "Go away."

"Pretty girl."

The smell of brandy enveloped me. I screamed. His hand clamped down on my mouth and nose. My fists beat him. I clawed his hands, arms, and neck. My voice made muffled sounds against his thick hand. His other hand slid under the blanket and up my thigh. I tried to shriek when his finger shoved inside me. I pushed my knees into his chest, but he pinned me with his legs, parted them with his knee. I struggled for breath, tried to bite him, but I couldn't. I punched his shoulders and head. Suddenly he hunched his body and thrust into me. Pain shot up my spine. I bit his hand until I tasted blood. Cursing and panting, he rode me like a drunk devil. Afterward, he lay heavy as a sack of potatoes on top of me. Suddenly he rolled onto the floor and was gone. For a moment my knees knocked together in humiliation and shame.

"Stop him. Kill him," I shouted. The hired hands sat up in bed and held their blankets to their noses. "Cowards," I yelled and ran to the top of the steps. But Mama wedged herself between me and the top step. I'd have to push her down the stairs to get through.

"Sigga, Sigga, Sigga." She dug her fingernails into my wrists and led me back to the bed, where she covered me with the blanket as if nothing had happened.

"Where were you?" I asked.

"I told you to wear a sweater over that dress."

In the far corner of the loft somebody laughed.

"What's wrong with you, Mama?" I whispered.

Instead of answering, she sang, "Elves tiptoed through the moss. They stole the woman. They pulled her deep down into the warm earth."

"Stop that singing." My heart pummeled my rib cage. A headache hammered my temples. Mama wiped my forehead with a wet cloth, still singing that stupid song.

"Why didn't you do something?" I snatched the cloth from her hand and shoved it between my legs and wiped the hateful evidence of Lárus off my body.

Mama spoke in a whisper. "He's the farmer's son."

"I hate you."

As if I'd hit her, she sucked in her belly, hunched her shoulders, and shuffled away. I was sorry for my words. But at that moment I did hate her. I beat the bed with my fist. I would cut his throat and throw his bloody body onto the manure pile. The place between my legs throbbed. My ribs ached. Damn. Damn. Damn. Lárus must die. I looked up at my dress on the bedpost. I wouldn't wear it. Under my blanket, I wriggled into my overalls. Workers, heads down, sat on the edge of their beds. I walked to the steps and descended into the kitchen.

The farmwife was kneading dough. I stared daggers at her. "Your son came to my bed last night—"

She punched the dough. "Hussy. You worthless hussy."

"I was in bed sleeping, when—"

"You pulled my son into your bed. And him engaged to the daughter at Upper Slope."

"He woke me up for practice?"

She pointed a floured finger at me. "Scum. Get out of my sight. Leave this farm."

My heart leaped. But fear followed. Suddenly I was uncertain. My voice quavered. "We have an agreement with you, my mother and I."

"No hussies on my farm. Get out."

"Where do I go?"

Her eyes brimmed with poison. "I'll arrange it. You'll go into domestic service in Reykjavik."

Reykjavik? Fat angels plucked harps. Heaven? Women earned money in Reykjavik. They walked on something called pavement or rode in boxy cabins with motors called cars. I ran upstairs. Mama sat on her bed, knitting socks. I placed my hands on her shoulders, raised her up, drew her close, rested my chin on her head, and talked into her hair.

"Remember I said I was going to Reykjavik?"

"No, Sigga," she said into my chest.

"Yes. I am."

Her knitting fell to the floor.

"After Lárus . . . and yesterday . . . the farmwife's sending me away."

Away. Harp music filled my ears and flooded my whole being.

"Fly my soul between heaven and earth. Jesus walk with me to Reykjavik."

But then I heard Mama snuffling. I reseated her on the bed, picked up her knitting, and placed it on her lap. My vision went zigzag. I'd thrown the puzzle pieces of our lives into the air. And now I was frightened. Would the pieces land in the right places?

"I'll be all alone," Mama said in a tiny voice.

I bit my lip. "You'll join me in Reykjavik." I reached under the mattress for my cloth bag. I threw in my nightgown, the overalls, the red sweater, and my sundress with the faded red roses. I tied the bag with a string.

"You'll come and get me?" Mama asked.

"Yes." I put my arms around her and squeezed her the way she used to squeeze me. I ran down the steps blinking back tears.

One last time, I walked the long, dark hall that smelled of dirt. My fingertips touched the rough walls. At the front door, the farmwife stood, bulky as a troll woman, and handed me an envelope. "A letter of reference for Rasmussen. He imports and exports. You'll take care of his wife and do some housework," she said.

Outside I found the farmer adjusting the cinch strap on the smaller horse. "You take the roan," he said. "She'll carry sugar, flour—maybe even coffee on the way back."

I swung my leg over the horse's back and settled into the saddle. When I saw Lárus unlatching the gate, I flew off my horse. Fists clenched, I pushed myself into his face until I felt his hot breath. "Despicable beast," I said and raised my arm to slap him. A strong hand caught my wrist.

"Sigga," the farmer said. "Get back on the horse."

As I hoisted myself back into the saddle, I saw Mama standing on the steps. So small. Ahead of me, at the gate, stood Lárus, his mouth twisted in a smile. But suddenly my hatred vanished in a rush of gratitude. He got me off the farm. As the horses plodded toward the main road, I fixed my eyes on the horse's rump swaying in front of me, then on the horizon.

Chapter 5

It felt like we'd been bouncing along for days and weeks. To the south lay the black beaches and the crashing surf. To the north, the land rose up in green and gravelly slopes. The sun hung in the sky directly above us. Finally, the farmer dismounted and disappeared behind some rocks. I clambered down from the horse, rolled onto the grass, and breathed in the smell of tiny plants with hard little leaves. Under the whoosh of the wind, I hugged my knees, felt the ache of my body melt away. The farm was hours behind me. I'd escaped. But at the edge of my happiness lingered Mama's sad face. I already missed her.

I pulled myself up to a sitting position and leaned against a lichen-covered rock. Purple moss campion blossomed on a green tussock. The farmer sat down next to me and handed me a chunk of bread with cheese. As I ate, I watched the grass on the other side of the road ripple in the wind.

"I'm sorry about it," he said.

"What?" I blushed. I knew what he meant.

"Here," he said, pushing a coin into my palm.

My fingers closed around the coin. I would shop in Reykjavik.

We both stood up. The farmer took out a flask and offered me a sip. I smelled the snuff on him, saw the shine in his eyes. The drink burned from my mouth to my belly. I tightened my grip on the coin.

When we stopped at a farm to spend the night, I wrapped myself in a blanket and rolled into a corner of the kitchen. I had to be awakened next morning. After a breakfast of coffee and bread, we headed out in a misting rain. Hours later, the sun appeared between the clouds. The sameness of the undulating rump of the farmer's horse made me sleepy. I dozed and woke up to a different landscape. We rode past bright-green, moss-covered lava rocks, surrounding black pools of water. Sheep skittered across the dusty road. A barking, curly-tailed dog ran toward us. The roof of a sod house sagged. On it stood a lamb on stiff legs.

As we approached Reykjavik, I smelled the sea and saw the snowy tops of Esja Mountain, at its foot the green water of the bay. Sod huts gave way to timber houses clad with corrugated iron. The horses slowed their pace. Houses came toward us in clusters, so different from the solitary farms I had known all my life, tucked behind a bluff or in a hollow.

Now the road was lined with small houses, shops, and a dairy. My heart pounded when I saw the sun shimmering on the pond in the center of town. We turned into a street lining the pond and stopped at a tall house with dragons carved into the wood under the eaves. I slid down the roan's belly and handed the farmer the reins. I ran my fingertips along a black wall, covered with moss and lichens, that surrounded the garden. Inside the wall, gnarled birch trees and red currant bushes grew out of black dirt. Purple and yellow pansies huddled against the house wall.

The farmer stood at the gate and waited while I raised the knocker on the door. A short, oily man appeared. His words rumbled up in an unfamiliar accent. "I'm Rasmussen. You're the girl?" He plucked the farmwife's reference letter out of my hand.

My chest tightened when I heard the farmer ride off, not because I liked him but because he was a familiar figure. I stepped into a hallway that felt like another country. Flowery paper covered the walls. Shiny wood formed the wide staircase and its carved railing. Rasmussen's eyes glistened under the sparkling chandelier.

"Five kronas a month with room and board. You will clean, cook, iron, and take care of my wife, Dagmar, called Diva. She thinks she's an opera singer." He rolled his eyes on the word "thinks." "Sang as a girl in Copenhagen—you know—around the piano at parties."

I knew nothing about marriage, but the way he talked about his wife made me uneasy.

"I'll have some outdoor work for you, too," he said.

"Gardening?" I would revive the pansies.

"Dock work. When the coal ships come in, you'll wear a man's sweater and cap and unload coal for a man's wage."

A joke? Men's clothes? I thought of Auður who wore breeches in the saga of Laxar Valley. Hadn't she been divorced for wearing men's clothes? Rasmussen took my elbow and led me up the stairs to a wide landing. Behind a closed door, a woman sang. Rasmussen swung open the door.

Against puffy pillows lay a plump woman with a doughy face. Her hair hung in dark ringlets, and she smiled like a little girl. Eyes shining, she extended a hand, jangling her bracelets. I clasped her thick fingers. Not farm fingers. Nobody collected that much meat on the bone on the farm.

Rasmussen spoke out of the corner of his mouth. "Today she's pretending to sing the opera, *Tosca.*"

Pretending?

Diva smiled sweetly. "I sing all the parts. Sometimes Rasmussen sings with me, screams as good as Emilio Biondi. Don't you, darling?"

Rasmussen ignored her and pointed at his watch. I followed him out. The floorboards creaked under our feet as we walked down the hall. Maids' Room, the sign on the door said. Rasmussen threw open the door, banging it against the wall. The room contained one large bed, much bigger than the one Mama and I had shared, and a wooden clothes closet. A dark-haired girl sat on the bed, holding a mirror to her face. Eyebrow hairs lay on a piece of paper next to her. With a black pencil, she drew a line where her eyebrow had once been.

Rasmussen gestured with both arms. "Edda from the Eastern Fjords and Sigga from the farm." Edda wrinkled her nose as if she smelled the farm on me. A shiny black dress lay on the bed, next to it a white apron and a small, stiff cap. I began to undo my overalls, but then I noticed Rasmussen's eyes on me. I folded my arms and glared at him. When he finally closed the door from the outside, I quickly stepped out of the overalls. The uniform felt silky and cool as I slipped it over my head. I buttoned it up to the neck and tied the strings of the starched, white apron behind my back.

Gazing into the mirror, I stroked the fabric over my hips, picked up the cap, and nested it in my hair. In the mirror I saw a tall girl with strong shoulders, small breasts, and a broad face. I recalled how Jónas had looked at me and smiled at my reflection.

Edda let out a low whistle. "You'll have no trouble finding a man."

"I don't like men."

"Why?"

I shrugged. Edda needn't know. I recalled the plumbing advertisements. "Where's the toilet?" I asked. Edda opened the door and pointed down the hall. Rasmussen stood at the top of the stairs, watching me. Abruptly he turned and disappeared down the steps. I entered the bathroom. In the center of the room was a porcelain bowl, above it a tank with a chain. My thighs trembled as I lowered myself to the wooden seat. As a child, I'd feared drowning in the outhouse. At Rasmussen's I would pee in safety. No newspaper strips here. I always hated the printer's ink on my thighs. I picked up a square of shiny paper.

Back in the bedroom, I closed the door and turned the key in the lock.

The light was out, and I curled up on my side of the bed. I felt the warmth of human breath between my shoulder blades. "Who are you?" Edda asked.

I whispered to the wall, "I worked on a farm until they sent me away. I have one relative. Mama." On the last word, my voice went ragged.

"You stole food?"

"The farmwife's son got drunk and—"

"Ohhh. I see."

I buried my head under the covers.

"Lucky you're not pregnant," Edda said. "Diva sends pregnant girls back to the farm."

I shuddered. I must never get pregnant.

Edda and I cleaned baseboards, washed Diva's lacy underwear, ground coffee, and dusted the porcelain figures of birds and dogs that crowded the sideboard in the hall. We shook dust cloths out the back door into the cold air until our noses were full of grit.

"Let's take a break and look at Danish magazines," Edda said.

I followed her into the little reading room next to Rasmussen's office. Danish magazines and local newspapers lay on the table between the chairs. I flipped through a magazine and admired drawings of men and women, their eyes closed, lips puckered. I'd have to learn Danish to read the love stories. In the next room, the floorboards squeaked under Rasmussen's pacing.

I raised my eyebrows at Edda.

"In the war, he lost some ships. He always worries about money," she said.

But on his cellar shelves he had cans of ham, red cabbage, and peas. Diva would never have to eat miltbread or pickled swim bladders. Bags of coal lined the wall. Rasmussen wouldn't heat the house with peat, seaweed, or dried manure.

"I'm saving for one of these," Edda said, pointing to a drawing of a woman wearing a small fur piece, a fox biting its tail. "And you—what do you want?" she asked.

I recalled last night's dinner of patty shells filled with creamed chicken and peas. I glanced up at the electric lights, recalled the shiny toilet paper. My bed was soft. I had everything I wanted. But underneath my satisfaction something struggled for air.

The tidy house felt like a cage. I fetched my coat, had to get outside. I breathed in the fishy ocean air. Just around the corner, I came to a small square. At its edge stood a gloomy, gray stone building. Parliament, the farmer had called it. A man wearing a skirt and some strange creatures were carved into the stone above the arched windows. At the center of the façade was the crown of the Danish king and the year 1880.

I took a side street and peered into the open door of a warehouse. Dozens of crates of flattened fish were stacked on both sides of the wall. At the harbor, men rolled barrels down the gangplank of a ship while seagulls circled against a bright blue sky. The men moved their arms and swooped forward to lift the barrels. I could lift barrels. Then I could sail on their boat beyond the horizon, into the world.

Carrying Diva's breakfast tray of coffee and oatmeal with prunes, I pushed open her bedroom door with my shoulder. When she saw the food, she turned her face to the wall. "Biksemad. I want biksemad," she said.

I hurried back down the stairs. In the kitchen, I sat down and ate Diva's breakfast. I arranged the prune pits on the side of the bowl when I noticed Edda watching me, hands on her hips.

"Diva wants biksemad," I said.

"Spoiled brat. Biksemad's just leftovers, something from her singing days in the pub."

"I thought she was an opera singer."

Edda smirked. "She sang in some sailors' pub in Nyhavn in Copenhagen. Biksemad was on special every single day."

She returned from the pantry with lamb fat, gristle, sausage, potatoes, and onions. After chopping and frying the whole mess, she plopped a fried egg on top and pushed the steaming plate in my direction. "And don't forget the singing juice," she said, drizzling a syrupy red liquid into a wine glass. The label showed red berries that didn't grow on the island.

Walking up the stairs with Diva's tray, I leaned forward and sniffed the red liquid. The sweet sharp aroma pinched my nostrils. Diva sat up very straight when I entered the room. A book slid off her belly to the floor. I picked it up and read the title, *Tosca, the Opera.* I watched her shovel the biksemad into her mouth and wash it down with the berry drink. Patting the bed next to her, she reached for the book. I climbed up and sank into the soft mattress.

"Don't stroll with a man, or you go back to the farm," she said out of the side of her mouth.

I shook my head. I'd never do that.

Diva opened the book to a sketch of a man holding a paintbrush. "Cavaradossi, the painter, was Tosca's boyfriend. Tosca's a singer, and Police Chief Scarpia wants to seduce her. Cavaradossi's hiding Angelotti, a Buonopartist, who has escaped from Saint Angelus prison."

I leaned over her shoulder. On the next page was a map of Rome. A river named Tiber ran down its center. West of the river were the words "Vatican" and "Saint Angelus Prison." And to the east, "Sant'Andrea della Valle."

"That's the church where the opera takes place," Diva said. "And just beyond that, on the Tiber bank, is the Jewish ghetto, home of my people."

"I thought you were Danish."

"Jewish, too. My people came from Spain to Denmark in the seventeenth century. They brought music, poetry, and art," she said, smacking her lips, shiny red now from the liqueur. "Opera's in my blood. Come sing opera with me."

I shook my head. I loved to sing, but Mama put a stop to that. When we sang in the loft, the hymns lifted me halfway to heaven. *Jesus, you are my savior. Walk with me.* I would put them off tune, Mama had said. I'd chanted rhymes with the men. "Rimmi, dimmi, dimm, dimm," in a furry, low voice.

"Scarpia arrests Cavaradossi," Diva said. "He will spare Cavaradossi's life only if Tosca submits to him. Tosca stabs him. He's dying, and she sings, ' *Ti soffoca il sangue?* Are you suffocating on your blood?'"

I hummed along with Diva's singing. *"Muori! Muori! Muori!* Die, die, die," when the door swung open and Rasmussen stood there, pointing a finger at me. "Sigga, you are the maid. Diva, you are the employer."

Fear sharpened the doughy lines in Diva's face. "We were only—"

I jumped down from the bed.

A few days later, I was fixing Diva's breakfast tray when Rasmussen walked into the kitchen. He carried an armload of clothes and dropped them on the table—a long, narrow undershirt, a man's sweater, a tweed cap with a visor, rubber boots, and overalls.

"They're unloading a shipment of Yorkshire coals. I want you to go to the dock and earn me a man's wage," he said.

I shook my head.

"You *will* go."

"But they'll find out I'm a woman."

Rubbing his oily lips together, he eyed my chest. "Flatten your breasts with the undershirt. Make your voice deep. Talk from your belly."

I stared at the men's clothes. "I won't."

He stepped toward me. "Yes, you will. I pay your salary. I own you, and I can rent you out."

"You don't own me!"

But he did. His hand gripped my shoulder. Sweat dripped down my back. I picked up the clothes and hurried to my room. Edda looked up from curling her eyelashes.

"He's never told you to shovel coal?" I asked.

"Me . . ." Edda thrust out her bosom. "I'd never pass for a man."

I tucked my breasts into the tight undershirt.

"Rasmussen will keep every krona you earn," Edda said.

My cheeks burned with shame. "I won't let him," I said and hurried downstairs. On the table I found Rasmussen's newspaper. He'd made a circle around these words.

> A coal ship is expected today. Coals are best quality. South Yorkshire Hards. For 40 kronas per ton, driven to your home from the ship. Place orders with Einar Thorgilsson.

I ran through the narrow streets into the space between the buildings leading to the harbor. A rust-streaked ship sat low in the water. Seagulls shrieked above. Men dressed in torn pants and thin sweaters stood at the door of the foreman's shed, beating their upper arms for warmth. I elbowed my way to the front of the crowd, wedged myself between a boy and an old man, bent over like a wheelbarrow.

The door of the shed opened. A large man in knee-high boots and a knitted cap stepped toward us. "You and you," he said, pointing to a couple of strapping fellows. They headed toward the ship.

The remaining men leaned forward and soundlessly begged, "Pick me, pick me."

I held my breath as the foreman ran his eyes over us, moving his pointed finger from left to right. At last it rested on . . . me. I touched my chest. Me? He nodded. I grasped a shovel as the old man next to me shuffled away. Poor creature. His wife would chop up the last of the swim bladders and serve them with porridge scrapings. The next day there would be no food. His children would stay in bed, hold their tummies, and groan with hunger. But my heart thrummed with joy. I'd been picked. I joined the men and began shoveling coal.

When the trough was full, the crane swung through the air and lowered its hook. A crew member attached it to the overflowing trough. Bits of coal dropped to the dock as the trough swayed above us before dumping its load onto the back of a waiting truck. I leaned on my shovel. My shoulders and back ached. Beads of perspiration formed white paths in the coal dust on the men's faces. I must look like them. I sneezed and wiped my nose, making black streaks down the back of my hand.

At the end of the day, I got paid almost twice a woman's wage. The coins jingled in my pocket when I walked. A trawler was docked nearby. It bore the name, *Sóley*. A tall crew member with copper-colored hair grinned at me from the deck. He hoisted a bag over his shoulder and bounced down the gangplank. I quickened my pace and headed away from the dock, but he fell into step with me.

"Hey, fellow. Shoveled a lot of coal?"

I ignored him, but he patted my shoulder. "Worn out, huh?"

"Don't touch me." My voice hit a high note.

"What did I hear? You're a—?" He peered into my face and scanned my body.

"No, I'm not."

He stopped walking and held out both arms, blocking my path. I tried to slip away, but he placed his hands on my shoulders and brought his face close to mine. "I've been at sea for two weeks, and I'd say you're the most beautiful woman I've ever seen. What's your name?"

I twisted out of his grip. "And yours?"

He grasped my wrist. "Sveinn Gunnarsson."

"That hurts," I said.

"Sorry, beautiful."

I smoothed my overalls. "Sigga's my name."

"My dear Sigga, what will you do with the money you earned? Buy a hat and new shoes?"

I couldn't admit Rasmussen would take it all. "I'm going home," I said.

"Can we talk some more?"

"No."

I walked away. But I heard his footsteps behind me. Every time I turned around, he was still there, watching me, laughing as if he knew I would turn around. The next time I looked he'd disappeared. I touched the coins in my right pocket, took a few out and dropped them into my left pocket. Rasmussen would get his money, but I'd save the rest for bus fare for Mama.

Chapter 6

Leaning out the window, I smelled the air and trembled like a cow confined all winter in the shed. I followed Edda out the door. On the steps, she linked her arm in mine. The breeze blew the sand from the partially paved sidewalks onto our legs as we walked briskly. At the center of the square was a clock, below it a picture of a woman in a twirling white skirt and the word "Persil," the name of the washing powder we used for Diva's nightgowns. We sat down on the bench. Edda offered me a cigarette. I turned it over in my hand, sniffed it. What a funny thing. When I inhaled, I coughed, but gradually I got used to the smoke. Halfway through, I liked the taste. With each exhale, my worries glided away. I smoked until the stub burned my fingers. I ground it under my shoe, closed my eyes, and raised my face to the sun.

"Like to stroll?" a deep voice asked. I opened my eyes. Sveinn, the grinning fisherman, stood in front of me in white linen trawlerman pants that widened at the cuff. Two buttons at the waist held up a white bib. He wore black clogs.

I recalled Diva's girl who strolled and got sent back to the farm, pregnant. Better to jump into the black water between the hull and the dock than return to the farm. I shook my head.

Edda jumped to her feet. "I'll go," she said, linking her arm in Sveinn's. He grinned over his shoulder at me as they walked away.

A few weeks later, I was on the dock again, collecting my man's pay, when I saw sea gulls circling the trawler, *Sóley*. I walked to the edge of the dock and peered into the boat's hold. Sveinn was tossing fish up to a line of crew members. The fish formed a silver streak as they flew from hand to hand until each fish landed on the back of the waiting truck.

"Hey," Sveinn called up to me, as he jumped over the side of the trawler and onto the dock. His bare arms were covered with clumps of salt and marked by tiny cuts. He grimaced as he dipped them into a bucket of water, then dried himself with a dirty towel.

I turned to leave.

"Wait for me," he said.

But I hurried away. Back at the house, I cleaned my face and hands in the cellar, took off the dockworker uniform and slipped into my maid's dress. Rasmussen met me in the kitchen, his palm extended.

My anger flared up. "I earned the coins."

"Pay me." His eyes shone like an oil slick. He lowered his voice. "Of course, if you join me later tonight, maybe I'll be more generous."

I threw a handful of coins on the floor. Growling, he bent to pick them up as I stalked out of the room.

Diva was happy to see me.

My shame overflowed. "I can't stay here."

"Why?"

"Rasmussen."

Tiny pink spots formed in her cheeks. "What can I do to make you stay?" I heard the pleading in her voice.

"Bring my mother here. She can cook, and clean, and sew for you."

"And where will *you* go?"

I blurted out a wish I didn't know I had. "I'll be a cook on a trawler, the *Sóley.*"

I wrote to Mama.

> *Please come. I've found a position for you here in Rasmussen's house.*

I kissed the envelope and brought it to the post office.

It had been a few weeks. No answer from Mama. I sat on Diva's bed, sewing buttons on one of her nightgowns.

"I'll teach you how to embroider," Diva said. "You can embroider insects and reptiles onto tea towels and sell them to Faroese fishermen. They love pretty things and will buy them for their wives back in Thorshavn. If you leave me, you can make a living sewing."

She reached into her sewing basket and took out an embroidery of Adam and Eve sitting under a tree. A snake with an apple in its mouth hung from a branch. A tiger, a camel, an eagle, and a stork watched the snake. Birds with red bellies and yellow heads sat on Eve's shoulders.

"For the wall?" I asked.

Diva shook her head. "A Seder towel, for the Jewish Passover meal."

"I don't know anything about Jewish."

"We are the chosen people of God. When King Herod began to kill all the newborns, God made sure his soldiers passed over the Jews' houses. That's why we celebrate Passover with a big meal called a Seder." She threaded a needle and handed it to me.

I stared at the needle. "I want to sew corsets," I said.

"Look under the nightgowns." She nodded her head toward the chest of drawers.

I jumped off the bed and rummaged through the bottom drawer until my fingers touched some fabric, coarse and soft at the same time. I pulled it out and ran my fingers along the boning buried in vertical channels at the waist. I held it against my body. I took some pins from Diva's sewing box and pinned the corset to my maid's uniform.

The door opened. Rasmussen's eyes locked on my corset. "A man's here to see you."

I flushed. "Who? I don't know anyone."

"Big fellow. Grins like a clown."

"Oh, him," I said, pretending not to care.

But I ran past Rasmussen and down the stairs. Sveinn stood near the gate as if he'd stepped back to look up into Rasmussen's windows. When he saw me, he made a mock bow and approached the steps. "Nice," he said, pointing at the corset, still pinned to me.

"It's Diva's." I unpinned it and folded it.

"Will you come walk with me?"

I hesitated. The fragrance of rain and sea hung on the air.

"Please," he begged, hopping up the steps until we stood nose to nose. Salt, sweat, and motor oil clung to him and his clothes.

"I'll get my sweater."

Upstairs, I threw the corset on the bed and pulled on my old double-darned man's sweater. As we walked quickly along the pond toward the mountains in the south, Sveinn's arm felt warm and steady against mine. I wasn't going against my principles. He wasn't Lárus, and he wasn't the hairy man.

"I want to tell you something," he said.

I braced myself.

"We were way out. The deck was slippery with fish, and a man fell overboard. We stopped the motor, threw out the cable. The sea was rough. We lost him. Then we saw his face in the water. He disappeared again, popped up. We yelled, 'Cable! Cable!' But it sank. We pulled it in and threw it out again. Finally, he grabbed it. We saved him."

I shivered. "Have you thought of safer work—like in a bank?"

A look crossed his face that told me working in a bank was the worst idea in the world. He squeezed my arm. "Money's in the pockets of trawlermen, not in the banks." He stopped walking and raised both arms, spreading the fingers. "Sigga, I only know your first name."

"My mother wouldn't give me my father's name."

"What do you call yourself, then?"

"My mother's name is Hansína, so on the farm they called me after her, Hansínudóttir."

"Most people know who their father is even if he's a shit heel."

I bit my lip.

We walked in silence except for the dull roar of the wind. "Speaking of fathers," he said as we rounded the pond into a more sheltered place. "Mine's trouble. Wants to run everything, but he can't run his own business. He tries to sell English marmalade and stale biscuits to people who can't afford bread."

But he had a father. "I'd like to meet him."

"No, you wouldn't."

"Why do you say that?"

His lips formed a thin line. His silence made me uneasy.

One day, I was on my way to the bakery to get sticky Danish pastries for Diva. A tall man with flowing white hair and a broad head, handsome as a lion's, walked toward me on the narrow pavement. He seemed to be talking to himself, shaking his mane in agreement with something he was thinking.

With each step, he raised his feet high like people back on the farm, scaling tussocks. When he passed me, I glimpsed light blue eyes and a long nose. I turned around and studied his square shoulders. Where had I seen him before? Then I remembered the photograph Jónas had shown me of a tall man who stood on the steps of the government building. Curiosity gripped me. I ran after him. But as I drew near, I stopped myself. What would I say? Anxiety clogged my throat. I turned and walked back toward the bakery. The smell of sugar cleared my head.

"Miss, how can I help you?"

"I'll have . . . the usual," I said.

With her eye on the next customer, the clerk wrapped up a loaf of bread and some pastries. I dropped my coins on the counter and hugged the fresh-baked bread, enjoying its warmth against my chest. On the way home, I stopped at the corner where I'd encountered the lion. But he was gone.

Back home, I set down Diva's tray of tea and pastries. Ignoring the food, she said, "Let me teach you how to embroider." She handed me a needle with gray thread and a piece of cloth. "Do you realize there are at least three shades of gray in a horsefly's wing?"

I sat down and stabbed the cloth with the needle. "I saw a man—" I said.

She took the cloth from my hands and sewed a few stitches. "Who?"

"He's tall. Wavy hair. Looks like a lion. Lifts his legs a bit when he walks."

"Guðmundur? He lives just up the street."

Guðmundur? The mitten shrinker who carved Mama's name on the lid of a box?

"He was talking to himself, like a crazy person," I said.

"Crazy for independence. Probably practicing his next speech. No more Danish king. That's Guðmundur."

"You know him well?"

"His wife, Herdís, sweet woman, comes here every now and then— feels sorry for me, I think. By the way, Guðmundur comes from the village near your farm."

My hands dropped to my lap. "He lives up the street? Where?"

Diva took my needle and thread and the towel from my hands and began to embroider gray wings. "In the large beige house with the brown roof."

I knew that house.

"The grasshopper can also be lovely on a tea towel, all green and yellow."

I put down my needle. All I could think of was Guðmundur.

I made a habit of passing the lion's house, but I couldn't think of a reason for knocking on his door. I tried to focus on the routine at Diva's. Mornings, I greased her voice with cod liver oil when she opened her mouth like a bird's beak. Her cherry liqueur chased away the fishy flavor. Mondays, I washed the floors. Tuesdays, I darned socks, mended frayed sheets, hemmed skirts, sewed on buttons, and reattached ties to featherbed covers until my eyes watered. Wednesdays, I chopped meat for biksemad and ironed towels and sheets. Thursdays, I prepared a thick brown sauce to pour over the weekend meat dishes. Fridays, I caramelized potatoes, dusted baseboards, cleaned toilets and sinks. Most days I sang with her.

One evening, I was in the cellar ironing the lace on her underwear when Sveinn's face appeared at the window. I let him in.

"I brought you something," he said, handing me a package.

I ripped off the paper. Inside was a dark blue sweater with a cable design.

"I was on a different trawler, long time ago, and it capsized. I was wearing that sweater. It saved my life. You should have it."

"Why?"

"Because you're saving my life. I think about you all the time I'm not with you." He grinned. Another joke.

"And when you're with me, all you think about is fish," I said.

I held the sweater to my nose and smelled the ocean, the fish, the fear, the killing cold. I pulled it on and smoothed it down my body. The cable design flowed over my breasts. He reached for me, tucked his nose between my neck and collarbone. "Ahhh, my favorite smells, you and the sea."

I pushed him away.

But that night I placed his sweater on my pillow and lay with my cheek on the pattern. How would his naked body feel against mine? I sat up and slapped myself. Don't ever think of him like that. He's not for you. I woke up with the cable design imprinted on my face, like those snakes I'd seen in Diva's magazines.

Rasmussen was out, and Diva slept. I grabbed my coat and ran up the street to the big house with the brown roof. I stopped at the gate and stared at the first-floor windows. Was he in there having breakfast? My heart fluttered, but my feet stuck to the pavement. Why am I here? Am I crazy? I noticed a woman kneeling on the steps that led to the front door.

Next to her was a bucket. She washed the last step and dropped the cloth into the bucket.

I recalled the lion's name. "Is Guðmundur at home?" I asked.

When she stood up, I saw she wasn't wearing a maid's uniform. "No, he's not. He went out to get a newspaper," she said, sweetly.

"Rasmussen down the street sent me," I lied.

She frowned. "Has Diva taken a turn for the worse?"

"Not at all. I have a question for Guðmundur."

"Come in." Her voice was warm. As I approached the steps, she wiped her hand on her apron and extended it. "I am Herdís, his wife."

"Sigga Hansínudóttir," I said.

I followed her up the steps and into a small parlor. Sweat formed under my clothes. Sveinn's sweater itched my skin. What would I say? I took off my coat and sat down in a chair with carved armrests. Herdís put away her bucket and took the chair opposite me. She had soft, brown curls and a small, round nose. My knee bumped against the claw-foot table leg. As I reached down to rub it, I saw the row of framed photographs on the shelf opposite. They all seemed to be of a young man who parted his hair on the right.

"Our son, Kalli," Herdís said. I'd pictured the lion as childless. "Kalli works on ships. He's first mate on *Hvítifoss*."

Sun glimmered through crocheted curtains and landed on one of the photographs of Kalli, giving it an unreal quality. I stroked the soft inlaid leather of the table. In its center was a round tin container with a small hole. I touched the shiny object with a fingertip.

"It's my friend's saccharine," Herdís said. "She visits me every day."

"Every day?" I longed for a friend, somebody I could be close to.

"Now, why did you come?"

"Well, you see—"

The door opened. In walked the lion. "Who do I have the pleasure—" His large hand reached for mine. Herdís slipped out of the room.

"Sigga. Sigríður, actually. I grew up on the farm, Upper Falls, near your village."

"Ah," he said. A shadow passed over his face. "Something rather sad happened at the falls, near your farm."

"You mean the baby?" I asked.

"Yes, that poor woman."

We all knew about the young woman who left her newborn baby behind the waterfall. The splashing water hid its cries. Mama sometimes hinted I was lucky not to be that baby.

"Can you help me bring my mother to Reykjavik?" I asked.

He looked confused. "You mean arrange a ride for her?"

"No. I've written her many letters, but I've never gotten an answer. Something's wrong."

"Tell me the name of the farm again."

"Upper Falls."

"And your mother's name."

"Hansína Theodórsdóttir."

His face didn't light up when I mentioned Mama's name, nor did he write anything down, not my name, not Mama's name, not the name of the farm. Herdís appeared in the door.

"It's time," she said. "They're waiting for you."

Again, his large, warm hand took mine.

Chapter 7

Up ahead, distant mountains appeared to rise up out of the sea like blue and purple giants. Sveinn stopped to pick some buttercups and blue-tufted vetch and handed me the bouquet. I nosed the flowers. He laughed at the pollen on my face. "You are nice to look at. Would you like to be the cook on my trawler, so I can look at you all the time?"

"Yes," I said.

"All day long you can boil potatoes in the galley." His hands slid down my back and lingered at my waist. The blood throbbed behind my ears. It scared me. I tried to push him away, but he drew me close, crushing the flowers. "The galley's small. Let's practice being in small places."

I broke free. "I'm going home." The bouquet of flowers fell to the grass. He held up his hands and staggered backward as if I'd hit him.

His words rang in my ears. "Are you serious about the cook job?"

The wind whipped up, throwing my words back at me. "Are you?"

"Yes!" he said. A startled godwit flew out of its nest.

I would see the world and gain my independence from Rasmussen. Sveinn grasped my shoulders. I swung an arm around his waist. Like two people in a three-legged race, we stumbled toward the fishermen's baiting sheds. We wound our way between beached boats. One shed was larger than the others. Sveinn opened the splintered wooden door. I bent my knees and rounded my back to enter the tiny hut. Dots of light shone through the holes in the corrugated iron above our heads. *Ouch.* My shin hit a bench.

We tore off our clothes and dropped them on the dirt floor. Shivering,

I lay down on the bench. One foot gripped the ground. The other flew out as I pulled him toward me. His salty, sweaty smell enveloped me.

"Am I too heavy?"

"Yes," I said as he pressed the air out of me. But I gripped his shoulders and braced my leg against the wall. I thought I heard my ribs crack under his bulk, but it was the rattle of the corrugated iron walls and roof. Wasn't there supposed to be pleasure? But it was all grunting and trying not to fall off the bench onto the cold dirt. Afterward, shivering so hard my teeth chattered, I couldn't find my other leg. Sveinn got to his feet and offered me his hand, but I couldn't stand up.

"What is it, Sigga?" he asked in a gentle voice.

"I can't find—"

As circulation returned to both my legs, I rolled off the bench. I found my skirt, but the button was missing. Crawling on the dirt floor, I ran my fingernails over pebbles, shells, dirt, and something still alive. A worm? Finally, my fingers curled around the small black button.

Outside in the daylight, I saw a fishhook in Sveinn's hair, plucked it out, and handed it to him. In silence we walked along the pond. Why did I do that? Now I'll have to marry him. I'll lose my independence even before I get it.

The ducks swam toward us, thinking we had bread crusts. Sveinn stopped, placed his arms around me and blew his hot breath into my hair.

"Why didn't we go to your house?" I asked.

"You wouldn't like it. Mother's dead, and my father's . . . strange."

"You mean he wouldn't like me?"

Something crossed his face that confused me. Love was a joke, and the joke was on me. But one thing was serious. The corset lessons. As a cook, I'd earn enough to pay for those lessons. "When do we sail?" I asked.

"Next Thursday. But we have a cook."

"You told me you needed one."

"Well—"

I punched his belly, not hard, but he winced. "Well, what?"

"I meant that once our cook leaves, *you* can be the cook. You're next in line."

He hadn't told me the truth. Something else gnawed at my dignity. "Next time let's meet at your home."

"I told you. It's my father."

"It's something else."

His gaze slid away from mine toward the pond. "Fish are my brothers and sisters. You can preserve them in the hold in two ways while you're catching more. You either salt them or ice them."

"All right, don't tell me."

Indoors at Rasmussen's, I tiptoed down the hall to my bedroom. Before going to sleep, I wrote a letter.

> Dear Mama,
>
> Soon I'll have work as a cook on a trawler. A man named Guðmundur will come and get you. I have work for you.
>
> All my love,
> Sissa

It was flu season, and Diva fussed. I checked her forehead several times a day, wrapped her in blankets, and sang to her the song of the iceberg that we used to sing in the loft. "Have you arrived, our country's ancient enemy?"

"Stop it," Diva groaned. "You're depressing me."

The heat was on full blast. I pulled the window shut.

Diva blew air upward from her lower lip, lifting the ringlets on her forehead. "You're roasting me."

What a brat. I didn't have time for her quirks. After weeks at sea, Sveinn was back. And he'd finally agreed to let me visit him at home.

"You've got to stay warm," I said. "Nobody's safe from the flu." I patted her bed cover and turned toward the door.

"Where are you going?" she called.

"Somebody's waiting for me."

"Somebody more important than me?"

I shifted my weight. "Yes. No."

"I've seen that lovesick calf, the trawlerman, hanging on the gate. Don't go."

I started to close the door.

"Edda's told me things—"

My hand was on the doorknob. "What?"

She spoke slowly, a trick to hold me. "She's seen him with a girl."

I shut the door behind me.

As I trudged over the packed snow, my breath steaming in front of me, a shadow landed on my happiness. I shook it off. I entered an alley and walked down a short slope to the back entrance, just as Sveinn had told me to do. His room was directly below his father's store. He opened the door immediately, as if he'd been waiting with his hand on the knob. He drew me into the warm room. On the nightstand, a kerosene lamp cast a warm glow.

He unbuttoned my coat, ran his hands down my back. But when footsteps sounded on the floor above, my shoulders stiffened. The pacing stopped. I closed my eyes and breathed evenly. "Relax," Sveinn said, tugging at my maid's uniform.

I pushed his hand away. "That's my best piece of clothing." My dignity was woven into its threads. Slowly, while he watched me, I undid the buttons on the silky dress, slid out of it, and placed it carefully on the chair in the middle of the room.

Finally, I stood naked in front of him. He reached for me, but stopped. His fingers touched the filigree cross I wore on a chain around my neck.

"Haven't you seen the sign of Jesus before?" I asked.

"It's unusual. Where did you get it?"

"Farmer."

"What farmer?"

"I was thirteen. He wanted me confirmed. 'No heathens on my farm.'"

"That's why he gave you the cross?"

The "why" of it lay at the bottom of my memory, covered with turf. I wouldn't tell him how I'd been alone in the living room nosing through his books, how my tiny breasts hurt when he pinched them, how the cross had been bought for his daughter, how his plea became my law. Don't tell about the touching.

That wasn't the shame of it. The shame was I wanted the cross so badly, I would never tell. I let Mama think Borghildur had given it to me.

Sveinn sat down on the bed. I joined him and pressed the back of my leg against the bed until it hurt. I was anchored. This was reality. I was no longer a pauper on the farm. I'd come here of my own free will. I could walk out the door if I wanted to. On the bed was a crocheted blanket. It was the ocean. I would dive in between the waves and swim for my life.

I lay down next to Sveinn and measured my body against the mattress' length. All those weeks he'd been at sea, I'd imagined this moment, how we'd lie together in a bed. I would run my hands over his head and his face. My fingertips would stroke his ears, his neck, his strong shoulders. And his hands would stroke my breasts, my thighs, between my legs. His bare chest would warm my skin. My blood would rush to meet his touch.

And it all happened just as I'd imagined. Afterward, dozing in his arms, I did not hear the footsteps on the stairs. But the sound of knuckles on the door startled me.

"We need more coal," a voice said.

Sveinn sat up and rubbed his head. "Not now, Papa." But the door opened, and a heavy-set, gray-haired man appeared. I pulled the sheet up to my nose and shivered under his gaze.

"Go away, Papa," Sveinn pleaded.

"Is that Fjóla?"

"Get out, Papa."

The merchant slammed the door so the pictures on the wall trembled. I sat up. "Fjóla?"

"Daughter of another merchant. Papa's got it planned, thinks I'll marry her."

I rolled Fjóla over my tongue, recalling Diva's words about another girl. "Will you?" I asked.

"No. I'm here with you."

"Will you marry me then?"

Not a proposal, just a question. But the look on his face pressed the air out of the room. I clutched the sheet in front of me and stepped onto the floor. I dressed quickly. The silky fabric of my uniform cooled my blushing skin. I was in my coat and at the door when he rolled out of bed and came to me. He nestled his nose into my collarbone. "I love you," he whispered.

I stiffened. "You don't."

Outside, the cold air stung my face.

I decided to stop arguing with Sveinn and sail with *Sóley* as soon as he needed a new cook. We made a truce as if Fjóla never existed. We were downtown at a special ceremony for the arrival of the statue of Ingólfur Arnarson, who discovered Iceland hundreds of years ago. A crowd gathered on the little green hill, Arnarhóll, to welcome the statue. We all gasped when it was revealed. The lion was there. I waved, but he didn't see me.

While everyone milled around trying to touch the statue, Sveinn said, "The cook left. Would you like to be our cook? I mean do you know how to cook?"

I clapped my hands. "Yes," I said. "I can cook. I do biksemad—the sailor's favorite."

When I told Diva the good news, the soft pout of her face collapsed inward. "Will you come back?" she asked in a weepy voice.

I kissed her perfumed cheek, told her I hoped so.

The next day the sun peeked through falling raindrops. I walked to the dock carrying my cloth bag on my shoulder. Sveinn stood in the prow of the *Sóley,* beaming as if he owned the ocean. I climbed the gangplank and stepped onto the deck. My feet felt the ocean rippling under the hull.

A tall fellow in a black oilskin brushed silently past us. "Fingers, my first mate," Sveinn said. "His hands are sensitive as a harpist's. He can count the number of fish in the net just by touching the cable." A freckle-faced boy rolled a barrel onto the deck. "That's Atli. I promised his mother that nothing—absolutely nothing—would happen to him."

A small dark-haired man sat hunched over a collection of winch parts—nuts and bolts spread on a cloth in front of him. Behind him hung a tangle of brown hemp laced with seaweed and bobbins. It smelled of brine and moldy rope. "Nonni's my machinist," Sveinn said. "Runs things on deck when we gut and gill and store the fish. And Haddi does everything else," he said, pointing to a sandy-haired man sweeping the deck. Haddi put away the broom and attached what looked like a liver barrel to the edge of the hold with a rope.

The deck vibrated as the boat's engine rumbled to life. Atli pulled in the mooring line, and *Sóley* glided from the dock. As Reykjavik Harbor grew smaller, I followed Sveinn into the pilothouse. The boat chugged past the jetties marking the outer harbor. We left Faxabay. The throb of the motor settled in my stomach and made a churning motion.

"We're heading north to the fishing grounds at Horn on the fjords," Sveinn explained. "In bad weather, we'll duck into Isafjörður."

"I better start the potatoes," I said.

Gripping the railing, I descended to the deck below, and squeezed into the galley. I washed the potatoes, picked one up, and aimed the tip of my knife at a black spot. As we sailed out to the open sea, I bounced against the galley walls. I cut the potatoes into small pieces and gouged out the black spots. I left them boiling in the pot, climbed the steps, and staggered across the deck to join Sveinn in the pilothouse. The land disappeared. The boat pitched on the heaving sea. A wall of gray water higher than the pilothouse rose up and crashed onto the deck. For a few moments, we were under water, but then the prow emerged and sea foam poured from the rusted scuppers and flowed back into the sea. The boat lurched. I fell against the wall of the pilothouse. Sveinn grinned as I pulled myself up by the railing.

"That's not funny. What if we capsize?" I asked.

He shrugged. "Somebody will save us."

"Somebody? God maybe?"

"Out here we play God. Once we found a live pig in the galley of a sinking ship, brought it on board, but it jumped into the sea. Fingers wanted to swim and save it, but I stopped him."

Picturing myself trapped in the galley of the sinking trawler, I staggered against the boat's slant. The gulls gave way to shearwaters flying just above the surface of the water, their blackhead caps skimming the tops of the waves. The fishiness of the ocean edged out the smell of the engine. As I held on and swayed with the movement of the waves, my stomach gradually settled.

When the trawler rounded the cliffs at Látrabjarg, the shrill sound of guillemots fussing with fulmars carried from the cliffs along the coast across the water. As we drew closer, I could make out the lighthouse at Bjargtangar. Orange-footed puffins puttered about the ledges.

Standing next to me at the railing, Sveinn nodded at the cliffs. "A killing place in winter. Ice forms on the boat, makes it heel over. Rocks splinter the hull. One minute a man's hauling in the net, the next he's washed right off the deck."

He held the railing with both hands and stared into the dark water. "Prepare trawl for launching," he called.

Atli, Haddi, and Nonni straightened out a bag-shaped net, long as the trawler, lowered it over the railing, along with weighted bobbins and boards. "Otter boards'll hold the trawl mouth open so it can swallow the cod," Sveinn said.

He shouted to the crew. "Launch. Full speed ahead." The otter boards sliced the dark green water. The bobbins clanged against the hull. The trawl opened like a parachute alongside the boat. The cables were ready all the way back to the winch drums, and the boat vibrated with the accelerated speed. Sveinn stared down at the swelling trawl in the water below. "Slow now!" he yelled.

The motor grew quiet. Fingers ran to the back block, grasped the cables, and held them as Haddi paid out cable, and the net descended to the bottom of the sea.

"She's there," Fingers said.

Haddi stopped giving cable. The motor gurgled.

The weather remained steady. Atli sat down on a crate and spread out the moldy rope of the extra trawl. I joined him. He pointed to part of a fish caught in the net, wiggled the crushed body loose, and tossed it over the side. "Signs of dead fish in a ghost net scare away the live ones," he explained.

A wave rolled under the boat. I recalled the stories of men washed overboard. I knew most sailors couldn't swim. I couldn't either.

"We've got something," Fingers said.

"Or we're stuck to the bottom!" Sveinn said back.

"It's heavy."

"Slow down. Hauling time."

Haddi wound in the cable while Sveinn turned the boat toward the haul. The winch creaked. The trawl, swollen with fish, rose slowly to the surface.

"Don't split it. Don't drop it. Don't bruise the fish," Sveinn said.

Hand over hand, they hauled half the trawl, then the other, over the side of the boat and gently eased it down onto the deck. Soon the silvery mass lay heaving and gasping on the deck.

Fingers approached the dying creatures and held up a squirming fish. He pointed to holes in its side. "Too many squatties in the water. They're ruining our catch," he said, throwing the damaged fish overboard.

Sveinn turned to me. "The spines of the ocean carp make holes in the cod, ruins them for the British market." And to the crew, "Get them in the hold before the next haul. Nonni, show Sigga how." He jerked a thumb at me.

"But I'm the cook," I said.

He squeezed the upper part of my arm and looked at me hard. "You need to learn. If I drown, you'll become captain of the boat." He grinned, but I thought he meant it. I shuddered. I didn't want to lose him.

Atli brought a basin up from the hold, pumped it full of seawater, and threw ice into it. Nonni picked up a wriggling fish and held it under my nose. I stepped back. Nonni snickered. He held the fish under the gill covers, belly up, and thrust the knife between the gills, probed the inside of the throat, and cut the pulsing vein. His knife slid downward, slicing the belly open to the spawn hole. "See. Simple."

Then he ripped out the guts, dumping organs and intestines into one barrel, liver into the liver barrel. Finally, he dropped the fish into the basin of ice water. The blood dribbled out of the cut-up body. "Don't let the fish poop leak out of the intestines into the fish. Doesn't go with fish and chips."

Nonni gutted another fish. "Make sure the blood's out of 'em. Stack and ice 'em carefully. No bruises. No rotting," he said. Blood ran down his arm as he showed me how to grip the guts and pull them loose. He slung the intestinal tangle into a barrel, then threw me a fish. "Okay, now kill one. Don't split the spine wrong, or we can't sell it."

Grasping the fish under the gill covers, I felt the life pulsing in my hand. With the tip of my knife, I probed the muscle and the artery. Finally, when the blood oozed out, I handed the fish to Atli, and picked up the next one. Haddi held out a sack of roe on two extended fingers, thrust them under my nose. At the sight of the tiny eggs, I felt sick. I jammed the knife into the fish's spine so hard that I broke the backbone, then turned the point of the knife until the blood dripped out. Ashamed, I gutted it quickly and dropped it into the bleeding basin.

"Light a fire under the liver barrel," Nonni said. "We'll need something to drink on the way." Atli filled the outer barrel with water, then lit a fire. I dug my fingers into the innards of the next fish, separated out the liver, and dumped it into the barrel. The organs slid together into a murky green liquid.

Atli glanced up at the pilothouse. He opened the tool chest bolted to the deck, took out a steel cup of nails, dumped them into the chest, dipped the cup into the cod liver oil, and drank deeply. "Don't tell the captain," he said and wiped his mouth on his sleeve.

Chapter 8

Nights I clung to Sveinn in the narrow bunk between wood and wall. As the boat rocked, I stroked his ears and ran my hands over his soft curly hair. I liked his smell. Diva would have labeled it "strolling."

The first haul was gilled, gutted, and arranged on ice in neat rows in the hold.

"If you peed into the hold, the Brits would still eat it," Nonni said.

"So why do you try so hard?" I asked.

Nonni pointed to the symmetry of the fish in the hold. "Don't you see the beauty in it?"

I climbed the steps to the pilothouse. Sveinn stared at the rain-pocked ocean. On the wall hung a picture of an open-mouthed, silvery, brown-and-yellow cod, a piece of hook-shaped flesh beneath its chin. I saw the resemblance but decided not to mention it.

"How can you tell when to lower the trawl?" I asked.

His eyes glowed. I'd tapped into his true love. "I hear a sound nobody else can hear. Cod song, I call it." He stroked the extra layer of flesh on his throat. "Cod likes to feel the ocean floor with his chin. Anyone can hear the surface swimmers sing—herring and capelin. I'm the only one who can hear the cod's song."

Fog had crept over the gunnels. It was time to haul in the next trawl. The winch creaked under its weight, and the full net teetered on the railing. Suddenly a wave crashed on the deck and hid the trawl from view. Sveinn's voice carried over the sloshing and sucking of the sea. "Don't spill the fish back into the sea."

Nobody noticed Atli's fingers between the cable and the railing. Nor did we hear Atli's scream as we pulled the trawl over the railing and dumped it onto the deck. Only then did we notice the blood oozing from the stub of the boy's index finger.

"Find it," Sveinn said.

We lifted each fish separately from the net, then crawled over the deck and swept it with our bare hands. But we couldn't find the finger. I pictured it dropping into the open mouth of a large fish. Nonni washed the wound with kerosene. Haddi scooped up ice from the hold, dumped it into a pillowcase, and held it against the bleeding stub. In the cool air, Atli's face was slippery with sweat.

"Lucky I drank that cod liver oil. It'll make me strong," he said through clenched teeth.

Sveinn placed an arm around the boy. "Sigga, would you like to get off at Hafnarfjörður when we bring Atli home?" he asked over Atli's shoulder.

"No. I'm staying."

Holding the boy against his chest, Sveinn leaned into a rolling wave. "Cable's a killer, especially in bad weather. Deckhand once got caught on it, flew overboard, hung onto the trawl. We winched him in. Second one wasn't so lucky. Got his arm caught between the block and the moving cable. Arm came off. Ship lurched, dumped him overboard. We saw him swimming with one arm, but he sank. We stared into the sea until we were nearly blind. He never came up. So, you see, you're lucky," he said into Atli's pinched face.

At Hafnarfjörður, Sveinn placed Atli in his mother's arms. Haddi and Nonni loaded more ice into the hold. Fingers pulled the rope in through the hawsehole as we chugged from the dock and headed south around Reykjanes and east along the coast toward England.

For the next few days, I stayed in the galley cooking saltfish and potatoes or stirring rice pudding or oatmeal. But when we docked in Fleetwood, I ran up on deck. I had to see the world. Gulls screamed overhead. The fish dock on the River Wyre emerged from the fog. I made out words painted on a wall. Fleetwood Grain Elevator. Lancashire & Yorkshire Railway. I sniffed the air for foreign smells, but the dock here smelled just like the one at home. The only thing different was the railroad tracks. I'd never seen those before. They glittered with fish scales.

Haddi moored *Sóley* so she lined up behind the other trawlers to unload. A truck labeled Leadbetters Fishmongers and Poulterers drove by. I helped the crew lift the cover off the fish hold. Men wearing black slickers and wool caps picked up fish, sniffed the gills, fingered the fish for limpness. A hand grasped my elbow. Sveinn handed me a piece of paper.

On it I read a couple of words. Chandlers. Otter boards. He pushed money into my pocket.

I headed out into the world. On the dock, I slipped on a fishskin and grabbed the side of a cart to steady myself.

"Easy luvvy," a voice said.

It belonged to a man with a weathered face. He wore a tweed cap and held a pipe between his lips. I showed him my note, and he pointed a stubby finger straight ahead. Trolley cars with numbers on the front moved on the tracks that ran down the center of the main street. Without waiting for the trolley to stop, a man jumped out.

I stepped into the street.

"Look out, luvvy," a woman said, pulling me back to the pavement before the trolley knocked my nose off.

Looking right and left, I walked until I came to a replica of a lighthouse. At its base was a sign, Trains to Blackpool Every Few Minutes.

In the road, horses pulled carts stacked with tins and boxes. A young boy in patched woolen pants pushed a handcart of canned goods. Canvas, suspended on metal structures, shaded storefront windows. Wind would've blown the canvas into the sea in Reykjavik. I peered into the windows of shops with strange names. Cooperative Society's Emporium. T. Walmsley's Plumbers and Paper Hangers.

I found the chandlers—Hodgson's Store, Shipping Supplies. Inside, I breathed in the smell of wood and dust.

The clerk was a rangy man with yellow teeth and red suspenders over a dirty white shirt. When he saw my note, he gestured to a dark corner where stacks of otter boards lined the walls, said he'd deliver the boards to the boat. Instead of thanking the man, I felt jealous. Sveinn was at home in this English world. I could be part of this world only by working in a smelly little galley. No. I wouldn't. I tightened my jaw and paid the man.

Women with shopping nets on their arms filed into a grocery shop. I followed them inside. I looked about and sniffed. What were they buying? They stood in line, holding tins of food. I peered at the strange labels— Lakeview Brand Whole Egg Powder, Maple Leaf Creamery Butter, Delicaf Dehydrated Coffee.

With my remaining coins I went to the butcher's and bought his last sausage. By the time I hurried back to the dock, Sveinn was filling the boat with coal. I was glad to go home. As we chugged out of the harbor and into the North Atlantic, I fried the sausage with onions and eggs. "Biksemad. Sailors' favorite," I shouted.

———————

Once the boat was unloaded and cleaned up in Reykjavik, we returned to the fishing grounds. If we got a big haul like last time, Sveinn would be the catch king. We launched the trawl again and again. The hold was almost full.

"One more launch," Sveinn said.

But when we started to pull it up and over the side, the wind shifted and pushed at us from the wrong direction. The bulging net pulled *Sóley* down toward the churning sea. Bracing myself against the boat's list, I nearly lost my balance.

"Cut it. Cut it," Sveinn yelled.

Halli and Nonni hacked furiously at the net until it sank to the bottom of the sea. Too late, though. A wave washed over us. Another pulled the boat over on its side. Now I was thrashing about in the cold sea. In the glimmer of light from the mast, I glimpsed Nonni and Halli clinging to the side of the hull.

"Move away from the boat. It'll pull you down," a voice shrieked.

How to move? I pawed the sea but got nowhere. I wasn't drowning, just freezing to death. Ice cold waves slapped my shoulders, washed over my head. Alone. Nothing but endless, freezing blackness. Sinking, I sent Mama a message. *I'm dying. I love you. I didn't mean to leave you alone on the farm.* She answered by singing in my ear. *Hættu að gráta hringaná.* Don't cry little girl.

I heard another voice. "Sigga."

But my arms and legs were too heavy. I couldn't move toward the voice.

"Come here," the voice called.

And there was Sveinn, bobbing in the water, holding onto an otter board. He pushed it toward me. I grabbed it and held on. "Don't panic. That will steal your energy," he said.

I fought my fear. I wanted to live. I wanted to sew a corset. A giant slurping sound filled the air. The trawler was sinking.

"Move away. Don't let it suck you down," Sveinn called. We pumped our arms and legs as *Sóley* sank, taking her lights with her. In the total darkness, I heard Sveinn's gasping voice.

"Remember the sweater. You're wearing the sweater. The sweater my mother knitted."

My legs turned to lead. My body hardly moved.

"Don't panic. Panic takes energy," he whispered in the darkness near my ear.

No panic. I lay my head on my ocean pillow to sleep. I wouldn't drown, just nap. My head was nodding on my chest when I heard a voice above us.

"Here. Two more."

A light glimmered. Hands gripped me under the arms, hoisted me up out of the water, and dropped me onto the deck. Sveinn landed beside me. Somebody stripped me naked, wrapped me in blankets, and carried me below. Somewhere, from under a heap of blankets, I heard Haddi and

Nonni. No sign of Fingers. I shuddered so hard, I thought I'd break all my teeth.

"We saw your light in the distance, so we knew you were there," somebody said. "When your light disappeared, we knew you'd gone under."

Sveinn grunted.

People waved and called to us from the dock. Heroes. That's what we were. Why? Because we were alive. When I stepped ashore, the ground felt hard under my feet. I scanned the crowd. Nobody, not even Edda, had come for me. The old merchant, Sveinn's father, and some other relatives surrounded Sveinn. With them was a young woman about my age. She wore a stylish suit, high heels, and bobbed hair the color of a field mouse. When she threw her arms around Sveinn and hugged him hard, I swore under my breath. Who—?

I approached her. She eyed me as if I were a jellyfish.

"And you must be the cook. My name's Fjóla." She grasped my hand with long fingers.

A bad feeling rose in my throat as if I were choking. Beyond the strange woman, I noticed the lion standing taller than the rest of the crowd. He wore an overcoat and a top hat. The government must have sent him to welcome us back. He shook hands with the captain of the boat who had saved us.

Out of the corner of my eye, I saw Sveinn walk away with the woman.

"Hey, aren't you going to say goodbye?" I called after him. But he didn't hear me. I stood there fuming. My stomach clenched. The lion stood close by, watching me.

"Excuse me." I ran behind the foreman's shed and vomited until nothing came up but strings of saliva. Strange. We were on land, and now I was seasick. I turned around. The lion had followed me.

"Come. I'll warm you up with some tea," he said. Wrapped in one of the boat's blankets, I walked with him to the main street. He stopped at a café I'd often admired from the outside. It was called Inga's.

"Or maybe hot chocolate with whipped cream?" he asked, pulling out a chair for me. The nausea had passed. Hot chocolate sounded good. At the next table, a group of people were speaking in a foreign tongue.

"German," he said. "All the best plumbers, carpenters, and electricians in town are German."

With the steaming hot chocolate and warm apple cake in front of me, I suddenly felt sleepy. I could barely keep my eyes open. Absentmindedly, he picked up his coffee spoon and took a big bite out of my cake.

Then he shook himself. "Oh, I'm sorry. I thought I'd ordered it."

Perfectly all right. I couldn't finish it anyway.

"Drowning is a terrible thing. I saw five men drowned. Young men. They lay on the beach. That was at Vík."

So he wanted to talk about *that* story. I knew it, too. "I think one of the drowned men was my father."

"Your father?"

An emotion I didn't understand passed over his face.

"Who is your mother?"

I pretended I hadn't told him before. "Hansína," I said politely.

He made a fist and knocked it against his head. "Hansína. Hansína. Hansína."

"Mama's still on the farm," I said. "Remember you said you'd help me bring her here.

"What farm?"

Was his memory failing? "Upper Falls."

He pointed a finger at me. "That's it. That's the name. I remember the name because the farmer used to come into town. He sold us angelica. Herdís made soup from it."

The nausea came on so fast, I ran outside and vomited into the gutter. I rose up and wiped my mouth on the back of my sleeve. I felt the lion's hand on my arm. I shuddered under his touch as my heart shifted in favor of Mama and against all men who pretended not to remember her. I wrapped the blanket tightly around my shoulders and hurried home.

———————

Every day Diva eyed me suspiciously. She kept telling me I looked pale. I couldn't keep it from her much longer. On the farm they called it "the morning sickness that can last all day." And where was Sveinn? Why hadn't he come to see me? One morning, right after giving Diva her breakfast, I ran down to the main street and made my way behind the old man's cracker shop to Sveinn's room and knocked on the door. No answer. I went around the front and entered the shop. The old merchant sat at the cash register, reading a newspaper. There was nobody else in the shop. I guessed there never had been. It wasn't the kind of shop where customers went.

"I am Sigga," I said.

His grimace signaled that he remembered me. "My son signed onto another trawler, *Lilja*. He's at sea."

Something pinched my heart. "Already?" I asked, but he turned away and pretended to serve some imaginary customers.

Walking home, I trembled. Sveinn might die. And he hadn't said goodbye. I began to sweat, and my face burned. I wouldn't marry a man who might drown. Besides, I couldn't trust him. I clenched my fists, ready to kill that Fjóla.

Every day I listened to the shipping news to learn the whereabouts of *Lilja*. When the trawler finally returned, I stood on the dock, waiting. Others waited, too. Casually I ran my eyes over them. Then I saw her. The woman in the boxy suit was waving at *my* man. He stood at the railing, grinning, waving back to her. In seconds, he was on the ground with his arms around her.

"Hey," I called.

"Sigga." He moved toward me, his arm still around Fjóla. Looping an arm awkwardly around my shoulder, he hugged me as if we were favorite classmates or maybe even close friends.

I spoke into his face, so the mouse-haired woman couldn't hear. "I need to talk to you."

He made a silly movement with his hands and glanced at Fjóla. His eyes sent her an "I'm sorry" look. She waved at somebody and wriggled out of his grasp. He watched her go then turned back to me.

"What is it, Sigga?"

"Who is she to you?"

His stupid grin drove my anger sky high. Then a familiar, gentle look passed over his face. He opened up his arms and reached for me. For a moment, I enjoyed the warmth of him, the smell of his sweat. I pulled away. "Who is she to you?" I repeated.

"Never mind. Nothing. You are my cook and my beloved." He reached for me again, but I stepped back.

For the third time I asked my question.

But he had no answer. Just the stupid grin.

"Is she the one your cracker merchant father picked out for you?"

I hoped for no. Instead I thought I saw him nod. My volcano spewed fire.

"If that's all you have to say to me, then this is my final message to you."

I raised my large hand high into the air as if I were about to hang sheets on the line on a sunny day. A brave man, my beloved didn't duck as I swung at his cheek with all the force of the anger inside me. The sound of the slap was so loud, crew members from *Lilja* looked up. He staggered backward, but he didn't fall. Instead he kept his eyes on me.

"I never want to see you again," I said. "If I see you on the street, I will cross to the other side." I stalked away. Behind me I heard him talking, but I didn't turn around. Soon, I no longer heard him.

Chapter 9

I saw the farm in a dream. Men were lined up on a bench. Women pulled off their boots, staggered backward, falling against the wall. Among the mocking men was Sveinn. He extended a leg and commanded, "Pull on me, woman." Sweating, I rolled out of bed and cast my vote for independence. I would *never* tell Sveinn about the baby. It was *my* baby, not his.

After breakfast, I picked up the dishcloth and dried the serving dish Edda had just washed.

"Diva told me you saw Sveinn with a girl," I said carefully.

Edda dropped her brush into the soapy water. "Diva imagines things."

I flicked the dishcloth at an imaginary horsefly. "I know who the girl is."

She gave me a long look, then plucked up the brush and scrubbed the bottom of a blackened pot. I untied my apron and hung it on a hook. Borghildur's reading from the saga of Laxar Valley came to me: To him I was worst whom I loved the most. With my nose in the air, I left the kitchen. Quickly, I ran up the stairs and into the bathroom and retched into the beautiful porcelain toilet bowl. Afterward, I sat on the bed, breathing and thinking, thinking. I recalled words whispered in the bakery about a woman who could *fix* women. Holding the railing, I walked carefully down the stairs. Edda was wiping the kitchen counter.

"I have a friend," I said. "Pregnant. Boyfriend won't marry her. Do you know of anyone who helps girls—"

"Helps girls?"

"Helps get rid of their babies," I whispered.

Edda pulled the plug in the sink. I barely heard her above the sucking sound of the water going down the drain. "The shacks, at the edge of the fjord. Maja'll take care of you—I mean her."

Blood crept up my neck and into my cheeks. I went for my coat.

"Money. You'll need money," Edda called after me.

Walking south toward the fjord, I inhaled the ocean air, heard the sea slapping the rocks. As I passed the baiting sheds and the beached boats, I tripped over frayed nets and cork buoys. Lumpfish, tied together in pairs, hung on drying lines, and the smell of rot rode the breeze. The ragged outline of the shacks came into view. Sveinn and I had often walked here.

I knocked and waited. A woman with a lit pipe between her lips opened the door. A ball of yarn and knitting needles poked out from under her arm. Her eyes went to my waist.

"Maja's next door," she said, pointing her pipe to a sod hut.

Children were arguing behind the door. A baby wailed. Nobody answered my knock, so I pushed the door in and entered a dark, narrow hall. The smell of dirt walls reminded me of the farm. "Maja," I called. A chinless man emerged from a back room. His long raincoat brushed by me as he disappeared out the door. A small boy stood against the wall.

"Is Maja at home?" I asked.

"Maaa ma," he called.

A slight woman with a baby on her hip appeared. "I can't help you today, dear. Come back tomorrow."

"How much will it cost?" I asked.

"Ten. It'll cost you ten, dear."

"Where will you do it?"

"My own bed, dear. You can nap afterward. Make sure you're gone when my husband comes home."

"Can I see?"

Maja took my arm and led me into the bedroom. The bed was a mess of wrinkled gray sheets and blankets. "I'll put on clean sheets for you, dear."

In the glimmer of light from the tiny window, I made out a small cabinet that stood against the turf and stone wall. "And what will you use?"

Maja handed the baby to the boy who seemed to follow his mother everywhere. From the cabinet she took a rectangular wooden box, the same kind that women used on the farm for storing knitting needles. She opened the box and took out a long, thin, silver-colored instrument that resembled Mama's crocheting needle.

I shuddered. Maja placed it back in the box.

"How far along are you, dear?" she asked.

"I don't know."

"I'll need the money before we begin, you understand, just in case—"

"Of course." I stepped back.

"Tomorrow's a good day for you, dear?"

"No." I shook my head. I let myself out the door and walked quickly away from the shacks toward the baiting sheds. My fists pounded my chest, waking up my heart, my blood, my baby.

Mama. Mama. Where are you? Eighteen years ago, she'd let me live. She hadn't placed me behind the waterfall to die. My hands slid down to my belly. I would not spread my legs for Maja's crochet needle. I made that promise to the tiny person who'd decided to live inside me. But I needed a husband. *Not* Sveinn. Never, not if he begged me.

The smell of seaweed rushed into my lungs, so rich with life it made me tired. I had to sit. At the baiting sheds, I lowered myself onto a cinder block just below the fish drying lines. A fish head brushed against my hair. Leaning forward, I ruffled through the grass until I found a sorrel leaf to chew. I sucked in my cheeks against its bitterness and closed my eyes.

"Dreaming?"

I opened my eyes. A small, weather-beaten man with a rounded back sat on a cinder block next to me, threading hooks onto a line. When had he arrived?

"I'm Jón, the Rower, representative of the little man," he said, pointing to a rowboat beached on concrete blocks. On its side, in messily painted black letters, were the words, Jón, the Rower.

"What?"

"I said I am Jón, and I represent the little man. Who are you?"

"Little? You mean little like you?"

He raised his eyebrows. I'd been dumb and rude. "I am Sigga," I said quickly. "In service with the Rasmussens." I couldn't keep the pride out of my voice.

With a red handkerchief, he wiped a tobacco drop from his nostril. "What do they pay?"

"Enough for this new skirt," I said, smoothing the fabric at my knees. He frowned.

"And room and board," I added quickly.

"The little man wears rags while Rasmussen dresses up?"

"Not rags. This skirt's high quality."

A furrow formed on his brow.

"Who's the little man?" I asked.

"You."

I flushed, recalling how Rasmussen took my man's wages. "What about the little woman? Do you help people like me?"

He studied me like some species of bird not seen on the island. His politics were strange, but I saw his other qualities. For one thing, he was so small I would be able to pick him up and move him from room to room. He hardly weighed more than my little calf. The thought warmed me. I'd loved that calf.

"Are you married?" I asked.

He hesitated. It was a simple question. Yes? Or no?

"I had a woman once . . ." His voice trailed off.

After midnight, I was lying in bed, drafting my marriage proposal to Jón when I heard the doorknob turn. Was I imagining it? I was glad I'd locked the door.

———

I found Jón sitting in the same place behind the baiting sheds, untying knots in his net. Beside him was a wooden cart shiny with fish scales.

Tying off a knot in the net, he gestured for me to sit down. I watched him attach pieces of metal to the nets.

"Keeps the net on the bottom of the fjord," he said.

I admired his undangerous life, so different from Sveinn's. Sveinn would roll on the waves, maybe even drown, while Jón sat in his boat and waited for fish to climb into it. Every evening Jón would come home, and we'd eat together. And from the safety of the nest I'd build with him, I would fight for my independence.

He dropped the net. "How many hours a day do you work for Rasmussen?"

Dusting, cooking rhubarb pudding, washing lace underwear, and singing with Diva wasn't work. "We start in the morning and finish in the evening."

His eyes sized me up. "I don't make a lot of money, a fish here and a fish there. Some we eat. Some I sell on the peninsula."

"Perfect," I said as if being dirt poor were a blessing.

He pointed to a cottage with cracks in the walls. "That's where I live." An outhouse door blew open and squeaked on its hinges. Corrugated iron, held down by stones, formed a roof. Chickens pecked at eggshells in the dirt, and a spotted cow grazed in the field next to the cottage.

"Is she yours?" I asked.

"Branda, yes. I have a son, Magnús. My mother, Bergthora, sleeps in the back room."

I was about to propose, but then he said, "Would you like to work with me?"

"Well, I've got some plans."

"Women don't have plans."

"No? I'm eighteen years old—a grown-up. I work as a maid. But soon I'll start my education."

His small eyes darkened. "Education?"

"I'm waiting for a spot in the corset construction class at Magdalena's," I lied. I still hadn't been to Magdalena's.

"Magdalena's? The convent? The nuns are sewing corsets?" He shrugged his shoulders. Hair grew out of his ears, a characteristic of trolls. But Jón was not a make-believe creature. His rubber shoes were firmly planted in the mud. He obeyed the law of gravity. I would be safe with him.

"Nuns?"

"Magga—she's Magnús' mother—always wore woolen knickers and a woolen shirt under her clothes, made them herself. Nothing secret about that."

If I married Jón, and he sold enough fish, I could pay for my corset construction lessons.

"Come meet my family," he said, placing his hands on his thighs and groaning as he pushed himself up.

As we climbed the broken concrete steps and entered the cottage, I noted I was a head taller than he. Rubber shoes littered the hall. Overalls and coats were piled up on hooks. The smell of sheep fat hung on the air, like at the farm. Rasmussen's hall smelled of floor polish.

Jón stepped back while I entered a small kitchen with a stove in the center. From the kitchen, a door led into the living room. A swollen couch sat at its center, next to it an armchair covered with a blanket. Pushed against the wall was a table, covered with books, newspapers, and loose paper. The window looked onto the fjord. From here I would be able to see Jón's boat on the water.

"Next there's Magnús," he said, taking my arm." In a small bedroom, a square-bodied boy of eight or nine, sat on the floor, surrounded by cut-out drawings of cars and boats. His dark hair stood straight up, stiff with oil and dirt, I guessed. His eyes were deep brown, a brother's eyes that would gaze with love at my baby. My heart beat faster. I needed this family.

In the bedroom at the end of the hall, Jón's mother, Bergthora, lay in bed wrapped in blankets, like dried meat rolled up in a bread bun. The bed across from hers was covered with nets, bobbins, and buoys. On a nail in the wall hung a yellowed calendar from 1909, seventeen years ago.

Jón waved a hand in the direction of his mother. "Welcome to the retirement home of Mud Road's only water carrier."

The old woman's eyes sparkled. "That calendar's from the year the government started piping in water and put us water carriers out of business."

I couldn't picture this little woman carrying water buckets with her matchstick arms.

"Hot water in our pipes. That's the next thing," she said.

"You must be strong."

"I carried two full buckets in each arm from the pump downtown all the way up to Mud Road. Did it for twenty years. Got two coins for each bucket, had to make seventy-five trips a day to earn a laborer's wage. Wasn't worth breaking your back for that. Finally, I learned to put a barrel of water on a handcart and ladle that water into buckets."

She took my hand and kneaded it as if she'd lost something. "Do you like to cook, dear?"

"Cooking's my favorite thing, after ironing," I said, lying twice.

"Then you'll enjoy my cookbook." She pointed to a composition book lying on the floor, open to a page covered with writings and drawings. I picked it up and flipped through it until I came to a recipe for dried cods' heads. "Jón's favorite," she said, watching me.

Today was Wednesday. Diva would be eating veal in wine sauce. Thursdays, salted lumpfish eggs with a silver coffee spoon. And the lovely rich brown sauce on the weekend with some kind of meat.

A sparkle came into her blue gray eyes. "After I stopped carrying water, I worked for a pharmacist, wrapping suppositories that parents put into their kids' bottoms to make them sleep at night. He kept the room cold so the suppositories wouldn't melt. Made my bones ache. They still do."

"Do you have a recipe for lumpfish?" I asked, handing her the book.

Skipping to the back of the book, Bergthora pointed to some drawings she'd made of lumpfish crawling at the bottom of the fjord: the large male and the scrawny female. Under the drawings were the words, Boil. Serve with vinegar and potatoes.

Jón took my arm and led me down the hall to his bedroom. Rumpled clothes lay on the floor. I pointed to the papers and pamphlets covering the bed.

"What's that?" I asked.

"Speeches on how to save the little man. I need a partner."

"To row the boat or to sweep your floors?"

"Somebody to get me out of bed in the morning."

In the living room, I glimpsed the sun sparkling on the water and far away the distant mountains leading their secret lives. Washing would be a joy here. The ocean wind would sweeten the smell of sheets and pillowcases on the line.

After I said goodbye, I walked down Mud Road. All the women had draped their bedding over the fences to air them out in the sun. These women would become my neighbors. And neighbors would give one more layer of safety to my child.

Once I was in bed, I pondered Jón's words. Work with me. Jón resembled a troll, but I would love him, and he would love me back. And my wedding gift to Jón would be Sveinn's baby. But as I began to fall asleep, images of Sveinn got in the way. The hair on his arms, his breath on my neck, the freckles across his shoulders, his strong embrace. My body grew hot with longing for him. It was past midnight when I finally fell asleep.

I rehearsed my marriage proposal as I walked quickly to the fjord the next evening. Jón sat in his usual spot near the baiting sheds. He looked up and ran his eyes over me. I returned his gaze without blinking. But inside me I blushed. I felt like a work animal, as if he were considering a second ox to yoke to the first.

"You still want someone to work with you?" I asked.

"Yes, a partner, somebody who can put a new latch on the outhouse door."

"I can do that," I said.

"You?"

Ignoring his disbelief, I plowed ahead. "If you'll marry me."

His head jerked back slightly, then he leaned forward and studied my knees, elbows, ankles, and shoulders. I held my breath.

"A good idea," he finally said.

A week later, Diva stood in the middle of her bedroom while I helped her into her blue silk dress.

"I want to make a good impression on your fiancé," she said, raising her arms so the dress slid over her shoulders and down her hips. Looking in the mirror, she sucked in her breath and drew her lips into a tight little smile. I took her arm, helped her down the stairs, and placed her on the reclining couch. She dabbed her eyes with a lace handkerchief.

Out on the street, a horse snorted. I opened the door. Jón stood on the doormat, his face dark from coal dust, his body dented like an old boot. With a corner of my apron, I rubbed his face until he squealed.

"A coal ship was in the harbor. I had to unload it," he said.

Really? Should I believe him?

"Bring him in," Diva called.

I gripped his jacket sleeve and pulled him into Diva's parlor. He stepped onto a handwoven throw rug as if it were the only spot of dry land in the room. When Diva jangled her bracelets, he lumbered across the floor and took her extended hand. Without a word, he picked up the suitcase that contained Diva's old coat, her dresses, her slip, the beastly shoes that pinched like clothespins, and the old corset. Underneath all these things lay Sveinn's sweater.

"My brother's horse, Brown," Jón said, helping me up to the cart seat. "I borrowed him for the wedding and the honeymoon." As Brown plodded past the pond, I blinked hard, recalling Diva's flushing toilet and Diva herself, and how our voices had blended in song.

"Honeymoon?"

"People go somewhere after a wedding. I thought we'd go to the cinema."

I placed a hand on my excited heart. I'd never seen a film.

Inside the cottage, dust balls flew up around my ankles. Grit crunched under my shoes. The light from the stove flickered against the wall, revealing what I hadn't seen before, a curled newspaper photo of a man. "Your grandfather?" I asked.

"No. Samuel Gompers, the American labor leader. He supported the little man."

"Tell me again. Who's the little man?"

"On a boat, the little man is everyone but the owner. At the plant, the little man is everyone but the owner. On the farm, the little man is everyone but the farmer."

I liked how Jón explained things to me. He wanted me to understand. Here in this cottage, I would be *somebody*. And so would our child. Sveinn was different. I'd been just an ear for his cod stories.

Bergthora half lay on the sofa. "I'm glad Jón picked a big girl. They last longer than small ones. Still, women of all sizes break under the cooking."

I swelled my chest and spoke bravely. "I'll boil the fish on Mondays, fry it on Tuesdays, make fish cakes on Wednesdays, bake fish loaf on Thursdays, and Fridays, when the fish is gone, we'll have blood sausage with oatmeal."

Bergthora clapped her hands. "And here's some advice for pleasing a husband: moisten your rye meal with sheep brains and fry it in suet. Add salt. It'll taste like wool if you forget the salt. Beware of heavy foods, like livered fish stomachs. They can sink a sailor."

She rolled onto her side and placed both feet on the floor. Grasping the side of the sofa, then the wall, she felt her way toward the kitchen.

I reached for her arm. "Are you all right?"

"Of course, dear. I'm on the downside of my coffee cycle now. I'll just cook the ram's testicles for after the wedding."

Jón carried my suitcase to his bedroom—our bedroom, a tiny dark room that felt like a cave. Shuddering under the weight of my new life, I opened the suitcase and took out Sveinn's sweater, raised it to my nose, and breathed in his smell. A crazy thought came to me. If I ran seven steps to the front door, I could escape from this broken little man and his strange mother. I would run down Mud Road and back to Diva. I pushed my heels into the floor.

Stay, I told myself. Blinking away memories, I crouched down in front of Jón's closet and slipped the sweater under some old boots.

I took off my undershirt, put on the slip, then Diva's old red dress. It was short on me. Finally, I squeezed my feet into the shoes and hobbled into the kitchen, ready to be married. Jón stood next to the stove, wearing a white shirt with suspenders and wrinkled black pants. He cracked his knuckles, a start signal for the life we would share.

At the magistrate's office, I promised to obey as Jón slid an adjusted curtain ring onto my finger. Mama. The word squeezed my heart. But now Jón and Magnús and Bergthora would be my family. And Sveinn's baby growing inside me. After we left the magistrate's office, Bergthora served the rams' testicles at the house. She sat down at the head of the table, closed her eyes, and pressed her palms together in silent prayer. I gave her a questioning look.

"Do you walk with God?" I asked.

Bergthora looked at me as if she hadn't understood the question. "I was praying that Magga—Jón's first woman—doesn't cast a spell on you, like the jealous queen did in *Njálssaga*. She made Hrút's prick swell so big he couldn't get pleasure from any woman but her, the queen."

Everyone laughed but me.

After the meal, Bergthora brewed wedding coffee. On the second cup, she sat up straight as a pole. "Go look under my mattress," she commanded.

I followed Jón into her bedroom. Under the mattress lay some old coins. Jón plucked them up and brought them to Bergthora.

"I put them there the year I carried my thousandth bucket from the well. It's for the cinema, for your honeymoon. Take Magnús with you. He's never been on a honeymoon."

Magnús was in the yard playing hide-and-seek with the chickens. "Want to see a film?" I called from the window. He ran up the steps and into the hall. He met us at the horse cart wearing a leather aviator cap with flaps that swung at his ears when he moved his head.

The film was about a rich landowner, Halla, who takes Eyvind, an outlaw, as her lover and flees to the mountains with him. When the fighting began on the screen, Magnús gripped the seat in front of him with one hand and punched the seat with the other.

It was my wedding night. I lay under the sheet in my new bed and watched Jón fiddle with buttons. He undid hooks and popped snaps until finally, his clothes—all but his long underwear—dropped to the floor. He raised the sheet, groaning a little, and rolled himself into the bed. He was only twelve years older than me, but tonight he resembled an old man. His hard hands and stiff arms gripped me—like levers and crowbars. I felt like a child wedged between the legs of a hard-backed chair. The hairy man. An involuntary shudder went through my body. But, reminding myself I would love this man, I stroked the knotted muscles of his neck and shoulders and felt the curvature of his spine. One shoulder was higher than the other. Gradually, I relaxed into sympathy for him.

"How did it happen?" I whispered.

"As a boy, on the trawler—I was twelve—I carried the intestine crate over my shoulder. Every time they gutted a fish, the crate got heavier. I always carried it on my left side. Finally, my back wouldn't straighten."

"And this?" I asked, touching his crooked right arm.

"Entrails covered the deck. Slimy things. Crate was heavy. I slipped and fell. We didn't dock for weeks. My arm healed crooked."

My heart warmed to him, my broken doll. His fingers trailed across my thickening middle. I held my breath. Had he noticed? Not yet, but eventually he would know. By then the baby would be ours, not just mine.

Chapter 10

On my second day at the cottage, I was getting used to Branda and her way of turning and licking me while I milked her. We would soon be friends. And I loved the chickens. I'd just finished naming them when I saw a familiar figure coming down Mud Road. Sveinn. I stopped breathing. I would run away. But I wasn't fast enough. He stopped at the gate of my cottage.

"Finally, I found you," he said.

"Why did you come?"

"Why? I thought we . . . I mean . . . I looked for you at Rasmussens. And suddenly I hear you're married to some little fisherman and living in this—" He waved at the corrugated iron roof, the outhouse, the muddy yard, the whole place I was trying to make into a home for myself.

"I—"

"You what? Tell me. What?"

I pulled myself together. "I asked you about that woman in the boxy suit. You wouldn't answer me. So I said goodbye."

He rubbed his cheek. I recalled how I'd hit him. A feeling of wrongness gripped my body. My baby must've felt it too because the nausea rose like a swelling wave. I placed my hands over my mouth and ran for the outhouse. I retched so hard I thought the baby would leap out of my throat. As I wiped my mouth with my apron, I glimpsed Jón coming out of the cottage. He walked up to Sveinn and talked in a loud and cheerful way.

"So, you're the catch king, second year in a row?"

I approached the two men.

Sveinn extended his hand to me. "Congratulations," he said through gritted teeth and turned to leave. I watched him grow smaller as he walked away from me down Mud Road.

I soon got to know my neighbor. Jón called him Ratcatcher. One day after school, Magnús came running inside.

"I kicked the ball into Ratcatcher's yard. I'm afraid to get it."

"Afraid? Why?"

"He's got rats on the line."

"Nonsense. I'll get it." I was eager to learn about Ratcatcher.

Carefully, I undid the latch on his gate, entered the yard, and picked up the ball. I saw several tailless rats pinned by their ears to the clothesline. From the corner of the yard came the sound of a man humming. Ratcatcher sat on a box, moving his knife against something he held in his hand. He was skinning a rat.

On an upended wooden crate lay a pile of bloodied rat tails.

"Why are you doing this?" I asked.

"Each tail gets me money from the city."

I swallowed down my nausea. Still, Ratcatcher was independent.

A few nights later I woke up to laughter at Ratcatcher's. I looked out the window. A man was coming from his basement carrying a box that rattled. Another held a bottle in each hand.

The government had banned alcohol. Ratcatcher must be making his own. His wife, Anna, wore the prettiest blouses on Mud Road. Ratcatcher had probably bought her a Singer sewing machine.

Jón and I had been married for a month, and he hadn't been out on his boat once. I milked Branda. I fried eggs. I found flour in the pantry, so I baked bread. We had food, but we needed fish. My baby needed fish.

"When are you going out on the fjord?" I asked one morning at breakfast.

He looked up from his writing. "Our party will take over the labor union."

"Yes. But we need fish."

"Sailors fall asleep in their food bowls. They fall asleep when they launch the trawl. They get washed overboard."

"Did you hear me? We need fish."

Jón banged the table with his fist. "We'll change the shift laws."

"We need coffee," I said. He was drinking hot water, spiked with milk. "What?"

Had I spoken Chinese? "That's the last of the bread. I need money for flour."

"Oh," he said. He took a piece of paper and a pencil from the shelf and began to make a list. Union. Shift laws. Strike. Pay raise. Pension. No mention of fish or flour.

I put my head in my hands. I closed my eyes and searched my heart. Hadn't I seen Anna going to work at the fish plant? Seconds later I was across the street, knocking on her door. She looked surprised to see me.

"Can I go with you to the plant?"

"Monday—look out your window. If the white flag's up, they need workers." She narrowed her eyes. "Jón won't mind?"

"He won't notice I'm gone."

When she touched my arm, I winced. I didn't like anyone feeling sorry for me. I had what I wanted. I would fix it.

"We'll go together," she said.

But it was Saturday. I couldn't wait until Monday to begin making a living. While Jón slept, I went to the closet and took out Diva's old corset. I placed it on the kitchen table and studied all the panels and how they were connected. I ran my fingers along the channels and the bones. I turned it over and counted the holes where the laces went. With a tiny piece of coal, I scratched a number on each part. With the kitchen scissors, I ripped the corset apart. My sweat was flying when Bergthora walked in.

"What are you doing, woman?"

"I'm teaching myself to sew a corset."

"No, you're not. You're destroying it."

I tore the loosened panels apart with my bare hands.

"The lack of coffee keeps me up at night," she said, and paced the hall. I ignored her, just kept on ripping and cutting. It was early morning, almost time to milk Branda, when I finished stitching the corset parts back together again. It was like a human body. All the parts had to fit together just right. I tried it on over my clothes. It was a little pouchy. Still, it was beautiful. I would learn to make one just like it.

Monday morning I stretched and sighed, knocking against the balled-up lump in the bed that was Jón. I padded across the cold floor from the bedroom, down the hall, to the kitchen window. Leaning out, I angled my shoulders and neck until I could see the flagpole at the saltfish plant. The white flag was up—a cry for help. Time to sun-dry the fish. I pulled on my overalls and covered my hair with a kerchief. Anna waited at the gate. We headed for the drying field. All my life I'd never had a girl-friend, except Borghildur and maybe Edda before she started making up stories about Sveinn. Giggling, Anna told me she was pregnant.

I linked my arm in hers. "That makes us sisters under the skin," I said.

The field, white with flattened fish drying in the sun, came into view. Women in white kerchiefs flew about, screeching like gulls as they spread the fish. Up out of this white sea rose a stack of layered, salted fish. Men rolled wheelbarrows of fish from the stack to the washerwomen who scrubbed off the salt.

Together Anna and I loaded freshly washed fish onto a pallet and carried it between us to the drying field. I felt a sharp pain through my rubber shoe when I stepped on a pebble. I tilted the pallet, and a fish slid onto the grass. When I bent to pick it up, a fish stacker pinched my backside.

I whirled around and slapped him so hard people stopped their work to stare. He rubbed the red welt on his cheek and scurried away.

"Nobody touches you, huh?" Anna asked.

"Not unless I say so." My chest tightened. I wished I'd slapped the hairy man.

After drying and stacking fish for sixteen hours, my hands were raw. I walked home with Anna on legs like jelly. I made a fist and pounded my back where it hurt. But I would do it again. One fish at a time, I would do it again. When I saw Jón standing in the doorway waiting for me, my spirits rose. Lucky me. I had a nice little husband waiting for me at home every evening. I closed the door behind me, gripped Jón under the arms, and swung him around. I made up the words as I sang. "King of my heart. King of the deep, dark sea. Saltfish, my love, fly above the clouds with me."

Hot and panting, I set him down on a chair and kissed the top of his head.

"Fishwoman," he said sweetly.

I took his hands, led him into the bedroom, and undressed him the way I'd always dreamed of doing if I'd ever owned a big porcelain doll. Careful of his aches and pains, I laid him in the bed. I undressed and crept into the bed beside him and wrapped my arms around him.

"Fishwoman," he repeated, locking me in a tight embrace. I felt safe and happy as I draped a leg over him. Jón—mine forever and ever.

I stood on a trestle at a long table and washed fish. Each woman had her own basin and washboard. A boy wheeled salt-crusted fish in a barrow and piled them onto the table. I scrubbed the salt off my fish and threw it into the slotted crate in front of the table. Done. The tallyman approached and checked my fish for blood spots.

Three men stood at the end of the trestle, chopping off heads and flattening the fish. They earned twice as much as I did. During lunch break, I went to the office behind the fish-washing station. The manager was making pencil marks on a piece of paper.

"I want to chop off heads," I said.

His gaze traveled across my expanding belly to my hands, red and swollen from the cold fish water. "Chopping off heads is men's work. Men have families to feed."

I thought of Jón lying in bed at home. "So do I."

"No, absolutely not."

I clenched my fists. He opened a desk drawer and took out a pair of two-thumbed woolen mittens and handed them to me. "I got them from a trawlerman, shrunk at sea with saltwater."

Angrily, I pulled on the mittens and returned to the trestle. Next to me a large, neckless woman flung out her elbows as she worked.

"Hello. I'm Sigga."

"I'm Lilla, the saltfish queen," she said from the side of her mouth.

"Is there money in that?"

She sent me a sharp look. "In what?"

"In being queen?"

"I get two kronas for every hundred fish. I wash a thousand fish a day. Watch me, girl."

A boy, with a shaky grip on a barrow, wheeled in more fish. Lilla took a large fish from the table, washed the salt off its back and under the fins. She turned it around, cut out the bones, and drained the blood from the throat and the spinal column. With the thumb of her mitten, she rubbed away the black membrane under the flap next to the head.

She watched as I placed a fish in my pan of water and reached for my brush. "Something baking in your oven, honey?" she asked.

I thrust out my belly for her to admire.

Chapter 11

Bergthora sat at the table, dipping a milk cracker into her coffee. I was stirring flour into melting margarine, preparing a sauce for the potatoes. Barrels clanged outside. The crew was here for the outhouses.

"Ah, bless their hearts," she said. "I remember the cold winter when everything froze, including the outhouses. The crew couldn't empty them."

I laughed as I added milk to the sauce.

"They transported the barrels of frozen shit and pee and drove them to the hot springs to melt the contents."

"Am I supposed to believe that?"

"I was there. It was 1918."

I added chopped-up potatoes to the sauce.

Bergthora had a dreamy look in her eyes. "Think of those poor louses in the shacks. No service. They dump their potties in the ocean," she said.

Maja's gray sheets came to mind. "You care about those people?"

Bergthora sucked the coffee out of her milk cracker. "My boyfriend, Ragbag, grew up in the shacks."

I dropped a smoked horse meat sausage onto the hot pan. A spicy smell filled the kitchen. "Ragbag? Your nickname for him?"

"He wrapped himself in dishrags, torn sheets, scraps of sheepskin, anything he could find."

Another resident of the shacks came to mind. "Do you know a woman named Maja?"

Bergthora rubbed her temples and looked puzzled.

"Her husband wears a long raincoat."

"Oh, Oddur. He hates Jón. Do you have more coffee?"

I filled the cloth filter bag with fresh coffee. Ever since I started at the plant, we had money for coffee. I set the water to boil.

"I call his kids the mushroom children," she said.

I poured her a cup of coffee. She watched the stream of hot, brown liquid.

"They resemble mushrooms?"

"Their skin looks like they never see the sun."

I shuddered at the memory of Maja's needle. That'll be ten kronas, dear. At the same time, a ridiculous wave of sympathy broke over me. Maja could have fed those kids for days with my ten kronas. The little mite inside me protested, did a grateful flip.

All Bergthora's features softened as the coffee entered her veins. "Magnús plays with them," she said. "Comes home with bumps and bleeding cuts. I sniff his hair. I smell mushroom kids on him."

"Why do you let him go there?"

"He likes to listen to Oddur rant about 'the little man.'"

"The little man? The same little man Jón's trying to save?"

"Yes. But Magnús also peeks at Oddur's pictures." She lowered her voice. "Under his bed in a locked box. Mushroom kids have the key."

Bergthora downed the rest of her coffee and bounced up to get more.

"What kind of pictures?"

"Ask Magnús. As a boy, Oddur was friends with somebody who's a bigwig in the government now. Whatever they did, it's on the photographs. That's how Oddur got an office job, calls himself Commissioner of Immigration."

"Then why does he still live in a shack?"

"Loyalty. He grew up there. Tortures his wife with a baby every year in a dirt floor hut."

I recalled the dark little rooms, the squalling kids. I couldn't understand anyone who didn't struggle to crawl up out of where he was born. "If Oddur has connections, why doesn't he get the sanitation crew to empty the latrines?"

Bergthora made a toast with her cup. "Purity of the Nordic race. Honor of the nation. Practical stuff like emptying poop doesn't interest him."

"An idealist like Jón? He makes me crazy with his little man stuff." She winced.

"I'm all for the little man," I said quickly. "But we've got to eat."

"Speaking of eating. It's Jón's birthday next week." Her voice dropped to a whisper. "He likes esophagus, stuffed with suet and chopped lung, good against coughing. Boil it for half a minute. Pickle it."

"I had enough of that kind of food on the farm," I said under my breath.

Bergthora reached into her undershirt and took out a pouch made from a dried sheep's bladder. She dropped a line of snuff on the back of her hand and sucked it up, first one nostril then the other. Her eyes teared and her head wobbled.

"His favorite food's lung pudding with a sweet, white sauce, spiced with a pinch of nutmeg if you can get it. Or cod stomach stuffed with cod liver," she said, mopping a brown droplet under her nose.

I dreaded ripping windpipes out of sheep's lungs.

It was peninsula day. I got Jón out of bed early and gave him some money. He'd go down to the dock and buy fish off the trawlers, load them onto his handcart, and fillet them for the hussies on the peninsula, wives of sailors out to sea, all lusting after him I feared.

By evening I was on edge. He was late. Finally, I heard fish-cart wheels grinding over the gravel. When he entered the kitchen, I sensed something different about him. His hard, little, black eyes had softened to the color of milk chocolate. Love? I'd seen it in the movies. I slammed down the haddock I was cleaning and sniffed his breath, his neck, his chest.

"You smell sour," I said.

"I was helping Magga move her whey barrels."

"And you fell in?"

His eyes traveled from me to the fish that lay on the cutting board. "That's not how you fillet a fish," he said.

"I think I know more about fish than you do," I said, scanning his face.

Then I saw it—the red lipstick smear on his cheek. I picked up the fish with both hands and swung it across his face. The scales were slippery. The fish slid out of my hands and fell to the floor.

He wiped the scales off his cheek. "You get one free slap. That was it."

"Then what?" I laughed in his face.

"You go back to where I found you, sitting on that concrete block."

"Ha. Ha. I found you." But I shivered. Had I swung my way out of my nest? Magnús stood in the doorway and watched us with dark, serious eyes. I picked up the fish and wiped the scales off the linoleum.

At dinner Jón explored the inside of his mouth for fish bones with his forefinger. "Fish school for you tomorrow," he said, pointing a wet finger at me.

"I did fish school on the trawler."

"This is different," he said.

I snorted.

Later, Magnús stood quietly next to me and dried the dishes. "Papa's fooling you," he said, looking up at me with serious eyes. "He smears lipstick on his cheek just to make you jealous."

Probably he was lying, but he was lying to make me happy. I touched the top of his head. "May I wash your hair?"

He surprised me by nodding happily.

I boiled water, mixed it with cold, and scrubbed his scalp with soap until he squealed. Rubbing his hair dry, I held him close to my growing belly. I parted his hair and combed it down flat. With his outsized grown-up teeth, he wasn't handsome. But I liked to gaze at him. My boy. My baby's brother.

In the hall, I found Jón's jacket, slipped my hand into the pocket, and curled it around a small cylinder. I took out the lipstick. It was bright red and worn down. I placed it in the top drawer in the bedroom, next to Borghildur's old lipstick. Jón was fast asleep when I finally crept into bed. I reached for him. He flung out his arms and said, "We will fight for disability pay and widows' pensions." I pushed him to the edge of the bed. Our baby needed the space.

The next morning, I wrapped Bergthora in two blankets against the morning chill and sat down with her on the front steps. Jón took a haddock from the cart, cut it between the gill and the throat, freed the gill from the head on the right side, and cut through the backbone and the small bones next to it. Finally, he cut off the head with a clean, cross-sectional movement and set it down on the step.

"Show-off," I said.

Bergthora covered her mouth, but I heard her laugh.

"You have to respect a fish," Jón said.

"Yes, master," his mother called out, doing a mock salute.

"Cut him along the lines of his body, the way God made him," he said, handing me a fish. "Your turn."

I placed my hand on my back and pushed myself to a standing position. Tongue between my teeth, I cut off the fish head without breaking the spine and filleted it, not leaving a single bone. His smile warmed me. I'd passed his test.

It had been a long day. Jón complained of his aching body. I heated water on the stove for his bath and helped him climb into the tub. Scrubbing the creases in his neck, I sang him the fish song I'd composed especially for him. "Salt and dry the big ones, big ones, big ones. Salt and dry the big ones, all day long." After the bath, I rubbed his body dry, placed him on a chair, and stroked the knotted veins in his legs with kerosene.

The baby settled into my back. I grasped the table and pulled myself up.

In bed, he whispered, "Fishwoman" and gently stroked my belly. His hard, thick fingers told me he liked me even though his tenderness seemed aimed at our baby. And thanks to the peninsula hussies, Jón was fit as a well-oiled machine. Fit for my bed. Grasping his shoulders, I placed a knee over his hip, angled my body to ease his entry. For a moment we were all together— Jón, the baby, and I.

Yet I dreaded the baby's arrival.

Chapter 12

After hours of pushing and panting, a squalling red-haired creature lay on my chest. Jón stood against the wall, hands in his pockets. "Like a fox," he said.

His uncertain look chilled me. I'd seen it on a ewe. The farmer had pushed the bleating lamb toward her udder. When the ewe turned her back on it, the farmer had wrapped the newborn in the fleece of a dead lamb from the same ewe and presented it to the mother. Recognizing the smell, she finally let her lamb suck.

I raised the baby up to Jón and held my breath. He shook his head. I lowered her again to my chest and felt her warmth against my breast. I looked into her red squalling mouth and told her the truth.

You're all mine.

"What shall we name her?" I asked, trying to pull him in with a joke. "Gill or Fin?"

No response. I lost courage and sank to the bottom of a dark pit. My dream of Jón as my baby's father floated away. The midwife placed the baby in the box Jón had built from pieces of driftwood. She stroked my belly. I gasped when the placenta slid out. Now I was shivering in the cool air as she wiped down my legs with a wet cloth. I looked up at Jón, still scowling. If only Mama were here. Or Borghildur. She'd told me how an ugly name can protect a child from the evil one.

I turned to face Jón. "How about calling her Tófa? Like the female fox?" Jón shook his head so hard I thought it would fall off.

"What about me?" Bergthora called from the living room.

"Bergthora's a fine name," Jón called back.

The baby slept in the crook of my arm. Darkness descended on me. I was back at Rasmussen's, listening to Diva warble, *Tosca, sei tu.* When I woke up, the whole world had changed. Jón was holding her foot and looking into her face. "*Sæl Bergþóra mín.* Hello little Bergthora," he said in a small warm voice.

My heart swelled. "Tosca Bergthora," I corrected.

With melting eyes, Jón studied the redheaded creature.

"*Tosca, sei tu,*" I sang, celebrating my baby's entry into the tribe of the water carriers. She would sleep in the room with her grandmother and would respect her above all other women for the thousands of buckets of water she'd carried. But first I would move all the ripped nets and bobbins from the other bed. My little family was fitting together nicely. Only Mama was missing. I must write her, beg her to come.

I rose from bed, wrapped a blanket around my shoulders, and joined the family at dinner. Sucking on fishbones, Bergthora said, "I hated that name Tófa. Nobody names a baby after a female fox."

Every time Tosca latched onto my breast, I squealed. When Bergthora saw my sore, cracked nipples, she said, "You need mouse ear."

Magnús had left his homework on the kitchen table and sat on the floor, arranging pebbles on the old carpet to form streets. Making the sound of a Model T's engine, he guided his driftwood car between the pebbles.

"Magnús," Bergthora said.

He jumped up and sat down at the kitchen table to do his homework.

"No. No. I want you to go to the edge of the marsh and pick some mouse ear."

His face brightened. He pulled on his aviator cap and ran out the door. Much later, he returned with a handful of plants topped with tiny white flowers. I followed Bergthora into the kitchen and watched her chop the mouse ear.

"If this doesn't work," she whispered, "you'll need a drainer. When I was a kid on the farm, we had a hired woman whose breasts got so swollen she couldn't feed her baby. Farmer sent for drainers. Two men hiked all day, crossing five streams. Finally, they climbed into the woman's bed and sucked her dry, one at each breast. Drainers have strong teeth because they get more milk than most children."

"That never happened on my farm," I said. My eyes grew moist. I longed for Mama. To cover my feelings, I focused on Magnús who was singing to the baby. "A car has two axles, a motor, and a cab. Tra, la, la, la, la. And four wheels."

I gritted my teeth and stared at the ceiling while Bergthora lathered the poultice onto my sores. I used to be brave. Now I was scared. What if that ceiling fell down on my baby? And the falcons. Every day they flew over the house hoping to steal my baby. Nights, trolls might enter the cottage, steal Tosca, leave me with a changeling. And when she slept, I checked on her, placed my mirror shard under her nose. If it steamed up, I knew she was still alive.

At the plant, I carried Tosca in a sling across my chest, trying not to hit her when I washed fish. One cold day when icicles hung from the gutters, I left Tosca with Bergthora. I worried. Hours later, I saw Magnús in the distance, crossing the marsh to the plant.

"She was crying," he said and handed me the baby. I draped an arm around his shoulders and held him close while I eased her onto my breast.

Chapter 13

A few months after Tosca was born, the postman stood on the steps. Sometimes he accidentally brought me Ratcatcher's mail—bills for 115 kilos of sugar for his distillery. But this time he handed me an envelope addressed to Mama, in my handwriting. I'd written it weeks ago to tell her Tosca had been born. The word DECEASED was stamped on the envelope.

I threw the letter onto the kitchen table. Bergthora looked up from her coffee. "Whaaa?"

But I couldn't speak. I ran out the door and splashed into the icy cold water of the marsh. Panting, I stared up at the sky. In the ragged clouds, I saw Mama's rounded back, her slim legs as she climbed over rocks, hunting for lost sheep, all the while knitting mittens. She'd been the only person in the whole world who loved me. Once I'd asked her, Was I an ugly baby? No. You had the most beautiful ears I've ever seen. They lay flat against your head.

I heard a rustling in the grass alongside the marsh. A godwit with a slender, rust-colored neck waded on tall thin legs, dipping its long yellow beak into the water. Its wings fluttered. Its speckled chest flashed as it flew up into the sky. As it became a dot in the distance, I saw Mama's sweet soul resting on its wing. My head grew heavy, and I looked down at the marsh grasses. Pearls stored for a special occasion spilled down my cheeks. The noise of my chattering teeth nearly made me deaf as I ran back to the cottage.

Just inside the door of the cottage stood a strange man in a rumpled suit. "I'm Guðmundur's secretary," he said. "He wants to see you."

I shook my head.

"It's about your mother."

I could barely lift my heavy feet to put on dry socks. The strange man helped me into my coat. We walked in silence to Guðmundur's house. Herdís led me into the parlor. Footsteps sounded in the hall. The lion's body filled the doorframe. In his hands was a large brown envelope. He gestured for me to join him at the small, round table.

"The farmer at Upper Falls sent this to Rasmussen. He brought it to me," he said, handing me the envelope. I pulled out a thin piece of official stationery from the county coroner in Skaftafellssýsla. My eyes blurred on the words.

> Your mother, Hansína Theodórsdóttir, died last week of
> consumption. She's buried toward the back of the church cemetery.

My entire childhood, she'd coughed until her bones rattled. For some people, coughing was a form of expression. You didn't die from coughing. Guðmundur's eyes were too much on me. Go away, lion. Go chase animals in the jungle. I fumbled behind my ear for a cigarette. Nothing.

Inside the large envelope, I found three sealed envelopes, all in Mama's square print and addressed to me. Had that ass Lárus refused to mail her letters? Or had she sealed them and decided not to send them? I opened the first one. Dear Sigga. She wrote about the rain that never stopped. The next letter was all about a new pattern of sweater she was knitting. I tore open the third envelope, expecting more weather news. But it contained only a piece of tattered paper. I recognized the paper Mama had called "the letter from your papa," the worn receipt from the village store: 2 kilos potatoes, flour, chicken netting, lard, sugar. I held it up to the light, scanned it for secret writing between the lines. Nothing. I turned it over. A word was scrawled on the back of the receipt. It hadn't been there before. I recognized Mama's handwriting. She had written a name, *Guðmundur*.

My lips trembled. I pushed the letters back into the envelope. Guðmundur, the faithful mitten shrinker—surely, that was who Mama meant. My vision blurred. The room spun. Man-killing waves rose up around me. I was drowning. I gripped the armrests of my chair, but the keel rose up out of the ocean. With my fingernails, I clung to the hull of the ship. A lion climbed up out of the ocean. It moved closer. I smelled its wet mane and screamed.

"I'll get you a cup of coffee," Guðmundur said and padded out of the room.

A chance to escape. I leaped out of the chair, felt my way along the walls, and ran out of the house into the cold rain. Once I was inside the cottage, I took the envelope from under my arm. In the bedroom, I pushed the envelope under Sveinn's folded sweater at the bottom of the closet. I would think about all this later.

The church on the pond gave things away in a program called Poor Help. I put in a bid for a baby pram. Every week I checked to see if anybody had donated one. Finally, a few months later, I got one. No fourth wheel. No brakes. But my heart was full of joy as I pushed it home.

"What are you doing with that?" Jón asked.

"We have a baby. Remember?"

"What about the fish cart?"

My palm tickled with the need to smack him. "I'm going to the shore to find a wheel. You can attach it."

"Me? Attach a wheel?"

I found one and borrowed some tools from Ratcatcher. Jón watched me attach it. I washed and dried the inside of the pram and bundled Tosca, pretty as a petal, into it. I turned left on Suðurgata, then pulled into Diva's garden, parked the pram under the gnarled birch tree, and carried Tosca up the familiar steps, the ones I used to wash with soapy water.

I ran past Rasmussen and up the stairs. "Oh. Oh. Look at that," Diva said when she saw Tosca. I placed the baby in her arms. She sniffed the top of her head, then shifted her gaze to my red, swollen hands. "You should have stayed with me. What's the news of your fisherman?"

"He catches a fish or two. I work at the fish plant. I try to fill in with sewing. I embroider centipedes and grasshoppers, like you suggested, on tea towels for the gift shop downtown. Foreign fishermen buy the strangest things for their wives."

She held my hand, turned it over, fingered the calluses. "Go into my closet," she said. "Find something nice for yourself."

I pawed through Diva's old silk ball gowns and finally held up a lacy blouse. "This?"

"Wear that and get a job at The Lingerie Shop."

I rolled up the blouse and stuffed it into my purse.

"And before you leave, take the magazines from under my bed. You'll find insects, reptiles, lots of ideas for your tea towels."

The door swung open. Rasmussen leered at us.

"Get some cans of food for Sigga. And help her carry the magazines," Diva said.

I hadn't forgiven the oily little man for taking my dock work wages, but I wouldn't waste time on bad feelings. He brought the magazines, then disappeared and returned with cans of red cabbage, peas, and Danish ham. Smiling in his tight, greasy way, he arranged the cans at Tosca's feet. I pushed the pram up the hill, favoring the three good wheels.

It was one of those long, bright spring evenings when the sun flooded the kitchen, but outdoors the air nipped your nose. I placed a platter of steaming fried haddock on the table. Bergthora sat with her napkin tucked into her neckline.

"Jón," I called. No answer.

I picked my way over the mud puddles to the baiting sheds. He sat in his usual place on a concrete block, talking, talking, talking. Two fishermen in torn clothes hugged their arms to their chests. I came up behind them.

Same old song from Jón. "You have no share in the profits—they're using you."

"At least we have jobs," the smaller one said.

Jón poured blood-brown powder onto the back of his hand, cupped it against the breeze, and offered it. Each man inhaled deeply. Eyes tearing, Jón passed a phlegm-clotted handkerchief over his nostrils. He turned to the older man. "Didn't we get you eight hours in the bunk out of every twenty-four?"

"Means nothing. They work us until every fish is in the hold, gutted and gilled."

"Dinner," I yelled. The men sprang to their feet and pointed their noses toward home. Jón reached for my arm and pulled himself up.

I pinned his arm to my side. "Why do you keep telling those men they're not happy?"

"I want them on my side, not Oddur's."

"To the devil with the little man," I said. "Women only earn seventy aura an hour drying fish while men earn a full krona. How's that fair?"

We passed a lump fisherman beaching his boat. His eyes were full of sympathy for Jón.

"Fishwoman," Jón said sadly. "You don't understand."

My volcano erupted. "I don't *want* to understand. I don't want to talk. I want to *do*."

I thought I was rid of those men. I was on all fours next day washing the floor. Jón sat in the shadows, rubbing his palms together, making a papery sound that set my nerves on edge when the front door opened. The snuff-nosed fellows shuffled into the kitchen. I jumped up and raised my fist at them. "Get off my clean floor."

The men stepped backward, out the door, and onto the step. The smaller one leaned in over the threshold. "I've decided to go with you, not Oddur," he said.

"Me too," the other one said.

I swung my rag at them, and they scrambled down the steps.

"Fishwoman," Jón said. "You chased away my friends."

"They interrupted my work."

"I won those men away from the nationalists. Now they'll vote for us."

"Hooray," I said, rubbing my temples against a headache.

Magnús emerged from the bedroom.

Five-year-old Tosca had been playing with Magnús' cars on the floor. When she saw him, she rose up on her heels and called, "Maggi, Maggi, Maggi."

He patted her on the head. At fourteen, he was still short and square like Jón. He held up a piece of paper. On it was a detailed sketch of a boat. The stick figure at the helm was labelled MAGNÚS.

"Nice, dear," I said.

He turned to his father. Jón's eyes darkened when he saw the drawing. "No boats for you, Magnús. You'll stay in school."

"But I want to fish with you."

"I'll tell you about fishing. You sit on a thwart with your chest stuck to your thighs from cold. Veins burst in your nose. One morning, you lie in bed like a hook that won't straighten. Wife pulls away your blanket. 'Get up.' You lie shivering in your underwear. She brings coffee, black as ink, pours it into the side of your mouth. You drink it until you can see your chest rising and falling. Your heart starts beating again. She rolls you out of bed. You stand up, but you're shorter than you were yesterday."

I glared at Jón, but he wouldn't stop.

"You can't reach your tobacco pouch where you put it on the shelf. She gets it for you, stuffs it into your pocket, pinches your leg to get the blood flowing. On the boat again, you crouch below the wind and pray for a bite."

Magnús crumpled his drawing and threw it on the floor. He strode across the room and slammed the door behind him.

"Why did you say that?" I asked.

Jón rolled his head against the wall. "I've got plans for him. If he stays in school—he just may get a chance to go to Moscow."

"Moscow! He's never even been north to Akureyri."

"The party will pay for his education in Moscow. When he comes back, he'll work for the party here."

"Magnús has his own plans. He wants to be a fisherman." I bit my tongue. I mustn't say what I was thinking. He's not like you. He'd be a real fisherman.

In the shed I found Magnús stroking Branda.

"I thought he would be happy with me," he said.

I placed an arm around him, the other on the cow's back. We stood like that for a few moments.

———————

Jón adored Tosca. He counted her freckles, combed her red hair, told me she resembled his great aunt, the only redhead in his family. When he should have been fishing, he took Tosca to the pond to feed our last bread crusts to the ducks.

After milking Branda Monday morning, I warmed up some water. Tosca was on the floor playing with cutouts from one of Diva's old magazines. Her hair stood out in a mess of tangles. Its red color cheered me, especially during the dark winter. And I purposely avoided using the Fedora soap that Bergthora said would lighten her freckles.

It seemed a shame to waste the water on sheets and towels. I glanced at Bergthora, nodding in the kitchen corner seat. "You haven't had a bath for a while," I said.

"Don't waste water on me."

But she didn't resist when I helped her undress. Her skin was pale and almost free of wrinkles, preserved for decades under wool. She stepped into the tub and slid underwater until only her lips, nose, and eyes were visible. Her mouth moved as she chanted, "Knead the milt into the rye meal, and you've got miltbread."

I left her to soak and began cleaning a fish for dinner. I fried onions and placed the fish in the pan. When something bubbled in the tub, I looked up. Bergthora was no longer visible. She had disappeared below the surface. I gripped her shoulders, pulled her up, and slapped both of her cheeks.

"You almost died," I said angrily.

"I found no coffee this morning. All I had was blood in my veins."

"Don't ever drown on me. You're my baby's grandmother."

She shook the water from her ears. "I was just resting." Leaning back into the water, she began chanting again. "Wrap the large intestine around the veins. Wrap them tight. Sew the underbelly around the veins and large intestine. Boil. Save it in sour."

I blocked my ears and turned my back on her.

Chapter 14

I made a habit of picking up Ratcatcher's discarded newspaper from the trash and reading the advertisements. One caught my eye: NEEDED– women with good legs for the revue, *The Kicking Nightingales*. Taxi Barn, Wednesday, 4:00 p.m.

I had good legs and no holes in my stockings. Using Jón's lipstick, I reddened my cheeks and forehead, then rubbed my whole face with udder cream until it glowed pink.

In the taxi barn, women in short skirts milled around, frowning and smoking. One sat at an upright piano. A man with a pad and pencil appeared.

"All together now, kick and sing," he said. I lined up with the rest of the women and gripped the shoulders of my neighbors.

The pianist pounded the keys. She sang the song, "I scream. You scream. We all scream for ice cream." I tried to follow the words and kicked as high as I could. I loved dancing. And I'd be paid.

But when the man read out names, he skipped mine. Something was wrong. "You forgot to call my name," I said.

"I've hired the girls I need."

I raised my skirt to my thighs. "If one of those girls gets sick, think of me."

His eyes rolled from the arch of my foot to my garter. "I'll call you," he said.

"No, you won't. I don't have a phone." I stormed out.

We were heating the cottage with peat and seaweed. I needed more work. On the way home, I balled up my courage and entered The Lingerie Shop. Bins overflowed with girdles, slips, and underpants. A shapely woman, swinging a measuring tape, popped up.

"Darling, what can I fit you for?"

I batted the tape away. "Magdalena? I'm looking for work."

"I need a girl to clean the shop," she said, eyeing my hands.

"I'll clean free of charge if you'll give me corset construction lessons."

She giggled. "Corset construction? I stopped offering those lessons years ago."

Disappointment pinched my stomach. Behind Magdalena's shoulder, I glimpsed a small room. A dark-haired woman leaned over a sewing machine, probably stitching corsets. How could I get into that room? I went to the shelf and pulled out a pair of thick, salmon-colored underpants with an undershirt to match. "Who buys these?" I asked.

Magdalena's beautifully made-up eyes rolled over my body and landed on my swollen fingers and broken fingernails.

"Who?" I repeated, gripping the ugly underwear.

"Everybody. They're warm."

"I can make them pretty," I said.

Her eyebrows rose.

"I embroider. I specialize in Danish creatures. Imagine butterflies, salamanders, hummingbirds embroidered on these underpants. Women will love them. At home they'll walk around in their underwear."

A sparkle appeared in Magdalena's eye. "Take some home with you. Come back with something beautiful."

I took three pairs off the shelf and tucked them under my arm. But, walking home, I thought hard. I needed more work. On Mud Road chickens scratched next to potato and rhubarb patches. Cows bellowed. Horses grazed wherever grass grew. I could reach into a cow's birth canal, turn a calf so the cow could deliver. I got paid in food—a blood sausage, a fish, or a couple of lamb chops. A light went on in my head. Why not human babies?

From that day forward, I listened for labor pains that floated out onto Mud Road from windows propped open to cool a sweating body. Within seconds, I'd be on the doorstep.

"Can I help?"

The midwife always nodded gratefully, told me to rub arms, legs, shoulders, heat water, and sing a hymn. I watched how she caught the baby and cut the cord. After a while, women called me directly and paid me with fish cheeks, liver sausage, and singed sheep's heads.

Picking driftwood one day on the shore, I tripped over a cracked leather bag. I took it home and cleaned out the sand and seaweed. I dropped a pair of scissors, a clean cloth, yarrow salve, and yarrow leaves into the bag. I was a healer now. My bag stayed in the kitchen, always ready.

It was an October afternoon, already dark. The wind moaned in the metal weather stripping around the front door. I was embroidering rainbow horseflies onto Magdalena's underwear. Next to me, Jón dozed. He'd been at the dock all morning, trying to persuade his friends to fight for shift laws and pensions. Bergthora, on the upside of her coffee spiral, sat on the sofa, knitting a sweater for Tosca, now age eleven.

Tosca's chest strained against the buttons of her dress. I always made the girl wear her clothes for as long as she could squeeze into them. This meant constantly moving buttons and hooks until she complained she couldn't breathe in a shirt or a dress. I visited Poor Help regularly and dug through boxes, but I rarely found something in Tosca's size. People usually handed clothes down to relatives, but I didn't have any. So I was grateful to Bergthora.

A knock on the door sent a thrill up my spine. Probably a neighbor wanting me to help pop piglets out of the back of a sow. I would catch the silky, sweet-smelling babies so their mother couldn't eat them. And when the pig was slaughtered, I'd get a slice of pork wrapped in newspaper. Instead, a small boy stood on the steps, his bald head shiny in the rain.

"Mama can't squeeze the baby out," he said.

Blue shadows lay under his eyes. His earlobe was ragged, and his chin sloped.

"Who's your father?" But I already knew.

"Oddur." Watching my face, he repeated the name. "Oddur."

"Yes, of course."

"Will ya come?" he asked.

Oddur wouldn't give me so much as a fishskin in payment. But the boy's eyes were full of pleading. Besides, Oddur might beat him if he returned alone. I fetched my delivery bag, threw in the horsehair rope for Maja to chew on, and pulled on my coat. As we walked through the tussocks toward the shacks, I asked the boy, "How was school today?"

"School?"

Ah, I forgot. Oddur kept his children home to teach them why the nationalists were better than the communists. I pictured them huddled together for warmth while he raved about the one-party system. The boy quickened his pace as we approached the sod and stone hut. A tattered car seat and a car battery lay in the yard. Dread came over me. I would turn around and go home. But the door opened. Oddur stood in the hallway wearing a raincoat as if he were about to leave. His hand grasped mine. He held on too long. I prepared to crack him across the face, but I heard a groan from the end of the dark hallway.

"Your wife," I said.

Oddur signaled to the boy. He padded along the dirt floor. I followed him into the same bedroom I'd visited all those years ago. A candle on a saucer provided the only light. The room felt moist as if sweat hung on the walls. Maja lay very still. In her eyes of pain, I saw a flicker of recognition.

"You never came back, dear," she said in a weak voice.

"My baby girl's eleven now."

Maja groaned under another contraction. Her quivering chin pointed to the ceiling. I took a handkerchief from my pocket and wiped her face. I stroked her trembling belly as the spent muscles of her womb contracted again. I turned her onto her side, rubbed her shoulders and the small of her back. Slowly she raised a knee and gave God one more chance. Take this blasted baby out of my body. But no crowning head appeared. The only sounds in the room were Maja's teeth chattering through her ragged breathing. Surgeons at the hospital could cut her open and lift the baby out. But they didn't visit the shacks.

In the hall, I found Oddur slumped against the wall.

"Take her to the hospital," I said

He shook his head. "Those doctors are Commies."

"Then you'll lose her."

"She's done it before. Nearly died each time."

My toes tingled with the desire to kick him in the groin. Instead, I walked to the stove, found a saucepan, cleaned out the oatmeal lickings, and filled it with water. I took yarrow leaves from my birthing bag and made tea in a cracked cup. In the bedroom, I placed pillows under Maja's shoulders and brought the cup to her lips. She turned away as her body tried again to expel the baby.

Toward morning, like an afterthought, a tiny wrinkled creature entered the world. I held the pathetic lump of life in my hands, pictured its future as Oddur's brat with a nose that ran green in all seasons. Maja whimpered as I laid the mewling baby on her chest and cut the cord. Even in these grimy circumstances, life might win. Eyes closed, Maja placed her hand on her baby's back. She groaned as she delivered the afterbirth. I hoped no part of it remained inside her.

But then the blood began to ooze from between her legs. The drops formed a thin stream that kept coming until she lay in a scarlet pool. I grasped the towel and pushed it against her crotch, holding it there until the warm, wet stickiness covered my hands. I reached for the pillow on Oddur's side of the bed. Kneeling between Maja's trembling legs, I pushed the pillow against the towel, but I couldn't stop this emptying out of life. I ran into the hall. Nobody answered my scream. Back in the bedroom I took Maja's hand. Her face had turned white. I recognized the beginning of absence. A gurgling sound came from her throat. A tremor passed through her body. Pain drained from her face as her features froze. I pictured her gliding through a crack in the mountains and sailing into paradise beyond Esja Mountain.

"Fly away, my love. Don't look back," I said, stroking her cooling cheek.

I wrapped the baby in a shirt that lay at the end of the bed. When I heard Oddur yelling at the kids, I walked into the hall and handed him the baby.

"Well?" he asked.

"She's gone."

Holding the baby with outstretched arms away from his raincoat, he made a sound of disbelief.

"When I report the death, I will explain that I recommended taking Maja to the hospital, but you forbade it."

"You're not much of a midwife, are you?"

The children crowded around me. The older ones were weeping. I wanted to hate them because Oddur had spawned them, but the lump in my throat got in the way. The boy who'd fetched me touched my elbow. For a second, I rested my hand on his warm, hairless scalp. I picked up my bag and walked out the door.

Outside, I faced the ocean and breathed in the cold, clean air. Beyond Mud Road, the clouds had parted allowing the sun to shine through. Mama's soul had flown upward on a godwit's wing. Perhaps Maja would join her.

Back home, I put my bag on the kitchen table. Bergthora sat on a chair leaning against the wall. "Did you save the poor woman?"

I recalled Maja's peaceful look, free of pain, free of Oddur. "Yes. I did."

———

It was a quiet, cold morning. As usual, Jón lay in bed, pulling his thoughts together. Tosca crept into the kitchen.

"My hair?" she pleaded. I reached for the hairbrush. While she ate her oatmeal, I brushed the tangle out of her wild hair and plaited it into a thick braid. At age twelve, she walked to school alone or with her friend, Helga, Ratcatcher's daughter. She was already in the hall putting on her shoes and coat when Jón's bed creaked and his feet hit the floor.

"I'll walk with you to school," I heard him say in the hall.

"You'll make her late," I said.

"No, he won't, Mama." Through the open window, I heard them chattering as they entered Mud Road. I slammed the window shut. I measured flour and other dry ingredients for brown cake, stirred the butter and sugar vigorously, banging the spoon against the bowl. On the radio was a serialized story about a woman who hit her husband with a bread board. She brought him unconscious to the hospital.

A sound at the door. "Fishwoman, I'm back," Jón said.

"Quiet. I'm listening."

The woman told the doctor her husband had fallen, but the doctor didn't believe her. I placed my ear against the radio. When the man regained consciousness, he mentioned the bread board. The woman was arrested. But he deserved the beating, I told the radio. He'd refused to work.

Jón spread his papers on the kitchen table.

"I'm baking," I said, placing my bowl in the center of the table and slapping together the wet and dry ingredients. I pushed the cake into the oven. "We need fish," I said, wiping my hands on my apron.

He divided his papers into two stacks: Shift laws for healthy workers. Pensions for disabled workers.

I fanned my face and ran to the bedroom. A good man. He's a good man, I told myself as I squeezed into a tight skirt I'd picked up at Poor Help. I wrapped up the underwear I'd embroidered with blue and green horseflies for Magdalena.

"Don't let the cake burn," I said on my way out. He didn't look up.

At The Lingerie Shop, I discovered Magdalena had rearranged the mannequins, so they formed a welcoming half circle of plaster women in pink corsets. Tables overflowed with pretty things.

"Can I help you?" a foreign voice asked. The woman emerged from the tailor shop.

I handed her the underwear. "Tell Magdalena Sigga brought it."

"I'm Klara."

"Do you . . . do you sew corsets?"

"A little. The machine helps."

"I'd like to stitch by hand."

Klara's lower jaw dropped. "By hand?"

"I grew up on a farm. Every evening we made things, mostly by hand."

"Magdalena will be here tomorrow. Come back? *Ja?*"

I walked backward out of the store, watching Klara examine the underwear.

Chapter 15

I stirred *skyr* into the oatmeal for dinner while Bergthora dozed in a kitchen chair. Next to her, Jón flipped through papers.

"Papa," Tosca called from the hall. "I have some math for you."

When she appeared, Jón held out his arms to her. Locked in his embrace, she wriggled an arm free and threw a math book on the table. "Papa, can you do the problems on page thirty-six? I don't know what they're talking about."

"Don't do her homework for her," I said.

He gave me a "Why not?" look.

Almost thirteen now, Tosca stood tall enough to kiss the top of Jón's head. "Papa likes numbers," she said to me.

I bit the insides of my mouth. Jón was what I'd wanted—a father for my little girl. My wish had come true, but . . . They leaned into one another. When Jón handed her the finished homework, Tosca said, "I have something." She ran to her bookbag and brought back a small card. She dropped it on the middle of the table.

It was a trading card in the trawler series, the kind of card included in cigarette packs. Anna, Helga's mother, bought cigarettes in packs not singles. Each pack had a card with a drawing of a trawler. I peered at the drawing. It bore the name of the boat. *Lilja.* Sveinn's boat.

Jón reached for the card. "That's Sveinn Gunnarsson's boat. He's the catch king," he said, shifting his gaze to me. "Didn't he come here once, years ago, looking for you?"

My stomach dropped.

Jón's eyes glowed. "Lucky girl. You got the best card. Nothing tops the catch king."

"And guess what? *Lilja's* at the dock now. Helga heard it on the shipping news. After school tomorrow, we're going to the dock—" Tosca's voice came out in a happy shriek.

"No," I objected.

Everyone turned to look at me.

"Why not?" Jón asked.

"You might slip on a fishskin," I said.

Tosca's warm hand touched my forehead. "Mama, you're feverish. Go lie down."

She was right. I felt hot, and my head ached. I hurried to the bedroom and knelt in front of the clothes closet. I found it in the same spot I'd placed it over thirteen years ago. My throat swelled as I ran my fingers over the rough wool of Sveinn's sweater. His daughter would want it.

We were eating breakfast when Tosca said, "I won't be coming home right after school."

I stirred my coffee. "Why not?" I knew why.

"Remember? We're taking our trading cards to the dock to match them to the boats."

"The dock's no place for a young girl," I said.

"Yes, it is. You unloaded coal on the dock when you were a teenager."

Why had I told her those stories? "Don't go."

"You can't stop me."

"Oh yes I can." I got to my feet, grasped the girl's shoulder, and raised my other hand. A look of terror crossed her face. I froze. She wrenched herself free and ran out the door.

I lit a cigarette and paced the kitchen floor, stopping sometimes to peer out the window. How would I glue the pieces together again? Breathing hard, I lit another cigarette and prayed, Don't let this happen.

I needed Diva.

Without a coat, hugging my arms against the cold, I ran down the hill toward her house. I flew into her bedroom. She patted the bed next to her. I climbed up and sat with my head on her shoulder.

"Something's wrong?"

"Tosca's gone to see Sveinn."

"Who?"

"The trawlerman."

"Oh, yes. So?"

"He's her father."

"And . . ." Her small eyes, fierce now, pinned me to the wall. "She doesn't know that?"

I shook my head.

"Why did you do this?"

I moved closer to her. "I wanted to make my own family with Jón, just the three of us—four with Magnús."

"No room for Sveinn?"

"Remember? He had another woman."

"And you let him go?"

"No. I punched him."

"You punched him instead of telling him you were expecting a baby?"

"He didn't fall down."

Her laughter jarred me. The look in her eyes made it hard for me to breathe. I'd been queen of my cottage. Now my crown rolled to the floor.

"Look," she said in a sharp voice. "I don't know anything about children or—" and she waved her hand at the window "—or the world out there. But not telling him and not telling her was wrong."

I hung my head.

"And what about Sveinn now?"

"I cross the street when I see him."

She slapped the mattress so hard her glasses fell to the floor. "The love of your life and you cross the street?"

Swallowing hard, I picked up her glasses.

"This is what I think," she whispered. "There's no shame in having a baby with the wind, like you did. But crossing the street—that's shameful."

A surge of anger saved me from sobbing. "I couldn't trust him."

Back home, I chopped onions and fried meat scraps. The door opened. Tosca threw her books on the table.

"I was at the dock," she said.

I cringed.

"A big red-haired man stood on the deck of the *Lilja*. He was looking at me."

I could picture him doing that.

"He got off the boat, started walking toward me, studying my face, like he knew me. 'I thought you'd never come,' he said. You know, like a mad man. Helga grabbed my arm. We ran away."

I leaned against the kitchen counter and held on with both hands.

"Why did he say, 'I thought you'd never come,'?" she asked.

Play for time. This will go away.

Tosca's face was in mine. "Who is he?"

I studied her green eyes and red curls. I recalled the story Magnús told me years ago of Tosca's first time at the dock. At age thirteen he'd brought her there to look at the boats. A red-headed fisherman kept staring at five-year old Tosca. Why? Magnús had wanted to know. I knew why, but I'd brushed it off.

Now I grasped my second chance.

"He's your father," I said.

The color behind the freckles drained from the girl's face. I reached for her, but she twisted away and stood with her back against the door.

"I hate you," she whispered.

I folded my arms over my chest, holding myself together. I'd let her live. But now everything I hadn't given her—the father, the grandfather, the brother, coats and skirts from Hamburg and Hull—rolled over me, crushed me. And Jón? When Tosca was a baby, we'd lain together in bed, Jón with his arms around both of us. She was his love. Because of a trading card, he was no longer her father.

"I'm sorry." I wasn't sorry about lying. I was sorry because the family I'd constructed was shattered.

She backed out of the kitchen. From the window, I saw her knocking on Helga's door.

Behind me, woolen socks swished on the linoleum. "Fishwoman," Jón said.

"You heard?"

He exhaled deeply, pulled a chair up against the wall, sat down, and closed his eyes. "Fishwoman—"

I placed a hand on his shoulder. He pushed it away.

"Fishwoman. You lied."

Lygari. Lygari. Liar. Liar. That was my label for Mama when she'd lied about Papa. Lies lay in our blood and clogged our veins.

"I wanted *you*, not Sveinn, to be Tosca's father."

I heard him inhaling, taking my words deep inside himself. Hours passed. He did not move. I took clothes off the line and folded them. I made coffee. I kneaded bread and peeled potatoes for dinner. I heard Tosca at the door. My blood turned cold.

"Hello, Papa," she said, whirling in and kissing Jón on the cheek.

He placed his arm around her waist, the way he always had.

She laid a hand on his shoulder. "Papa, when you did my mathematics homework yesterday, you did it wrong. The teacher was very upset. I didn't tell her you did it, though."

I saw the love in her eyes as she waited for an answer.

"Papa, did you hear me?"

"Show me what I did wrong," he finally said.

Tosca fetched her bookbag from the hall, pulled out the math papers, and placed them in front of Jón. "See the red marks. You did a terrible job," she said, a laugh in her voice. He picked up the pencil and began to rework a problem. She rested her head against his.

I waited until Tosca was alone in the kitchen to take Sveinn's sweater out of the closet. It looked just as I remembered it with the cable design down the front. I raised it to my nose and imagined I smelled Sveinn on it—the motor oil, fish, and sweat. My heart quickened. I wanted to keep it. For a moment, I fought with myself. No, she should have it. Holding it in both hands like an offering, I brought it to the kitchen.

"I have something for you."

She looked up.

I extended my arms. "It belonged to Sveinn."

Tosca jumped up from her chair and took the sweater from my hands. She pulled it on over her school sweater and smoothed down the cable design over her chest, just like I'd done years ago when Sveinn had been mine. I rolled my eyes toward the ceiling, exhaling my shameful jealousy.

"What kind of man is he?" she asked.

I thought of a word that might apply to any man who did not beat his wife with a belt buckle. "Nice," I said. "He's nice."

Like a warm day in winter, Tosca twirled on one foot and chanted, "Nice. Nice. Nice." Suddenly, she gripped my shoulders. "Do I have a grandpa?"

Reluctantly I told her about the seller of stale biscuits and crystallized syrup. "His name's Gunnar Sveinsson. He runs the little colonial goods shop on the main street." All Tosca's life, I'd vowed to keep the toxic old man from us. And now, the surly merchant had crept into my family.

"I'm going to show Sveinn his sweater," Tosca said. I followed her to the steps and watched her splash through puddles, holding the hem of her man's raincoat high out of the mud.

Chapter 16

It was two years since Maja had died, and the memory still haunted me. I'd thrust my midwife's case under the sink and hadn't delivered another baby since that day. I felt the cold autumn wind on my face as I walked down the steps. In the shed, the smell of dusty hay, manure, and the hard-packed dirt floor soothed my nerves. I tied Branda's legs together with a greasy string, rubbed my hands with udder cream, and pulled on the teats. As streams of milk banged the bottom of the bucket, I sang to the cow, "My eyes and your eyes. You know what I mean—"

A sound at the entrance caused me to stop singing. I hadn't seen Oddur since the death, but I immediately recognized his chinless profile. "What do you want?" I asked.

"You ask me? You killed my wife. Don't you have something to say?"

I recalled Maja's bloodless face and how her mouth had sagged in death.

"I want you to tell Jón—"

"No. I won't tell Jón."

"—to stop recruiting followers for his Stalinist club in my neighborhood. We in the shacks are nationalists. We won't fall for Jón's international tricks."

I picked up my full pail. "You fraud. You don't give a toenail for the little man."

"We'll provide work for dockworkers and factory workers without Stalin's filthy money," he said.

"Look at you. Best pals with that nasty little Hitler."

"We're just patriots. It's Jón who's selling us to the foreigners."

"Foreigners?" I shouted, swinging the pail, taking care not to spill a drop.

"The Komintern in Moscow. That's Jón's boss."

"Shut up."

He held up his hands. "Komintern's drooling over our little island, telling Jón how to deliver us into the arms of Moscow."

"Get out. Get out."

"Tell Jón to stay out of my neighborhood," he said, stepping out of the shed.

"No," I screamed after him.

Jón was sitting with his ear to the radio when I entered the kitchen. The announcer's voice came out of the radio.

"Dozens of people were injured during a meeting of the city council last night. A mob gathered outside the door and burst into the meeting hall. People fought with clubs, chair legs, and fists. By the time the police finally brought the situation under control, the injured were crowding into clinics and the hospital."

Jón clapped his hands. "Afterward the council caved, agreed to provide more jobs."

"By breaking heads, you got your way. I hate violence."

"Fishwoman, you've got hot blood. You love violence."

"Did I ever hit you?" I'd always wanted to. My blood simmered. "Those stupid make-work jobs? Two men take turns with the same shovel?"

"So, each one will work part-time. At least they won't starve."

I took off my greasy milking apron and washed my hands. "What's the Komintern?"

He raised his eyebrows. "You really want to know?"

"I'm asking."

"It's the Communist International. They're helping us establish a party that will guarantee a good life for the little man."

"And woman?"

He laughed.

"If I hit the city council with a chair leg, will my wages improve? No. They still won't let me cut off fish heads at the plant for a man's wage."

"Fishwoman," he said, rolling his head against the wall, staying inside the grease stain he'd put there before I married him.

"Oddur visited me in the shed."

"Ah," he said deep in his throat as if I'd mentioned King Kristjan X.

I pointed my finger at him. "Watch out. Clubs. Chair legs. Your men scared people. Oddur will promise order, and votes will go to the nationalists."

He smiled sweetly. "Main thing is the little man eats."

Shaking my head, I went to the pantry and took out leftovers from Sunday's salted lamb and beans. During dinner, Oddur's voice came out of the radio.

"We'll fight back against the communist mob that attacked the council. The nationalist party will restore order to the nation."

"See what I mean?" I said.

Later in bed, he spoke to me in the gentle tone he used when he said things I didn't want to hear. "Fishwoman."

I covered my head with the blanket, but I could still hear him.

"It's about Magnús. The party will send him to Moscow for training. He'll come back and save the little man."

I sat up straight. "He wants to be a fisherman."

"He sails in two days."

"No. No. No." I punched the mattress with both fists. "How dare you?" I got up and paced the kitchen, smoking and cursing.

Two days later, I was in the yard scrubbing fish scales off the planks of the cart and drying them with a rag. Tosca moped in the doorway when Magnús came down the steps, carrying Jón's cardboard suitcase. When I saw my boy's face twitch like it used to just before crying, I spat, just missing the chickens. He threw the suitcase onto the cart and grasped its handles.

Jón and I walked on either side of Magnús out Mud Road toward the harbor. I dragged my feet. By walking slowly, I could keep my boy longer.

Too soon, the road dipped toward the dock, the goodbye place. Memories came to me of Sveinn's grinning face growing smaller and smaller as he sailed away.

"Why must I go?" Magnús asked.

Jón frowned. "Don't be an ass—it's an opportunity."

"I'd rather fish."

Clouds formed between Jón's eyebrows. "On a good day you get four fish—one to salt, one to fillet, the other two to sell. But what happens on a bad day?" He didn't wait for an answer. "The best you can do is go to the dock and let the foreman beat you at cards, get on his good side. He selects you for shoveling. Once. Twice. Then what?"

Magnús shrugged.

"You climb into the hold of the trawler and start shoveling. You grip the handle of your shovel with your left hand, push down hard with your right. Your back screams for mercy. The foreman rewards you with more work. You think that's bad?"

"Stop," I said.

"Bad's the day he *doesn't* pick you. You let him win your last coin at poker. He still chooses the man next to you. You raise your hand. 'Hey, what about me?' He points to the man behind you."

Liar. Jón preferred playing cards in the shed with the other rejected laborers. Not being chosen gave him time to recruit the little man. At the gangplank, I hugged Magnús and whispered into his ear, "Don't believe what they tell you."

Jón glared at me. "He's going to Moscow for an education, Sigga."

I heard the edge in his voice. My family had a crack down the middle. I would make it heal. Magnús appeared at the railing. Björn, the pink-cheeked son of the dock crane machinist, joined him. He'd be his classmate in Moscow. Throwing away two fine boys, instead of one, didn't console me. The ship eased away from the dock. My groan blended with the ship's whistle. I glanced at Jón. I expected to see happiness. Instead, I saw the face of a sad, old man.

It was noon on the day after Magnús left, and Jón was still in bed. He hadn't been out on the boat all week. A dark cloud hung low over the fjord. Wind lashed the cottage, and raindrops pelted the windowpane. I ran outside and took the sheets from the line. Coming back in, I bumped into Jón. He wore his oilskin coat, hat, and boots. His eyes looked wild as if he couldn't see me.

With the laundry basket, I blocked his way. "Where are you going?"

"I need to go fishing."

Exactly what I'd wanted him to do for thirteen years, but today the ocean was in a man-killing mood. I dropped the basket and drew him close.

His voice sounded like cloth ripping. "Move."

"Storm's coming up."

"Good for fishing."

I struggled with him until we nearly fell down the steps. He twisted out of my grip and ran. I chased him, caught him by the shoulders, and held him against my chest. "Jón—"

"Move," he shouted.

"Forgive me."

"I can't."

"Tosca was in my belly the day we met. I thought—I thought you knew."

His voice was a hoarse whisper. "She was my daughter. Now she's not."

"She's *still* your daughter. She loves you. And . . ." In a tiny voice I said the words I'd saved for an emergency, like coins in a piggy bank. "And . . . I love you."

He shook me off and walked stiffly toward the boats. I tackled him again.

"Leave me be," he said. With a surge of strength, he threw me to the ground and ran away. I'd never seen him run before. I chased him and wrestled with him while he tried to launch his boat. He struck me in the face with his fist. I fell backward and hit my head on one of the concrete blocks. I lay still for a moment. When I opened my eyes again, his boat was out on the fjord and Bergthora stood over me.

"Why did you let him get away?" she screamed into the howling wind. I scrambled to my feet.

"You couldn't stop him? A cripple?"

I hurried away from her. Rain lashed my face. At the shore, I scanned the rolling waves edged with white. I glimpsed his tiny boat, sinking and rising on the pockmarked water. "Jón. Jón," I screamed. But instead of rowing to shore, he became a dot on the billowing waves. Just as my eyes began to hurt from fixating on his boat, the darkness swallowed him. Hugging my arms, I walked back to the cottage.

A noise on the steps. My heart froze. Tosca entered the kitchen, grinning. "Where's Papa?" she asked. "The teacher told me to stop letting him do the math. He makes too many mistakes. Isn't that funny?" She ran down the hall calling him. When she got no response, she came back to the kitchen. Now she stood in front of me. "Papa?" she asked.

I told her. "He went to sea."

Tosca slumped into a chair and buried her head in her hands. I put my arms around her, consoling myself by holding her slender body against mine.

All night the storm howled. We sat at the kitchen table, waiting.

Toward morning, the storm quieted. As usual I milked Branda. When I came out of the shed, I saw some boys coming up from the shore. They said they'd seen bits of wood from a boat swirling among the rocks in the cove. It didn't mean anything, I told myself. It wasn't Jón's boat.

But two days later, a lumpfisherman stood on the steps. I recognized him from the baiting sheds. "Jón's body washed ashore," he said. "He's on the grass just above the fjord."

Tosca's voice sounded in my ear. "Mama, come."

Bergthora hung on my arm, and Tosca trailed behind as we walked toward the fjord. I didn't want to see him. I could look away. But suddenly he was there, lying in the grass in front of me. His bloated body seemed larger than it had in life. Instead of forming a tight little knot, his body seemed relaxed and free of pain with arms and legs loosely flung out. His eyes glistened as if he were alive, looking forward to his first cup of coffee. But a bloody froth had formed at his nose and mouth. My legs went soft like rubber. Tosca wept on my shoulder and wiped her nose on the sleeve of Sveinn's sweater.

At the funeral, I wore Jón's jacket. It squeezed my armpits, but when I moved my arm, his smell rose to my nostrils and comforted me. Bergthora leaned against me. "The minister's not talking about Jón," she whispered. "Jón walked with Karl Marx, not Jesus."

I told her the minister must've mixed up his corpses.

Jón had been a noisy man. His sounds often got on my nerves. But that evening, after the funeral, I missed the swish of his dry hands when he rubbed them together, his groaning and creaking when he stood up, his trumpeting snuff juice into his handkerchief, his constant sighing. He'd cleared his throat hundreds of times a day. Sometimes I wanted to choke him. Now in this new silence, I heard myself breathing. My sweater sleeve whooshed against my apron. The linoleum creaked underfoot. Water crashed through the cloth filter into the coffee pot. Coals snapped like branches in the stove. Fish bones clicked on my teeth.

Before crawling into bed the first night, I placed Jón's long underwear on his side of the bed, under his jacket. I burrowed my nose into the jacket's armpit and breathed. Loneliness felt like a crushing boulder on my chest. I never thought I'd miss the loft. But I hungered for the clack clack of the spinning wheel treadle, the click of knitting needles, the rasp of wool combs, the chanting of rhymes rimmi dimmi dimm dimm, and the soft mooing of my little red calf in the shed below. And for Borghildur's deep voice reading from *Egilssaga*. And all around me the grumbling of old men.

My knees against my chest under my blanket, I felt pain in all my muscles as if I'd been ripped up by my roots. I'd lost everything—the noisy workers back on the farm and the family I'd cobbled together.

In the shed next morning, I sat on the cow skull stool and leaned my forehead into Branda's warm belly. A rustling sound came from the entrance. Damn him. Not now. I froze when Oddur's hand touched the back of my neck.

"He's gone. We're both alone now. Perhaps we could—"

"Get out."

But he tapped his fingertips on the back of my neck. The hairs rose on my arms. I jumped to my feet, set the pail aside, and threw the milking stool at his head. It hit the wall and fell to the dirt floor. He stumbled over the threshold and out the door. I shook so badly I nearly dropped my pail as I stumbled back to the cottage.

At the kitchen table, Tosca wept quietly. I placed a hand on her shoulder and laid my cheek against hers. "Help me clean the house," I whispered. Like a creaky old woman, the girl rose to her feet. In memory of Jón, we did what he'd hated most. Tosca scrubbed the baseboards and swept up dirt. I corralled dust balls and set them free in the yard. I broke up colonies of spiders that built webs on the windowsills. Under the sink, I found Jón's other pair of socks soaking in a pan of gray water. I rubbed them together, wrung them out, and emptied the dirty water. As the water gurgled down the drain, I felt a loss. I'd thrown away the last of Jón.

Behind me, the radio blared. "Chancellor Adolf Hitler urges all Germans to boycott Jewish shops."

Bergthora called from the back room. I found her in bed with her blanket up to her chin. Her composition book lay open on her chest. I read the words, *Lunch after Jón's Funeral.*

"I've written down all of Jón's favorite recipes," she said in a hoarse whisper.

I sat down on the edge of the bed and brought my ear to her mouth.

"Jón's father also drowned, fell overboard. He'd been gutting and gilling all night. Fell asleep on his feet."

"Why did Jón do this?"

She pushed her head into the pillow as if to get away from me. "It was an accident."

Tosca had suddenly become Sveinn's daughter. This was not an accident.

"You know," Bergthora said, "I'm glad Jón sent Magnús to Moscow. He's safe there. If he were here, he'd be fishing, maybe drowning. Roll me over. I've got some coins under the mattress."

"I took them a few weeks ago. You were sleeping."

"My life savings."

"No. You gave us your life savings years ago."

Fear edged Bergthora's voice. "We'll starve."

"No. We won't. Is something wrong with your eyesight? Did you think Jón put food on the table? I worked at the fish plant and the dock. I delivered infants and calves. I embroidered insects on tea towels and sold them to Faroese fishermen. I even sold fish on the peninsula to Jón's woman, Magga, all so you could drink your coffee."

She closed her eyes. Her cheeks sagged, forming wrinkles at her ears. I shouldn't have said those things about Jón. He was her son.

I patted her hand. "I'll find food, and we need coal." I got to my feet. "According to the news, no coal boats are at the dock today, but I can still pick up a few stray pieces." I took the teaspoon from the sugar bowl, dropped it into my burlap bag, and headed out.

At the dock, I passed kerosene barrels where small boys crouched like cats, eyes gleaming in coal-streaked faces. I went down on my knees, picked up coal bits that had hit the ground on both sides of the trough, and dropped them into my bag. With my teaspoon, I pried up coal pieces wedged between the dock planks.

"Can't fill a stove with that," a deep voice said.

I recognized the dock foreman, the one I'd worked for when I posed as a man. He gestured for me to follow him. In the shed, men sat at the table playing poker, their coins piled in front of them. They waved at me. They knew me from the days I'd fetched Jón home from politicking. Against the wall lay the coal dredger, a net held open by a metal arc attached to a long pole.

Together the foreman and I carried the net to the edge of the dock, lowered it over the side, and dragged it through the black, oily water. It came up black with coal scraps. I dropped them into my bag before the cat-eyed boys could snatch them. I dipped the net over and over again.

Back home I found Tosca staring glumly at her homework. Oddur's voice came from the radio and filled the room.

"It only takes a few drops of foreign blood to destroy our fine Nordic race. We cannot be vigilant enough about keeping out people of non-Nordic races. We must—"

I turned it off.

Chapter 17

With little work at the fish plant, we lived on Branda's milk and eggs from the chickens, potatoes, oatmeal, pickled liver and blood sausage, and an occasional fish that Sveinn gave Tosca. One morning, I was feeding the chickens potato peels when a familiar figure entered Mud Road. I drew in my breath. It was Sveinn.

His lip curled as he ran his eyes over the sagging shed and the outhouse. "Hasn't changed since I saw you here thirteen years ago."

"Please, Jón's dead."

His eyes softened. "Sorry."

"Tosca's at school," I said.

He looked startled, unfamiliar with school. "Do you have children? Other children?" I asked carefully.

"Gunnar's eleven years old."

I blinked my eyes, tried to widen my view of Sveinn to include this boy.

"I also have a son," I said. "My stepson, Magnús, is in Moscow." I couldn't read the expression on his face. "Magnús is a fine young man," I added, ready to go to war for him.

"I know that. I've seen him downtown, holding Tosca's hand, talking to her."

All those years of silence hung between us.

"Why didn't you tell me?" he asked at last.

I brought up an excuse, pumped it full of poison, and aimed it at his heart. "You saw me on the street with a redheaded child. You never asked. You never claimed her."

"She appeared on the dock."

I nodded.

"The second time I saw her I was sure."

"No. *She* was sure about *you* because I told her."

"She wore a man's raincoat. And overalls, like the clothes my wife offers the poor."

"We aren't rich," I said, expecting him to shame me with his look.

But instead his eye seemed to turn inward as if he blamed himself. He practically whispered his next words. "She appeared again. And you know what?"

I shook my head.

"She'd come to the dock when she was just a little thing. With Magnús."

"Yes."

"This time was different. She started to unbutton her coat. For a moment, I was afraid she had no clothes on underneath. You know like the dames do in the red-light district in Nyhavn. 'Stop, little girl,' I wanted to say. But she held her coat wide open. And I saw what she wanted me to see. My old sweater, the one I gave you."

His mention of the sweater sent an old warmth for him pulsing through my veins. When I touched his hand, he turned to face me.

"What did I do?" he asked.

"I don't know. What did you do?"

We both laughed.

"I couldn't speak," he said.

"Unusual for you," I said gently.

"I just held out my arms. And she walked toward me, let me hug her. I held her against my chest. Her hair smelled of fish, just like my own hair. Isn't that funny? The smell?"

"Yes, funny."

"I wanted to give her money, but I thought it would shame her. I asked, 'Would you like a fish?' She nodded, said you wouldn't mind."

I tensed.

"She said you had told her I was nice."

"You are nice." I reached for his arm, just to steady myself.

He shook his head. "If I was nice, I'd have climbed the steps to your cottage years ago, pounded on the door, demanded to see my daughter. But I didn't. What can I give her now?" he asked, looking at me, waiting for me to say something like, Hope for the future.

But my needs were practical. "New shoes. A pretty confirmation dress. A winter coat not designed for a man."

His eyebrows shot up. "Tell me more about her," he said.

"Every night she cries her eyes out for her papa."

He flinched at the word *papa.*

"Come and visit and talk to her. I'll give you coffee."

"Another time," he said, turning abruptly.

As I watched him walk away from me, out Mud Road, my body sagged under the weight of my feelings, as if I'd been working all day. I had to move about. I fetched my hairnet and apron and headed for the fish plant. The white flag wasn't up, but maybe I could get some work anyway. I walked fast. Gradually, blood pumped into my muscles, and I felt at peace. I hadn't earned the feeling. My little girl and her father had brought it to me. My cheeks grew warm. Sweat prickled my skin. I'd held my breath for about thirteen years. As I exhaled, my body welcomed the unexpected joy.

At the plant, I cracked the ice in my basin and washed fish until the water became murky with salt and scales. I got clean water. When I returned, Lilla the saltfish queen, stood motionless on the trestle. A fish lay in her basin.

"What's wrong?" I asked.

She jerked her head in the direction of the tallyman. "He earns twice what I do and strokes my knee while he counts fish. Here he comes now."

The tallyman pointed to the unwashed fish in Lilla's basin. "Well?"

"I quit," Lilla said.

I gasped. Nobody quit. It was a death sentence. What would she live on? But Lilla took off her gloves and untied her apron.

"Where will you go?" I asked.

"Gut plant. They wash in warm water there. When your hands turn to ice, come join me."

A few weeks later, my red, sore hands were so swollen that if I held them up to the night sky, they covered the moon. I warmed them under Jón's jacket and headed for the gut plant. Lilla stood on the loading dock with a bunch of other women, all wearing white coats. They looked like doctors on a smoke break, but I wouldn't let that scare me.

"Hey," I called out.

Lilla took my hand and led me inside the plant. I almost slipped on the slick floor. The gut smell blended with the fumes from the smokehouse next door. "If you work here, you'll stink so bad people will cross the street."

"Good. I like my privacy."

Crates bearing labels from village slaughterhouses were stacked against the wall, full of dried sheep intestines, packed in salt. A large tub of cold water stood in the middle of the floor with bunches of intestines hanging on hooks along its rim. Each woman had a tub of warm water next to her. To soften up the intestines, I guessed. I longed to sink my hands up to the elbows in that water.

The women looked up when Lilla passed, waiting for orders. "How did you get to be foreman so fast?" I asked.

She placed her hands on her hips and swayed slightly. "The other lady slipped on an intestine, broke her hip. I had the bossiest voice." A tall woman with a sour face stood at the table next to us. "Krissa, my best scraper," Lilla said.

The sour woman lifted a gray bundle of dripping intestines out of her warm tub and laid them on a table that stood on an angle. With a rubber scraper, she pushed the waste and mucus out of the wormlike things into the slop bucket below the table.

Lilla stopped next to an empty work table with a basin of water next to it. "My other good scraper dropped dead of a heart attack. Can you fill in?" she asked.

"Yes," I said. My lucky day. I couldn't wait any longer. I went down on my knees and immersed my arms up to my elbows in warm water. It soothed my skin. I was eight years old again, lying in that washtub of warm water while Mama soaped my neck. Pleasure rippled up to my earlobes.

"Get up, girl," Lilla said, handing me an apron as I scrambled to my feet. She brought a handful of guts on a hook and attached it to the rim of my tub. "If you tangle these, you're out."

I tried to smile. She didn't. Women lost their jobs every day. I needed the money. I plucked up a couple of intestines, laid them on my table, and ran the rubber scraper along the length of the intestines' smooth surface. As I worked, I sang a song I'd heard on the radio, "giddy giddy baba, giddy giddy boo, giddy giddy baba, do you love me true, ooh baby, oooh."

Krissa glared at me, and I sang louder.

I was enjoying my new job when Lilla's voice boomed through the plant. "Everybody to the main table." I brought my scraped-out intestines to the large table in the center of the room. Lilla pointed to a two-pronged spool. "If you wind an intestine sixty times without ripping it, you have first quality gut and get paid more."

Tongue between my teeth, I counted as I wrapped, One, two, three . . . sixty.

I felt Krissa's icy stare.

At the end of the day, I walked home slowly, rubbing my stiff neck. A cat followed me, sniffing the smoked meat flavor of my legs. At the cottage, I found a towel and some green soap and walked to the tall grass at the fjord. I slipped off my clothes and splashed into the cold sea. Teeth chattering, I waded in up to my thighs. I rubbed in the soap and dashed icy water on my puckered flesh. Wriggling and twitching, I dried my body with the towel. Above the sound of the sea, I heard a man laugh. Oddur stepped out of the tall grass and walked toward the shacks.

Chapter 18

My heart beat hard as the ship approached the dock. Magnús was coming home. Now I saw passengers waving from the railing but no sign of him. Two crew members threw out a cable and moored the ship. The gangplank wheels screeched as the crew pushed it into place. A blond woman bounced down the gangplank and stepped onto the dock. Behind her came a slender man with fine features and curly hair. The woman turned to him and spoke in a foreign language.

"Jewish refugees. Bah," a man standing next to me said.

A woman squeezed his arm. "Not Jews. Germans," she said.

"They take our jobs."

"Quiet," the woman said. "Nine Jews. Is it a problem?" She waved furiously at one of the passengers.

The foreign blond woman stopped talking and kissed the good-looking man on the mouth, like in the movies. A taxi pulled up. She climbed into the back seat. The foreign man watched her drive away. His face was sad.

"Meier. Meier," he called and walked right into me. I rubbed my shoulder.

"Excuse me," he said in English. I glimpsed his hazel-colored eyes before he disappeared into the crowd.

A suitcase landed in my cart. A stocky, bearded man said my name. I blinked. "Magnús?" I reached out to hug him. He made a tiny movement as if to pull back. He'd changed. It wasn't just the beard. He grasped the handles of the fish cart. On the way home, he gazed at the groups of shabbily dressed men loitering on street corners.

"How was the voyage? Seasick?" I asked.

No answer, just a grunt. At the boarded-up bakery, he smiled for the first time and said, "Everything's down at heel here—"

"We're stuffing our old shoes with newspapers, patching our patches. When women wash their kids' clothes, they leave the kids in bed because they don't have a second pair of clothes."

He smirked. "Not everyone's poor," he said, pointing to the big houses along the pond, where Diva and the lion lived.

When we got to the cottage, Magnús stood on the steps and inhaled the air that blew in off the fjord. Inside, he studied the stains on the walls, the floor, the ceiling, the cracked windowpane. A copy of *The People's Press* lay on the table. I was glad I'd plucked it out of Ratcatcher's garbage.

Magnús flipped its pages. "I'll turn this thing into a real newspaper," he said.

"You'll need typewriters," I said.

"Moscow'll send money."

"Can Moscow buy me a toilet?" I waited for his laugh.

But his voice was flat. "Bathroom fixtures are not part of the revolution."

"You lost your sense of humor," I said.

Bergthora shuffled into the kitchen and rubbed Magnús' head as if he were still ten years old. "Let's have some coffee," she said and opened the cupboard. I knew she was looking for the unchipped cups.

I began with a warm-up. "Things have changed here."

He narrowed his eyes at me. "I got your letter about Papa. I wanted to come back for the funeral, but they wouldn't let me."

I sat down and folded my hands. "Everything happened so fast."

Eyes still locked on mine, he said, "Papa spent his life waiting for good weather. Why did he go out in a storm?"

I shrugged. I had no answer.

Bergthora piped up. "Tell him what else is new."

Glaring at her, I skittered out on thin ice. "Sveinn, the trawler captain. He's—"

Magnús interrupted. "The one who looked at Tosca funny?"

I nodded.

"I knew it. Even as a kid I knew it, but you shushed me."

I heard Tosca's quick, light steps. Now she stood in the doorway studying the strange bearded man. When she recognized Magnús, she rushed forward and threw her arms around him. He leaned back and studied her. "When I left, you were a little girl."

Now she was taller than Magnús. None of their features were similar, as if they were not only from different parents, but descended from different tribes. Tosca pulled up a chair close to Magnús, placed her forearm against his, and gazed up at him.

"Did you miss me?" she asked.

He smiled.

"I missed you," she said and snuggled against him.

I woke up in the middle of the night to the sound of sobbing.

"Olga. Olga."

I got out of bed and knocked on Magnús' door. "Are you all right?" No answer.

Next morning, I found him in the kitchen writing.

"Working?" I asked.

"I have to make a speech," he said.

I stroked the back of his neck. "Who's Olga?"

He winced under my touch.

"Olga?" I repeated. "You called her name last night."

He stared at the pattern on the oilcloth table cover. His voice was ragged. "She had black hair, a chalk-white face, and a slender body that curled itself like a question mark around a cigarette."

"Go on."

"I was at Olga's. Snowflakes fell softly on the skylight above until it was completely white." He dropped his voice and looked around. "Olga was in contact with social democrats in Germany. For the Komintern, social democrats were the enemy—"

I slapped the table. The Komintern. It lived in Moscow but followed my family home.

"I woke up to banging on the outside door three flights down. Boots clomped up the stairs. A loud knock. I got dressed while Olga opened the door. Two police officers walked in. 'Get dressed,' one of them barked at Olga. I didn't like how he looked at her. The other officer fingered her framed photographs and leafed through her books. He tucked her journal into his pocket."

I took a cigarette from behind my ear, lit it, and inhaled.

"The officers dragged Olga down the stairs, pushed her into the back seat of a black car. It sped away. I tried to follow them on foot to Lyubjanka prison. 'Where is she?' I asked the guard. He shook his head. For months, I visited Lyubjanka several times a week. Nobody had heard of Olga. I was walking on Red Square when a classmate came up beside me. He steered me down a side street into a noisy cafeteria. 'Stop looking,' he said. After that I drank a lot of vodka."

I exhaled. "You can't work for these people."

"If I don't, I end up at the bottom of a freezing lake with weights attached to my ankles."

The next night Magnús called Olga's name again.

Once the slaughter season ended, work slowed at the gut plant. Since 1937 and the Spanish Civil War, the Spanish had lost their taste for *baccala*. So we didn't salt much cod at the fish plant. Whatever money I could pick up, I spent at the dock on fish to sell on the peninsula. But it wasn't enough. We slept in our sweaters. Bergthora lay in bed praying for coffee. Magnús went to work, typed all day, but he hardly earned a krona. I guessed he was doing volunteer work for the Komintern.

Meanwhile I had my own nightmares of Jón coming up out of the sea, trailing seaweed. "Fishwoman, you killed me."

Behind him stormed Sveinn, red-faced as Thor, the god of thunder. "Liar. Evil woman." And Magnús sobbed, "You killed my father."

Worst of all, Tosca mouthed the words, I hate you. I hate you. I hate you. A burning river of red-hot lava rolled over me.

"Don't you recognize the volcano in the Laki craters that killed thousands? Your fault," a voice said.

Bergthora's wailing as she mourned her son woke me. Wrapped in sweat-soaked sheets, I shivered in the thin daylight.

I pondered my power. Was I strong enough to make all of them unhappy? I saw myself as a little girl lifting a calf. I am strong, I told myself as I planted my feet on the cold floor. I put on Diva's lacy blouse, got my heart kicking with a strong cup of coffee, smeared on Jón's lipstick, and headed for The Lingerie Shop. My heart pounded as I climbed the steps. Magdalena's red knitted dress hugged her body perfectly. I envisioned the excellent corset she wore underneath.

"What can I fit you for, darling?"

Silly woman didn't recognize me. "I'm Sigga. Did you like the horsefly embroidery?"

Her eyes brightened. "The ladies loved the flies. Do you have more?"

"No, but I can embroider grasshoppers, Japanese beetles, sticklebacks, and reptiles, also daisies and butterflies," I said, rattling off everything I'd seen in Diva's magazines.

Money signs sparkled in her eyes. "Come in Wednesday next week. I'll give you a needle and colored thread. You can work in the tailor shop with Klara."

My heart sang. I had a foot in the door. Soon I'd be sewing corsets. I skipped down the steps onto the pavement and almost bumped into the lion. He looked handsome with his mane gently lifting in the breeze.

"You look like sunshine, Sigga."

"I have a job sewing in The Lingerie Shop."

His teeth gleamed. He must brush them after drinking coffee. Mine were turning yellow. He startled me when he touched my arm. "Have you been to see your mother's grave?"

Unshed tears crept into my throat. I shook my head.

"I need to go to the village tomorrow on business. I have a car. Would you like to come with me? We can drive up to the church. You can visit her grave."

My eyelids ached. "Yes," I said. "I'll come."

I saw Ratcatcher's family peering out their kitchen window when the lion's black car pulled up. I slid into the front seat. The engine roared out of Mud Road, splashing through the mud puddles, scaring the chickens. We were well out of town, crossing the moss-covered heath, when he said, "Tell me about your mother."

I glanced at his wide, honest face. What did he want to hear?

"She could knit faster than a bird can fly. But—she was afraid of everything."

"Afraid?"

"The worst thing was . . ."

He waited.

"The worst thing was . . . I'd promised to bring her to town, and I didn't."

This was it. The hard, little knot I could not get past. I covered my hot face with my hands, peered through my fingers at the dark sand to the south, the grassy toes of the mountain to the north. The countryside seemed both familiar and strange. I realized everything I loved, everything but Mama's bones deep in the earth, was elsewhere, not here.

In the village, the lion bought me coffee and cake at the gas station café. I looked out the window and envisioned Mama picking her way among sharp stones in her thin sheepskin shoes. Outside, the sea wind caught my hair as we walked down a gravel road, shiny black from the drizzling rain. We passed several small wooden houses before the lion stopped at a gray, two-story concrete house.

"This is where I lived," he said. "What was the name of your farm again?"

"Upper Falls, named after the tiny waterfall in the cliffs behind the farm."

"I recall people coming from out that way. They sold mittens, scarves, eggs."

"Mama sold angelica."

A frown line formed between his eyes. "It was a long time ago," he said.

"Mama was small, nervous, with hunched shoulders. You would remember that."

His smile and the warmth in his eyes surprised me. "Yes. She wanted me to fix things."

"Fix things?"

A lock of hair fell onto his broad forehead, and he looked young. That was how Mama must have seen him. I followed his gaze, now riveted on a second-story window. "She wanted to leave the farm, wanted me to find a way around the law that bound laborers to the farms."

"To leave? She wanted to leave?" I shook myself. That wasn't Mama.

He seemed lost in memory, perhaps seeing himself all those years ago, a tall young man, with a small, weather-beaten woman nestled in the curve of his arm. Their bare skin was bathed in a rose-colored light. I saw it through his eyes, felt his memory reverberate in me. I recalled the name Mama had written on the back of the shopping receipt. Guðmundur. Had she meant the mitten shrinker? Or this man? I must choose. The vision of the couple at the rosy-colored second floor window couldn't be denied. It was just a matter of making a decision. I chose the man who stood next to me as my father. This is what the vision of my mother's willing, warm skin told me. Violence against my slender mother had not been the cause of my birth. I had been conceived in love. I vowed to keep this choice of mine close to my heart forever.

The lion placed an arm around my shoulder, and we walked away from his former home. Stepping on the black lava pebbles, we headed toward the crashing sea. The wind continued to whip my hair. Under my feet, the pebbles creaked each time the sea withdrew, sucking the water back into itself. Fulmars screeched in the cliffs above. I tried to keep my focus on these sights and sounds. Yet now the ocean itself grew fuzzy around the edges. I was back in the icy water with Sveinn, clinging to the otter board. Now I was running alongside the heaving water, screaming Jón's name. The glistening pebbles came up toward me. They pulled me down. My knees buckled. The lion placed his arm around my waist, caught me before I sank into the surf.

"This is where it happened," he said as if I hadn't heard it before. "It was May 10, 1911. The weather was bad with the waves breaking close to shore with hardly a gap between them. A Danish ship was anchored out beyond the breakers with goods for the stores in the village. We had to unload those goods. Oarsmen launched two rowboats, pushing the prow into a gap between waves, then rowed furiously to get past the breakers before the next wave capsized them."

His voice trailed off but came slowly back.

"When they tried to launch the third boat, the waves rolled in so fast there was hardly an opening for a rowboat. The ocean was wild. The men on shore tied a cable to the prow of that boat, so they could pull it back in. The oarsmen pushed the boat in between the waves and rowed as fast as they could. But a huge wave capsized the boat and turned it over. The men sank, struggled back up, climbed onto the keel of the boat. It turned over again. The men on shore, who held the cable, fought against the waves as they pulled the boat in. When it was over, seven men lay on the beach. Five of them dead. Two were brothers."

He was pale and breathing hard, staring at the place where the men had lain.

"Mama told me about the accident," I said.

He seemed pleased by this. "Did your mother come to the village after that?" he asked.

"Yes, many times."

"I thought so."

In silence we walked to the car, and he drove up the hill to the church.

"Here's where they all lie," he said as we stepped out onto the gravel. We entered the small cemetery behind the church. I was glad when he walked away. I wanted to be alone with her. I found a small wooden cross with Mama's name cut into it, Hansína Theodórsdóttir. I hadn't spoken to her for years. Mama. In my voice, I heard the pitiful cry of the lambs, separated from their mothers. Ma-ma-ma-ma. In response to that cry, Mama's sweet song rose up from the grave. *Hættu að gráta hringaná.* Don't cry little girl.

I looked out over the cluster of houses in the village to the green hills dotted with small farms, and all the way to the black sand and the white surf. The smell of fresh earth and grass filled my nose. I didn't hear him approach, but I sensed his presence next to me. I reached for his hand and squeezed it, not a gesture of affection, just a silent pact between my spirit and his.

Several days later, the foreigner, Fritz, stood on my steps. He handed me an awkwardly wrapped package. "Magdalena, she give me your address," he said slowly, testing each word.

"You speak very well," I said.

"Klara teaches me."

"Come in." Walking behind him, I sniffed myself. I'd been to the sausage factory yesterday. Did I smell like a holiday leg of smoked lamb? I pushed wisps of hair behind my ears, rubbed my lips together, sucked my teeth for food scraps. I fumbled with coffee. While it brewed, I ripped open the package. A piece of frayed and discolored pink cloth fell onto the table. Odd shapes were stitched together, forming a corset. In some places it was soft and smooth. The bones inside the channels felt hard as chicken bones.

"Klara gives it to you. So you can learn," he said.

I raised my eyes toward heaven. Mama, can you believe my good luck? Two corsets.

"You like Korsett?" he asked, coming down hard on the "tt."

I nodded. Sighing, I stroked the fabric. It was a work of art. Slowly I shifted my gaze to his brown-green eyes, his soft, curly hair, and his skin. I'd never seen such beautiful skin. It wasn't the pink and gray shade of most people I knew. Nor was it splotchy like the skin of some on the farm. Fritz had a healthy even color, as if he'd absorbed sunlight and held onto it forever.

"How did you come to the island?" I asked.

"My friend, Meier, was already here. He sent me a letter. 'Come to the Danish colony,' he said."

"This is *not* a colony," I said. My hands shook as the lion roared inside me. "We only share the Danish king. And in 1944 we'll be a republic."

"I am only quoting Meier—" he began, his voice apologetic.

"Go on," I said, reducing my voice to a purr.

"Social democrats got Meier work. He say, I will find something, too. I read Meier's letter to my parents. 'Come with me to Reykjavik,' I tell them. I go down on my knees. *Nein. Nein.* My father does not even look up from his newspaper. 'We'll be fine,' my mother said."

"Have you heard from your parents?" I asked.

His face darkened. "Meier's father. He is standing in front of his shop. Nazis put a sign in his window. *Jüdisches Geschäft.* Jewish Shop. Still, I see Aryans enter the store."

"What are Aryans?"

"Blond people with pink faces. Like you. People who are not Jewish. Storm troopers kick in the window. Throw Meier's father on the ground. They kick him."

He wiped his forehead with the back of his hand.

"My father, after Hitler put the ban on going to Jewish doctors, he had just a few patients left. All Jewish. My mother—all she does is wash our floors. All day. She goes into the bakery at Rosenthalerplatz. Dirty Jew. Somebody say it. She come home, crying, crying. So we have no bread, only old crackers. At night we hear voices below our window. My mother cries. I go to the window. In the torchlight, I see the Hitler Jugend. Their faces like masks. They sing, 'Jewish blood will spurt from the point of a knife.' My mother? She is shaking and shaking. Still they refuse to come with me."

Fritz stopped talking and raised his eyes to a crack in my ceiling. After a long silence, he lowered his eyes to mine and said, "I do not know what has happened to my mother and father. It is a terrible feeling."

"My mother is dead," I said, as if that could console him.

"And your father?"

"I'm not sure."

His eyes grew dreamy.

"Are you happy here?" I asked.

He twirled his hand, neither yes nor no. "Have you some Nazis here?" he asked.

"Not Nazis, just nationalists."

"What?"

"It's a small party, some shop keepers and unemployed people. They like to fight the communists and say they're patriotic. I think they wish they were Nazis and Hitler would send them money, just like Moscow sends the Commies money. The nationalists are not friends of the Jews. So watch out."

His hazel eyes contained a burning look. "I know about one nationalist—*Ein Mann ohne Kinn*. The chinless one. Oddur, the Jewcatcher."

I dropped my hands to my lap. "How? How does he catch Jews?"

"Like this. Let us say some people here they are fixing radios. A Jew comes here. He fixes radios faster and better. People complain. 'That Jew,' they say. 'He take our business.' They are nagging and kvetching to maybe the union or to some association. Jew only has six-month residence permit. It has run out. Chinless one hears about it. Radio-fixing Jew gets deported."

Cold fury formed in the pit of my stomach. I heard Bergthora's feet crossing the floor. The old water carrier poured herself a cupful of cold coffee, drank it down, and poured herself another. She sank heavily onto a chair at the end of the table.

I turned to her. "Fritz says Oddur is a Jewcatcher."

Bergthora leaned forward. "Remember, Sigga, I told you about those photographs. Now Oddur has an office and the ear of Bouncy—" She moved her hand up and down. "I call our prime minister Bouncy, just like a rubber ball."

Fritz pushed back his chair. "I must work early in the morning."

"Where do you work?"

"Margarine factory."

I walked him to the door and watched him put on his boots. He had nice boots. They must've cost a lot. When he was gone, I brought the new corset into my bedroom and placed it in the closet next to Diva's old corset. "There you are, my sweet darling. Join your sister. Together, the three of us will sew our way to independence," I whispered.

Chapter 19

Months after Magnús returned from Moscow, he came home every day with newsprint fingers from editing the newspaper. He ran meetings where heads got broken. And the Komintern or whoever pulled his strings in Moscow, made him take a seat in the parliament. His colleagues hated him because he was always on the wrong side. And he hardly earned a krona.

It was after midnight. I waited for Magnús to return from a meeting. I heard him outside and brought the kettle from the stove, filled two cups with water, and spiked them with a shot of Branda's milk. We'd run out of coffee money.

Like a storm blowing into the kitchen, he entered. "Those goddamned nationalists. But they serve a purpose. They create solidarity among the comrades." He sat down and cut some liver sausage, ate it from the knife blade. "I met a woman at the meeting."

My eyes widened.

"Klara, one of the Jewish refugees."

"Klara? From Magdalena's?"

He nodded, reached for a slice of black bread. "Everybody drummed the floor with their rubber shoes when I arrived. I raised my fist. They call me Magnús Fist, and the crowd got to its feet. They roared. Klara appeared, sat down right in front of me. After that, I aimed every word at her."

His eyes glowed, and his face was flushed.

"You're in love."

"I asked them if they'd seen the Nazi destroyer in the harbor? I held up the red cloth with a black swastika, told them what happened yesterday, how I climbed the mast to get it."

Jón would have been proud, I thought.

"I threw the flag on the floor and spat on it. A man leaped onto the stage and peed on the flag."

"For God's sake."

He raised his voice. "The back door flew open. A cold wind filled the room. Men in uniform marched in, boots clicking on the floor. Oddur walked up to me and said, 'You desecrated the Führer's flag.' I said, 'Take it then' and threw the pissed-on rag at him. People laughed. Somebody swung a chair. Klara jumped up and took my arm."

Sipping on the spiked milk, I asked, "Why didn't she run away?"

"Her hair's dark as coffee."

"I know. I sew with her."

"She's the only Jewish tailor in town, but Oddur's trying to deport her."

"What?"

"Last week somebody showed her an editorial about Jewish tailors and how they're competing with local tailors. 'Is there any way I can help you?' I asked. 'Yes,' she said. 'Marry me.'"

"And why not? You're single," I said.

He slipped a finger inside the neck of his sweater. "I'm married to my work. The party. The newspaper. The parliament." He hunched his shoulders and glanced at the window. It was open a crack.

I rose and snapped it shut. "No spies here," I said.

"Let's pretend I believe in the revolution, the party, all that." A look crossed his face.

"I thought you did."

He tightened his jaw. "After the revolution, you won't have to sell fish or clean intestines."

"But it's honest work, not like working for Moscow."

He looked hurt, but I couldn't stop. "When you came home from Moscow, the price of fish was down. Shops were boarded up. Starving kids chewed boiled shoe leather and fishskin. People couldn't go to work because they had no clothes. You smiled at that. Why?"

With my hands folded, I waited for his answer.

He spoke slowly. "The closer people were to starving, the more grateful they'd be to me for raising them up."

"It sounds so, so . . . unlike you."

"Papa wanted me to form the party and get into the parliament. Now he's happy, sitting up in heaven, singing power to the proletariat."

The hair rose on my arms at the thought of Jón sitting in heaven next to St. Peter. Speaking ill of me? I hoped not. Magnús picked up his newspaper and pretended to read it. When I said good night, he didn't look up.

In my bedroom, I took out both corsets—Diva's worn old corset and Klara's leftover corset—and studied them. Each piece was perfectly stitched to the next piece. These strange, tight garments pushed up women's bosoms, tightened their tummies and bottoms, restricted women in painful ways. But for me—well, corset construction would set me free. Smiling to myself, I folded the corsets and slid them back into the closet.

———

Klara was stitching corset parts on a machine. I wanted to help. But Magdalena bustled in, her arms full of underpants and shirts.

"Darling, I'm so glad you're here. Flowers and butterflies are just what these clothes need."

I sat down on the tailor shop sofa, threaded a needle, and plunged it into an underpants leg. "Somewhere Over the Rainbow" came out of the radio. My heart sang along as I embroidered pretty colors on a butterfly wing.

During our coffee break, I took a long look at Klara. "Why did you come to Reykjavik?"

"I'm from Berlin, just like Fritz. When Hitler did bad things to Jews, I ran to Denmark. I knew Denmark believed in freedom. But no more Jews. 'Try our old colony,' they said."

"Are you afraid of being deported?"

"My residence permit expired long ago," she whispered.

"Marry my stepson, Magnús. Then you can stay here."

Her eyes grew round. "Magnús Fist? The communist?"

"He's for the little man, like his father was."

She set down her cup. "I'm a social democrat. Communists don't like us."

I recalled Magnús' recent tirade against the bourgeois sellouts. "Don't tell anyone that. Marry Josef Stalin if you have to."

Klara looked at me sideways.

Fritz appeared in the door. "*Bist schon zurück?* Are you already back?" Klara asked.

"I clean margarine machines. Then chef say, 'Go home.'"

"I've got to deliver this corset," Klara said. "*Bleib hier.* Stay here, Fritz. Help Sigga."

She wrapped the corset in brown paper. Fritz took out a small dictionary. He seemed to be underlining words.

"Is that how you study?"

"Every day I learn three new words in your strange language. Today I learn, *vörubíll, söðull, púki.* Truck. Saddle. Goblin."

"Why goblin?"

"Hans at work taught it to me."

"Don't listen to him. He's trying to get you deported, teaching you crazy words, so you will insult somebody."

He slammed the dictionary shut.

"I saw you on the dock when you first arrived," I said.

"At the *bryggja?* The harbor?"

"Yes. I was picking up my stepson, Magnús."

"The revolutionary? Pardon me if I ask. Is he a little, you know, loco?" He spun a finger at his temple.

Anger tickled the back of my neck. "No. Just political. His father was Jón the Rower."

But he wasn't listening. He spoke as if out of a dream.

"When I arrive here, I smell fish in the air. Houses, they are the color of sand. No trees. It did not look real. More like a kid, he make it. He cut houses and trees out of paper, and he paste them on the sky. I see it, how rust runs down the house walls. Brown streaks. Smoke is coming up from the chimneys right into the clouds. I step onto land. It feels so hard—how should I say—so real. Jelly. My legs are like jelly. The dock pushes into my heels."

"There was a woman with you," I said. "Blond. Was she also a refugee?"

"Ah, Ursula. The opposite. Yesterday, I am at the plant. I am drying the machine parts, when I see the foreman. He is a Nazi. Pardon. I mean nationalist."

I sat up straight.

"He is talking to Ursula. She comes to my table. I can smell her eucalyptus breath. 'Are you happy here?' she asks."

"Are you?"

The color rose in his cheeks. "Being here in this *komisches Land*, funny country. It is better than being dead."

Better than being dead. The words stung my heart. "I heard you call the name Meier."

"I live with Meier. Tomorrow after work I meet Klara and Meier at Inga's Café. Come too. I will buy you coffee."

Silk stockings swished, and Magdalena entered the tailor shop. "Ooh, you sewed a salamander?" she said, fingering one of my embroidered knickers.

"No. Japanese beetle." I found it in Diva's magazine.

"I just ran into Guðmundur," she said, eyeing me harder than I liked. "He and my dead husband were in politics together. He told me I was lucky to get your help, said you'd been to sewing school. Diva's."

I also do opera, I started to say, but the door to The Lingerie Shop squealed, and Magdalena ran to greet a customer.

Chapter 20

Often I stole money from my tight budget to see a film. I always learned something. When I saw Ginger Rogers dancing backward, I told myself I could do that if dancing kept my family from starving to death. Martial arts I learned from a Chinese film. At home I practiced kicking.

I'd just returned from selling fish on the peninsula. Bergthora was sleeping, and Tosca was at school. I rolled up my skirt and aimed my foot at the groin of an imaginary enemy on the opposite wall. My leg hung in midair when I realized I wasn't alone.

Magnús stood in the doorway, smiling in his new tight way. "Winning the war against evil?"

I lowered my leg and straightened my skirt.

"I'm getting married tomorrow morning."

I made a whooping sound. "To whom? A duck on the pond?"

Quacking and flapping his arms, my boy jumped around the room, leaping over the sofa like he had when he was little. I took him in my arms, the way I used to. We danced until we collapsed onto the sofa. He talked excitedly.

"I sit at my desk, typing. Rain's banging against the windows. Door flies open. It's Klara. She pulls a paper from her pocket, hands it to me. I read it out loud. 'Your residence permit has expired. By order of the chief of police, you will depart Reykjavik with *Litlifoss*, October 6 at 9:00 a.m. Your police escort will arrive at 7:00 a.m.' Three days from today. Klara's looking at me with big eyes. 'Can you help me?' she asks in a tiny voice."

I'd never seen Magnús so lively.

"Wait. Listen. I tell her, 'I can steal eggs from an eagle's nest, swim through freezing water, fetch you hot lava from a volcano, but I can't save you from Oddur.'"

"Poetic, but—"

"She rips the letter from my hands and walks out the door. I go back to my desk. Then it hits me. I'm a fool. I run after her, splash through puddles, bump into people, knock a kid over. She's walking fast. Finally I catch up with her, touch her shoulder, say her name. She turns around. Before I can speak, she says, 'Yes. I will marry you.' Just like that. We go straight to the magistrate's office. A small man—sleeps in his clothes I think—comes out of the back room. 'Not today,' he says. 'Tomorrow morning at nine.' We walk out holding hands."

I hugged my boy. "You know what this means?"

He shook his head.

"We've got to clean your room."

I got dust cloths and a broom. I handed him a cloth. "Take the spider webs out of the windowsills. I'll sweep under the bed, chase your dirty socks into the open."

The magistrate's office was musty as an animal's den. The furniture resembled grumpy bulls. But Klara shone like sunshine. She would be the Jewel of Mud Road. After the ceremony, when it began to rain, I held both my hands over Klara's head to keep her wedding hair dry.

I rushed into the cottage before the newlyweds and covered the kitchen table with my Christmas tablecloth. I'd embroidered it with a foreign insect called praying mantis. After the male and female make love, the wife eats the husband. At the center of the cloth, I placed a bottle of Ratcatcher's home brew.

Magnús leaned against the kitchen wall and told unfunny jokes. Klara laughed joyously. I leaned forward and studied her perfect teeth. She would give me beautiful grandchildren, but she was simply too perfect for my old cottage. With my foot, I covered the old crack in the linoleum floor. I also leaned back against the wall to hide the grease stain from Jón's hair.

"Does your back hurt?" Klara asked in a sweet voice.

I shook my head and rolled my shoulders.

Magnús raised a cup of Ratcatcher's brew first to the yellowed newspaper photo of Josef Stalin and then to the curled photo of Samuel Gompers. "To the workers' paradise."

Such garbage, I thought.

He toasted Klara. "To my new partner in the Popular Front that unites all parties of the left against the fascists."

I raised my glass to the Jewel of Mud Road.

"We will fight the Nazis together," Klara said, taking Magnús' arm. Perhaps love would smooth the prickly skin Magnús had grown in Moscow.

After everyone had gone to bed, I turned on the radio.

"The Jews have ruined the banking system. They're at the root of the Depression and unemployment in Germany. Don't let the same thing happen here." Oddur's voice had a whine to it.

Next morning, Klara entered the kitchen, her hair hanging loose, a pink glow on her cheeks. I guessed she was headed for the outhouse and handed her an old copy of *The People's Press.* Peering through the window, I watched her navigate past the chickens.

I was glad for the newlyweds' harmonious chatter. But as the days ripened into weeks, their sharp voices woke me up at night. I heard Magnús accuse Klara of making love to Fritz and Meier in the tailor shop. Crazy. That's what he was.

One morning, months later, Klara and I were alone in the kitchen. Her face was pale, her eyes puffy. Her hands shook when she picked up her cup, slopping the coffee over the rim.

"Hvað er að, elskan? What's wrong, dear?" I asked.

Blushing, she said, "If Magnús and I . . . if we had a little one, a baby . . . I think maybe . . . *ich denke vielleicht* . . . life could be different between us."

A baby? I shook my head. I knew they'd tried. I'd heard them torturing the bedsprings. Sveinn and I had had a baby, and for thirteen years we didn't speak. But Klara's words hit a nerve. Poor Jón. If we'd had a baby together, perhaps he'd have stayed home that night.

"Remember when that woman was trying to get residence permits for those Austrian-Jewish orphans?" Klara asked.

I pressed my lips together, went to the stove, and stirred up some oatmeal. I'd wanted one of the orphans, a sibling for Tosca. I recalled the editorial.

> Don't these do-gooders realize that the Austrian-Jewish children
> will grow up? Have children of their own? Ruin the race?

Klara must have been thinking the same thing. She sat down and slumped in her chair.

All week, I stayed home and stitched green and yellow grasshoppers for Magdalena. When I brought her the underwear, I found Fritz in the tailor shop.

After Klara tallied the sold underwear and shelved the new grasshopper sets, she said, "It's closing time. Fritz and I are heading out to Inga's to meet Meier. Want to join us?"

I hadn't been to Inga's since that day years ago with the lion. The café looked the same, but something was different. A small man at a corner table was hunched over schoolwork.

"That's Klensch," Fritz whispered. "Another refugee. He tutors kids in German."

"Can he make a living doing that?" I asked.

"No. He can't pay his rent. His landlord complains to the authorities. That will be trouble."

A short, dark-haired man waved us over to his table by the window.

"Meier," Fritz said. They all started speaking German.

"Hey," I said, and they switched to a mixture of English and Icelandic.

Meier poured me a drink called grapefruit. It felt like bubbles coming out of my nose and rising to the ceiling.

A large, fat man said, "Inga, more soup—"

"Does he own the place?" I asked Fritz.

"A refugee. Cello player from Hamburg."

"Bad manners, though."

"Jewish musicians have it good. Never get deported. Why? They make music, cheer everyone up in the winter."

A shrill laugh shot up. I craned my neck. Ursula, the square-headed woman with the big teeth, stood next to a man half-hidden behind a newspaper. When he lowered the paper, I saw it was Oddur. Abruptly he stood up, took Ursula's elbow, and led her to the door. Through the window I watched how Oddur's raincoat dragged along the wet street.

Meier tapped the back of Fritz's hand. "She's why I told you to keep a low profile."

Fritz frowned like a belligerent little boy.

I recalled May Day a few months ago when the communists and the nationalists marched. I joined the crowd that lined the street. We waited for the parade. Fathers put children on their shoulders. Women ran into the street. A kid rode a bike down the center of the road. Holding the flag-staff with both hands, the flag-bearer led the troops. Behind him came the uniformed marching units. Men in gray shirts with red swastikas stitched on armbands clicked their boots on the street. They played drums and sang German hiking songs, *Das Wandern. Das Wandern.* Suddenly Magnús and his followers jumped out from the side street. They wore special shirts and sang the *Internationale,* louder and louder until they drowned out *Das Wandern.* A slender man stepped right in front of the nationalists' flag-bearer. It was Fritz.

"Fritz," I yelled. He didn't hear me. The flag-bearer swung his stave. Wood hit bone. Fritz fell to the ground. I broke through the crowd to reach him. But he jumped up, ran down Fischersund. I lost him.

The door of Inga's opened, and newspapers blew off the tables and onto the floor. A large man stood in the open doorway. He carried a silver-tipped walking stick and wore a green coat that reached almost to his ankles.

Fritz made a muffled trumpet sound. "Announcing the new German consul, Rainer Dietrich."

"Shut up, Fritz," Meier said.

Too late.

Dietrich pointed his walking stick at our table, crossed the room, and stopped next to Meier's chair. Leaning forward slightly, he said, "Heil Hitler. *Ich bin Generalkonsul Dietrich.*"

"Heil Hitler," answered Meier. Klara mumbled something.

Dietrich ignored me. My shabby clothes told him I was just a local. But to Fritz he repeated, "Heil Hitler."

"Guten Tag," Fritz responded.

Pink spots bloomed in Dietrich's cheeks. "We say Heil Hitler—"

Fritz looked up at Dietrich and said calmly, "This is Reykjavik, not Berlin."

The only sound was silverware clattering in the kitchen. Meier's leg brushed against mine as he kicked Fritz. Dietrich rapped the table. Whipped cream billowed out of Fritz's cup and into the saucer. I couldn't understand Dietrich's German, but I saw the color drain out of Fritz's face. Dietrich's eyes swept the room once, and he walked out. The door closed behind him. The sound level began to creep upward.

"Idiot," Meier said into Fritz's face. Without a goodbye, he left us.

A couple of days later, I was deep-frying *kleinur* in suet. I heard the wind whipping Ratcatcher's wash next door. I longed to be outdoors drying saltfish in the sun, but there wasn't much work at the plant. These days the trawlers packed cod in ice instead of salt and supplied the British fish and chips market.

Klara burst into the kitchen. It was midmorning. Why was she back from work? Her face was puffy. "They deported Klensch and Meier," she said.

I recalled Meier's shin kick under the table.

"Fritz and I went to the dock. The police car arrived. Two officers led Klensch and Meier to *Litlifoss*. Once they were on board, only Klensch appeared at the railing. We called to him and waved, but he just stared straight ahead. Ship's whistle was so loud, I covered my ears and watched it sail out to sea."

She handed me the editorial page from today's paper.

> Foreigners have been expelled. The authorities have exerted
> themselves against vagrants who wandered here from Germany.
> They thought we wouldn't notice them.

The timing puzzled me. How had the editor known ahead of time what would happen this morning?

Bergthora ambled into the kitchen. Her cheeks were gray with lack of coffee. I pushed the editorial under her nose. "Do you think Oddur wrote this?"

"Probably. He's a smart man."

I slammed the bowl of fried *kleinur* down on the table. "You always have something nice to say about that piece of scum."

"And now you're worried about your Fritz?"

"Not *my*," I said, stuffing one of the warm pastries into my mouth and chewing fiercely.

Pouring coffee into our biggest cup, she sat down and placed the back of her hand on Klara's cheek. "I am sorry about your friends." She turned to me. "The only way to save him is to find a decent local girl who will marry him."

"Decent?"

She sat up straight as a pillar. "I'm decent and available."

The anger drained out of me. I punched my mother-in-law's shoulder until she squealed.

At that moment, Tosca walked in. "Stop it," she said. "Stop punching Grandma."

At the tailor shop next day, I found Fritz sitting on the sofa next to Klara. She put a finger to her lips. I sat down on the other side of Fritz.

"Meier told me I could get work here," he said. "I was happy. No Hitler. But this place, it is very poor. I am just arriving. I see a man marching down the cargo gangplank. A barrel of kerosene is on his shoulder. What's keeping his pants up? A piece of string. I see it. A piece of string. Freedom it is. *Ja.* But how should I say it? It is freedom down at the heel. At last I see Meier. I am so happy. We each take a suitcase and carry it on our shoulder to Meier's *Wohnung.* But people are staring. Why? I ask it to Meier. He get irritated. 'You are a foreigner. Your shoes. Your jacket. Your haircut. Keep your head down. Don't make a fuss.' That is what he say."

Fritz's shoulder shook against mine. That day on the dock he'd bumped into me.

"That first night on Meier's sofa I am missing Berlin. Raindrops hit the window hard. It is not like at home. In Berlin the rain it come down softly. It is sliding down the pane in wiggly lines. As a boy, I give the raindrops names. They run races on my window. Here we have angry rain. It cuts us like knives."

Klara went to her sewing machine while Fritz kept on talking.

"Meier's sofa it has no legs. It sits on concrete blocks. Newspapers and books, they are everywhere. No coffee table, just a board on crates. One crate has a blue label. On it I see a picture of a blond child. She is spreading Atlas margarine on bread. That's where you will work, Meier tells me, Atlas Margarine Factory. No, I say. I am a philosopher. I teach. Ungrateful ass he calls me, says I am making a fuss. He tells me about a Jewish couple. They fix watches, have a good business. But they make a fuss. Go yap, yap about high price of fish. Local people complain. Yap, yap couple takes customers from them. Oddur, the Jewcatcher—he deports them."

Did the bottom crawler really have that much power?

"Meier tells me packing margarine will raise me to—how shall I say—a higher level of self-knowledge."

Klara rustled through the trash. "Here it is." She pulled out a newspaper and read from the editorial page. She must have read it carefully before with a dictionary because she pronounced every word perfectly.

Is the island to become a place for nurturing foreign vagrants?
They're settling here as workers in industry or commerce. Some

even run independent businesses and hire others. The authorities
are not supervising these activities despite their oversight
responsibilities. For the good of our people and the purity of our
race, this must change.

The muscles of Fritz's face tightened, then sagged.

A few days later, the sun sparkled on the scales of the fish I'd just
bought from a docked trawler. The seagulls shrieked above my head. I
was haggling over the price of halibut when I saw Fritz, shoulders sloped,
looking out to sea. I called his name.

He turned his head slowly.

"Is the margarine factory closed today?'

"I am soothing my nerves."

"What do you mean?"

"Out of timber so crooked, from which man is made, nothing entirely
straight can be built. Immanuel Kant said it."

"I don't know about timber," I said, waving my hand at the mountains. "No trees here."

"Will you permit that I walk with you?" he asked. His voice was unsteady.

"Come. You can help me sell fish." We headed up the hill away from town.

"Ursula, she come to the factory," he blurted out.

I envisioned her square head and big teeth.

"She was on the boat with me. Ursula tell me she will photograph
birds here. Now she is tracking me."

"Tracking you? Why?"

"She knows I am Jewish."

I was piecing it together. She must work for Oddur.

"We are just arriving. The boat is pulling up to the dock. I am looking
for Meier through my binoculars. She comes up beside me on the deck.
'May I see?' she asks. Sweet is her voice. Of course, I say. I put the binoc-
ulars in her hands. She sees the letters engraved on the little silver plate.
'G.E.E. What's this?' she asks. Gotthold Ephraim Eisenmann, I tell her.
Fritz is my nickname."

His mouth formed a grim line.

"Gotthold? Why is it important?" I asked.

"Jews often name their babies after the playwright, Gotthold Ephraim Lessing. It is—how shall I say it—a fashion."

"A fashion for Jews?"

"Ursula knew this fashion."

We arrived at the house of my first customer. Dandelion yellow hair, nightgown unbuttoned, she trilled, "Hello." I filleted her fish, wrapped it in newspaper, and handed it to her. Without taking her eyes off Fritz, she gave me a coin. I pushed my cart down the road.

"We get off the boat," he said. "Officer takes my passport, studies all the stamps—Vienna, Rome, Paris. Takes out his notebook, writes something. I wait a long time. At last, he gives it back to me. He takes Ursula's passport, doesn't look at it. He stamps it."

"What did this mean?" I asked.

"Keep your head down. That's what it means." His voice broke.

Chapter 21

It was late November and moonlight shimmered on the ice in front of the cottage. A thin layer of snow covered the fish cart beside the chicken coop. I cleared the steps because Klara had invited another Jewish refugee from Berlin to talk about the Nazis. Dr. Weissmann was very important, she said.

Fritz arrived after everyone was seated. His face was covered with stubble. His hair was shaggy. When he took off his coat, I noticed his shirt was spotted with coffee stains. My hand on his elbow, I directed him to the last empty chair.

"That's Dr. Hans Weissmann," I whispered, pointing to the white-haired man seated on the sofa between a woman, her hair up in a bun, and a teenage girl with braids. Fritz plopped himself down on the chair and stared at the family. The girl lowered her eyes under his gaze. Weissmann began to speak in German. After every few sentences, Magnús translated. In Moscow, he hadn't learned much Russian, but he'd picked up German, maybe thanks to Olga.

"I woke up to the sound of breaking glass," Weissmann said. "Damned cat. We'd had guests, and we'd left the glasses for the morning. I didn't want to wake my daughter and wife, so I tiptoed to the kitchen. But the glasses stood on the counter. The cat was asleep."

He stopped. His daughter nudged his arm. "Then *I* woke up," she said softly.

Weissmann patted her hand and continued. "We pressed our faces against the window. Down on the street, men were shouting. Dogs barking. Crash. Screams. Glass breaking. The window at Steinmetz's tailor shop was gone. And the police?" He slapped his forehead. "I knew it then. The police didn't help Jews!"

Fritz covered his ears.

"The synagogue was in flames." Weissmann's voice trailed off.

I glanced at Fritz. His hands covered his face.

Weissmann's wife picked up the story. "Next day, the SA arrested Jewish doctors and professors, my husband, too."

Fritz pushed back his chair. It crashed to the floor. Stumbling over people's legs, he made his way out of the living room to the front door. I got to my feet and pushed my way between the guests. I ran down the steps into the yard. He stood quite still, his head lolling on his chest like a soft cloth doll.

He raised his head and muttered a name to the sky. "Meier." He said it again and again. "Meier. Meier. I'm sorry."

I placed my arms around him and pressed my chest against his back. A shudder rippled through his body. I held him until he stopped shaking and his spirit grew quiet. Taking his hand, I led him up the steps and into the kitchen. In the living room, Weissmann droned on. Fritz sat down on the chair where Jón used to sit, leaned his head against the wall, and closed his eyes.

"Stay there," I said. I ran into the bedroom and fetched a sweater I'd been knitting. I finished it off and slid the yarn from the needles. I held it against his chest. "I got the yarn from Diva, just the right colors. Brown, rust, and orange, the colors of my favorite bird, the godwit."

He gave me a vacant stare.

"I've always wanted to fly," I went on. "But I can't seem to get off the ground." I eased the sweater down over his head and arms, straightening the ribbing at his waist, feeling the warmth of his belly under my fingers.

He rubbed his hands over the sweater as he eyed the candles, flour, matches, brown sugar, rusted sheep shears, and soap on my kitchen shelves. It must look shabby to a rich man from Berlin. Gradually he shifted his gaze to my eyes.

"Meier . . . he was a good cook," he said quietly. "Chopped onion with eggs, my favorite food. Every day when I come home, he asks me, 'How was work?' And I always complain. 'All day I am scoring and packing margarine. I put it into crates and carry the crates to a flatbed truck. People talk. I can't understand them.' Every day I whine, whine, whine. Meier is—" He stopped.

"What?" I asked.

"Like my mother, always taking care of me. I tell him about Hannes at the factory, how he rolls up a piece of butter paper, places it under his nose, parts his hair with a fingernail, does a Nazi salute, and points to the foreman's back. I am boiling inside. Every day, I am boiling inside. In Germany I was a coward. But I tell Meier, 'Here in this country I will kill a Nazi.'"

"Remember we don't have Nazis," I said. "Just nationalists."

He didn't hear me, just kept on talking at my back while I sliced the cakes I'd baked for the guests—one rhubarb and one oatmeal.

"I am walking home one day, when I see a notice nailed to a telephone pole. I take out my dictionary. 'Social democrats, socialists, and communists. Join the Popular Front against the fascists. Meeting Thursday, second floor above the Diamond Cinema.' I run home. 'Meier,' I say, 'I must go to this meeting.' He says, 'You're an ass.'"

I served him a slice of each of the cakes.

"'Keep quiet. This isn't your country.' That is what he say to me. But that evening I write the words of the poet Rainer Maria Rilke in my journal: 'It is our fate to be opposite and nothing else.'"

I handed him a fork.

"Next morning, I leave early for work. In the center of town, I smell onions frying at the sausage stand. Gulls screech at the harbor. And singing. A soprano is singing. *Ach Du Lieber Augustine, Augustine, Augustine.* Suddenly I am looking into Ursula's face. 'Why are you still here?' I ask. 'I am commissioned to do another photography project,' she says."

"Sigga, I think I am her project."

He cut his slices of cake into large pieces and scooped them into his mouth until his cheeks bulged. He chewed and chewed then pushed away the empty dish.

"The day they take Meier and Klensch, I walk to a place that overlooks the bay. I see it then, the ship, *Litlifoss,* inching slowly out to sea. I see it following the curve of the earth."

I took a cigarette from behind my ear and offered it to him. He shook his head and got to his feet. After he was gone, I smoked my cigarette alone.

―――――――

The summer of 1939 had been the loveliest I could remember. Now it was September. Sunshine sparkled on the sea. My sheets billowed on the clothesline in the ocean wind. Children played ball and rode bikes on Mud Road. The chickens—my darling girls—were out of the coop, cackling and pecking. I was airing out our bedclothes on the fence when I heard the radio from the open kitchen window. "Hitler's Reichswehr hammers Poland. Germany did not respond to the ultimatums of Britain and France. These countries have declared war on Germany."

I climbed the steps quickly. Magnús looked up from the radio. His eyes were red-rimmed.

"Poor Poland," I said.

An angry look crossed his face. "Poland started it."

"Is that the party line?"

He placed his hands over his ears.

I moved closer. "Your father spoke to me last night in a dream. 'To hell with both of them—Hitler and Stalin.' That's what he said."

Magnús jumped up. He pushed me away when I tried to follow him. From the doorway, I watched him toe his way between chicken droppings.

I should have warned Klara, but at dinner her eyes brimmed for poor Poland.

Magnús went to the window and shut it tight. His back against the sink, his arms folded, he spoke in a low voice. "Both of you are living in some kind of fairy land. Let me tell you about poor Poland. I was in the newspaper office trying to breathe. It's hard to keep a clear head in that place. Those stacks of newspapers eat up the oxygen. I waited for the telegram from Moscow. It didn't come. I was free to write what I wanted. I typed, 'German tanks crossed the border into Poland. Germans fired on helpless civilians. Poles on horseback fought back with swords.' Your poor Poland, right?"

Tosca's eyes took on a deep green color. "Calm down, brother," she said.

He pointed his forefinger at her. "This is a message for you, little girl. The door swings open. It's a messenger with a telegram. I read it, folded it into a little wad, pitched it into the wastebasket, ripped my paper out of my typewriter, and rolled in a new one." Leering at us, he said, "Hitler and Stalin made a pact. Now the Nazis are suddenly our friends. So what should I do?"

Nobody answered him.

"Huh? Huh? I want to live. I followed the party line."

He leaned into Tosca's face and touched his nose to hers. "So I wrote, 'A band of Poles attacked German tourists. But the German Army put down the uprising. The Red Army helped the Germans restore peace in Poland.'"

Klara shook her head. Magnús gave her a look.

"So Björn comes up behind me. Remember Björn? He was with me in Moscow—cigarette fingers and coffee breath. 'But the Polish people—' he starts. I don't even look at him. I just point to the wastebasket. 'Party line's in there.' I write my fairy tale while Björn rummages through the wastebasket."

Bergthora sat up straight. "Magnús, since you're so close with the Nazis these days, can you use your connections to save Fritz?"

I saw his clenched fists. For a moment, I thought he would hit his grandmother.

I made my voice light as whipped egg whites. "Bergthora, why don't you marry Fritz? Save him from deportation?"

We all laughed, all but Magnús.

———————

I sensed the U-boats prowling around the island. Neutral. Ha. I knew it from Sveinn. Our trawlers fed the fish and chips market every day in Britain. The Nazis didn't like that. The boat debris from U-boat attacks washed up on shore—life jackets, pieces of railing, hatch covers, nets. Sometimes I plucked up boards that floated in the surf. At home I nailed them to my chicken coop, praying they weren't from Sveinn's trawler, *Lilja*.

It was a dark day. Wind whipped the rain against the cottage, and news of Poland moaned out of the radio. I sat indoors, embroidering happiness onto Magdalena's underwear, tiny green caterpillars on the underpants, flying butterflies on the undershirts. Once I had a small stack under my arm, I set out for The Lingerie Shop. Splashing through puddles, I thought of Jón. I wasn't one to visit the graveyard, but today the tombstones beyond the lichen-covered wall called to me. I pulled open the squeaky gate and made my way down the narrow, muddy path between graves until I came to the overgrown plot where Jón lay under a wooden cross.

"Well . . ." I started.

No answer but the sound of raindrops hitting the ground.

"I told Magnús about how you crept into my dream last night."

Still no answer. My irritation grew. "The stuff about Hitler and Stalin, did you really mean it?" The wind whipped up. A branch broke off a tree and splashed into a mud puddle. I heard Jón exhale on the word. Fishwoman.

"If that's all you have to say . . ." I kicked the concrete that surrounded his plot. But then I regretted it and patted the dirt that covered him. "*Svona. Svona, Jón minn.* There. There, my dear Jón."

Inside The Lingerie Shop, rain dripped from my coat onto the wooden floor. The only customer was pawing through the garter belts. I handed Magdalena the bunched-up underwear. "Oooh." She pulled out an undershirt with a yellow butterfly embroidered between the breasts and waved it singing, "Ta-da."

She showed the customer the little worm on the underpants. "Beautiful? No?"

"I'm glad you like them," I said. "Can you pay me now? It's slaughter season. I need money for some ingredients."

The garter customer fingered the stitches on my butterfly, then glanced at my swollen hands. My clumsy hands couldn't make anything that beautiful, I heard her thinking. I was just the delivery girl. I whispered a lie. "I bought the yellow thread in a special sewing shop."

"I'll take the worm and butterfly pair," she said.

My heart fluttered. I'd never wanted to make a living embroidering, but here I was.

"Your husband will love you in that." I said it loud enough for the three customers who just walked in to hear.

Feathery fingers touched my side as Magdalena dropped coins into my pocket. Oh no. Too casual. I took out the coins and counted them.

"That will be one third of the payment," I said. "I'll get to work on the next batch."

From the shelf, I took down three sets of plain underwear, pushed them under my sweater, and buttoned my coat over them. I waved my hand to the customers, calling, "*Farvel, mine damer,*" a Danish phrase I'd picked up from the magazines. As soon as I was out the door, they would ask Magdalena, Who was that?

During the fall of 1939, daylight was a broad gray slice between the rainy dawn and the gloomy night. Poland was lost. The Germans hadn't landed on the island yet, but if they did, I feared Fritz wouldn't last long.

To cheer us up, I had a slaughter party. Klara laid out a block of suet, bags of rye flour and oatmeal, a pitcher of sheep's blood, and a package wrapped in paper and tied with string. I undid the string, pulled back the paper, and touched the pile of sheep's stomachs, folded like moist white washcloths, with gray rubbery tissue smooth on the outside and patterned on the inside. God's miniature architect had crept through the creature's entrails and designed this six-sided pattern.

I nudged Bergthora. "We'll make enough blood pudding to last the winter."

Ratcatcher's door slammed. A few seconds later Helga bounced into the kitchen. Giggling, she slid out of her dress. Underneath she wore a black lace slip, too big for her. I'd seen it at Magdalena's. Now I wanted it. My fingers itched to rip it off the girl's body.

"Mama, if he squeezes me, Mama, what should I do?" blared out of the radio. Helga wiggled and sang.

"Put this on, girl," Bergthora said and pitched a balled-up housedress at Helga's head.

I measured rye flour and oatmeal, then dumped the grains into a bowl. Tosca poured in the blood and stirred the mixture with a wooden spoon until it became a rust-red soup. Helga shimmied across the kitchen, scooped up the suet squares with both hands, and dropped them into the mixture. My ears perked up. Somebody had knocked on the door. I pushed my fly-away hair behind my ears and pinched some rosy color into my cheeks. As my heart pounded my ribs, I opened the door. Fritz stood on the steps, rain dripping off his face. Wind whooshed into the cottage, blowing coats off hooks.

"Shut that door," Bergthora shouted.

I pulled Fritz into the cottage and led him into the kitchen. The women made an ohhh sound as they stared at him as if he were a new stove. I touched him here and there as I fussed around his ribs, his waist, his slender back, finally tying the apron strings in a bow.

Swaying, Bergthora gripped the doorframe. "Let's start. I'm falling asleep on my feet." I'd cut back on her coffee this week. I needed the money for blood and grains.

I spooned the mixture into a sheep stomach and handed it to Klara for sewing. She held a large needle to the light, threaded it, stabbed it into the thick, white organ, pulled out the needle, and plunged it back into the animal tissue. Her big, square stitches formed a ridge on what resembled a miniature, lumpy soccer ball.

I handed Fritz my spoon. "You try."

Wincing, he picked up a stomach between thumb and forefinger and dropped a dollop of the rust-colored mixture into its center. His lip curled as he squeezed the stomach into a ball. Quickly he handed it to Klara. After cutting and knotting the thread, she dropped it into the pot. The windows steamed as the stitched balls thudded gently against the sides of the pot. The smell of an animal's insides filled the room. It took me back to the farm, how I'd loved and hated the slaughter season, how I'd hung onto Borghildur's bloody apron until I was old enough to help. "Dipsy Doodle" blared out of the radio. Helga sang along. Tosca jumped to her feet, and the girls danced down the hall. We didn't hear Magnús come home. He snapped off the radio. The girls groaned. Without a greeting, he headed for the bedroom.

"He's had a bad day in the parliament," Klara said and followed him.

Good riddance. Magnús would cast a shadow on our happy evening.

But from the bedroom soon came the sound of quarrelling. I slapped the wall. "Quiet." I turned the radio on, high volume. "Giddy giddy baba, giddy giddy boo, giddy giddy baba, do you love me true, ooh baby oooh."

The girls jumped up and danced again. The way they shook their bodies made me uneasy. I cleaned off the table and set out oatmeal cake with coffee. The girls joined us.

Bergthora touched the back of Fritz's hand. "You know that Oddur lives nearby?"

I switched topics fast as I could. "They're showing *King Kong* at the New Cinema." Goblins glittered in Bergthora's eyes. "Sigga and I are both widows—"

The girls dropped their forks. Doubled over with giggles, they headed for the sofa. Bergthora got to her feet, raised her coffee cup, and said good night.

"Nice family," Fritz said.

I held my head high. "I made it myself."

"What? You make it yourself? Ehh? Like a Korsett. Ha. Ha. You patch it together?"

The lovebirds in the next room were shouting curse words. To drown them out I horselaughed at Fritz's joke. When he raised his eyes to the old crack on the ceiling, I followed his gaze and shuddered. The water stains to either side of the crack had grown.

"It reminds me of——" he said.

I felt a tremor of irritation. "You always say something is like something else. Why?"

"This is how we speak in the university. It's, it's . . . to show how smart we are."

A joke? I often walked past the university and felt sorry for the dried-up weaklings who spilled out of that building. Couldn't do anything but talk.

"It reminds me of——" He made circles with his hands. "——of Sistine Chapel in Rome. Michelangelo painted it."

"Michelangelo? Whaaa?"

He leaned his head back and pointed. "It is called 'Creation.' God has created Adam. Now God extends his hand to Adam. On your ceiling. Don't you see?"

I saw a crack that would soon let water in. I needed to climb up on the roof and fix it.

"In Rome it is my favorite thing, this ceiling. I am not a strong believer. But I like this idea. God gives his hand to little man."

Little man. I blinked away the image of Jón.

"I am glad you came here tonight," I said.

"Why?"

"For me the slaughter party is about living with our sheep."

"Tell me about the sheep."

Was he making fun of me?

"The sheep," he repeated.

"When I was a girl on the farm, I gripped a sheep between my legs. I felt its life on my skin, its warm belly throbbing. I slid the shears into the greasy wool. I was careful not to cut the animal as I eased the wool from its body."

"And the slaughter?"

"I vomited when the women drained the hot blood from the carcass. It smelled like metal. When the blood ran into the basin, we had to stir it to keep it from forming lumps. Nobody wants to eat blood lumps in their sausage."

He paled.

"When I was a little girl, I peered through my fingers at the women working on the carcass. They pulled out the innards, separated the steaming kidneys from the lungs, peeled the fatty membrane from the organs. It was disgusting, but when they boiled the innards, I was suddenly so happy I danced and clapped my hands."

His face was blank. I tried to explain the joy.

"The sheep was dead, but we would survive."

The wind rattled the glass in the windows. Fritz's face drooped.

"You see, my whole life is about survival. Finding coal, getting a fish, selling a towel, cleaning a gut, feeding my child. If I have to murder a sheep to survive, I'll cry as I clean my knife blade. But my heart will sing. I'll have meat."

"I grew up in a city," he said. "You know what I like about this island?"

"Curds or whey? Rain or snow?"

"The politics."

I groaned.

"Reminds me of my father. 'We social democrats must never ally with the communists against the Nazis.' He says it over and over again. 'Not even to save the republic?' I ask. He shakes his head, calls me a Bolshevik Jew."

Yik, yik words. Bolshevik Jew.

"One day my father realizes he is wrong. One whole month he does not speak. At last he points his fork at me and says, 'We should have made an alliance with the communists against the Nazis. Right, Fritz?'"

"And your mother?" I ask. "What did she think?"

"My mother? She like to hang prints by Jewish painters like Lesser Ury on the wall—of Berlin prostitutes and steamy train stations. My father's nerves? Ach."

"Before I met Diva, I didn't know what a Jew was," I said.

He banged his spoon against the sides of his empty cup. "I do not know either. I am seven years old. One day I kick the ball out of the school playground into a weed garden. 'Jew!' It is a big boy yelling. After school, I get my teddy bear and sit down to cocoa and cookies with my mother. 'What's a Jew?' I hold up my bear, so she can tell him the answer. But she brings me to the hall mirror. 'There's a Jew.' I cry and cry and blow my nose into the fluff on my bear's back."

"I never had a father," I said. "I only had a letter from him that my mother carried in her pocket. But it was a fake. My mother lied to me."

"You are still angry at her?"

"Yes. But when I feel that anger, Mama looks down from heaven, calls me Baba Yaga. You know the witch. Too big and ugly for my own cottage. I have to sleep with my big feet out the window."

He laughed, thought I was joking.

"Just one of my dreams," I said.

But I held onto it, gazed into Fritz's hazel eyes and saw myself there, climbing on top of my piled-up mistakes. From there I would save my family. I realized he wasn't thinking about me. He was looking inward.

"Did you make peace with your father?" I asked.

"One day I think he's at the clinic. I hear a sound from his bedroom. I open the door. He is sitting on the bed. In his hands he has an Iron Cross. It is a medal from the German government. He is stroking it. He does not look up. 'I got it in the trenches in the Great War. It means I'm a real German.' That is what he says. Next day I cannot sit still in school. I hurry home, go into his bedroom. I search through his drawer. My hands touch leather and steel. It is a military belt. I read the words engraved on the buckle, *Gott mit uns.* God be with us. Can you imagine this? It is the thing that held up his pants in the Great War. He is German. It is his religion."

My hands, big as frying pans, lay on the table.

Chapter 22

It was morning on December 1, 1939. Magnús sat across from me tight-jawed and frowning. The radio told of Finns wearing snowshoes and stabbing Red Army tanks with kitchen knives. The Red Army left a trail of blood in the snow. Funeral music. My spirits sank. Russians were clobbering Finland. We'd be next.

I lit a mourning candle. "For the Finns."

"The Red Army put down border skirmishes in Finland," he said.

"They murdered unarmed people."

He flinched.

I got up to fetch coffee and gazed down at the familiar cowlick, the one I'd fought with years ago when I used to cut his hair. By the flat look in his eyes this morning, I knew that he knew the Soviet Red Army had butchered Finland. And he could never admit it. The Hitler-Stalin Pact had a grip on my boy's tongue.

"Poor Magnús," I said.

"The others'll call me a traitor—"

"They don't mean it."

But the other parliamentarians meant it. It hurt me to think how they hated him when he defended the Soviets.

"There's oatmeal in the pot, dear," I said, closing the door behind me. Outside, daylight edged into the darkness as I made my way across town to the flat Fritz had once shared with Meier. I knocked. No answer. I knocked again. At last, Fritz opened the door. His face was creased, still folded up for the night.

"Would you like to come to the funeral march for the Finns?" I asked.
"I don't like funerals," but he stepped aside to let me in.

Ignoring his mood, I entered a room that resembled Magnús' newspaper office. Stacks of old newspapers lined one wall. A few open books lay scattered on the floor. All over the sofa were underlined newspaper clippings, Fritz's way of learning the language, I guessed.

I followed him into the kitchen. His hands shook as he spooned coffee into the pot. The lid clattered to the floor. He covered his ears as if the sound hurt him.

"It's not exactly a funeral," I said.

He whirled around. "You and your family—"

I bristled. "My family?"

"I used to go to Magnús Fist's meetings. I thought he'd fight the Nazis. But now he supports the Nazis and refuses to criticize the Soviets."

Heat rose on the back of my neck. "He's in a tough position—"

"Is he afraid of Moscow?"

I spat out the words. "Magnús isn't afraid of anything."

But he was. I'd heard his nightmares. He'd cried in my arms the day they called him Kuusinen after the Finnish traitor Otto Kuusinen, who helped the Soviets invade Finland. Poor Magnús was supporting the Nazis and the Communists, and he hated both of them.

"He's scared of his own party," Fritz said.

Magnús had shown me on a map where he thought the bones of party line opponents lay at the bottom of chasms and icy lakes.

"If you don't want to come—"

"Relax," he said over his shoulder and disappeared into the bedroom.

I heard him opening and closing drawers. I picked up a large book with a colorful cover, *Paintings* by Marc Chagall. I flipped the pages and studied the paintings. A monster fish flew over a river while playing a violin. A man held the hand of a woman who flew like a kite through the air above him. I turned the page. A woman in high heels and a lacy dress flew over tiny houses.

"Voila," Fritz said, planting himself in front of me. He wore the orange godwit sweater I'd given him. "You like Chagall?"

"I like his flying people."

"As a scholar—" he said.

I rolled my eyes.

"As a scholar—you see, I'm not a believer."

"How will you get into heaven?"

He shrugged. "I won't. But as a scholar, I've read parts of the *Torah*—the first five books of the Jewish bible—and even the *Zohar* mentions flying."

I pointed to Chagall's happy couple. "I mean this, real flying."

He came up so close I smelled the hairs on his arms. My blood quickened. I raised my face to his. But he wanted to talk. "When desire unites male to female, the universe is blessed, and joy reigns above and below. That's from the *Zohar*. It's about flying."

I threw the book on the sofa and stepped toward him. I placed my hands on his waist, moving them over his ribcage, up under his arms, drawing him to me. I kissed him lightly. His lips tasted of cinnamon. He stepped back.

"What's wrong? Do I taste like . . . like dried fish?"

"Like rhubarb cake," he said.

I realized he had the power to hurt me. Blinking hard, I focused on a framed photo of a fountain with a statue of a man riding a sea monster. An alligator's mouth sprayed the man's toes with water. Alexanderplatz was printed bottom left. A young woman stood next to the fountain with her arms around a little boy.

His breath tickled my neck. "My mother."

"She's pretty."

"Was pretty. Let's go."

Outside, we joined the dark line of people heading downtown as the midmorning sky changed from charcoal to gray. At the square surrounding the Jón Sigurðsson statue, men and women stamped their feet for warmth. A speaker steamed the cold air with his words: "The rapacious dictatorships have now collaborated to press the lifeblood out of one more neutral country."

The muffled sound of wool on wool filled the air as the crowd clapped. We walked slowly with the other mourners down the dark street toward the Finnish consulate. A stocky figure, his head wrapped in a scarf, appeared. A familiar voice teased. "New boyfriend? Hah?" Magnús stepped in front of us.

"Cocky little upstart," I said, laughing.

But Fritz bristled. "Nazi sympathizer," he said into Magnús' face.

I pulled on Fritz's arm, but he shook me off and grasped Magnús' shoulders. "I was in Berlin in the *Weimar Republik* with the Reds. Stupid like you. They want to 'liberate' us from our freedom? Like in the Soviet Union?"

Magnús slammed his fist into Fritz's chest. "Ungrateful Jew."

Fritz lunged forward and gripped Magnús' throat. "You say that when Klara asks you to pick up your socks?"

Magnús swung. Fritz ducked, rose up, and hit my boy so hard he fell to the ground. Fritz dropped to his knees and straddled Magnús, pinning his arms.

"What's this?" a gruff voice said. A police officer pulled Fritz to his feet. "Who are you?" When Fritz didn't answer, the officer led him to the police car.

On the ground, my boy looked small, a party hack, no match for a man who lifted crates of margarine all day. I knelt next to him and stroked his swelling cheek. "Why did you pick a fight?" I asked.

He shook his head.

"If this leads to Fritz getting deported . . ." I said.

Behind me the police car drove off. Magnús scrambled to his feet and loped away like a wounded dog. I'd have to swallow my pride and call on the only person who could help. I wrapped my scarf over my face and walked up the hill to the building where I'd once brought Tosca to visit Sveinn. My heart hammering, I knocked. *Don't be home,* I prayed.

Sveinn opened the door. He looked startled. "Something happened to Tosca?"

"No. To Fritz."

"Who?"

"He's a Jewish refugee, a friend of Klara's, my daughter-in-law."

His expression softened. I entered a living room brimming with red velvet, overstuffed chairs, pillows embroidered with flowers, and crocheted doilies. Small oil paintings of trawlers hung on the walls. Embroideries of red roses in full bloom covered every chair. On the wall hung yellowed photographs of ancestors. Wedding pictures of Sveinn and his flower pot wife lined a shelf, along with pictures of a boy, their son I guessed. I searched the shelf until I found a photo of Tosca tucked into the corner of a picture frame. It was a curled strip of four blurred photos, the kind you snapped in the booth downtown at the photographers. Her flattened nose told me she'd been too close to the lens.

"So?" Sveinn asked.

"Fritz beat up Magnús, my stepson. The police arrested him. His residence permit expired a long time ago. Isn't Police Chief Bergur your friend? Can you please talk to him?"

He shook his head. "I talk to Bergur every day but not about refugees."

"Please. Before Oddur finds out and builds a deportation case against him."

"You want me to bail out your boyfriend?"

My cheeks burned. "He's not my boyfriend."

"Then why do you care so much?"

"He's a German Jewish refugee. Oddur wants to deport every Jew he can."

"Why did he beat Magnús?"

"Maybe he's suicidal. I don't know."

Sveinn gestured toward an overstuffed chair. I sank into it. He sat in the chair opposite me, his legs spread wide as if to make room for his belly. "I don't like people who beat Magnús. Years ago, he came to the dock, holding the hand of a little redheaded girl who kept babbling, probably asking silly questions. And—I never forgot this—he always answered her."

My skin prickled at Sveinn's version of the story I'd once shrugged off.

He fetched his coat. In silence we walked to the jail. In a brightly lit room, Bergur sat in a chair chatting with another officer. His eyes grew round when he saw us together.

"A friend of Sigga's family has been mistakenly arrested," Sveinn said.

Bergur drew back his chin. "Mistakenly?"

"His name's Fritz."

"Actually, it's Gotthold Ephraim Eisenmann, called Fritz," I said.

Sveinn raised an eyebrow. "You know him pretty well, huh?"

Bergur opened a door and disappeared. When he returned, Fritz was with him, holding his socks and shoes, looking smaller and thinner than a few hours ago. The three of us walked out into the crisp December darkness.

I'd seen Klara baking the bread she called challah early that morning. When I arrived at the tailor shop in the afternoon, I saw the same bread on the table, still wrapped in a towel. Klara was sewing. Fritz sat on the sofa, his head in his hands.

"Hello," I said. Fritz didn't seem to hear me. I was counting and folding underwear when I heard heavy footsteps by the girdle bins. Oddur stood in the doorway. His eyes were on Klara.

"I hope your residence permit is in good order," he said in a husky voice that gave me chills.

Like an angel, Magdalena flew up behind him. "Sir," she said. "This is the tailor shop. It's private. If you're not interested in a girdle, please leave my shop."

Oddur ignored her. "You. I've seen you before," he said to Fritz.

Magdalena raised her voice. "Sir, I repeat, if you're not interested in a girdle, get out or I'll call the police."

Oddur pointed at Fritz. "Or maybe I'll call them on you."

Magdalena gripped Oddur's arm. "When the Germans land here—" he said. The door of the shop slammed behind Oddur as Magdalena escorted him out.

I turned to Klara and Fritz. "What's this about the Germans?"

"They talk about it at Inga's," Fritz said. "Consul Dietrich's planning for it."

Klara cleared the sewing table and unfurled a white tablecloth. "Dietrich's building up a fifth column," she said, unwrapping the challah bread and breaking it into pieces. "You know, a welcoming committee—for when the Germans land. Nice people, too, people who went to university in Germany. Most have no idea Dietrich's working for Heinrich Himmler."

"Heinrich—"

"Just gossip. That's enough."

"Want to celebrate Shabbat with us?" Fritz asked.

Out of a bag, Klara took a silver goblet, candleholders, candlesticks, and a bottle of red wine. "Compliments of Magdalena's boyfriend in the British consulate."

On the tablecloth, Klara placed the wine and the goblet. The challah loaves went to the center of the table. I pushed the candles into the holder and Klara lit them. "I'll do the blessings and prayers," she said.

"I am glad. I don't know prayers," Fritz said. "All I know is Hegel and Descartes."

Klara smiled sweetly. "You're just a passport Jew, assimilated, afraid to be Jewish."

Fritz looked hurt. "Isn't everyone afraid to be Jewish?"

"Even before Hitler, you probably told people you were just German. You bought a Christmas tree to fit in. Right?"

"How did you know? We assimilated. Here I can't because—"

My head spun. What were they talking about?

Klara interrupted. "On Shabbat, Jews recall the story of creation. In Genesis, God creates heaven and earth in six days and rests on the seventh day. It is a mitzvah for Jews to light candles to usher in the Shabbat."

Fritz studied his hands.

"Two biblical references, Exodus 20:8 and Deuteronomy 5:12, tell us to observe Shabbat."

"My father . . . he calls religion a fairy tale," Fritz said.

Klara slapped the table. "*Hör auf mit dem Quatsch.* Stop the nonsense. In a religious ceremony, we don't mention fairy tales."

She lit each of the candles, then waved her arms above them three times. Covering her eyes with her hands, she said, "Blessed are you, Lord, our God, King of the Universe, who has made us holy through His commandments and commanded us to kindle the Shabbat light." She uncovered her eyes. "Repeat after me. *Shabbat Shalom.*"

I sat close to Fritz on the sofa so that our legs touched. I chanted with him, "*Shabbat Shalom.*"

"Now hug and kiss one another."

I placed my arms around him, drew him close, and kissed him on the lips. He looked surprised, but he didn't pull away. In the corner of the room, Klara struggled to open the wine bottle. Fritz startled when the cork popped.

"Now the father of the family blesses the wine," she said, handing Fritz the bottle and a little book. "Pour two ounces of wine into the Kiddush goblet and say the wine blessing."

Fritz read in a strong voice, "Blessed are you, Lord, our God, King of the universe, who creates the fruit of the vine."

Klara repeated the blessing in Hebrew. "*Baruch atah Adonai, Elohaynu, melech ha-olam, borei p'riy ha-gafen.*"

Fritz drank the wine, refilled the goblet, then offered it to me.

"Now, everybody wash your hands," Klara said.

"What?" Fritz said.

Klara pushed us into the bathroom. Over the sound of running water, I heard her say a blessing in Hebrew. When we returned to the tailor shop, Klara was thanking God for the challah and salting it.

Sharing it with us, she said, "We often have chicken and fish, sweet carrots, asparagus. Today we must imagine those things."

"In that case . . ." I went to my bag and unpacked the sliced blood pudding and liver sausage I'd brought for a snack.

Klara winced. "These foods are not, how shall I say, traditional."

Chewing on the challah, Fritz said, "I do not care what is traditional."

Under her breath, Klara said, "*Dummkopf.*"

I shuddered, recalling how Oddur had looked at Fritz.

Chapter 23

On May 10, 1940, I woke up to the sound of a motor in the sky. I ran outside in my nightgown and stared up into the heavens. I'd seen pictures. It was an airplane. And we didn't have an airport. German airplanes dropped flyers on Copenhagen a month ago. Do not resist the occupation. It was our turn. Heinrich Himmler was here, and he'd take Fritz.

I pulled on some clothes and left a message for Bergthora to milk Branda. At the harbor, the sea air was laced with the smell of onions sizzling at the sausage stand. Yellow Studebaker taxis lined the road to the dock. A red-eyed couple, left over from last night, climbed into one of them and drove off. At the dock, a crowd peered at the horizon. I wormed my way to the front. Three destroyers were approaching the outer harbor. Tires squealed next to me. A black Mercedes halted. The doors opened. A man and woman scrambled out—German Consul Rainer Dietrich and Ursula. Both of them jumped back into the Mercedes and sped off.

"Get ready for Heil Hitler all day long," a man next to me said sadly.

"How can you tell the ships are German?"

"Intuition. Look for bowl-shaped helmets, gray uniforms, boots buckled over the pants legs, stocky guns."

I searched the crowd. Where was Fritz?

Like tiny hard-shelled insects, humans crawled out of the side of the ships and into the lighters below. The small boats plowed through the choppy water. I held my breath. Men in greenish-brown uniforms, not gray, stepped ashore.

"*Verdammt nochmal.* Damn it again," a familiar voice next to me said.

"Fritz." I placed an arm around his waist and pulled him close.

A soldier stepped ashore. "Blimey. No polar bears?" he asked the crowd.

Fritz whooped. "It's the British Royal Marines." He gripped me under the arms and swung me around.

Some young men shook their fists at the marines. "Invaders. You are violating our neutrality." But the marines kept coming. Soon dozens of pale men on rubbery legs marched toward the center of town.

"They're left over from the Great War," Fritz said. "Long-barreled guns and broad-brimmed helmets."

A civilian in a black coat came ashore. Word went around. British ambassador. Two men in dark coats, white silk scarves, and top hats got out of a black car. They shook hands with the ambassador. All three climbed into the car.

Fritz placed an arm around my shoulder. "Churchill has insulted you. No? He's occupied a neutral country. But look! He sends an ambassador. Shows respect for your—how do you say it?—sovereignty."

Fritz was safe, but we'd lost our independence.

We followed the soldiers. Small boys in short, woolen pants chased them. Others, dressed in mechanics' overalls and aviator caps, carried sticks shaped like guns on their shoulders and marched beside the soldiers. Gawkers, pressed against storefronts, watched the singing soldiers. "It's a long way to Tipperary. It's a long way to go."

Smoke billowed up from the chimney at the German consulate.

"Documents. I think Herr Rainer Dietrich is burning documents," Fritz whispered.

We hurried up the hill. Soldiers were banging their rifle butts against the door. At last, the consul opened the door. He wore a bathrobe. He'd changed clothes since I saw him at the dock earlier that morning.

A bowlegged marine climbed the wall next to the door and struggled to remove the insignia of the Third Reich from the wall. We walked down the hill. Men in pajamas spilled out of the Salvation Army building, hugging their arms against the cold. We stopped at the telegraph/

telephone station. A soldier was swinging an ax against the door. Men climbed through the broken doorframe. A night watchman stood nearby.

"We'll pay damages," an officer said to him.

In front of Hotel Eden, several young women chatted. When a breeze lifted their skirts, they swung their hips and giggled. Just beyond Eden, at the pond, soldiers marched into the big elementary school. Children were being sent home.

"Soldiers need the school for offices," Fritz said. I heard joy in his voice. I wanted to be happy, too, but I remembered Tosca.

I turned to him. "I've got to go home."

Fritz held my arm. "Not yet."

A group of soldiers gathered in front of Hotel Baldur. They watched two soldiers hang a white banner with a red cross on it from the second-floor window.

"A little more to the left," a soldier called out. Others carried cots, rolls of bandages, typewriters, and radios into the hotel.

A short, plump man in a dark suit raised his fist. "This is my hotel," he yelled.

"We need a hospital," the commanding officer said.

A notice was nailed to the lamppost. We both peered at it. Fritz read it aloud.

"We regret this inconvenience to your nation. We will only stay as long as absolutely necessary. The Commander."

Throngs of soldiers poured out of the ships. Short and scrawny, slope-shouldered, bowlegged in knee pants, they grinned at us through bad teeth. Some of them had fear in their eyes.

Magdalena stood on the steps of The Lingerie Shop, swinging a glass of wine. "Come drink a toast with me."

Fritz was halfway up the steps when he turned around. I shook my head. But I hated to see him sad. "All right. Just for a minute."

We climbed the steep wooden staircase to Magdalena's flat above the shop and sat down at an ivory-inlaid table, covered with a semicircle of silver spoons from around the world. On the walls hung posters from Gibraltar, Sardinia, and the Dingle Peninsula. Magdalena filled three thumb-sized glasses and raised hers.

"Compliments of John."

The drink smelled like rotting driftwood. As its warmth turned my chest into a glowing oven, I forgot my precious daughter.

"To the British Royal Marines," Fritz said, emptying his glass down his throat. Magdalena poured him another. "Who's John?" he asked.

Magdalena swung the bottle. "He's with the British consulate—soon to be the embassy."

A Brahms rhapsody came out of the radio. The prime minister's voice interrupted the program. "Our government insists on its neutrality and rejects the British occupation. Nevertheless, I ask that you treat the British like any other guests."

The lion must be weeping. All that trouble getting independence from the Danes.

"Guests? What an ass," Magdalena said, wrinkling her nose.

Downstairs, a door opened. The sound of shuffling feet.

Magdalena shot up from her chair. "No. No. You won't commandeer my shop," she shouted as she ran down the stairs. Fritz and I followed her. My head spun from the brandy. Klara, not soldiers, stood in the middle of the shop. Her left eye was swollen shut.

"What happened?" I asked.

But I knew it was Magnús. His nervous system teetered on the Hitler-Stalin axis.

"I was dancing with joy when Magnús came home. 'The Brits will protect us from the Germans,' I said. He called me names. I said his politics are stupid. He hit me."

I drew the Jewel of Mud Road close, and she sobbed against my chest.

"*Schweinehund,*" Fritz said, slurring the word.

"Stay here tonight, dear," Magdalena said. "I've got to go and chat up the new ambassador." Singing to herself, she whirled out the door.

Fritz and I led Klara to the tailor shop and placed her on the sofa. I made a wet compress from corset scraps.

Holding the cold cloth over her eye, Klara said, "I sensed the British were coming. Days before they landed, I secretly lit my Shabbat candles and thought about the golem of Prague and how it saved the Jews."

I poured wine into the Kiddush goblet.

She raised her hands in protest. "Not the goblet. It's not Shabbat."

Next to the sewing machine was a coffee cup, empty but for a brown rim in the bottom. I transferred the wine from the sacred goblet to the cup and handed it to Klara. She drank deeply. "The British are the golem come to save us from the Germans," she said.

Sounded like nonsense to me.

Fritz held the back of the sofa to steady himself. "Remember, Klara? In the story, the golem gets *ausser Kontrolle.* Out of control."

They argued in German about the golem until I took Fritz's arm. "Come. You're drunk."

On the way out, he knocked brassieres to the floor, bent to pick them up, and fell against the girdle bin. He sat there laughing until I helped him to his feet. Holding his arm, I led him down the steps. My arm linked in his, I headed toward the harbor. The sharp sea air would improve his balance.

Cots, stoves, ammunition, clothing, cans of food, radios, blankets, and pillows lay in piles, shiny from the light drizzle. The crane swung overhead with a Jeep dangling from its hook. Soldiers shooed us away.

At the post office, soldiers were piling up sandbags beneath the windows. An arrow pointed to an air raid shelter in the basement. On the corner of the building was a box with a horn attached. The box bore the label Air Raid Whistle. A group of red-lipped schoolgirls stood next to the box, giggling and eyeing soldiers. The breeze lifted their short skirts. I remembered my daughter and hurried home.

———

The British had pitched their tents on the gravel at the end of Mud Road and everywhere else in town. From inside the cottage, I could almost hear the soldiers breathing. Because it rained a lot, they slept in puddles and hung their clothes to dry while it drizzled. One evening, I passed a collection of tents and heard singing.

"Pack up your troubles in your old kit bag and smile, smile, smile."

A flap of one of the tents flew open in the wind. Inside, I glimpsed men wrapped in blankets, picking food out of tin cans, and playing cards. A soldier came out of the tent and brushed past me. He ran around the tent, hammered pegs into the mud, then ducked back inside and pulled the flaps shut. In spite of the rain, a few soldiers warmed their hands over a fire in a tin barrel.

I shivered in the cool morning air as I fed my chickens. I called out their names, "Minna, Dodo, Bibi," and they trod the thin rubber of my shoes. Somebody was shouting beyond Mud Road. I ran to the edge of the field. Men were marching, holding fence posts against their shoulders. Their mossy-green outfits told me they'd escaped from the nursing home. I must bring them back. I moved quickly and silently across the field, mustn't scare the old men. A bully barked orders, and the runaways formed a line.

"Look out, men. The gal's got her knickers knotted," a voice yelled.

They all turned to look at me. Soldiers. Not old, either. One of them pointed a gun at me. "Howdy," I said. I'd heard it in a cowboy movie.

"Blimey, the gal's friendly," the soldier said, and lowered his gun.

Just after the occupation had started, I was buying fish at the dock when I saw the Germans I'd seen at Inga's—the plumbers, carpenters, electricians—crowded together, guarded by British soldiers, waiting to board a ship. One of them, taller than the rest, wore a long green coat and carried a walking stick. I realized with a start, the Brits had arrested German Consul Rainer Dietrich.

Back home, I asked Magnús, "Where are the Brits sending the Germans?"

He frowned. "Some island off Britain. Isle of Man. Isle of Wight. No telling."

"Do you think Fritz is safe?"

"Safe? Don't be a fool. The Brits invaded us. A neutral country. They'll send Jews back to Germany if they feel like it."

Klara walked in. Magnús pretended not to see her.

"I was coming out of the shop and tripped on the loose step," she said, shaking the rain out of her hair. "I don't know where he came from, but a soldier gave me a hand, helped me up."

Magnús slapped the table. "You are collaborating with the enemy."

Klara looked at him as if he belonged in an asylum. "These men are here to protect us—"

"From whom? The Danes? Didn't we fight for hundreds of years to get rid of the Danes? And now you're kissing the boots of the greatest colonial power in the world."

"They're here to keep Heinrich Himmler away," Klara said.

Groaning, Magnús held his head with his hands. "Can't you see? Can't you see?"

But we didn't see it his way.

That evening Bergthora's fish cakes, frying in the pan, steamed up the windows of the cottage. After dinner, Tosca was muddling over math problems when somebody knocked. She jumped up. I heard Fritz's voice, then Tosca, begging him to help her with math.

"No. I am a philosopher."

She came back pouting.

Fritz entered the kitchen. "I just quit the margarine factory."

"Why?" I asked. Now he'd surely be deported.

"Imagine this. I am still in bed. Somebody knocks on the door. From the window, I see a man in uniform, behind him a Jeep. Soldier sits at the wheel. I open the door. My heart, honest I tell you, Sigga. Boom, boom, like a drum. Will he deport me? 'Lieutenant Gillespie, Officer of the Royal

Marines,' he says, looks at a piece of paper. 'Are you Gotthold Ephraim Eisenmann?' I say, 'Yes, I'm called Fritz.' He taps his head. 'In the other war, all the Germans were called Fritz. And now I'm asking Fritz for help.' He laughs like that bird here on the island—the loon."

I took two cigarettes from behind my ear, gave him one.

"I'm celebrating. You know why, Sigga?"

I drew the smoke deep into my lungs.

"I am on German Consul Rainer Dietrich's blacklist."

"Because you're Jewish?"

"And—a troublemaker," he said, proudly. I decided not to mention Meier's deportation.

"What will you do for them?"

"They want me to read Dietrich's handwriting. Of course, I agree. Off we go in the Jeep to the German Consulate. Sigga, my heart turns to ice when I see what is on the table—a pile of notes in Dietrich's handwriting. One of them says something like this: 'The residents of this island are a corrupt, lazy breed. No Norse gods. They reproduce fast. Do not marry much. Illegitimacy rate is 23%. Celtic heritage is evident. Dark hair, blond, an occasional redhead. Poor as paupers. Not much for sale here. Can't buy a tire or a pair of shears or even motorcycle goggles. Wretched place. No Aryan race.'"

He puffed on his cigarette.

"The note, it is addressed to Heinrich Himmler. Dietrich divides people into categories. Under 'Reich Supporters' he puts, of course, Oddur. Next to his name, 'Will promote our racial cause after I am gone.' Meier and I are under 'Reich Opponents.' Lots of insults, like, 'The arrogance of these 120,000 people thinking they can establish an independent state.' Calls the local people 'decadent and physical cripples.' Writes that women pluck their eyebrows and paint their faces like clowns."

Clowns? I recalled Edda plucking her eyebrows.

"And next to Ursula's name, it says, 'pro-Reich.' They ask me, 'Do you know this fellow, Oddur?' I tell them, 'I know him, like a dog knows a string of cans tied to his tail.'"

———————

Whenever I walked out Mud Road, I heard the soldiers, coughing and sneezing. I saw them crawling out of wet tents and cooking canned food over barrel fires. They hung their dripping clothes on lines and wore them damp. I was glad when Fritz finished his job at the consulate and began assembling Nissen huts for the soldiers. Slowly, they moved into the huts. Still, everyone felt sorry for them, everyone but Magnús. One morning I was crumbling a cake of *Ludvig David* chicory into the coffee pot. A peaceful murmuring came from Magnús and Klara's bedroom, but gradually the tone changed.

"You're whores for the British," Magnús yelled.

Klara answered quickly. "And you're a whore for Stalin."

Something heavy landed on the floor.

"Building huts for soldiers pays better than your stupid make-work jobs—two men sharing a shovel. What nonsense."

"You are stupid," he said. The door flew open. Magnús hurried past me and onto Mud Road.

In the bedroom, I found Klara pulling her cardboard suitcase out from under the bed. Pressing against me on either side, Tosca and Helga peered into the room. I pushed them away. "Ever since he came back from Moscow with the red bug in his pants—" I said.

Klara gave me a look of disgust.

"—he hasn't been normal."

She snapped the locks of her suitcase.

I tried a different approach. "Magnús was a gentle boy. But now he kisses Stalin's ass." Again, I'd said the wrong thing. Grimacing, Klara carried her suitcase down the hall to the door. As she reached for the latch, I stepped in front of her. "Don't go," I pleaded.

In the kitchen, Tosca turned up the radio, "Giddy giddy baba, giddy giddy boo— "

"Stop that noise," I yelled, taking my eyes off Klara. She slipped her hand behind me, gripped the latch, and was gone. From the kitchen window, I watched the Jewel of Mud Road walk away.

I guessed she'd sleep on the sofa in the tailor shop.

I turned around. Tosca was bent over with her skirt lifted while Helga dipped a small brush into a jar of brown liquid. I recognized the gravy browning that Sveinn's father had taken off his shelf and given Tosca for her birthday. *Stupid old man.* Helga painted a dark line down the back of Tosca's white leg. And then another down her other leg.

"Perfect," she said, stepping back and looking up at me for approval.

Tosca stood up straight, keeping her skirt raised. "Mama, doesn't it look just like stockings?"

It looked better than the thick brown socks most girls wore. In fact, my girl's legs looked too good. She was thirteen, but the painted stockings turned her into a woman in a soldier's eyes. I groaned.

Helga fanned the dark lines with a newspaper. "Hold your skirt up until it dries."

Tosca tucked her skirt into her underpants. "Dancing will help it dry. Come, Mama."

She whirled around and took me in her arms, and we danced to the radio. Later, I watched the two girls cross the road to Helga's house, their bare legs looking slightly blue in the cold. And I saw what I didn't want to see—the slight sway in Tosca's hips.

The radio announcer interrupted the music with news. "The English Channel was unusually calm as 900 some ships and small craft sailed from Calais to Dunkirk, evacuating 338,226 men from France to Britain."

Chapter 24

It was one of those long summer days in June, a day when the sun came out in the morning and hung on all day and narrowed into a gray shimmer during the night. I stood reading copies of the paper displayed in the window of the newspaper office. People were being killed all over Europe. Hitler had marched into Belgium, Holland, and France on the same day the Brits arrived here. And on that day Fritz's favorite person became prime minister of Britain. His name was Winston Churchill.

I picked my way around one of the ditches that crisscrossed the city, ready for the pipes that would bring natural hot water into everyone's home. But thanks to the German occupation of Denmark, the pipes lay in the hold of a ship, moored in the harbor in Copenhagen. The waiting ditches stayed open. If your boyfriend was a soldier, you could find privacy in a ditch in dry weather. But in the rain, little kids could drown in them.

With about twenty thousand British soldiers in town, money flowed. How could I get some of that money to feed my family? I climbed the steps to the bank, sat down in a patch of sun, and stretched my legs. I had a hole in my brown stocking. Customers stepped over me, grumbling, but I ignored them. I needed silk stockings. With my long, slender calves in silk stockings, I would be able to sell soldiers anything. Alcohol was an example. The soda pop factory brewed six-percent beer just for the soldiers and sold it at seventy-five aura a bottle. And Ratcatcher sold his brew around the clock to soldiers.

"*Halló stúlka.* Hallo, girl," a soldier called from the other side of the street. I opened my eyes and waved back.

Behind the soldier a basement door opened. The sound of "The White Cliffs of Dover" filled the street as a soldier stepped out, carrying a newspaper cone of fish and chips. A few weeks ago, the place had been a laundry room.

"Mama."

Tosca's red hair glowed. In the sunshine, her face was freckled as an oystercatcher's egg. She had on the new coat Sveinn had given her, taken in at the waist. It frightened me how it showed off her budding figure. She grinned at me in the lopsided way of a child, Sveinn's child.

Across the street a group of soldiers had formed. One of them whistled. Tosca unconsciously ran her hands down her chest like the little girl I wished she still was. I thought of throwing a blanket over her. I would hide her from soldiers. Like the mother duck, I'd flap my wings—look at me, take me—while my pretty duckling stayed safe in the nest.

I scrambled to my feet, took Tosca's arm, squeezed it so tight that she squealed, "Ow, Mama." Arm in arm, we walked down the street, peering into shop windows.

At the Leeds store, I pointed at a coat in the window. "Nice huh? All I've got is Jón's old tweed."

"Try it on. Make payments," Tosca said.

I shook my head. I didn't need a shopkeeper staring at my elbows poking through my sweater. We kept on walking. A wall of sandbags rose up at the end of the street. Gun barrels and helmets peeked over the top. I tapped a sandbag. "Hey, fellas."

No answer.

"Poor guys," I said. "Bored to hell in these forts. If we could give them what they want."

"You mean . . . ?" she asked, blushing.

I tapped my forefinger against my lip. "I mean fish," I said quickly. "And laundry."

We entered Mud Road. I hoped I could whisk Tosca inside to do her homework. But my heart sank when I saw Helga running toward us.

Between her thumb and forefinger, she held the stub of a mascara pencil the girls shared. Giggling, they ran off.

Soldiers were playing soccer with the boys from Mud Road. All around them steel Nissen hut frames, cemented into foundations, awaited roofs and fronts. Tents were pitched on every patch of open space. Underwear and T-shirts flapped on clotheslines next to the tents. A soldier was taking dry clothes off the line.

I called to him. "Those pants still look dirty. How did you wash them?"

"We don't wash 'em. Just soak 'em and hang 'em up to dry."

I stepped close enough to smell his tobacco. "I can do your wash. And dry it." Before he could answer, I wrote down my address on the back of a receipt, handed it to him, and pointed to the cottage. "109 Mud Road," I said.

Business came faster than I expected. I was cleaning oatmeal lickings from the sides of the pot when I heard boots stomping on the doorstep. I opened the door to three smiling soldiers. Each one carried a bulging pillow case. I invited them in.

"It's a dreich day," one of them said as they watched me make coffee.

"Like home," another answered.

Just then Magnús walked in. He took a step backward as if he'd entered the wrong cottage. "What the devil?"

"These young men are my friends. My stepson—"

Ignoring my introduction, Magnús kicked a knotted wash bundle into the living room. "So what's this, then?"

A soldier jumped to his feet. "Just leave yer breeks with the wummin," he said. They headed for the door.

In the hall, a soldier whispered to me, "He's a bit pit oot, ehh?"

Another gripped his shoulder, shouting, "Up yer kilt."

I told them to pick up their wash on Friday.

Magnús' eyes rolled toward the ceiling. I took a cigarette from behind my ear. On the exhale I said, "I'll do whatever I can to make a living off the occupation."

"It's not only immoral—" he began.

I put my hand on his forehead as if to check for fever. He slapped my hand away.

"Supporting the Nazis because of a stupid Hitler-Stalin Pact. That's moral?"

"All this so-called British work—washing clothes, building roads, constructing huts—is competing with local business."

"Since when is a communist worried about local business?"

I saw right through his Moscow made-up, phony self. And he knew it. He hated that about me. He unfolded a piece of paper and placed it on the table. "I spent all night making this flyer."

Protest intolerable work conditions under the Brits.
Strike for better wages and shorter hours.
Stay home August 15.
WORKERS COMMITTEE OF THE SOCIALIST PARTY

"Don't do it," I said. "The Brits will send you to prison on one of those islands."

Wheels rumbled over gravel outside the window.

"Back her up," a voice said.

I ran to the window. A truck pulled up to the camp at the end of Mud Road. Soldiers unloaded steel bars, cement, wood, and corrugated iron. A familiar figure stood and watched.

"Fritz," I called. He didn't hear me.

At the mention of Fritz's name, Magnús sprang up. I followed him.

"You've joined the invasion force?" Magnús asked over the clatter of building materials.

"I build airport runways and huts for them."

"Under the next government, you'll be up for collaboration with the enemy."

Shut up Magnús. You're making a fool of yourself. But I held back.

"I thought the fascists were the enemy," Fritz shouted.

"British employers abuse the workers."

"They pay us."

"Look," Magnús said, "I'm trying to like you because you and your people got shafted in Europe. My wife's Jewish."

Fritz raised his voice. "And you celebrated the occupation by beating her."

Magnús clenched his fists and closed in on Fritz. But Fritz raised his hands as if to surrender. Magnús backed off. I sighed with relief.

As soon as Magnús left for work, I tucked my skirt into my underpants, dropped some Sunlight soap into the water, stepped into the tub of soaking uniforms, and stomped on them singing, *"Take me to the fish shop. Take me to the sea."* I heard a knock on the door.

I climbed out of the tub, toweled my legs, and adjusted my skirt. Two soldiers stood on the steps.

"You do wash?" the taller one asked. The other one held a lumpy bag. The next minute they were inside the cottage, looking around, glancing down the hall. I sighed with relief. Tosca was safe at school. They dumped balled-up socks and dirty underwear on the floor.

I pointed to an old fruit carton in the corner. Obediently, they picked up their clothes and threw them into the carton. I led them to the front door. But three more soldiers arrived.

One of them handed me a bottle of gin. "Miss Sigga. We got dirty clothes."

I gave up on throwing them out. I gestured toward the kitchen table and served them coffee in cracked cups with milk crackers and butter. A soldier opened the bottle of gin and poured it into the coffee. They lit their pipes, joked, and laughed. My kitchen smelled of men.

A short soldier with slicked-back hair said, "Sigga, I need somebody to teach me the language. All I can say is, '*Ég elska þig*. I love you.' Can you teach me more?"

A blond fellow, his cheeks ruddy from gin, punched the soldier. "Bloke's just after a pretty girl."

"Shut your geggie. You're hammered," the short one said.

I had to get rid of them before Magnús returned. I faked a cough. "Influenza here in my house. You catch and cough until you die." They all stood up at once. After they were gone, I opened the window wide to let in the ocean air.

Every day I heated hot water on the stove and filled every basin and bucket I had. Soaking wash filled up the entire cottage. I scrubbed clothes on my washboard and wrung them until my knuckles turned to raw meat. Most days it was too rainy to hang things on the outdoor line, so I wove wash lines from old nets, string, and worn-out horsehair cables and strung them across the living room. I spread *The People's Press* all over the floor to catch drips. Cursing, Magnús stepped around buckets and ducked under washing lines.

When I discovered lice in the soldiers' clothes, I hauled them across town to the hot springs and washed them in boiling thermal water. One spring morning, I had so much wash that I borrowed my brother-in-law's horse, Brown. Old now, he'd been young when he helped us celebrate our honeymoon. As Brown plodded past the marsh, slower than a human walking, I breathed in the smell of freshly cut grass and awakening soil.

A red phalarope flew up out of the marsh, then lowered its flight, circled, dipped its beak into the water for plankton. I shaded my eyes to admire it. I loved this bird. From its free and easy ways, I guessed it was a female. The female phalarope made a life for herself. Flashier than the male, she did the courting. She laid eggs, then flew south in search of a new mate while the male hatched the eggs and fussed over the babies. Jón and I had both been male phalaropes. We needed a second child, so we could each have one.

A woman, weighted down by a basket of wash, walked along the side of the road. From her basket hung the green-brown sleeve of a soldier's shirt. "*Góðan daginn, þvottakona,* Good day, washerwoman," I called as I brought Brown to a standstill next to her. She threw her basket into the cart and climbed onto the seat. Slowly Brown moved forward.

"Giddy baba, giddy boo, giddy baba, do you love me true—" I sang.

The woman's head swiveled around. "Did you learn that from the foreigners?"

"It's my daughter's favorite song," I said.

Brown lumbered past the Shell Oil tanks with the little windows painted on them to fool the Germans. The smell of hot tar thickened the air. Shovels clanged and gravel rumbled out of the back of a truck as men made the runway for the Brits' airport.

"I'll get a permit and fly on my own wings," I told my companion.

She moved to the edge of the seat as if I was contagious.

At the washhouse, she jumped down and joined the other women lugging overflowing baskets of clothes. Children hung onto their mothers' skirts. The women pushed them toward the benches against the wall, told them to drink the sulfur coffee. Steam rose up from the earth, and the hot water was channeled into cement tubs, covered with grates. The whole place smelled of rotten eggs. Over to the side, some women cooked food in the hot water. A woman draped overalls across the grate and beat them with a wooden paddle.

She sang tenderly, "Oh, Mama dear, what if he whispers, 'I love you?' Mama dear, what should I do?"

I dumped my wash into the water.

"Criminy, it's warm in here," a male voice said.

"Ach, away ye go."

Two soldiers hesitated in the doorway, then sat down on the benches next to the children. A woman took a coffee pot from the grate and filled cups for the soldiers. One of them grasped a thigh that wasn't his. A woman, my passenger, smacked him. The soldier placed his hand back on her thigh. This time she did nothing.

Two young girls appeared in the doorway. Their sleeveless summer dresses showed their pale arms puckering in the cold. They had no wash. Instead, they found seats among the soldiers. I squinted to identify them. One of them resembled Helga. My heart fluttered. Was Tosca with her? I peered again. No. They were somebody else's daughters.

Back home, I found Magnús waiting for me. He waved a half-wrapped chocolate bar with bite marks where the first row had been. He turned it over and pointed to the words on the back. Made in Great Britain.

"And this?" He held up a crumpled envelope. On it was a caricature of a bear doffing his hat and the words, Brown Bear Stockings.

I gasped. "Where did you find that?"

"In the wastebasket."

I glanced at the clock. Nearly dinnertime. Where was that girl?

"You party with enemy forces."

"They drop off their wash."

"I saw the gin bottle," he said.

I checked the clock again. Where was she? I started to heat up yesterday's fish cakes. Magnús talked to my back, moving when I moved, raising his voice.

"The soldiers are turning women into whores. They shoot people. They killed a kid for climbing into a Jeep. A soldier shot Ratcatcher in the leg when he chased a rat into one of the camps." He slammed the chocolate bar on the table, breaking it into small pieces.

I whirled around, aiming the spatula at his face. "Listen to me. We have no money since the saltfish sales dried up. Soldiers pay me to do their wash. I sew on buttons and repair tears in their uniforms. If I were a man, I'd be pouring gravel into roads, building Nissen huts and an airport. But I am *not* a man."

Magnús stuffed most of the chocolate bar into his mouth and chewed until his teeth turned brown. He'd always loved chocolate.

———————

Sveinn showed up early one morning just after Tosca had left for school. Fortunately, it was a nice day and all the soldiers' wash was flapping outside in the ocean breeze, not dripping in the living room.

"Keep Tosca away from the soldiers," he said.

"Of course." Under his stare, I tried to recall where she said she was going after school.

"Some twenty thousand British soldiers are on the island."

"I've noticed," I said, placing a cup in front of him.

"Keep her away from them."

"I heard you the first time."

"I've run into Magnús. He tells me they come to the cottage."

I slammed a plate on the table with a piece of stale cake on it. "Listen to me. Soldiers are camped in every field, on every vacant lot, down alleys, and between houses. They ride the buses, crowd the sidewalks, drive in the wrong direction up one-way streets, go to the cinema, the swimming pool, the bathhouse. They crash their Jeeps into horse-drawn milk carts. I trip over the linchpins that hold their tents. How can I control what the soldiers do?"

The look in his eye told me he didn't believe me. I was exaggerating. "So you say soldiers are everywhere. You can't avoid them? My wife doesn't seem to run into a lot of soldiers. But your life's overflowing with soldiers. Because of that my daughter's is, too."

"Your wife? Your indoor plant? Does Fjóla ever leave the house? How would she know?" Somehow talking about Fjóla made me uncomfortable. I held the edge of the table.

"Steady now." His warm hands clasped my wrists. "I'm talking about our daughter."

I promised to keep our daughter safe.

The following evening, I pushed the door open to Tosca's bedroom. The girl sat on the bed. Her eyes sparkled as she held up a shimmering silk stocking.

"Where did you get those?"

No answer. Her mouth formed a pout. I yanked the stockings out of her hands. She threw herself on the bed and rolled against the wall, sobbing. I slammed the door behind me. I hid the stockings under the pillow on Jón's side of the bed—a place she'd never look. If I couldn't stop her from going where the stockings led her, at least I could slow her down.

The next day, after I put more soldiers' clothes to soak, I walked Tosca to school. At thirteen, she didn't need that. I did. I watched her disappear inside the building. While she was in school, she wasn't in a café with a soldier. Calmer now, I went downtown. Under my arm, I had a small stack of embroidered underwear in four different shades of green and yellow. I'd embroidered lizards and snakes, prettier even than butterflies. The ladies would fight over them.

The Lingerie Shop was crowded with customers. Magdalena hurried toward me. Her nose was shiny with perspiration, and her voice came out shrill. "Oh darling, they all want corsets."

My heart did a backward flip. This was my chance. The women stroked the corsets on the mannequins, holding pink lace nightgowns against their bodies, asking each other questions. "How does it look?"

"Tell me the truth. Will Steini like it?"

Klara was at the cash register, taking money and wrapping packages. Women were lined up.

Magdalena whispered in my ear. "Occupation's a blessing. The town's full of men. Money's flowing. Our women can afford corsets again. Can you help Klara sew corsets?"

I placed both hands on my chest to keep my heart from escaping. I tried to sound calm. "I am busy these days," I said carefully. "But I think I can fit it in."

Exhaling with relief, Magdalena hugged me.

I spent a few happy hours in the tailor shop with Klara, distracted from worrying about my precious girl. I learned how to measure a woman's bust, waist, and hips. Klara showed me how to cut the fabric and assemble the panels for a corset. After Magdalena closed the shop, Klara and I sewed for a while. Suddenly I remembered Tosca and went for my coat.

I was halfway out the door when Magdalena called after me, "Dress nicely tomorrow. You can wait on customers, take their measurements."

Going home, I walked on air. I was an employee. I would sew corsets. Passing the newspaper office, I peered in and caught the headline and the beginning of an article.

> A Morals Committee of prominent citizens is examining the
> extent to which the occupation force has degraded the women
> of the island. The police are conducting regular raids on various
> guesthouses in town where soldiers rent rooms by the hour.

I started to run. Outside the city bathhouse, I almost tripped over the pile of boots, backpacks, canteens. I weaved my way through the groups of soldiers, who stood on the street corners smoking, calling to every woman who passed. I bumped into a soldier who had an arm around the waist of a young girl, his face bent over hers.

"Excuse me," I said. He looked up. So did she. "Helga?" But it wasn't Helga. My shoulders sagged with relief. A soldier touched my arm. I shrugged him off and kept on running. The squeal of a saxophone came from a fish and chips place. I ran past a lit-up window, saw couples dancing. I stopped. This café hadn't been here last week. In fact, Sveinn's father's biscuit shop had been here a week ago. The old man must have rented out his shop. I thought of my promise to Sveinn and got a choking feeling. The occupation was everywhere. Finally, I was home.

I stepped inside and stood in the hall. "Tosca."

Her voice was small and childish. "Yes, Mama."

She and Bergthora sat at the kitchen table, studying one of Diva's magazines. Under the light from the single lightbulb, they both looked beautiful.

Chapter 25

I fixed the zipper on my old black skirt and put on a new red cardigan over Diva's lacy blouse. I'd skipped movies for five months and thinned Bergthora's coffee to afford it. But something was missing. Of course—the Brown Bear stockings under my pillow. I rolled down my thick brown socks and placed my bare feet on the floor. When I saw my long toenails, I shuddered. They would cut right through my stockings. I found my tiny scissors and hunched over my toes. Bergthora peeked in.

"Do you have a stomach cramp?" she asked.

"Toenails," I said, snipping them and talking into my bare knee.

"You sound terrible. I've got something in my cookbook for stomach cramps."

I sang, "Giddy giddy baba, giddy giddy boo" and slid my legs into the silky stockings. "I'm working in The Lingerie Shop today."

The water carrier's mouth formed an O.

"No more bellies hanging, bosoms drooping. Thanks to the occupation, our women can afford a corset."

Bergthora tossed her head. "Devil's gotten into those hyenas."

I attached the stockings to my garter belt. As I walked, my legs made that swishing sound, like Magdalena's legs, the sound of success. I took out the stub of lipstick, dabbed my cheeks with red. I rubbed them, spreading the color, making my cheeks pink as Christmas apples.

At the store, I found Klara bent over the sewing machine. On the sofa and the table lay the corset materials—outer fabric and lining fabric cut into panels, steel boning, eyelets, and laces.

"I see you've already cut the panels. You've gotten the lady's measurements?" I asked, pretending to know about corsets.

Klara nodded. "How's Magnús?"

"He lost his job at *The People's Press*. He's driving a taxi for soldiers and their women."

"But he hates the occupation. The soldiers. The British."

"He's probably a terrible taxi driver."

She raised her eyebrows and pointed to a piece of paper. "I have measurements for five women. Can you cut the outer fabric and the lining fabric for the panels?"

I picked up the shears and began cutting.

"The pattern. The pattern," Klara said.

"Oh, of course." I cut for hours until my hands ached and my wrists trembled. I heard men's voices out in The Lingerie Shop.

"What size are her boobies?"

"Idiot. About the size o' me 'ands. Har har."

"Ooh, she'd like that. And some knickers to match?"

I peered into the shop. Three soldiers were laughing and play-punching one another. One held a brassiere up to his chest. Another fingered underpants embroidered with Japanese beetles and praying mantises. The third soldier caught sight of me.

"Hold on mates. There she is. Sigga. Sigga."

I withdrew into the tailor shop, but they barged in. "We stopped by your cottage. Brunhilda said you wuz here," the noisy one said.

"Bergthora," I corrected. "Come by next week for your wash."

On their way out, the soldiers pushed one another against the underwear bins. "Titty ha," one of them sang. The other two yelped with laughter. Magdalena entered the tailor shop and fixed her eyes on me.

"I don't want soldiers in my store. Understood?"

"Understood."

"They seem to know you. Do they?"

"Not really."

But she watched me put the scissors away.

I walked quickly up the hill. Soldiers stood in knots at every corner. Some lingered in the graveyard. A jeep, full of yelling soldiers, passed me. Sveinn had said his wife hadn't noticed any soldiers. Perhaps she wore blinders when she shopped. Back at the cottage, I found Bergthora sitting on the sofa behind the basins of soaking wash, knitting and talking to herself. Beside her sat Tosca. Her eyes went straight to my stockings. I hurried away.

By May 1941, I was accustomed to soldiers laughing and talking noisily in the street. Today was different. They were quiet. I saw two soldiers wiping their eyes, and I caught the words, "Jerry" and "the Mighty Hood." At the newspaper office I read the headline in the window.

The German Battleship *Bismarck* Sinks HMS *Hood*,
Pride of Britain, in the Denmark Strait

Later I read the whole article, how she exploded, broke apart, and sank with her hull standing straight up out of the water. For a few days, the town was quiet as the soldiers mourned. Klara and Fritz wore long faces. They talked about Churchill as if they knew him.

Then the British HMS *Royal Ark* sank the *Bismarck*, the largest battleship ever built in Germany. Joy erupted in the street. Soldiers began whistling at girls again.

In July, the Americans arrived. They weren't strangers to me. I knew them from the movies. Yanks had long straight legs, broad shoulders, big white teeth. They wore pressed uniforms. Smiling for no reason at all, they talked like cowboys through their noses.

"Why are the Americans here?" I asked a short, bowlegged British soldier, who watched me fold underwear.

"So we can go to Europe and get our heads blown off," he said.

I looked at his serious face. "Don't say that."

"It's true. We'll be dead. Yanks will get all the pretty girls."

The Americans didn't need me to do their wash. They brought washing machines. But many Brits stayed. So I still had customers.

Fritz was shoveling gravel for roads near Hvalfjörður, the deep fjord where the occupation anchored ships. He kept his ear to the ground and picked up gossip. That's how he knew when his hero, Winston Churchill, would arrive. On August 16, 1941, Fritz came to fetch me. By the time we got downtown, a crowd had formed in front of the parliament house. I kept my eyes on the little balcony where the great man would appear. Next to me, Fritz shifted his weight and cracked his knuckles.

At last the door to the balcony opened, and a short man, round as a barrel, stepped out. He wore a captain's hat and a navy pea jacket. His words rolled out like a grumble, and he made a V sign with both hands. When Churchill disappeared inside the parliament house, Fritz looked longingly at the balcony.

He pulled on my arm. "I want to see him review the blended troops," he said.

As the bus rattled toward the big road, Suðurlandsbraut, Fritz hummed the British national anthem, "God Save the Queen". I no longer worried about him getting punched in the face by Magnús. Just last month Hitler had attacked the Soviet Union. The Hitler-Stalin Pact was over. Magnús didn't have to like the Nazis any more. Klara could move back into the cottage. What a blessing for my family.

Fritz and I pushed our way to the front of the crowd until we could see Churchill's cigar, his apple pink cheeks. When British and U.S. soldiers marched by, he saluted.

"He's happy. Do you know why, Sigga?" Fritz asked.

"Because he's got lots of soldiers to play with?"

"And . . . and . . . the bulldog thinks Roosevelt is now with him."

His exuberance made me giddy. Among the marching soldiers, I spied one of my wash customers. "Hey," I called out, but the soldier stared straight ahead. When the review ended, we walked back downtown. Fritz stopped in front of Inga's, but I hesitated. "Ursula might be here," I said, peering into the window.

"She ran away to the Western Fjords. The MPs are still looking for her."

We entered the café, but I still didn't feel safe. A group of noisy men sat at a table in the back. I recognized the heavy cello player and other Jewish musicians—the refugees who never got deported.

"Notice the mood here," Fritz whispered.

I shook my head.

"Everyone waits for the bang that will bring Roosevelt into the war." He clapped his hands together, making a big sound.

"Bang?"

"Listen, Sigga. When we pour the gravel into the roads, we talk. One day Hitler will torpedo a U.S. boat. Bang. It will be an accident. Roosevelt will send the isolationists to hell. He will bring the U.S. into the war."

"The U.S. is already in the war," I said, pointing to some Yanks outside the window.

He smiled. "Ah, but it is not official."

Then I saw Oddur, getting up from a table. Quick and sly as a rat, he moved along the wall, making his way to the door. His raincoat flapped against the legs of our table. I moved my head so he wouldn't see my face.

My throat tightened. "I must leave," I said.

Fritz looked surprised, but he didn't try to stop me. I walked quickly. I was at the foot of Suðurgata when the door of a dance café flew open. Two uniformed men burst out. Choking, punching, kicking, they rolled onto the street. A crowd gathered. People tried to pull them apart. Women screamed.

Boys shouted, "*Dreptu hann.* Kill him."

Military police officers beat the men with clubs until blood flowed from their noses and mouths. Two girls in skimpy dresses huddled against the wall crying.

I hurried home. Tosca wasn't there. I ran across to Ratcatcher's and banged on the door. Anna opened it, her eyes frightened.

"Where are they?" I shrieked.

Tosca's voice came from a back bedroom. "I'm here, Mama."

"I was just checking," I said, lowering my voice, straining to sound normal.

Anna's face relaxed.

"By the way," I said, "if you're ready to throw away the newspaper, I'd love to see it."

She disappeared into the kitchen, came back, thrusting a newspaper into my hands, then closed the door tightly.

Back in the cottage, I discovered an open letter in the paper from the surgeon general.

> The Morals Committee has been tracking immoral behavior of some 500 women, ranging in age from 12 to 61. We are aware of women by the dozens on the lowest level of whoredom.

That lousy Churchill, bringing all those soldiers here. I got to my feet, wrung out some wash, and prepared my tub for rinsing.

Chapter 26

I sensed Oddur was in the shed even before I'd reached for the cow's teats. He emerged from the shadows and touched the back of my neck with his fingertips.

"I saw you with your Jew," he whispered.

"Get out!"

But he didn't. "I've got what your Jew's missing," he said reaching into his pants and tweaking the foreskin of his purple limb.

"Take your ugly dick out of my shed."

He patted his crotch. "Perhaps you and I can come to an agreement."

On my feet now, I picked up my dung shovel.

"My connections, you know. We can prove your Jew's been involved with some little incident, like rape, unless, of course, you and I—"

I swung the shovel against the side of his head. He fell to the floor. Dead. Joy pulsed in my veins. But he was alive and crawling out the door.

My hands trembled as I milked the cow. When I brought the pitcher into the cottage, I found Sveinn in the kitchen talking to Bergthora.

"Where's Tosca?" he asked when he saw me.

"School."

"We've had seventy pregnancies caused by soldiers since they arrived," he said. "The surgeon general complained to the commander of the occupation. Do you know what he answered?"

I set down the pitcher and placed my hands over my ears, but I still heard him talking.

"'I'm surprised the figure's not seven hundred, the way women here throw themselves at the soldiers.' That's what he said."

"Stop it. I've fed and protected our child for fourteen years. Suddenly you're the expert."

He gestured toward the tubs of soaking soldiers' clothes. "You call that protecting?"

"I need the money to feed your daughter."

"If something happens to her, it'll be your fault."

"I can't control forty thousand soldiers, who fill the streets, the buses, the shops, the movies. They skate on the pond, swim in the pool. They dance boogie-woogie, jazz, jitterbug, even in your own father's biscuit shop. Whole country's gone berserk."

He touched my cheek with his forefinger. "Calm down," he said gently.

———————

By the fall of 1941, U.S. forces had settled into camps all over town named after some old battles. These camps had streets that crisscrossed and bore strange names like Hollywood and Broadway. I agreed with Magnús. Soldiers had taken over our country.

One morning, Bergthora called me to her bedside.

"Can't get out of bed," she said. "The occupation makes my joints ache."

A cup of double thick coffee didn't help. "You need seaweed broth," I said.

Pocketing my knife, I headed out. At the inlet, I watched green, brown, and purple seaweed undulate in the water each time a wave lapped the shore. I waded into the icy water, grabbed a bunch of tangled seaweed strands, and cut until I had an armload.

With my arms full of seaweed, I approached the lumpy sandbag fort the Americans had built to guard the fjord against German invasion. Incredible. Why would Germans come into the fjord? I passed the fort as close as I dared. I probably smelled like smoked lamb. But men liked the smell of meat, I told myself.

A soldier paced in front of the fort and sang something about Texas and a girl. The muzzle of a gun poked through the gap in the sandbags. Abruptly, the singing soldier raised his gun and aimed it at me. I dropped the seaweed, put my hands in the air. I saw a tic in his jaw. Grimace. Release. Grimace. Suddenly he swiveled away from me and aimed his gun at the fjord. Out on the water a rowboat bobbed in the place where Jón had once fished.

Sweat broke out on the back of my neck. "No. No. Don't shoot."

"Kill the Krauts." *Crack*. The sound of gunfire flew across the water.

A soldier leaped out of the fort and slammed his rifle butt against the shooter's head. He fell face down. I dropped to the ground and grasped the shooter's legs. Together we pinned him to the ground. Two boys came running out of the shacks. Each grabbed a foot while I lay on the shooter's legs. The boys chattered happily while the shooter sobbed into the dirt. A Jeep pulled up. Military police handcuffed the shooter and threw him into the back of the Jeep.

I scanned the fjord. The rowboat emerged from behind a jetty of rocks. The fisherman was back on the thwart. He was safe. Still, my heart banged against my ribs. I picked up my seaweed and took the long way home across the meadow. In the field, a horse rubbed its head against a fence as the breeze ruffled its chestnut mane. I approached the animal and nuzzled its velvet nostrils. Its musky smell calmed me. A stone wall surrounded the farmer's field. From behind it came the odor of rotting fish. I peered over the wall. The ground was covered with fish heads, their mouths locked open in a smile, fertilizing the rocky places. Life would grow from this field of rot.

Back home I let the seaweed simmer on the stove. When the broth was ready, I brought Bergthora a bowl of it. While she ate, I told her the story of the crazy soldier who thought he was killing Germans on the fjord. By the time I got to the part about the military police, she was asleep.

I was punching eyelets into the back of a corset. On the table next to me were a couple of completed corsets. Klara and I filled orders as fast as we could while Magdalena took measurements in the store. I looked up from my work. A stocky soldier with black shiny hair stood in the doorway of the tailor shop.

"Can I help you, sir?" Klara asked, patting her hair into place.

"Name's Mort. Can you help me find a birthday gift for my sister?"

"Does she live in a cold climate?" I asked.

Mort grabbed his shoulders with both hands. "Brrrr. Cincinnati, Ohio."

I got up and led him to my underwear sets. "Would your sister prefer reptiles or butterflies?"

"Butterflies," he said. "She's my little sister. I want something as pretty as she is."

I liked Mort's open face and his shyness. In his dark brown eyes, I pictured his little sister, a stocky girl, with bobbed black hair. I flipped through the underwear, showed him moths, green caterpillars, snakes, and beetles.

"I want that one," he said, picking up an undershirt with an orange and black butterfly.

Mort watched me wrap the clothes, but when I returned his gaze, he looked down at his shoes. "You've been so kind," he said. "I don't suppose we could talk."

He wasn't cocky like most soldiers.

"Talk?" I asked.

"Over a cola, across the street?" he asked.

I knew the place he meant. Every time its door opened, music filled the street. "I'll meet you just past six."

He held his sister's package against his chest and smiled in a sweet way.

At six, I put on my coat and headed across the street. I descended the steps to the noisy little basement café. Mort sat at a small table behind two bottles of cola. He looked grateful to see me. The table and chair felt sticky under my fingers, but I sat down and leaned toward him. "Tell me about Ohio."

"We've got a front yard, where Mom grows tomatoes and peas," he said shyly. "We eat good back home."

His mother baked pies, and the people of Ohio played a game called baseball from early morning until late at night. If they weren't on a team, they studied something called baseball cards.

The English part of my brain went blank. Then a line from a John Wayne film came to me. "This is a hold-up."

Mort snorted with laughter until the cola came out of his nose. "Chattanooga Choo Choo" played in the back of the room. Still gasping, he reached for my hand. We danced in the tiny space between tables. The music warmed my aching muscles. Under the reddish glow of the light bulb, another couple danced. The woman's face looked hard.

"Krissa," a voice yelled from the back of the room. Of course, Krissa, the bitch from the gut plant.

A soldier toppled a chair as he reached for Krissa. Krissa's partner drove his elbow into the man's chest. A flick of the wrist. A blade flashed as he opened the man's belly. A gasp filled the room. An ambulance arrived, and the medics lifted the wounded man off the dirty floor. I couldn't finish my cola. The sides of my mouth stuck together. I led Mort outside. We crossed the square in front of the parliament building.

Mort was talking to himself. "Mom. Oh Mom."

"I'll walk you home," I said. "What camp do you live in?"

"Shiloh," he whispered.

From between the buildings, the lion appeared. Instinct told me to cross the street. Instead I raised my head high.

"Sigga," he said.

"Guðmundur."

Frowning, he nodded to Mort. "Sigga," he said. "We've struggled so hard for independence from the Danes. We tried to behave like a sovereign nation and stay neutral in this war. And now this." He didn't point to quivering Mort, but I knew what he meant by "this."

I was glad Mort couldn't understand.

"Don't sell us out," the lion said. "It was bad enough having the British trampling all over the place." A crowd of laughing soldiers with girls on their arms walked past.

The lion disappeared down a side street. He had a point. I took Mort's arm.

"We show movies at the camp. Want to come?" he asked.

I loved movies. I loved escaping into worlds that seemed more real than mine. "Yes, but not today." From the entrance to the camp, I watched Mort make his way down the main gravel road with rows of Quonset huts facing one another. When he entered one of the huts, I turned and went to the cottage.

It was slaughter season. I took time off from corset making to earn extra money. Village slaughterhouses sent boxes of salted, hardened sheep intestines to the gut plant. I sang extra loud as I scraped intestines, "Giddy giddy baba, giddy giddy boo, giddy giddy baba, do you love me true?"

Lilla walked up, hands on hips. "Main table, ladies."

I carried the clean, wormlike organs to the long table at the center of the room. Krissa stood next to me. I hoped we could become friends after what we'd experienced together. But no. As we wrapped intestines around spokes on a spool, counting—one, two, three—up to sixty in a slow rhythmic way, I sensed the tension in Krissa as if she herself were being wound up on a spool. I counted faster.

"Too fast," Krissa said.

The wheel spun faster.

"Are you deaf, soldiers' whore?"

"What did you say?" I asked.

"I saw you at the café. You're a soldiers' whore."

Anger exploded in my chest. "And I saw you, bitch."

Krissa's shoulders tightened. Her fists clenched, but I was faster. I reached into the cold-water tub, gripped a handful of leather-hard guts, swung them up out of the water, and slammed them against Krissa's head and chest. She yelped. I swung again. Blood trickled down her face. I chased her to the exit, whipping her shoulders and arms.

"Drop the guts," a voice yelled. Lilla thrust herself between us, seized my arm, led me to the door, and pushed me outside. "Go home. Don't come back until you can control yourself."

I breathed hard all the way home, recalling the rush of pleasure I'd felt. I'd wanted to kill her. A poisonous hatred lodged in my throat, choking me. I could smell my own stink as I thrust my hands deep into my overall pockets and pushed them against my thighs.

After the fight with Krissa, Lilla didn't want me back—not yet. And once we got past the backlog in corsets, Magdalena didn't need me but two days a week. I went back to buying fish at the dock and pushing my handcart over the rutted road to the peninsula.

Today was a windy, rainy day, but I still made the trip. Strains of Mozart came from the Weissmann's house. I rubbed my chapped knuckles and reached for a big haddock. Slapping it onto the board, I grasped the knife and cut from the pectoral fin to the backbone. I spun the fish around and sliced along the backbone, careful not to cut the bone. Sliding the blade past the rib cage, I bore down until the point came out at the belly. Keeping the blade flat against the spine, I sliced all the way down to the tail. Perfect. I stepped back to admire my work.

Frau Weissmann appeared in the doorway with two cats squirming in her arms. "You should play with the symphony," I said.

"Ooooh, I play terribly."

I didn't answer. Foreigners were always looking for compliments. When I folded a sheet of newspaper over Frau Weissmann's fillet, an ad caught my eye.

Dance in the Red Cross Building at Snorrabraut Tonight

I handed Frau Weissmann the wrapped-up fish. The cats yowled, and she batted them with the package.

"Has Klara returned to Magnús yet?" Frau Weissmann asked. Nosy woman. I never should have told her about the Jewel of Mud Road. Did she think wives came and went like the seasons at the cottage?

"The Hitler-Stalin Pact drove them apart," I said.

"Ah. A political marriage."

I blew on my chapped hands, grasped the cart handles, and hurried to my next customer.

Back home, I took the remaining gills from my pocket, dropped them into the pan with some margarine, and added potatoes. As I stirred the bubbling mixture, I thought about money. It was everywhere. How could I steer it in my direction?

I divided the gills and potatoes between me and Bergthora. As I ate, I remembered something I could sell. I needed an excuse to go to the camp. I wanted to go to that dance tonight. I went to the bedroom and pulled out the bottom drawer where I kept embroidered handkerchiefs to sell to Faroese fishermen. I'd embroidered a different island bird on each one, with duplicates of my favorites—the phalarope, the godwit, and the loon. I spread them out on the table.

"Nice," Bergthora said, fingering the feathers of a loon.

"Soldiers call them souvenirs."

I scrawled the names of the birds along with the words "by Sigga " on scraps of paper. I folded each handkerchief, stacked them with the handwritten labels in between. At the gate to the camp, the guard stopped me. I inclined my head in the direction of Mud Road. "Remember me?" I whispered. "That night at my house? Oooh, you were hammered."

He'd never been to my house, but an anxious look crossed his face, and he waved me in. I quickly found Mort's hut.

Cots were arranged along the wall. Under each one stood boots and snowshoes in neat rows. In the center of the cramped, musty room, a soldier fed coals into a round stove. Home Sweet Home said the embroidery that hung on the wall. Sweethearts back in Ohio stitched them by the boxful, Mort had told me.

I stood next to the stove, took out a handkerchief, and waved it at the men. "Buy one for your sweetheart," I said, moving my leg, showing my knee. Soldiers rose up from their cots. I talked out of the side of my mouth the way I imagined people did in Ohio. "Here you are stuck on this icy rock. And your sweetheart back home's starting to forget you? Send her a souvenir."

"Let's see those," a sandy-haired soldier said. Another one came up behind him, shoved the first with his elbow.

"Hey, I get first choice."

The door opened, and Mort walked in. He beamed when he saw me.

Sandy-hair looked up. "Hey, Mort, you know this lady? She just walked in. No warning. We coulda been exposed, in our underwear."

"Shut up, Mel. Look what she's got."

"Gifts for your girlfriend," the second soldier said, fingering an embroidered thrush.

"Gimmee a pair," Mel said. "I got two girlfriends. How much?"

I hadn't thought of a price. "Pay me what you can." Men dumped sock money out on their beds. They took money from under their pillows. They emptied their pockets. All the coins went into my bag, much more than I would have made from the Faroese fishermen.

"Hey, save one for me." It was Mort. He took a bill from his pocket. "Keep the change." My bag was full of money, and the soldiers sat on their cots studying the birds. Mort touched my elbow, escorting me to the door.

Mel cupped his mouth and called out, "Come on, Mort, show your stuff."

Mort bowed low, took me in his arms, and hopped around the room, singing in a voice sweet and smooth as honey, "Oh baby, you mean more to me than the whole state of Ohio."

I scrambled to keep up with him as we jumped around the little hut, the bag of coins clanging against my thigh. The soldiers whistled and cheered.

"Make your move, Mort. Don't let her go," Mel shouted.

Mort stopped and looked me in the eye. "There's a dance tomorrow."

"Will you take me?"

"Nine o'clock."

The soldiers clapped.

I ran home. Bergthora sat at the kitchen table copying recipes into her cookbook. I emptied the money onto the table in front of her. "I sold all of them."

"How?" she asked.

"I showed them my beautiful legs."

Tosca stood in the doorway watching. "Where?" she asked.

I couldn't lie. "Shiloh Camp."

A look of horror crossed my girl's face. "Mama, you told me to stay away from soldiers. And you—" She turned and ran toward her bedroom. I followed her, but the key turned in the lock. I banged on the door. She wouldn't open it.

Back in the kitchen, I slumped in my chair while Bergthora counted my coins.

The iron hissed as I moved it over my black dress. I'd worn it to Jón's funeral, and it was already tight then. It was almost nine o'clock. Mort would soon be here. Magnús walked in the door.

"Did somebody die?" he asked, pointing to the dress.

I put down the iron and took my lit cigarette from the sink edge. "Yesterday I sold all my handkerchiefs at Shiloh Camp. One of my customers is Mort. He's from Ohio."

Magnús snorted. "Ohio? All my taxi customers are from Ohio. They fuck girls in the back seat."

"Don't talk to me like that. Mort's missing his mother and his sister. So I agreed to go to a dance with him."

"You did what?"

"Mort's a nice boy. He's lonely, so I'm going to the dance with him."

"Have you forgotten that my little sister lives in this house? And you . . . you are going out with soldiers?"

"Not soldiers. Just Mort."

I picked up the iron again, smoothed the wrinkles in the hem, wriggled into the dress, and tugged on the zipper. When it wouldn't budge, I turned my back to Magnús. "Help me," I said, sucking in my breath and lifting my shoulder blades. Slowly and carefully, he pulled up the zipper.

"How can you—?"

Laughter came from Ratcatcher's house. I took Magnús' arm and led him to the window. Three soldiers descended Ratcatcher's steps. One carried two bottles. "They are our allies, here to protect us from the Germans."

Magnús looked bewildered.

"I read it in your paper," I said. "Last year you called the soldiers filthy scum who invaded the island. Now your paper says they're our allies. They travel in convoys, deliver weapons and Jeeps to the Red Army in Murmansk. But I can't talk to soldiers? You need to catch up with your own policies. "

"Talking's okay," he said. "Just don't let them do what soldiers do." He picked up a matchstick and cleaned under his fingernail.

"What soldiers do?"

"You know what I mean," he said, breaking the matchstick and dropping the parts into his empty cup.

"What do you know? You scared your own wife away."

He got up and kicked the chair against the wall.

I followed him into the bedroom. He sat on the bed's edge and held his head in his hands. I placed my palm on the back of his hot, angry neck, the way I had when he was a boy. "I'm sorry," I said.

But I couldn't stay focused on my shame. You are my sunshine, sang in my head. Soon I'd be dancing with Mort.

My shoes pinched my feet, and my dress pressed my breasts together. On Mort's arm, I walked unsteadily toward a large hut. The sign read, **American Red Cross Recreation Center**. A woman with a white Red Cross cap nesting in her hair smiled from the doorway. She gripped my wrist and pulled me in the direction of the hut.

"Welcome, dear." Her fingers tapped a message on my wrist. The hut's short of females. Go in.

I answered with my eyes. Let go, bitch.

She was a spider for the Red Cross. Girls were her prey. She would feed them to soldiers. I clenched my fists. If this spider pimp woman ever touched Tosca, I'd rip all her legs off. As I followed Mort into the hut, I heard the spider calling out behind me, "Admission's free."

Red and white streamers hung across the room. Couples moved to the sigh of a saxophone. Under the table, I kicked off my shoes. When the saxophonist stopped, a record played, and everybody in the room sang along.

I led Mort to the dance floor. He swung me around until sweat dripped between my breasts. My dress cut my underarms. My face was hot. I needed to breathe. I waded through the crowd until the cold outside air enveloped my body. I laid my burning cheek against the cool metal siding of the hut and watched the spider pimp woman pull girls out of cars.

Back inside, I saw couples leaving the floor to kiss in the dark corners. But Mort wanted to dance, so I closed my eyes and glided across the floor. I forgot everything but the sense of the music in my body. When I opened my eyes, I saw a tall soldier with a long, thin face and a beak-like nose, standing at the back of the room. He stared at me.

Mort was telling me about his cat.

"What's her name?" I asked.

"My mother has three—Dulcimer, Harpo, and Gretchen."

The soldier's eyes were still on me. Remembering Lárus and the hairy man, I shivered.

"Mort," I said.

"Dulcimer's the strange one. She'll purr and then suddenly turn on you."

"Take me home."

He looked surprised. "Harpo's like a member of a different species," he said. The two girls I'd seen outside now sat at a table with a group of ruddy-faced soldiers. Mort trailed behind me, talking in a dreamy voice. "Dulcimer's treacherous. She'll pretend to play and then—"

"Did you see that soldier?" I asked. "The big one?"

"He's a loner. Probably harmless."

I held his arm as we walked along the pond. He pointed to the church with the sharp green steeple. "All the locals seem to be Lutherans," he said. "I can't even find any Catholics."

"You want Catholics?"

"No, I want Jews, somebody to pray with."

"I know someone named Fritz, but I don't think he prays."

He rolled the name off his tongue. "Fritz? A German name?"

"Fritz ran away from Germany."

"Ah, a refugee? Do you have other refugees?"

"A few. Mostly musicians." My heart tightened at the memory of Meier and Klensch. "Some got deported."

"Why?"

"This is what I heard on the radio. 'We island residents have precious blood from the Vikings in our veins. A single drop of Jewish blood will contaminate our blood.'"

He frowned. "Do you believe that?"

I squeezed his arm. "The nationalists do. I'm an independent thinker."

Tiny snowflakes swirled in the wind. Laughter glanced off the frozen pond. A line of soldiers and girls held one another at the waist. They skated single file, forming a creature with dozens of legs and a flickering tail.

By the time we climbed the steps to the cottage, I was taking short breaths. The dress pressed on my rib cage. I needed a corset. I didn't invite him in. Instead I bent down to kiss him, but he turned away.

"Bedtime," he said, glancing at his watch.

"What?"

"I get up early."

He disappeared down Mud Road. I'd suffered all night in the dress, crushed my feet in those shoes. I felt abandoned. Alone. And my daughter? Where was she? I walked down the hall and peered into her room. Bergthora was rolled up and faced the wall. But Tosca's bed was empty. I recalled the girls at the dance hut, and my heart froze. I must go and find her. Then I saw the note on the table.

I am spending the night at Helga's.
Love, Tosca.

I was relieved. She was still on Mud Road.

I toed my shoes into the closet and stood at the window. Snowflakes fluttered down big as coins. In the shadows, somebody moved against the outhouse. Him again. The tall soldier. I ducked behind the curtain. But he saw me and moved toward the door. I ran to lock it. Pounding on the door, he raised his voice into a high-pitched scream. He kept screaming like that until somebody shouted, "Shut up."

Gunfire. And Ratcatcher's voice. "He's down."

I opened the door. The tall soldier lay on the ground writhing. Ratcatcher stood next to him, clutching his gun. "Just a leg wound. He's a big rat, but the city won't pay me for his tail." In the doorway at Ratcatcher's, I glimpsed Tosca and Helga in their pajamas. When they saw me, they disappeared into the house.

After the military police fetched the soldier, I couldn't sleep. Instead, I paced and smoked. Finally, I ran my fingers along the bookshelf until I found my old poetry book, the one I'd made on the farm, copying poetry from the evening readings in the loft. I sat down on the sofa and read love poems. Love? Where was it? Sveinn had chosen Fjóla. And I'd buried Jón.

I woke up on the sofa with a crick in my neck. Tosca walked in. "Good morning, darling," I said as friendly as I could. But I didn't like her looks . . . as if she'd been up all night. "Where did you get the stockings?" I blurted out.

The girl's eyes were belligerent. "That is not your business."

My anger boiled over. I jumped up, grabbed a fistful of her hair, and pulled it back so tight that her eyes formed green slits. I shook her head until she yelped with pain.

"The stockings?"

"I'll never tell you."

I threw her onto a chair. "Listen to me. I'm trying to keep you from getting hurt."

"No, you're not. You just want all the soldiers for yourself. You're wearing my stockings, you tart."

Tart burned. I swung at her, but she ran for the door. I wouldn't follow her to Helga's. Instead I stood in the hall, clenching and unclenching my fists. I'd wanted to kill her. My own baby.

After I fed the chickens and milked Branda, I knew what I had to do. I changed into some clean clothes and headed for the police station. Chief of Police Bergur sat at his desk. He recognized me immediately.

"You are Sveinn's friend, Sigga," he said, shaking my hand.

"Sveinn is my daughter's father. Our daughter is fourteen."

"A daughter?" He pointed to a stack of files on his desk. "These files are all about people's daughters."

The phone rang. Bergur picked it up and shouted into the receiver. "How old is she? Thirteen? Name?" He took notes. "If we find her, I'll call you."

He slammed down the phone. "The world's gone crazy. We're living in hell. The other day, a local wandered into one of the camps. Got shot. Every single day, our men fight with the soldiers over girls. And the little girls think it's a game. They can't stay out of the barracks. Soldiers pass twelve-year-olds around for chocolates, oranges, silk stockings—"

"Stop. Please stop."

"Sorry. I only have sons."

The phone rang again. Bergur picked it up. "Soldier beating up a local? Call the military police." He hung up. "Thank heavens for the MPs. Yankee MPs are brutal. Knock your teeth out. Handcuff you. Then they ask what you did."

"Bergur," I said.

Flipping through his files, he didn't seem to hear me.

"Bergur!"

He looked up. The phone rang. He ignored it. "Yes, you were saying."

I hesitated. I was afraid of the answer, but I had to know. "Bergur, I read it in the paper, how some committee keeps a list of girls involved with soldiers. Right?"

"We're tracking them. Plan is to save them from themselves. Remove them from temptation. Besides, if they're promiscuous, they're a health hazard. We'll send them to a nice farm."

"Nice?" I swallowed hard. "Is my daughter's name on your list?"

He reached into the drawer and brought out a thick file. "Her name?"

"Tosca Jónsdóttir."

He peered at me over his glasses. "Jón? Didn't you say she was the daughter of Sveinn?"

"I married Jón before she was born, and Jón claimed her as his daughter." Bergur frowned. "Address?"

"109 Mud Road." I held my breath while he studied his papers.

He raised his head. "Nobody at that address on our list."

My shoulders relaxed.

"Wait a minute," he said, opening the folder again. "Mud Road. Mud Road. Here it is. Somebody on Mud Road is on our list. Helga, fourteen years old, lives at 107 Mud Road." He looked up. "You know her?"

The blood pounded in my head. "Helga's my daughter's best friend."

"We're tracking all the women and girls on our list. If your daughter's with Helga, she may wind up in a raid."

The phone rang again.

I ran out the door, down the hill to The Lingerie Shop. Women in hats and fashionable imported coats milled around, fingering the lingerie. Magdalena and Klara, cheeks flushed, were taking measurements. Magdalena nodded furiously at me and talked around straight pins in her mouth. "Stack of orders in the back room."

I hurried to the tailor shop and began stitching panels. But the machine kept getting stuck. I cut threads, tore up seams, started over again. I was bent over my work, cursing to myself, when I heard Fritz's voice behind me.

"Goddamn it. I can't do this," I said and threw the whole mess on the floor at Fritz's feet.

"Whooo," he said, humming Beethoven's "Fifth" under his breath. I knew it from the radio. He went to the little cabinet, where Klara kept her outdoor shoes, and took out the half-empty wine bottle. He emptied the coffee cup in the sink and poured me a cup of wine. I drank deeply and felt it warm my body. For a moment, I forgot about Tosca and the soldiers.

Fritz held his cup in both of his hands. "Today I see something big," he said. "You know I am working on the roads near Hvalfjörður. Lots of destroyers at anchor there. Every day I listen to the talk. It is raining. Everything is gray. The ground, the sky, the water in the fjord. And then I see a busted-up destroyer sailing into Hvalfjord. That's it, people start whispering. 'What boat is it?' *Kearny.* That's the name. U-boat put a hole in her side. She's a mess. All around me, they are talking, talking. They say she carries eleven dead Americans inside. I ask myself, Are the Americans in the war?"

He closed his eyes, muttered something.

"What did you say?" I asked.

The corners of his mouth curled upward. "And Roosevelt will enter the war. Churchill will be sooo happy."

I raised my cup for more wine.

Next morning, the wind bellowed in from the north and formed snowbanks against the Quonset huts in Shiloh Camp. I peered into the thin gray light and glimpsed the sentry at the entrance to the camp. Snow was piled high on his hat and his gun barrel. Shouts came from the camp. Soldiers held hands and bowed their heads against the gale. A trash can lid and other debris flew through the air. The soldiers ducked. A fierce wind ripped a sheet of corrugated iron off a hut roof and sent it hurtling into the storm. I strained to see through the swirling snow. A soldier fell to the ground. Two soldiers picked him up and carried him between them. When the wind shifted and slowed, I went to milk Branda. Returning with a full pitcher, I found a curly-haired soldier on the steps.

"Mort's hurt," he said.

That ass. He'd rejected me. "How?"

"A sheet of corrugated iron flew into his neck and sliced him good. Doc stitched him all night. He asked for you."

I put the milk in the kitchen and followed the soldier to the hospital hut. The spider pimp woman sat on a hard-backed chair next to Mort's bed, reading aloud from a hunting magazine. When she saw me, she moved to the next bed, saving her place in the magazine with her finger. Mort's eyes were slits in the bandages. A purple swollen hand rested on the sheet.

"A roof hit me," he whispered. He mumbled something I couldn't understand. I brought my ear to his mouth. "I want somebody to pray with me," he said.

I could get him a priest, like the Irish one in the movie who sprinkled water on the drunk just before he died.

"I want a Jew, not a rabbi. A Jew who's a believer."

"I'll find one," I said, kissing my fingertips to him.

At the door, spider pimp woman pretended to straighten gun magazines in the rack. I narrowed my eyes at her, pictured myself jabbing a pitchfork into her heart.

I walked down the center of Suðurgata in the deep tire tracks in the snow. At The Lingerie Shop, I hesitated, took a deep breath, plastered a smile on my face, and climbed the steps. I went straight back to the tailor shop. "Remember Mort?" I said. Klara looked up. "He got hurt, wants somebody who's Jewish to come and pray with him. Can you do it?"

Klara's face lit up. "I'll go after work," she said.

Chapter 27

Just before Christmas, I found Tosca alone in the kitchen baking cookies. "Where's Helga?" I asked as I dumped underwear pairs on the table.

Her lips trembled. "I think they sent her to the farm for loose girls."

"What happened?" I asked.

Her face was bright red. "I-I don't know. Some kind of raid."

"You weren't there?"

Eyes fixed on the floor, she shook her head.

I moved closer. "Stop it. Stop talking to soldiers. Don't even look at them. I'll thrash you with Jón's belt."

Her head jerked up, and she faced me with cold green eyes. "If you touch me . . ." She threw the spoon into the batter bowl and ran from the room, crying. Jón never wore a belt. He'd held up his pants with suspenders.

A burning smell came from the oven. I took out the cookies.

With Helga at the farm for loose girls, Tosca stayed home most evenings. For Christmas, I saved up for a leg of lamb. Christmas Eve it was sputtering in the oven when Tosca walked in and announced she would spend Christmas with Sveinn and Fjóla.

"Why?" My voice was shrill.

Her red hair crackled under the ceiling light bulb. "To get away from you," she said.

I narrowed my eyes to hide the sting of her words. She went to the bundle of twigs that was our Christmas tree and fetched the wrapped package I'd placed there for her. When she was gone, my shoulders sank. I needed more human beings. I went for my coat.

At Shiloh Camp, moonlight glittered on the kerosene cans filled with gravel stacked against the huts' walls for insulation. Snow covered the piles of tin cans, rolls of barbed wire, and broken-up crates. I poked my head in the door of Mort's hut. Buckets of coal flanked the potbellied stove in the center of the room. On one of the beds, Sandy threw down a card. Mel protested and quit the game.

A soldier lay on his back, reading a magazine. "Hey guys, listen to this. Millie sat naked from the waist down, her legs spread wide. Wearing blindfolds, the men pawed the air, looking for her. Then she giggled and—"

"Where's Mort?" I asked.

Mel looked up. "It's Sigga, woman of my dreams."

"Millie grabbed the hand of one of the men, placed it on her knee, ran it along her thigh to its prize in the forest. Whooopee." The reader threw the magazine on the floor.

"Shut up with that trash," Mel yelled.

Mort sat on a cot in the corner, eating something from a can. He still wore a bandage on his head. A red scar ran across his neck.

I sat down next to him. "Would you like to come for Christmas Eve? We have leg of lamb." Clumsy me. "You don't celebrate Christmas?"

"Yes, we do. In Ohio, Christmas Eve's a Jewish holiday." He gestured with his head toward Mel and Sandy. "Can they come too? They're stuck at the North Pole without Santa Claus."

This would be fun. "Hey boys, be welcome at 109 Mud Road."

Back at the cottage, Klara hung silvery caramel wrappings on the bush branches. The sound of fat bubbling around my leg of lamb and Magnús snoring on the sofa filled the cottage. I chopped up potatoes, onions, and pieces of turnip. When the soldiers arrived, I brought them into the living room. Magnús sat up and stared angrily at them. The soldiers laughed and plunked down bottles of gin. Soon they had their arms around one another. They swayed on the sofa and sang a sad song. "I'm dreaming of a white Christmas."

When Fritz walked in, Magnús brightened. "Would Kant forgive me if I shot up both the U.S. and British camps and slit the soldiers' throats?"

he asked. "I mean, how does that fit into Immanuel Kant's categorical imperative?"

Fritz glanced at the singing soldiers. "Not at all."

"Didn't you tell me Kant doesn't blame the individual who does the wrong thing as long as he acts out of good will . . . even though the consequences may be bad?"

"I never told you that," Fritz said.

Magnús gestured toward the soldiers. "I hate those guys."

"Stop it or you'll get nothing to eat," I said, turning to the kitchen. I took the leg of lamb out of the oven, stuck two forks into the meat, and lifted it onto a holiday platter. I arranged the potatoes, onions, and turnips around the meat. I was carrying the platter into the living room when my toe hit the broken place in the linoleum. I fell forward. The lamb and the vegetables slid off the platter and lay on the floor, steaming. On my belly in the lamb juice, I sobbed.

The door opened and Fritz stood above me. "*Das macht nichts.* Does not matter."

He shut the door behind him. Together we pushed the meat back onto the platter, picked up the vegetables and arranged them around the meat. We scrambled to our feet. Fritz handed me the platter and held the door open for me.

As I entered the living room, Fritz whispered, "Now you must smile."

Everyone looked up. The soldiers burst into "Jingle Bells." Klara, Magnús, and Bergthora joined in, pretending to know the words.

As I carved the meat, Bergthora asked, "Did you dump the sliced fish stomachs into the lamb juices like I told you to?"

I nodded. I must have left them on the floor. We ate the lamb down to the bone. Still smiling, I served the rice pudding. Mel reached for the bottle and poured gin over his pudding. "Great dessert, Sigga," he said, slurring his speech and dropping his forehead into his bowl.

Magnús turned to Sandy. "Are you still putting communists in prison in New Jersey?"

"Actually, we're working with the Soviets now. Ever hear of Rosie the Riveter? She builds tanks and boats. We send them to Murmansk to help the Soviets beat the Germans."

Before Magnús could answer, I stood up and said, "Time to dance around the tree." I took Mort's hand and Mel's. Stumbling over chairs, we sang, "This is the way we wash our clothes, wash our clothes, wash our clothes." Bergthora coached the foreigners on hand motions. "Now sing after me. 'This is the way we comb our hair, comb our hair.'"

Full of gin and food, I fell into a deep sleep after the guests left. Hours later I heard fingernails scratching the windowpane. I sat up. The Christmas Eve troll was at the window. Ever since I was a child, the troll had haunted me on Christmas Eve. I knew the rules. No matter what the troll said, I mustn't turn around and look at him. I would die if I did. Now the troll chanted, "Fair seems your hand to me. Hushabye, my clever maid." I raised my hand, stroked the chapped sore skin, touched the broken fingernails. I was tempted to look the troll in the eye and thank him for the compliment. But I pushed down on my thighs and kept my back to the troll. Through my teeth, I hissed out the words Mama had taught me. "My hand is fair because it has never touched filth, Hoblin, my goblin and hushabye."

His voice rose in anger. "Fair seems your foot to me. Hushabye, my clever maid."

I raised my foot and stroked the cold, dry skin as I spoke. "My foot's never trod filth, Hoblin, my goblin, and hushabye. Stand and be turned to stone, nobody's loss but your own."

The troll cursed bitterly as he turned to stone. I fell asleep again. A chinless figure in an oversized raincoat haunted my dream. His rubbery lips pressed against my cheek. His thick fingers stroked my neck. I startled awake. I lay still, staring at the ceiling. What had awakened me? I heard a thin wail below my window. I got out of bed and hid behind the curtain. I peered out the window. But it wasn't Oddur. Limping near the chicken coop was the tall soldier. Moonlight glinted off his ax blade. My door was bolted. I was safe. I crept back under the covers and waited for him to go away. But something nagged at me. Fritz. Was the dream about him? I'd begged him to sleep on my couch. Walking through the town at night wasn't safe—not for him. But he'd insisted on going home. He was in trouble. I pulled on my clothes. In the kitchen, I pocketed my fish knife.

Magnús appeared. Rubbing his eyes, he said, "I heard a sound outside."

"Crazy soldier's back." I headed for the door.

"You can't go out there. He's dangerous."

"I must. It's Fritz."

He gripped my wrists. "I won't let you go."

I hesitated but only for a second. "Distract him while I run away," I said. "He'll chase me. Run between us. He's drunk. He'll fall. Shout for Ratcatcher."

His eyes gleamed with hatred for the occupation. As I ran down the steps, the soldier raised his ax and bore down on me. But I was faster. Behind me, his ax skittered across the icy ground. I ran past the frozen pond, between the buildings, and into Fritz's side street. Silhouetted in the lamplight was Oddur. He held a blindfolded man in a headlock. Fritz.

I drew my knife. Oddur didn't see me until I closed in upon him and pressed the tip of the blade into his neck. "This knife's filleted better-looking fish than you," I whispered. Blood trickled from the wound. Oddur turned to me, loosened his grip on Fritz, who slid to the ground. I raised my knee and drove my foot into Oddur's groin. He stumbled back, slipped and banged his head on the ice and lay quite still.

I kneeled beside Fritz and cut the cords from his wrists. Lowering myself to his chest, I whispered, "We must leave before Oddur wakes up."

"And the foreman—"

"Who?"

"The foreman from the margarine factory. He beat me, tied my hands. He is fetching a car to drive us some place."

I raised him up and placed an arm around his waist.

Leaning on me, he walked slowly. "How did you learn to kick like that?"

"I saw a newsreel about martial arts."

"You are—" he said.

"A powerful kicking donkey?"

"Yes."

By the time we entered Mud Road, I was exhausted. At the foot of the cottage steps, lay the tall soldier. Magnús stood over him, cursing. "Get the hell out of my country."

I helped Fritz up the steps, placed him on the sofa, and covered him with a blanket. Bergthora stood in the doorway, clutching her nightgown. "Make him some tea. I'm going to the camp," I said.

The sentry sat in his box, his head lolling on his chest. "A soldier's lying at the bottom of my steps," I said.

The sentry's head snapped up. "What's his condition?"

"Maybe dead. He wouldn't be if you'd kept him in prison. Allies fight Germans. We fight the occupation force."

"Calm down, ma'am. I have a paper for you to fill out."

I batted the paper away. "One of your soldiers is bothering my chickens. Come get him, or I'll bury him in my yard, dead or alive."

"I'll send the MPs," the sentry said.

By the time I got back to the cottage, the soldier was sitting up and rubbing his head. A Jeep pulled up and MPs jumped out. The muscles in my legs hurt as I climbed the steps. It was Christmas morning, and I was grateful for two things. Fritz was alive. And Tosca wasn't here.

I was in the shed milking Branda when I heard squawking from the chicken coop. My darling girls—Minna, Dodo, and Bibi—were hungry. The shed door opened. Oddur walked in and stood so close to me, I felt the warmth of his body.

"This time I have the knife," he said.

I felt the cold blade against my neck. "Take it away," I said.

He pressed tighter. "We almost got him Christmas Eve. Then you came along."

I spoke in an even voice. "Why do you hate him so?"

"You or your daughter might give birth to something that would ruin our fine Nordic race. That's why."

I cringed at his mention of Tosca. "Nordic race! Look at your own degenerate offspring." Yet on the last word I felt a tenderness for the tiny scrap of humanity I'd pulled into the world, his last-born child.

"I'll make a bargain," he started.

"No bargains. I wish I'd killed you."

"Nasty. Nasty. You really hurt me." He lifted the blade off my neck. "Look," he said.

I watched as he stroked his crotch.

"I'll spare Fritz if—"

Music from the opera crept into my memory. I envisioned Scarpia's eyes gleaming like Oddur's as he grabbed the singer, Tosca. Mine, mine, mine. Tosca had refused him until she realized that her lover's life rested in Scarpia's hands.

Oddur rolled his pelvis. "Just once, darling."

The only sounds in the shed were Oddur's hard breathing and Branda's uppers and lowers grinding as she ate. I pictured the pleasure Oddur would have dropping Fritz's body into a chasm. I recalled a grimy little man who singed sheep's heads among the rocks at the shore. "Spread your legs just once, and I'll give you a sheep's head—a whole one."

I did things for my family. "Not here. Outside," I said.

"In the cold?"

"Under the northern lights. So romantic."

"Where?"

"On the big rock at the mouth of the fjord at eight o'clock tonight."

His hand touched my shoulder. I stood up and pushed him away.

"We do it once, and you'll never touch Fritz or me again?"

Nodding, he put his knife away and was gone. Back in the kitchen, I put down the milk and filled a bowl with scraps for the chickens. As I approached the coop, I cackled and waited for my girls to come running. But they didn't. Silence. I set down the food bowl and bent under the coop entrance. My foot touched something soft. I almost stepped on the bodies of my chickens. I scooped up the bloody carcasses. Holding them against my chest, their blood dripping down my apron, I carried them out of the coop into the moonlight. Their necks had been wrung. No fox could do that. I pictured Oddur's stubby fingers on their necks. I rocked them in my arms and crooned, "My poor, dear girls."

On a nail at the coop entrance, a white piece of paper fluttered in the breeze. I ripped it off the nail.

Until tonight, darling. O.

Dirty bastard. I held my chickens up to the moon and screamed for revenge. Gently, I carried them into the pantry and covered them with a burlap bag. I thought of burying them in the yard with a prayer and a small, wooden cross. But I was poor. I had a family to feed. In memory of my chickens, we would eat them for several days.

I dug my nails into my palms and seethed with hatred. I sat down on the sofa next to Fritz's feet. "Stay still," I whispered. "I'll sing you a lullaby." Fritz closed his eyes as I sang, *"Bibi og blaka."* He fell asleep before I'd finished. The top button of his shirt was unbuttoned, and his slender neck was exposed. I recalled Oddur's knife blade and how it had felt on my own neck.

A sound at the door. Tosca was home from Sveinn's.

"Poor Fritz had an accident," I said when she saw him on the sofa.

"I am sorry." She took his hand. Then she placed it on his chest as if he were dead. "Mama," she said. "I miss Helga."

I looked at her hard. "Stay away from soldiers, or you'll be sent away too."

"I'm careful, Mama." The song "Little Brown Jug" blared out of the radio, and she took off dancing.

"You are not careful. Who gave you those stockings?"

Ignoring my question, she danced across the room. I followed her, grabbed her shoulders. "Did you hear me? Bad things happen to girls who go with soldiers. They end up in the barracks. They get raped."

When she laughed in my face, I shook her shoulders until her teeth chattered.

"Stop," she shouted. "You have no right to push me around."

I bristled. "I am your mother."

"No. No. I'm not stupid. Gin bottles. Cigar stubs. You are not my mother. You're a . . . you're a—"

Crack. I slapped her so hard she fell against the wall. I came after her and slapped her again. I was on top of her when Fritz struggled up from the sofa and pulled me off. I stepped back and leaned against his chest. Sobbing, the girl ran out of the cottage.

Fritz dropped onto the sofa and groaned. "I must go home now."

"One more night," I begged. I wanted him safe while I bought his life under the lizard's loins. I bit the sides of my mouth at the thought.

For dinner I fried up some scraps of fish and threw some potatoes in the pan. I went into the bedroom and put on a special dress for the occasion. I checked the clock. Almost eight. As soon as we'd cleared the dishes away, I dropped a pack of cards on the table. "Bergthora," I said. "Teach Fritz how to play 500. I'm going to Ratcatcher's to see Anna."

The moon lit my way over the tussocks to the fjord. Up ahead, I glimpsed his chinless profile outlined against the sky. He walked toward me.

"There," I said, pointing to the tallest rock. The tide was coming in, slapping the rocks. I climbed to the top. He clambered up behind me. Once I had a foothold, I turned and pulled the reptile up and over the ledge. For a moment, he lay on the surface of the rock, panting.

"You're an exciting woman," he said, climbing to his feet.

"Men have told me that," I said politely.

With a turn of the wrist, he reached inside his pants and raised his stiff limb to the moon. Chanting something, he stepped toward me. I smelled dried fish on his breath, and the mustiness of the shacks on his clothes. He fumbled under my dress. I shivered uncontrollably as he reached between my legs. I raised my pelvis. Below, the waves crashed noisily on the rocks. He thrust at me.

I staggered backward. "Wait. I'm not ready," I said, gripping his waist.

I imagined him as John Wayne, slid my hands down his hips, moved my fingertips to his crotch, stroked him. He gasped and began thrusting again. I leaned over him, moving my mouth toward his hardness. Above me, he panted with anticipation. But as my lips touched his soft, musky skin, revulsion gripped me. My hands slid to his thighs, his knees, his ankles. I growled as I gripped his ankles and pushed my shoulder against his body. All my strength rushed into my arms. I lifted him off the rock, into the air, and flung him out toward the sea. "Fly, chicken killer," I screamed. And for a glittering moment, he flew, backlit by the moon. When he crashed on the rocks below, I leaned over and watched the sea claim him.

My heart drummed. Out of my mouth came Diva's words from the opera, the ones Tosca sings after stabbing Scarpio to death. "*Questo e il bacio di Tosca!* This is Tosca's kiss." The waves broke on the rocks below, and Oddur's body rolled in the surf.

I climbed down from the rock. The thrill of revenge thrummed through my veins. Oddur was evil. I'd done a good thing. Above me, the sky was full of stars. I felt a gush of joy. Up ahead, the shacks formed a crooked line against the sky. On that line I saw the tiny image of the infant I'd once pulled into this world and laid on its dying mother's chest, an orphan now. I would never forgive Oddur for making me do that. His still warm ghost wrapped its tail around my conscience and squeezed. Happiness drained out of me. I whimpered into the night air as I climbed the steps to the cottage, holding the railing with both hands.

Tosca walked into the kitchen, looking like she'd been thrown from a cart and run over. I saw the mascara smudges, the missing top button, and the stockings—torn now.

"Where were you?"

"At Sveinn's."

From the shipping news, I knew Sveinn was at sea.

"No, you weren't," I said.

Sulking, she made herself coffee. I didn't have the energy to fight with her. I was waiting for something.

Oddur's body washed ashore on the sea-smoothed pebbles north of the fjord. His obituary appeared a week later.

> A brave man who rose up from poverty, dared to voice his opinion, to be different, dared to be disliked. A nature lover, he liked to walk near the sea, climb the rocks. An untimely death for a patriotic man.

It was signed, Gunnar Sveinsson, Sveinn's father, the moldering merchant, who had given Tosca a dusty jar of English marmalade on her last birthday. I showed the paper to Bergthora, who sat across from me.

"His children. Poor mites," she said, dabbing her eyes.

I propped open the window and inhaled the cold ocean breeze. Behind me, she kept talking. "Ah, the photographs. His blackmail game is over. They can close his office." My heart swelled with a blend of pride and guilt when she said, "Fritz will be safe now. Nobody else will make cases for deportation like Oddur did."

In the weeks after Oddur's death, I went to The Lingerie Shop every day and did whatever work was needed. Nobody asked me to wash the doorknobs and drawer handles with soapy water, but I had to keep moving. I didn't want to think. I swept the floor, washed it, folded the merchandise, and straightened the shelves. I sewed corsets until my eyes bugged out.

But at night, in my dreams, slimy creatures sank their teeth into my shoulders, plunged knives between my breasts, and ripped my heart out of my chest. I woke up drenched in sweat. I had to tell somebody, so I practiced confessing into the darkness. "The bottom crawler and I were lovers. When we got passionate, I hugged him so hard that—"

Not lovers, I corrected. "I mistook him for a calf. I just wanted to see if I could lift him." Then what?

"He jumped out of my arms."

Why was he in your arms? the voice wanted to know.

I woke up to somebody shaking me. Bergthora stood next to my bed. "Stop screaming," she said.

One morning about two months after Oddur's death, I smelled something right out of a sheep's stomach cooking in the kitchen. I found Bergthora stirring sheep fat onto a pan.

"Oddur's youngest brat was at the door yesterday begging," she said. "I'm cooking belly bag for him." At the word "begging," my nausea took on shape. I ran to the outhouse and brought up breakfast. I staggered back to the cottage. I needed Diva.

I entered her bedroom without knocking. A fashion magazine lay on her chest. It rose and fell with her breathing. I cleared my throat, and she opened her eyes and smiled.

"How are you and your beautiful girl?" she asked.

I shook my head. "I don't know. I just don't know." I climbed onto the bed and sat so close to Diva that the hairs on her arm stroked my forearm. I closed my eyes and visualized my life with nothing in it but the sea and the sky and maybe one godwit walking in the marsh. How had things become so complicated?

Diva tapped the back of my hand. "And how are you making ends meet?"

"Corsets. These days I do corsets."

Her gaze warmed my forehead as if she read my thoughts from left to right. "Your dream has come true. Something else?"

"I sell fish. In season I go to the gut factory. Thanks to your teaching me to embroider, I do underwear and tea towels. Magnús and Klara bring in some money. We're surviving."

That was a lie. I was barely breathing these days. Oddur was dead. Tosca hated me. And Fritz? I wouldn't think about him. Had he been worth another man's life?

Diva fixed her small, dark eyes on me. "And?"

"You heard what happened to Oddur, the immigration commissioner?" I asked.

She wrinkled her nose. "God rest that devil's soul."

"I saw him die," I said.

The room filled with silence. But inside the silence, Diva murmured the words Scarpia sings when he seduces Tosca. "*Via, mia bella signora, sedete qui.* Come, lovely lady, sit down."

I sang Tosca's angry response. "*Non toccarmi, demonio.* Don't touch me, you demon."

In a deep voice, Diva mimicked Scarpia's words as he clutches Tosca. "*Tosca, finalmente mia!* Tosca, mine at last."

I whispered, "*Questo e il bacio di Tosca.* This is Tosca's kiss."

For a moment I felt nothing but my memories torturing my nerves. Under the noise of waves crashing on the rocks and washing over the bottomcrawler's body, Diva took my swollen hands, held them up to her face, and sang to them. "*O dolce mani, mani suete e pure.* Oh, gentle hands, hands sweet and pure."

"No," I said. "Not sweet and pure."

Diva kept her eyes on my hands. "You gutted and gilled fish, you held your baby, you washed your stepson's hair, you shoveled coal, and—" she studied me with soft eyes, "—you took care of me."

"And they—"

Diva interrupted. "Why did you name your baby Tosca?"

That opened a different wound. "I wanted her to fight back, like Tosca in the opera."

"And what caused you—?"

"He was evil."

"Evil? Are you sure that's the reason?"

"Bad things happened to me."

"Long ago?"

I nodded as Diva's dark eyes investigated the corners of my soul.

"I see," she said. "It sounds like Oddur paid for more sins than his own."

Chapter 28

"How was school today?" I asked.

My daughter raised her face to mine, and my heart skipped a beat. Her eyes were outlined with black. Make-up covered her whole face. She looked foty-five years old, not fourteen. I reached forward and pinched her chin between my thumb and forefinger. "What's that stuff on your face, baby girl?"

When she slapped at my hand, I held on, pinching hard until I hurt her. I knew I was leaving a bruise. A knock on the door. I let go. Helga walked in.

"You're back," I said sadly.

"Back from prison," she giggled. The farm hadn't changed her.

Tosca was wriggling into her coat. "We're going for a walk," she said.

"It's late. It's dark." I ran to the door and opened it. "Look at the weather." A wind gust blew clothes off the hooks. Driving rain soaked the floor. The girls rushed out the door. I grasped the tail of Tosca's coat and got a sharp elbow in the chest, slipped and landed flat on my back. Scrambling to my feet, I tried to chase them, but I was too late. They slammed the doors of a taxi and took off, splashing mud and gravel. Groaning, I buried my face in the wet coats in the hall.

I'd go downtown, search every café, every dance place, every hotel, the barracks of every camp. But I'd never find them. Whimpering, I entered the kitchen.

Bergthora appeared. "She'll be back for dinner."

"Don't talk to me," I said. I took out my colored threads and sat down on the sofa. With quick, stabbing stitches, I embroidered pythons and cobras onto tea towels. Bergthora sat next to me, noisily sipping coffee, grating on my nerves. After she went to bed, I stared at the rain pelting the windowpane and lost track of time.

My head was nodding on my chest when headlights played on the windows. Thank God. I peered out. Once I got my hands on that girl, I'd slap her to China. But Sveinn got out of the taxi. He ran up the steps, left the taxi motor running.

The blood left my head. I opened the door, clutched the doorframe, and yelled at him. "Is she dead?"

"No. She's at the hospital."

"What happened?"

"I'll tell you on the way."

I gripped his arm and held on. She's alive, I told myself.

He turned to me. "Bergur did a raid on that big house near the National Theater. Soldiers were there. Women. Girls—"

"She slipped out."

His eyes held no forgiveness. "I begged you."

"I told her, 'Never go with soldiers.' I sniffed her clothes. I beat her. I threw her against the wall."

He fixed me with a hard gaze. "I asked you to keep her safe, not hurt her."

My anger boiled over. "I didn't fight to keep her safe just because you asked me to."

"No?"

"I tried—" I slapped the leather seat. "I tried to keep her safe from soldiers because—"

He grasped my wrist. "Because what—?"

"Because I didn't want a soldier to make her pregnant and leave her, like you did me."

He let go of me and dug his fingernails into the seat. The taxi pulled into the hospital driveway. I followed Sveinn to the entrance. He asked for Tosca's room number at the front desk. We climbed the steps and walked silently down the corridor. At her room, he stepped back.

"You go in first. You're her mother." Mother. The word chilled my spine.

In the hospital bed, Tosca seemed to have shrunk into a very small person. Her head was bandaged, her face bruised. One eye was closed and swollen. I rushed forward and took her hand. Her lips moved. I placed my ear to her mouth. "What are you saying, darling?"

"I just wanted to dance."

"You told me you were going for a walk."

Of course she'd wanted to dance. We all wanted to dance. I heard "Little Brown Jug" in my head, recalled how Mort swung me around.

Sveinn walked to the other side of the bed. He touched her foot, held it through the blanket. "I'm here, too," he said. I realized I knew nothing about how they talked to one another.

Tosca pulled herself up to a seated position and fixed me with her one good eye, then Sveinn. She lay back down and sighed. "Everything hurts."

I heard a smacking sound from the other side of the bed. Sveinn was punching his hand with his fist. I picked up a newspaper that lay on the bed. Somebody had made a circle around an article.

> Soldiers of the occupation are degrading our women and girls. They are creating a moral crisis. Under the guise of protecting us from the Germans, they are threatening our independence.

The lion's warning about Mort came to me. Had he written this? The paper grew hot under my fingers. I handed it to Sveinn. He read a few lines, rolled it up, slapped his hand with it.

"Degrading our women. That's what soldiers do."

Tosca cleared her throat. "Not degrading us. It was me. I wanted to be with them. I loved the music, the dancing, the jokes, the drinks. They burn your throat, Mama. They didn't kidnap me. I went to them."

My broken heart swelled with pride. Good girl. Don't be a victim.

"Mama—"

I moved in close. "Yes, darling."

"I'm not a nice girl."

"Don't—" I said quickly.

"I want to tell you—both of you—what happened."

"Not now," I said.

"I want to talk, Mama."

Sveinn fetched chairs. I braced myself.

"Helga and I passed that place on Laugavegur, the Blue Star Café. The door opened, and the song "Peggy the Pin-up Girl" was like a magnet, Mama. It pulled us in. People were swinging each other, singing. The jitterbug is fun. Do you know the jitterbug, Mama?"

I nodded. Sveinn glared at me.

"A woman jumped up onto a table. She wiggled her hips and sang all the words. Can you believe it? Helga and I were just about to leave. Honest. Just about to leave." She stopped talking and stared at the green wall as if she'd forgotten what happened next. "Two soldiers came up and asked us to dance. Nobody ever asked me to dance before. Their names were Fred and Will. I started to say no. But then they played one of my favorites, 'Boogie Woogie Come Ashore.' You know it, Mama?"

"I've heard it," I said carefully. "On the radio."

"People ran to the dance floor. So did we. Fred said my hair was the color of an orange peel. He spun me around, dipped and swayed. Do you know he can wiggle his ears? Dancing made us hot, so we had cola. But it tasted funny. Time to go home. But my knees wobbled. 'Let me help you,' Fred said. He took my arm."

Sveinn patted Tosca's hand. "You must be tired. Rest now."

Tosca made a fist and punched the mattress. "I must tell you the whole story now."

Sveinn's shoulders tensed.

"We kept walking. I was so dizzy. I didn't know where we were. I wanted to go home, but the words stuck in my throat. We stopped in front of a big old house. A cat sat in the window, cleaning its paw. I knew it was a nice house because of the cat. I could rest here. Fred took out a deck of cards, said we'd have fun. An old woman wearing the national costume opened the door, braids looping up at the back. 'Can I rest for a minute?' I asked. She gave us keys. 'Midnight. Be out by midnight.'"

I ground my teeth. I'd rip that woman's heart out.

His finger on his lips, Sveinn said, "Stop now."

Her voice quavered. "But I must."

I stroked her arm, talked between clenched teeth. "We're listening."

"We played cards. I kept falling asleep. Fred gave me an orange drink. I drank some of it, but I couldn't drink any more. My mouth didn't work. Everything went dark. This is the part that confuses me. I was crawling around in a cave. And it was full of hairy trolls."

Anger became a growling animal inside me. I would chew those soldiers to pieces.

"My head spun in circles. Hairy trolls danced around me. They dug their fingernails into my skin. I fought them. They hit me. I kicked them. I tried to strangle them, but there were so many. I grabbed two of them by the hair and banged their heads together. They screeched so loud the old lady came running. The lights came on. Police Chief Bergur picked me up off the floor. I heard the 'nino' of the ambulance."

Her unbandaged eye studied me. "Mama," she called out. She clutched my arm with both hands. "Mama," she repeated. A nurse peered into the room. I patted her shoulder, pleaded with her to rest. "Mama—listen, I fought them off," she screamed into my face. "I fought them off. I'm still your nice girl."

The word "nice" shot out of her. It sparkled for a moment and fell smoldering to the floor. The eager look on her face cut my heart. I wiped my eyes with the back of my hand. After all the broken-down shoes and torn clothes I'd made her wear, she didn't owe me nice.

Sveinn's face had lost its shape. "It's time to go," he whispered.

I bent down and kissed Tosca. "Magnús will pick you up tomorrow." No answer. Her good eye gave us a flat stare.

After Sveinn dropped me off, I paced the floor, smoking and talking to myself. I was ready to explode. Somebody must pay. I went to the door. I heard a voice behind me.

"What's going on?" Bergthora asked.

"Bad. Bad. Something bad." I ran down the steps into the mud.

She followed me, pleading, "It's night time."

At the camp, I yelled at the sentry. "The rapists. Give me the rapists."

He raised his gun. "Go home."

"The rapists. I'll kill them."

The gun barrel was centimeters from my nose. "Don't make me shoot you."

I clenched my fist. A small hand gripped my arm. "Come home," Bergthora said in a gentle voice. "They really shoot people."

The sentry looked relieved. "Thank you," he said to my mother-in-law.

Leaning on Bergthora's arm, I limped home. She sat on the sofa with me while I tore at my hair. "It's my fault," I said.

"You tried. I saw you slapping her around."

"I failed," I whimpered.

Bergthora stood up. "Don't pity yourself."

I closed my eyes. Red, yellow, purple, and green flashed on the inside of my eyelids. Trolls stomped on my brain. I should have tied the girl to a chair, nailed driftwood planks across her bedroom door, raised a barbed wire fence around the cottage, locked her in the cow shed. When I heard footsteps, I opened my eyes.

Magnús was staring down at me.

"Tosca and soldiers—" I started.

"Bastards."

I struggled to sit up. Magnús was at the kitchen window, his head outside, yelling in the direction of the camp. "Fuck the occupation."

I rose stiffly to my feet, went to him, and placed my hands on his waist. He turned. Our noses almost touched. "You brought them into our home, you . . . you . . . " he said.

I pressed my forehead against his. "If you dare call me a filthy name, I'll break both your legs and hurl you out the window."

He stepped back. "They ruined my sister," he whispered.

"Not ruined. Never ruined. We don't know exactly what happened, but she's still our precious girl."

At the center of my fury, a tiny dot of peace formed. It grew as I studied my stepson's face and glimpsed the love he'd shown the girl from the day she was born. I'd made a lot of mistakes, but choosing Magnús as a big brother for my baby was not one of them.

When Magnús brought Tosca home the next morning, I looked up from scrubbing uniforms over the washboard. The bruises on her face had bloomed to purple. "Hello, darling. Do you want oatmeal?"

No answer. She went to her room.

Later, I found her lying on her side, staring at the floor. She spoke in a dull voice. "When the nurse brought my clothes this morning, I could barely put them on. They smelled so bad. I can't stand my own smell."

"Darling, don't say such things."

"Leave me alone."

A voice came from the other bed. "Bury the shark until it smells like the devil's ass."

"Quiet, Bergthora," I said.

"Hang it out to dry for at least twelve months, and let the poisons drain out. Shark has no kidney. Pees through its skin. Can't eat it fresh."

"Stop it."

"I'm praying for my girl."

Later, when I returned to Tosca's room, the water carrier was snoring quietly. I sat on the edge of Tosca's bed and brushed my lips against her earlobe. "Don't ever let a man bring you down," I whispered.

A choking sound. "No man will want me now."

"What man would you want? That is a more important question."

"Mama, you don't know anything. Nothing like this ever happened to you."

My own story ripened. It was ready for telling.

"On the farm—you know I grew up on a farm—Lárus, the farmer's son, came to my bed. I fought him, but he was stronger. The farmer's wife found out and sent me away. I hated Mama for not protecting me. I never saw Mama again. And for a long time, I hated men."

She turned to face me. "Is that why you didn't name me after your mother? Because she didn't protect you?"

"Perhaps."

"Did Jón like my name?"

"Yes."

"Did he like me?"

"You were only eight years old the day he took you out in his boat. He talked for three days about how you'd pulled in a fish, how you had his fisherman's blood."

"I miss Papa. If he'd been alive, this wouldn't have happened to me."

Something passed between us as I saluted the ghost of my younger self flinging words at Mama. From that place would come the gift I could give my girl, the gift of my hard-won wisdom.

"Don't you think you'd have still gone dancing with soldiers?"

My question gave way to her own question. "Why didn't you marry Sveinn?"

The spaces between my fingers grew and shrank under my gaze as I conjured up half an answer. "He was engaged to Fjóla. And the old man—his father—hated me. I couldn't live with that."

The image that flew into my mind was a familiar one. Mama was climbing over rocks, searching for sheep, knitting socks as she sang. That folded piece of paper lay in her apron pocket, my father's so-called letter. A discovery shivered up the back of my neck. The letter was designed not to deceive, but to console her little daughter. I breathed comfortably as if a fish bone lodged in my throat for years had finally come loose.

Tosca's voice broke into my newfound peace.

"Did you ever wish I didn't have red hair so I wouldn't resemble Sveinn?"

I gripped the side of the bed until my fingertips hurt. Out of the tiny pain I pulled the truth that kept changing for me. Of course, I'd wished she looked more like Jón, so she'd fit into the little family I'd made from the pieces that didn't really fit together. But something was new here.

"I loved your hair," I said. "I let it grow until it became a mass of bushy, wild red curls. Imagine a tiny girl with all that hair."

Tosca's smile felt like the beginning of forgiveness.

"And your green eyes reminded me of him. I always listened to the shipping news. When the announcer mentioned the location of Sveinn's trawler on the fishing grounds, I breathed a sigh of relief."

Her face brightened. She sat up straight. "I want to see him."

I hurried out of the room. In the kitchen, I found the old lipstick and applied it thick and greasy. My knit cap looked like what you'd wear for milking, so I tweaked it to an angle like I'd seen on a mannequin at Magdalena's. You silly thing. He won't care how you look.

"Mama."

I ran to her room.

"Remember when I told you I was a nice girl?"

I held up both hands. "Don't—"

"The doctor at the hospital said I wasn't . . . I wasn't raped."

I stood quite still. I mustn't tell her I didn't believe her. With 50,000 soldiers on the island, nice had lost its meaning. We were all just surviving. I placed the back of my hand against her cheek.

"I want to see Sveinn," she said.

I hurried out.

At the harbor, the wind blew in off the sea. I climbed the steps to the Fisherman's Café. With both hands I pulled open the door against the wind. The place smelled of fish frying in suet. Sveinn sat alone at a table in the back. Fish skin lay in a yellow pool of fat on the plate in front of him.

"How is she?" he asked, pushing away his plate.

"Still in bed."

His eyes held mine. I saw in them his image of me drinking gin with soldiers, dancing with them while our girl was beaten up in the old patriot's brothel. Slap me, I thought. Make me feel pain, so I can start to heal.

"She wants to see you," I said.

"I told you to keep her away from soldiers."

I winced. "Do not accuse me like that." A fisherman at the next table stared at me. "Just because I'm a fishwoman and not your prissy butt Fjóla."

The way he flinched told me his flower pot wife did not make him entirely happy. Why else was he eating here? My fingers brushed the back of his hand. "I talked to Bergur. He told me things," I said.

"Me, too. I know about the twelve-year-olds, wearing make-up and mascara, posing as women, who go into the barracks and get passed around. For chocolate. They do it for chocolate."

"I know. I know."

"I told you no soldiers." The entire bulk of his weight landed on the last word.

I pushed back my chair, stood up, and leaned over him. "Soldiers are everywhere. On the buses. In the alleys. In the movies. How can I, one woman, control fifty thousand soldiers?"

"How is it that other women don't keep running into soldiers? My wife Fjóla—"

"But Fjóla hardly goes out, right?"

I must have raised my voice because the Faroese fishermen at the next table clapped for my performance. They hummed a song, then added words, about a harpooned, dying whale.

"The ocean ran red with blood."

Sveinn took my hand. "Sit down. Please sit down." Dark circles collected under his eyes. He hadn't slept either.

I obeyed, but I leaned away from him. "Can I tell her that you'll come?"

He nodded, but I still groaned under the weight of the trouble between us. I sensed it coming, his going back to the start of it all.

"Why didn't you tell me about my daughter?" he asked.

"You must have known you had a baby inside me."

His eyes softened. "How could I know?"

"You must've known," I said, trying to convince myself that the secret of her birth, of her very existence, wasn't all my fault. I didn't want to be an evil person. I was tired of stretching the truth so thin I could see the whole fjord through it.

Sveinn arrived at the cottage that afternoon. While he talked to Tosca, I eavesdropped outside the bedroom door, but I couldn't catch the words. I went back to embroidering spiders and their tiny prey. It was fine work, and my eyes watered from staring at the stitches. I had just closed my eyes and leaned back in my chair when Sveinn entered the kitchen and sat down across from me.

"Well?" I asked.

I took cigarettes from behind my ears, lit both of them, and placed one in his mouth. Together we blew smoke that blended together and clouded my vision of him.

"You know," he said. "Years ago, we were docked in Nyhavn, when a whore handed me a card with her phone number on it. A funny card. On it was a drawing of an old woman with a wide, double chin. When I tilted the drawing, a miracle happened. The old woman turned into a young girl with big breasts. By squinting, I could see both images at the same time."

I exhaled and saw him as he was today, his paunch, his thinning hair, the broken veins in his cheeks, his eyes rimmed with wrinkles from living under the sun and staring at the sea. I squinted and saw him as he'd been—his copper-colored curls, his freckled smooth skin, his clear green eyes, his big grin and white teeth. And I envisioned our strong, young bodies locked together in pleasure.

Did he see my dry, gray-streaked hair, my broken, stained teeth, my face full of the hard life I'd lived almost entirely without him? I'd never been beautiful, and now I was changed. Something terrible had happened. In spite of everything, I felt a sort of peace. And that peace belonged only to us.

"What did you say to her?" I asked.

"I said what I think you wanted me to say."

"What?"

"You are beautiful and nothing will ever change that. No man. Nothing in this world—"

"And? Something else?"

"I love you, and I always will."

My own father would never say those words to me, but sensing the magic they must hold for my daughter was enough for me.

A few days later, I was ready to go to The Lingerie Shop when Sveinn arrived.

"Where is she now?" he asked.

"Asleep."

"I have something to tell you," he said.

"Wait. Let me make some coffee." My hands shook as I spooned the coffee into the bag. Finally, I filled our cups and sat down.

"You were listening in the hall the other day when I talked to Tosca," he said. "But I don't think you heard what she said to me."

I tilted my head in his direction.

"She asked why I didn't marry you if I knew you were pregnant. I told her I came back after three weeks at sea, and you were already married to a little man and living in a cottage. I went to see you. Remember? You ran away to vomit in the outhouse. That's when I thought maybe you were pregnant, but I wasn't sure. I was an idiot. I didn't ask the right questions. You asked me once to marry you, and I made a joke."

He wiped his palms on his thighs.

"It was long ago," I said.

He fixed his eyes on mine. "I have missed you every day of my life."

I didn't hear Tosca arrive, not until she pulled out a chair and sat down. Sveinn touched the bandage on her head. "When does this come off?"

"Maybe next week. Those trolls sank their teeth in deep."

Back on the farm, we always blamed the trolls for things we didn't understand. She'd inherited that from me.

"Mama," Tosca said. "Sveinn says I can't sail with him until after the war."

Silently, I thanked him for that. Jón had never been able to resist Tosca's demands. Under her whining and wheedling, he'd always given in to her. Sveinn stood up and leaned toward her with folded arms.

"Listen to me, precious daughter. If the Germans torpedo your boat, swimming won't help. You can't breaststroke back to shore. Lucky ones cling to a raft until they can't stand the cold any longer and roll into the sea. Some survive, like the guys they found on a raft off Greenland. Stiff as boards but alive."

"You're trying to scare me," Tosca said.

"Yes," he said, chopping the air with a pointed finger. "That's how the animals in the jungle protect their young."

Tosca smiled. Maybe she enjoyed his scolding. A sign of love?

"We were about two hundred miles from shore when we got the call," Sveinn said. "A tanker had been hit, probably British. Suddenly we were sailing into hell. The ocean was on fire, waves roaring. Up close, another sound. I brought the rescue boat so close I thought the skin would melt off my bones. Stopped outside the ring of flames, pulled some men from the water. Then the terrible sound came from the center of the fire. My blood froze. The wind flattened the flames, and for a second I saw them, tiny figures in life belts, but there was nothing I could do to help them. I can still hear the screams."

His face grew red.

"The tanker was sinking. People hung from rope ladders on both sides of the ship. Dark people, from India, screaming foreign words. It was about to explode, ready to suck us under. We could only save a few more. Had to make choices. One man's life meant another's death."

Tosca's eyes were riveted on Sveinn.

"I sent out boats. Men were pulling out burned survivors. A few more. Just a few more. The deck was so hot under my feet, I could hardly stand it. I was risking my men's lives. Survivors were hanging from the mast. It was over. I turned away from the tanker. It exploded, fiery as a volcano.

Ship parts flew into the air. Sea was burning, like hell. Men were screaming, begging for mercy on their souls. All around us bobbed jabbering
dark-faced people with their turbans still on. Finally, a big ship, a destroyer
took them. Each one shook hands with me and bowed as he left my boat."

He sat down and pointed a finger at Tosca. "That's why I don't want
you to sail with me until after the war."

"I must go to the shop," I said. On my way out, I kissed each one on
the crown of the head. "Tosca, fix breakfast for your father."

Chapter 29

I found Magdalena holding her tape measure under Herdís' arms. Herdís brightened when she saw me. "Guðmundur asked me to tell you he'd like to see you." I nodded and hurried past the girdles into the tailor shop.

Fritz sat on the sofa. "Klara, she goes to make deliveries," he said. "I am between jobs. Finished the roads. I am waiting to start laying the hot water pipes."

"Ahh, at last. Hot water in Reykjavik."

"Klara told me about Tosca. I am sorry."

"You were there for Christmas. We had soldiers. Remember?"

"But Tosca wasn't there."

"I should have been more careful."

"In Berlin, we call this false guilt. You are only her mama, not God." Only.

The word almost knocked me down. I pushed it away. "In the spring, will you go on a hike with me?" I asked.

His eyes lit up. "I love hiking. In my student days, we hiked for days in Brandenburg."

"On the farm, the only time we 'hiked' was when we looked for lost sheep. Will you hike with me up Esja Mountain? We can get a new view of Reykjavik."

"I'm excited," Fritz said and kissed me lightly on the lips. He tasted of sugar. He must have stopped at Inga's on the way.

I pushed my way through a crowd of soldiers and girls. A soldier offered me his arm. "Ahnt you a beauty, lovey?"

"She's mine. I saw her first," another said.

I slapped them away. Breathing hard, I headed up Hverfisgata, walking fast and pumping my arms. I passed the National Theater and didn't stop until I came to the big ugly house Tosca had described. Yes. A cat sat in the window cleaning her paw. A figure moved through the room behind the cat. I climbed the steps and rang the bell. An old woman dressed in the national costume opened the door. She wore a silk apron over her skirt. On her double row of gray braids sat a velvet black cap with a tassel down the side.

Her tiny black eyes probed me. "Yes?"

"I came to see your whore house."

"This is a respectable hotel," she said.

I spat into the flower bed next to the steps. "You rent rooms to soldiers and teenage girls. Is that respectable?"

"You are mistaken," she said.

I stuck my foot in the door before she could close it. "My daughter was one of your teenaged so-called customers last week," I said, shouldering my way inside.

The woman backed away. "Your daughter's not telling the truth, then."

"The truth is she ended up in the hospital. Police came. You remember the raid?"

"Ohhhh. You must keep your daughter home. Did you know she'd become a whore?"

I grabbed her arms and flung her to the floor. Straddling her, I grabbed her braids, pulled until her eyes narrowed to slits, and banged her head on the floor. Behind me, through the open door, I heard giggling. Soldiers with girls were climbing the steps. When they saw me on top of the old woman, they stopped laughing.

"What is this?" a soldier asked.

"She fell down and hit her head," I said. "I was checking her pulse."

I got to my feet. Chief of Police Bergur was striding up the walk.

"Run," one of the girls yelled. The soldiers followed.

"Sigga?" Bergur said. "What are you doing here?"

"This woman's running a brothel for teenagers," I said. "Arrest her."

"Is that your business?"

"I'm helping the Morals Committee. You saw those little girls running away."

"She's killed me," the old woman shrieked.

"You're alive," Bergur said, helping the pimp woman up.

"I told her I knew she was running a whorehouse. Maybe she fainted," I said.

I smoothed my clothes and walked down the steps with a straight back. But my head was pounding. Recalling that the lion wanted to see me, I turned into the street along the pond. As I climbed the steps, I pushed hair wisps behind my ears and checked my coat for missing buttons.

Herdís greeted me at the door. "He'll be glad to see you," she said, smiling. She led me into the small parlor where we had talked the first time. The lion was bent over some writing. I sat down and studied my hands. The bitch pimp woman had scratched me.

He put down his pen.

"Your wife told me you'd like to see me."

"Yes. Yes," he said, rubbing his hands together. He gave speeches for a living, but with me he often seemed tongue-tied. "Tell me the news of you," he said politely.

"My daughter danced with some soldiers. She drank something bad and got into trouble."

Horror crossed his face. Didn't he know this happened every single day since the occupation began?

"She's only fourteen."

"Fourteen," he said. The number seemed to mystify him. "Horrible, just horrible."

While the lion fumbled through his feelings, I aimed my words at his lukewarm heart.

"Tosca—that's her name—is very upset about what happened."

His icy blue eyes warned me to back off. I would not.

"Her father, Sveinn, has come to talk with her. To tell her she's beautiful."

"Good idea," he said, rolling his eyes over the shelves that lined the walls, as if he could find a solution there to the tension between us. "Sigga," he said, shifting his gaze to me.

I held the sides of my chair. "Yes, Guðmundur."

"She's your daughter, so she must be beautiful."

Sometimes the sun's rays that come late in the day at the end of summer are the kindest ones. "Will you come and talk to her?" I asked.

"I don't think I can do that," he said, shaking his head.

I got to my feet.

He took my hand. His touch startled me. "I want to tell you something." He gestured toward a shelf of framed photographs of a boy. "This is my son. His name is Karl. We call him Kalli."

I'd seen the photos before, but I hadn't dared ask about them. Now I went to the photos and studied each one hungrily, taking in Kalli's features—the broad face, the large nose, and a smile that might sway people to vote for him. The hair was thick like the lion's, but it was cut short. Not a mane, just a haircut. "How old is he?" I asked.

"He just turned thirty-seven," the lion said.

I noticed some more recent photos. On a small side table stood several framed photos of Kalli as a young man. On one of the photos, Kalli held a child on his lap. Next to him stood a tall, attractive young woman.

"Unfortunately, he is no longer married. His little boy is three," the lion said.

I couldn't stop looking at the photos.

"He sails on cargo ships, says it is his patriotic duty to bring food to the island."

I remembered. Herdís had mentioned a ship. Kalli was a rough, hard worker, like me. Our blood flowed in the same way. "What ship is he on?"

"*Hvítifoss*. He sails the western route to New York, like we did in the

Great War, avoiding the blockade, the U-boats."

I'd often heard *Hvítifoss* mentioned on the shipping news.

"I thought you should know about Kalli," the lion said quietly.

I wanted to kiss him, but I knew better. "I am glad you told me," I said, shaking his hand. On the way home, I hugged the idea of Kalli. One day, I would meet him. As I passed the southern part of the cemetery, I twirled around, holding an imaginary Kalli in my arms. Soldiers had caught my scent and followed me, but I danced away from them.

Later that week Herdís came to the shop to try on her corset. As I laced her up, she said, "Thank you for visiting my husband. He's always in a good mood after seeing you."

"It was my pleasure."

"You are a widow, my dear?"

I nodded with pins between my lips.

"Were you never afraid of the ocean?" she asked, turning around and raising up her arms as I pinned fabric.

Talking around the pins, I said, "Yes. But my husband drowned near shore, in the fjord." The hot blood of loss and guilt flooded my cheeks. Herdís must have noticed because the worry line deepened in her forehead.

"My son . . . our son . . . signed on with *Hvítifoss*—"

"Guðmundur told me."

Slipping out of the corset, Herdís laughed awkwardly. "He's a free spirit," she said.

I folded up the corset. I sensed she wanted something more than a corset from me.

"The western route will be safer," I said. "Less chance of torpedoes."

She winced at the word "torpedoes."

Fritz and I climbed the rocky slope, picking our way between heather and sedge. Our feet brushed against the hard, little blossoms of purple saxifrage that grew among the pebbles. Below us, rays of sun shimmered on the water and highlighted the red roofs and white walls of the farms. I slowed my pace and sat on a rock. Fritz joined me, and we leaned close together. Lichens, rough under my fingertips, resembled brown, yellow, and rust-colored paints that had been spilled and blended on the rock. Moss nestled soft as a cat's head in the rock's crevice.

"Tell me more about this fellow Socrates," I said.

"Dialogue. That is Socrates. It was his way to the truth."

"The person who talks longest wins?"

"No. No. Truth comes out of the talk."

"Did people believe Socrates?"

"I don't know."

I touched his thigh with my fingertips. "You know what?" I said.

He caught my hand in his.

"You won't need to marry me after all. Or Bergthora."

"No? Really," he said, chuckling carefully as if he sensed eavesdroppers.

"You're laying pipes for the government. They won't deport you." Besides, Oddur was dead. But I wouldn't speak of that.

"Ah, pipes," he said dreamily. "You shall have a wish come true, a wonder. Hot water will flow right out of the faucet and straight into your bath."

I studied the gray boulders that stood up out of the green grass below. My world was full of miracles. "How do you do it? I mean the pipes."

He followed my gaze. "I shovel lava and pumice to create a foundation and make a channel in the lava chips. On top of that, I place the steel and concrete Bonna pipe. Next, I fill the channel with porous lava. Voila, Sigga gets a hot bath." His green eyes sparkled like the sea on a sunny day. He took my hand. "It will be my gift."

"Every time I take a bath, I'll think of you."

"One day, will you let me run the water?"

My face grew hot. "Ah. Maybe."

"You have done so much for me. For you I can run the water." He cleared his throat. "I have something to tell you."

I was glad for the change of subject. "Tell me."

"Meier's alive. I'm sure of it. I'll never see him again, but he exists."

I narrowed my eyes to slits of skepticism.

"He's a rock," Fritz said. "A rock that gradually becomes sand, then dust, then reappears again to build something new."

This sounded goofy.

"Do you think of Jón in that way?" he asked.

Visions of Jón lying in the grass, his face glazing over, made me shudder. "No. I think of him out on the fjord, waiting for a fish, falling into the water and not coming to the surface. The ocean washed him up on the shore and left him there. When I saw him dead, his eyes glistened like a kid looking at a Christmas tree. Can't think of him as a rock."

"His death must have been terrible for you."

It was, but not like he thought. "He was like the sick old dog on the farm," I said. "When that dog finally died, he lay on the grass, with no more pain. That was Jón."

I couldn't explain how losing Jón had been like losing all the safety I'd built up in this world. He was a plodder, like the old horse, Brown. Nothing could happen to a man who led such a small life, a man who caught one fish at a time. A safe life. And I'd thought I could make a family out of that idea. But I'd been wrong. My only consolation was that after he died, he felt no more pain.

"We must go. The sun, it is setting," he said.

I followed him down the mountain, saw his slender shoulders move with the slope of the hill. He stopped and waited for me. And now we walked side by side. I rubbed the back of my neck.

"Tired?" he asked.

"Every muscle in my body aches from hunching over the sewing. Thanks to you and your hot water pipes, I'll soon have warm water for a bath. That'll cure my aches."

"Ah," he said. "You will lie in the warm water, and I will wash your hair and soap your skin. I'll dry you with a soft towel and rub you all over with a sweet-smelling oil."

I blushed. Still, the idea that another human being might rub me with soap, scrub my neck, clean between my toes and inside my ears was as fantastical as the saltfish of my dreams that flew over the town. In all my years of washing fish, cleaning intestines, scrubbing clothes, bathing Jón, Tosca, Magnús, and Bergthora, nobody—except Mama once—had ever bathed me.

Walking home alone, I reviewed the bath plans. While he was mixing the water, I would stay in the pantry with the door closed. First, I would apply the lipstick good and thick. I would undress and wrap myself in the big towel, the one I'd used for drying Jón. I'd clutch the towel at my neck, step forward with my left foot, and enter the kitchen. My right foot would follow. I would cast away the towel. For one shimmering moment, he would gaze at my long, beautiful body. Then I would step into the tub. His eyes would linger on my shoulders and travel down to my small but exquisite breasts. I would immerse myself in the water, lie back, look up at the water stains on the ceiling, his imagined Sistine Chapel, and finally into his eyes.

Chapter 30

A small crowd had gathered on the dock. *Hvítifoss* was approaching land, returning from New York. I liked the excitement of welcoming back local people who had been out in the world. But this time I had a special reason for being here. Kalli.

The cold wind blew through my coat as I paced the dock with my arms crossed. At the same time, I was warm with excitement. How would Kalli look today? A lion like his father or a pretty lamb like his mother? Would he look like me?

"Hello, dear." I peered through the November darkness. It was Herdís, holding the arm of her husband. "So nice you could come to welcome the ship. It always makes a big difference to the passengers and crew to have a crowd welcoming them home."

Did she really think I was here for patriotic reasons? I wanted Kalli, not with my curious brain but with a desire that had lived in the pit of my stomach ever since I was a child asking Mama for relatives, for Papa, for anybody. I wanted to be connected to the earth, rooted. Not just Sigga, a child of a secret father, with no siblings, no grandparents, no family but a redheaded daughter, Tosca.

Herdís turned to her husband. "Don't you recognize Sigga in the dark?" She dropped her voice. "Sigga's sewing a beautiful corset for me."

The lion took off his glove, shook my hand, and held onto it. On the farm, I was known for my big hands. Once I'd loosened an angelica plant, I could pull it up out of the earth with my bare hands. I felt it more than saw it. The lion's hand was bigger than mine.

"You know, Sigga," he said and pointed into the darkness. "Out there, on that ship, are some brilliant young people, returning home. Doctors. Engineers. They will build up our country, help us achieve our independence."

I joined his happy mood. "I will sew towels, corsets, and underwear for them. And when they are hungry, I'll sell them my beautiful filleted fish."

The lion laughed. I'd never heard him laugh before.

Herdís hugged her husband's arm. "Seeing Kalli again will be just like Christmas."

My blood quickened. All three of us peered at the black water and the charcoal sky as if we could see him out there. Around us relatives spoke the names of loved ones. Excitement bound us all together. A father, a son, a daughter would be home. The ship was close to shore, I heard somebody say. We moved to the edge of the dock and searched the sea for the ship's lights. But this was wartime. No lights. Tomorrow the shops would be filled with food, clothes, shoes. Customer lines would wind around the block.

A boy peered through binoculars at the invisible place where the black sky met the dark ocean. He handed the binoculars to his mother, calling out, "Look. Look. It's Papa's ship."

A cheer went up. The boy's mother handed the binoculars to the next person. After that, the binoculars traveled from hand to hand. Two giggly young wives, arms around one another's waists, waved and began to shout the names of their men. All around me, people said the names of a husband, a son, a daughter. I breathed his name. Kalli.

Then it happened.

Out on the ocean, red and yellow blazes lit up the darkness. The crowd screamed, then went silent. It couldn't be a torpedo, not this close to shore. I stared at the fire at sea. Our ship? Families huddled together. Next to me, the lion's wife buried her face in her husband's coat and sobbed. Lights from Allied planes filled the sky, and a destroyer's lights, like silver pinheads, dotted the ocean's surface. They were chasing the devils. They would rescue survivors. Everyone waited for a miracle.

I wanted to say something comforting to the lion and Herdís, but my lips trembled. I could not speak. I had no words of comfort. I knew the procedure. Sveinn had told me how chasing Germans came first, picking up survivors last. Typically, the Nazis torpedoed a ship and left the freezing survivors clinging to the rafts for hours while the Allies chased down the U-boat. Survivors often rolled into the sea.

The horizon glowed red as aircraft lights played over the water. Word went out. The chase after the U-boat was over. The survivors were on their way to shore in a rescue boat from the destroyer. A weak cheer went up as the dinghy chugged into the harbor. Only a few figures, wrapped in blankets, sat huddled on the boat. A few cries of happiness were heard as families embraced the survivors. After the hugging, most of the relatives were still waiting. This would be the only boat, somebody said. Everyone who had survived was already here. I covered my ears against the sound of sobbing.

A survivor, a young man, broke away from his mother's arms and approached the lion. "You're Kalli's father?"

The lion nodded.

"He wanted me to tell you—if he didn't make it. After the torpedo hit, he helped others find life belts. *Hvítifoss* was sinking fast. He kept finding more belts, and he made people put them on. He held their hands as they stepped into the lifeboat. Afterward, I didn't see him. We were all scared, but Kalli was fearless."

The lion stepped forward, reached for the boy, drew him to his chest, and held him. After a long moment, he released him. Herdís hugged him also. Then the boy's family reclaimed him. The lion placed his arm over his wife's shoulders and led her away. I watched them until I could see them no longer. In the pit of my stomach, the old emptiness yawned. As I walked home past the graveyard, I spoke his name. Kalli. Kalli.

When I woke up, I peered into the morning darkness. I knew what I had to do. Food would ease our sadness. I pulled open the night table drawer and took out a pad of paper and a pen that Jón had kept there in case he got new ideas for saving the little man in the middle of the night.

I wrote some words and tore up the paper and started over again. I tried again. No. Not good enough. By the time I'd finally written something, the floor next to the bed was littered with balled-up pieces of paper. My handwriting was never good, so I printed the following words:

Dear Guðmundur and Herdís,

Please accept my sincere condolences for the loss of your son. May I invite you to a special dinner to honor the memory of Kalli. As you know, I am not rich. But it would be a great honor for me if your family and mine could come together and honor the memory of your fine, brave, beloved son, Kalli.

Yours,
Sissa

On my way to The Lingerie Shop, I walked past the lion's house and slipped the note under the front door. An hour later, Herdís showed up at the shop, her body bent under the weight of her sorrow. I saw the note in her hand, recognized it as the one I'd written. In silence she handed it to me. It said, *Yes. Guðmundur.*

"When can you come?" I asked carefully.

"Thursday, the day after the funeral," she said, her voice breaking. Her body swayed. I caught her before she fell to the floor. As I held her in my arms, a yearning hit me so hard I didn't know where to put it. I couldn't express it to Kalli's mother. Yet—

I blurted it out. "Do you have a photograph of your son?"

I'd seen photos of him in the lion's parlor, but I longed to see his face again.

"Yes. Yes," she said and fumbled in her purse. Finally, she dug up a dog-eared photograph. "There," she said, handing it to me. "Isn't he handsome?"

It was not a new photograph. On it, Kalli seemed to be about twenty years old. Yet I studied his eyes, the space between his eyes, his broad grinning mouth, his slightly crooked teeth, his jaw and his chin. I blinked hard against my tears.

"Yes," I said softly, "very handsome" and handed the photograph back to her.

I puffed on a cigarette as I took a halibut off the cart and brought it into the kitchen. I rolled down my stockings, put on my worn sheepskin shoes. I wanted the dinner to be special, so I consulted a yellowed, curled-up recipe I'd clipped from the newspaper. But when the radio played my favorite song, I put my cigarette on the sink and sang along, "Giddy giddy baba, giddy giddy boo, giddy giddy baba." Tapping my foot, I cleaned and filleted the fish. "Do you love me true, oh baby oooh." I fried the gills and roe and melted suet in one pan, butter in another.

Squinting over the cigarette smoke, I stirred the batter for the currant cake. Then I beat Branda's cream until it stood up in stiff peaks. When the fish was ready, and the cake was in the oven, I looked at the clock. They would soon be here. Pearls of sweat broke out on my forehead. "Five more minutes," I called to Tosca, who was in the living room sweeping and dusting. Bergthora measured coffee into the pot. It would be ready when we needed it.

"Magnús, quick. Clear the steps," I said. "There might be ice." Klara was on all fours in the living room, rummaging through the bottom drawer of the chest, looking for the Christmas tablecloth.

My hair was in a tangle, and sweat poured off my face. I went into the bedroom and put on my black skirt. It was tight, so I undid the top button. Over it I wore my clean blue sweater with the elbows darned green. I heard talking on the steps.

"When do we get our hot water?" Magnús asked. Fritz must have arrived. No more fist fights with my boy. I thanked God.

"You will be my first customer," Fritz said.

His hand lingered on my waist as he kissed me on the cheek. "Go help Klara set the table," I said quickly. He hurried away. I soon heard them chatting in German.

Finally, we were ready. The table was beautiful with a lit candle in the center. I glanced out the kitchen window, but all I could see was Magnús putting away the shovel in the shed. What if they didn't come? My heart flipped over and landed painfully, wrong side up.

Then through the window, I saw the headlights. I heard frightened chickens clucking. I smoothed my skirt and patted my perspiring face with the corner of my apron.

"They're here," I yelled as I opened the door and watched the lion assist Herdís out of the black car and up the steps.

"Come in," I said, extending my hand to the lion and fluttering my fingers behind my back—a signal for everyone to step back. Herdís practically fell into my arms. I embraced her until she let go. She shivered visibly. Klara fetched the bristly gray and brown shawl I'd knitted from unspun wool, very rough but warm, and wrapped it around Herdís' shoulders, and led her into the living room. She sat down on the broken-down sofa, wedged between two springs. Bergthora joined Herdís as if to show her the sofa was safe.

The lion sat down in the armchair I'd retrieved from the house of a neighbor who had died. His children hadn't wanted it because it didn't match the fabric of their sofa. Magnús perched on the armrest of the sofa. The rest of us sat on hard-backed chairs placed around the room. I recalled the gift bottles I had from the soldiers.

"Would you like some gin?" I asked.

The lion nodded yes. Klara offered glasses to the lion and Herdís. But when she offered one to Bergthora, my mother-in-law said, "Hell, no. It's hard enough for me to stay awake after three cups of coffee."

We all laughed, and we kept laughing and laughing long after it was no longer funny. Laughing kept us from having to talk.

"Thank you for inviting us," the lion said and raised his glass. He and

Herdís emptied their glasses and looked as if they'd like more. But I signaled to family members, and we all brought our chairs back to the table and placed our glasses next to the plates.

I walked around the table filling glasses with non-alcoholic malt beer. After I placed the fish and the vegetables on the table, I raised my glass. For a moment, I could think of nothing to say. My mind conjured up visions of Kalli. He'd been a little boy on the day when Mama knocked on the lion's door and offered angelica for sale.

"To Kalli's memory," I said.

I raised my glass to each person at the table. Diva had taught me this. After we all swallowed the frothy sweet drink, I glanced at Klara. "Do you have a prayer for Kalli?"

Klara's brown eyes glistened in the candlelight as she struggled to say the Icelandic words. "*Allt hold er gras og öll gæði sem af því koma eru blóm á engi. Grasið sölnar og blómið visnar vegna þess að andi Drottins blæs á það—Sannlega er fólkið gras. Grasið sölnar og blómið visnar en orð Guðs er eilíft.* All flesh is grass, and all the goodliness thereof is as the flower of the field; the grass withereth, the flower fadeth because the breath of the Lord bloweth upon it. Surely the people is grass. The grass withereth, the flower fadeth; but the word of our God shall stand forever."

The lump in my throat threatened to choke me. The lion seemed to be listening, but I saw his lips tremble. Magnús told us what a fine young man Kalli had been. How he'd done his best for his country by traveling all the way to America to import food for us. This was odd because Magnús hadn't known Kalli.

I said, "*Gjörið þið svo vel.* May you enjoy your food," the signal to start eating.

The lion nodded. We talked a great deal about the weather. A disagreement arose between Klara and Bergthora about whether it had rained on Wednesday. Nobody else cared.

We had finished all the fish and potatoes when I glanced at the lion. His shoulders shook. I touched the back of his hand. Tosca jumped up from her chair and flew to him. She put both arms around his neck and muttered something in his ear while he sobbed. When he grew quiet and wiped his eyes, she led him to the sofa. They sat and talked quietly while Klara and I cleared the table and served the coffee and rhubarb pudding.

Suddenly I remembered something. "I have some nice cigars," I said. "*Bjarni fra Vogi* brand, payment for fish from a customer on the peninsula."

I climbed up on a chair and took down an old wooden box of cigars I'd been saving for years. I wiped off the dust, lifted the lid, and offered it to the lion. Even Herdís and Tosca took one. Under the cigar smoke that blended over the kitchen table, Herdís leaned toward me and whispered in my ear.

"The corset is very comfortable. I'm wearing it today."

When the cigars were smoked down to stubs and our throats were dry and our voices raspy, Bergthora said, "I have a special dish in honor of Kalli."

Gripping the backs of our chairs, she made her way to the pantry. I heard her moving pots and dishes in the cold, little room. Finally, she brought a platter of small gray-white things and announced proudly, "Pickled sheepshead bones, softened in sour whey all winter, soft as pudding."

In his usual polite manner, the lion picked up a soft bone. "Have one, dear," he said to Herdís. Both of them chewed in silence. The lion took a second one. They looked relieved when the plate was empty.

The lion turned to me. "Sigga," he said. "Rasmussen told me Diva taught you to sing."

"Diva sang and I hummed."

He ignored my words. "Can you go to the beach where the fishermen died? Remember, you and I were there?"

Of course I remembered.

"Can you go there and sing the sailors' song for my son?"

I was stunned. "Why don't you do it?" I asked.

He shook his head. "I can't sing."

"I can't sing either," I said.

"Yes, you can, Mama," Tosca said quickly. "Remember 'Giddy giddy baba—'"

I pictured the beach, how the lion and I had stood on the black pebbles. The words about humans lost at sea sang in my head. Nobody would hear me above the surf. "Yes," I said. "I will go." I glanced at Fritz across the table from me. "Will you go with me?"

He nodded.

"You will take my car," the lion said. He rose from his chair and signaled to Herdís. I stood in the doorway and watched Magnús lead them slowly down the steps. When they were gone, I turned to Bergthora. But she was gone. On the table lay her cookbook. I sat down and turned to the title page. *A Water Carrier's Memoir and Cookbook*, by Bergthora Magnúsdottir. Under that: "Dedicated to my granddaughter, Tosca Bergthora Jónsdottir."

I'd seen most of it before, the pages of favorite foods cooked for her family and her boyfriend Ragbag—trash sausage, belly bag, miltbread, curly dock soup, pickled sheepshead bones, lung pudding, cod stomach stuffed with cod liver, boiled and pickled sharks' fins and tails.

In cramped handwriting, she'd described the circumstances surrounding each meal.

> *October 1916. The first time I cooked belly bag for Jón was the day he came home from the sea. His friend washed overboard. Never found him.*

I flipped through the book and found three pages of recipes dedicated to the days after Tosca's birth.

> *1927. My granddaughter has hair red as a sunset.*

But then I noticed something strange. Among the recent entries, the words *mushroom children* were penciled into the margins with dates. The foods were similar to those Bergthora had served us. The entries occurred about once a week after Oddur had died. She must've delivered the food to the shacks. Or the boy whose nose ran in all seasons had fetched it.

I understood then. Often I'd returned home and found food on the table but no Bergthora. Then she'd pop up from nowhere. She'd been for a walk, she said. I never questioned her disappearances. The last entry contained the pickled sheepshead bones and today's date under the heading, *In memory of Kalli.* I went to the water carrier's room and placed the book on the chair next to her bed. I watched her thin chest rise and fall in sleep, and my heart filled with gratitude for her life.

The wipers labored through the blur of early morning rain on the windshield, offering occasional glimpses of the road. Fritz drove. I sat next to him, hands resting in my lap. To sing the song, I'd have to extend my hands. Too bad my fingernails were dirty and broken.

The rain was only a drizzle when we got out of the car. Fulmars screeched on the ledges of black cliffs. The air smelled of ocean and seaweed and wet stones. Like trolls wading, lava formations rose up from the water. We walked on the black pebbles and dark sand that led to the sea. The surf bubbled like soapsuds, and the shore pebbles creaked against one another when the sea pulled back into itself. I stood at the ocean's edge, the water licking the toes of my shoes, and focused on the very spot on the horizon where I imagined the foreign world began.

"Don't laugh at my singing," I said.

But I laughed at myself until my whole body felt loose and comfortable. Standing on my toes, I leaned toward the roiling surf, and raised my large, calloused hands, the hands that had brushed Tosca's hair, patted Jón's backside, swung guts at the bitch Krissa, and gripped Oddur's ankles and thrown him into the sea. I fought the sadness that overcame me. I pictured Mama knitting in heaven and took a deep breath. I threw my head back, projected my voice upward, and sang the words into the wind. "*Alfaðir, taktu ekki aleiguna mína. Alfaðir, réttu út höndina þína.* God, don't take all that I own. God, extend your hand to me." I sang it for all of them. Kalli, Jón, Meier, Mama—and Oddur.

As I sang, Fritz moved close to me as if to protect me. After the last note, I remained still and stared at the ocean. A puffin flew over the rocks, its feet like orange rudders. A fish dangled from its orange and black beak. A skua shrieked, flew at the puffin's beak, snatched part of the puffin's catch, and flew off with the scrap of stolen herring.

I made a fist at the skua. "Hey, monster."

"Now they'll both live," Fritz said.

Next to us, shiny black basalt columns resembled stacked elf chairs. The ocean shimmered glassy green, and Fritz's eyes held a hint of its color. The wind shifted, and rain sprayed our faces.

On the way home, Fritz drove fast with self-confidence. Even when the tires skidded in the gravel, I trusted him. The sun hid behind the clouds, and the wind buffeted the car. We were almost back in town when the clouds parted into soft white tufts, revealing the sun. It glimmered big and gold, like the memory of something nearly forgotten and the promise of something not yet known.

As we drove past the first sod huts at the beginning of town, I asked, "Would you like to come to the cottage for coffee and crepes in memory of Kalli?"

Fritz nodded. When we arrived at the cottage, Tosca placed a bowl of deep-fried twists in front of him.

"They're still hot," she said.

While I waited for the water to boil for the coffee, I glimpsed Bergthora on the sofa, holding a children's book. Next to her sat a small boy.

"Can you help me with the crepes?" I called to Bergthora.

"I'll make them," she answered.

Slowly, my mother-in-law rose to her feet and led the boy into the kitchen. He wore ripped woolen pants that came to his knees. His socks hung about his ankles, showing bruises and cuts on his legs. He must be a scrapper. I knew him. I'd held him once, even before his mother had. Three years old now and still alive. Following Bergthora around the kitchen, he set out flour, butter, sugar, and milk. He seemed to know where everything was. A thought came to me. He must have baked here before. He climbed up on a chair and watched Bergthora stir the batter and ladle it onto the hot pan.

I couldn't take my eyes off the boy, the youngest of the mushroom children, the one I'd expected to die. In the shine of his bald head, I saw my whole busy life, my struggle, my constant worry about food and money, and my losses. With a serious expression on his face, he followed Bergthora's every move. I raised the back of my hand to my nose and felt my warm breath on my skin. I breathed slowly and evenly as my pride, anger, and hatred withdrew—at least for a short while—in favor of this moment.

"It's ready," the mushroom boy called out in a small, shrill voice.

He carried the platter of crepes in both hands and placed it on the table.

About the Author

Solveig Eggerz, a native of Iceland, is a storyteller, writer, and teacher. Her award-winning novel, *Seal Woman,* based on historical events, is set in Iceland, Germany, and Poland. Solveig teaches creative writing to diverse populations, ranging from the Writer's Center in Bethesda, MD, to blind students in Iceland, to incarcerated persons in Northern Virginia. As a member of Storytelling 2.0, a group of four women storytellers, she travels the East Coast telling stories to adults. In public schools, she introduces children to folk and fairy tales. Working with Heard, an Alexandria, VA, non-profit, she weaves folk tales into the writing program at Northern Virginia jails. She is a former reporter for the *Alexandria Gazette-Packet,* and her essays and stories have appeared in *The Delmarva Review, Palo Alto Review,* and *The Northern Virginia Review.* A speaker of three languages and a babbler in Italian, she holds a PhD in Comparative Literature from Catholic University.

To learn more about Solveig Eggerz,
please visit her website **http://www.solveigeggerz.com/**

Acknowledgments

To my fine and dynamic US publisher, Michele Orwin of Bacon Press Books; to my brave Icelandic publisher, Helgi Jónsson of Tindur; to Sandra Bond, my agent for *Seal Woman*, who always believed in my writing; to Fred Ramey of Unbridled Books, who gave new life to *Seal Woman* and paved the way for *Sigga of Reykjavik*. I am grateful for the writings of Thor Whitehead, Gunnar M. Magnuss, and Herdís Helgadóttir and for the information I gathered at Skógar Regional Folk Museum in southern Iceland. Warm thanks to my friends and cousins in Iceland who walked with me through museums, answering my endless questions; and to the librarians at the library of the University of Iceland who assisted me throughout years of reading old newspapers. Thanks to my writers group of fifteen years, the Holey Road Writers, for their patience in reviewing the manuscript. And to the Writer's Center of Bethesda, Maryland, where I worked with two excellent writers, Ann McLaughlin, who never let me stop writing, and Robbie Murphy, who told me to expand my short stories into a novel. And to Alice McDermott who told me to change direction, which I did. Thanks also to Steven Bauer for his imaginative perspective.

I dedicate this book to the memory of Guðný Óskarsdóttir, who took care of me when I was small and she was young, and when we were "big," became my closest friend.

Book Group Questions

1. What role does Sigga's anger play in the story?

2. How does Sigga's childhood and her relationship to her mother relate to the choices she makes in Reykjavik?

3. How would you describe the impact of her stay with Diva on Sigga's development?

4. How do Sigga's conflicting goals cause her trouble?

5. In what manner do Sigga's choices regarding family and work relate to her goals?

6. Describe the irony of Sigga's quest for independence through sewing corsets.

7. How does Sigga's choice of husband relate to her early relationships to men?

8. Why does the Allied occupation of Iceland in World War II pose a moral dilemma for Sigga?

9. What aspect of Sigga's nature causes her attraction to the refugee Fritz?

10. How is Sigga's childhood quest for her father different from her adult quest?

11. How do the two father quests differ, Sigga's and Tosca's?

12. What role does Sigga's mother-in-law, Bergthora, play in Sigga's search for family? What role does her stepson, Magnús, play in that search?

13. How has Sigga's concept of family changed by the end of the story?

If you would like the author to address your book group,
contact her at **solegg24@gmail.com.**

Praise for *Seal Woman* by Solveig Eggerz

"In this fierce and poignant novel, Solveig Eggerz deftly transports her readers between Germany and Iceland as her heroine struggles to come to terms with her past and present."
—Margot Livesey, author of *The House on Fortune Street*

"Solveig Eggerz takes us to a littoral world where ancient legend touches everyday life as surely and constantly as the North Sea meets the East Coast of Iceland."
—Dan Yashinsky, author of *Suddenly They Heard Footsteps: Storytelling for the Twenty-First Century*

"I found this book almost impossible to put down; Charlotte's secrets will haunt you for a long time."
—Robert Bausch, author of *Out of Season*

"The blend of knowledge about Berlin during the war with rural life in Iceland and with the development of Charlotte is intriguing, gripping, thought provoking."
—Dorothy U. Seyler, author of *The Obelisk and the Englishman: The Pioneering Discoveries of Egyptologist William Bankes*

"Set in the tough but beautiful landscape of Iceland, a wonderfully written story about the triumph of love, strength, and art over crippling loss."
—Barbara Esstman, author of *A More Perfect Union*

Awards for *Seal Woman*

First Prize Fiction, Maryland Writers Association, 2003
Finalist 2009 Eric Hoffer Award
"Editor's Choice" November 2008 *Historical Novels Review*
Book-of-the-Month, January 2010, American Association of University Women
The Icelandic version of *Seal Woman* (*Selkonan*) was nominated by Krummi, an Icelandic literary organization, for its Red Feather Award for interesting sex scenes.